Deacon's Horn

By

Cary R. Bybee

Published by Bybee Books
Lebanon, Oregon
U.S.A.

This book is a work of fiction. While I strived to keep history, science, geography, and Biblical truths true and accurate, any resemblance to real events or situations or actual persons, living or dead, is coincidental.

Deacon's Horn
Copyright ©2003 by Cary R. Bybee

Published by Bybee Books, January 2004

Edited by Bea Kassees and Tina L. Miller
Page layout by Tina L. Miller
Cover art and design by Steve Gardner
Copyright ©2003 Bybee Books
Cover Photos Copyright Photo Spin, Digital Stock, Digital Vision

ISBN: 0-9744398-3-5 (soft cover)
         0-9744398-4-3 (hard cover)
         0-9744398-5-1 (electronic book)

Library of Congress Control Number: 2002095841

Previously published in March 2003 by 1st Books Library.
Previous ISBN's:
         1-4033-8653-6 (soft cover)
         1-4033-8654-4 (hard cover)
         1-4033-8652-8 (electronic book)

Printed and published in the United States of America

This book is printed on acid free paper.

Dedication

This book is dedicated to my Grandfather
Orville A. Bybee (1912-1999)
An awesome man who provided me with guidance, insight, kindness, and
love for so many years of my life.

Grandpa, I know that you are looking down from Heaven.
I hope I can pass your legacy of love
on to my own grandchildren some day.
I love you.

Other books by Cary R. Bybee:

The Last Gentile
The Final Witness
The Library Man

Acknowledgements

Bea Kassees of Millennium Christian Shows—Thank you for your tireless dedication to this ministry and your many thoughtful prayers.

Tina L. Miller of Obadiah Press—Thank you for helping us make our work more worthy of God.

Steve Gardner—Thank you for the wonderful cover designs.

Dustin and Melissa Mitsch of Written Communication.com—Thank you for the terrific web site.

Chapter 1: The Aftermath

July 14, Day 2: Scott Turner sat staring out of his 17th story office window at the drizzly evening sky. Cloudy days like this had never bothered Scott in the past. He generally went through each day in such a hurry that he rarely noticed the weather, but today was different and the rain only made it worse.

Scott could still see Zach's casket lying there knocked off its foundation with the lid wide open. Zach should have been in that casket. After all, Scott had seen him get hit by the car, and he had come to the viewing to say his goodbyes. Zach had looked so peaceful lying there in his new suit.

Scott rubbed his tired eyes with the back of his hand. It had been 24 hours since that horrific moment when the ground began to shake ferociously, forcing Zach's coffin to fall off its stand and revealing nothing but an empty gray suit. Zach's body had vanished along with his wife, Valerie, and his son, Timothy. In fact, all around the world in every country people had instantaneously disappeared. People from Scott's office were gone, as well, including Stephanie Miller, Zach's young assistant. He had been looking directly at Stephanie when the ground began to shake, and instantly she had vanished. The people of the world were only now beginning to understand the magnitude of how many had disappeared.

Scott picked up his television remote and pressed the power button. As he scanned through the channels, the news was nearly the same on each. Buildings leveled by the quake were too numerous to count. Fires raged out of control in major cities in every part of the world and at many oil refineries. The effects of the earthquake were being felt on every part of the planet.

Outside the city of Tacoma, Washington, a nuclear power plant had a structural failure that resulted in a core breech and fed the local environment a massive and lethal dosage of radiation. In Japan there was a similar core breech that dumped the deadly radiation into the Sea of Japan, instantly starting the horrible process of killing the sea life. The number of broken dams was not yet known, but flooding was tremendous and fatal to the many low-lying areas of the United States and other countries. Literally millions of homes and apartments around the world were completely demolished into mounds of rubble.

Yet the carnage from the massive earthquake and subsequent tidal waves was only a portion of the total disaster. In many cases, as millions of people disappeared from the earth, they left behind moving vehicles without drivers to control them. There were millions of automobile collisions.

In the sky overhead planes were left to fly themselves as the pilots and co-pilots simply vanished from sight. Large jetliners crashed into homes, churches, office buildings, and even playgrounds.

As Scott listened to the news, his jaw slackened at the numerous disaster scenes flashing before his eyes. He listened carefully to one reporter as he tried to speculate on where all the vanishing people had gone. "There is a growing belief," said the senior anchorman, "that millions of people have been abducted by aliens from another planet. This may explain," he continued, "why it appears as if more children were taken than adults. Furthermore, it may explain how the earth could have experienced a simultaneous earthquake on every continent. Perhaps the aliens aligned themselves around the world and, with some unknown power, these beings from another planet coordinated the abduction of a large part of the world's population."

How ludicrous, Scott thought. *If they had watched Zach's show on the Return of Christ, they would know where everyone went.* He turned the channel to his own news station. They were reporting the same nonsense.

Finally Scott found a station where the news reporter was interviewing a minister from a local Chicago church. "Is it possible that the Rapture has occurred?" the reporter inquired with an incredible amount of worry in his tone.

"No. Absolutely not!" said the preacher as he shook his head.

"Then where have all the people gone?" the reporter asked. "Surely, sir, you don't believe the alien story, do you?"

"It's not my first choice," the minister replied. "Perhaps God has chosen to punish all of those people for some wrongdoing. After all, He didn't remove you or me," he said with a smile.

"But so many people!" said the reporter with amazement, "and so many children!"

Scott flipped the channel one more time only to see before him a picture of Carl Perkins. Scott idolized Carl as a great man and a friend of God. "Reverend Perkins was found dead in his home," said the young female reporter as she stood outside Carl's spectacular mansion. "Apparently Mr. Perkins died of a drug overdose. He was found this morning by an unidentified government official who was sent to the Perkins home to find out if he knew why all of the people had disappeared."

Scott flipped the television off and dropped the remote control to the ground. He buried his face in his hands and began to cry, not so much for Carl, but for himself. *What was the prayer that Pastor Thomas prayed at Zach's funeral? Why didn't I listen?* His mind screamed out in anguish. *Why didn't I give my heart to Jesus the way Zach's son, Timothy, did only seconds before…before what?* Scott thought with a loud sob. *Before Jesus Christ took the Christians to Heaven!*

"God!" he said aloud. "What is to become of us—of me—now?" Scott laid his head on his desktop and wept uncontrollably until he finally fell asleep from exhaustion.

Chapter 2: The Repentant Man

Day 3: Joseph stood holding his breath as Zach came closer and closer towards him. The field that Zach walked through was covered with white and yellow flowers. The grass was tall and green—incredibly green unlike any color he had ever seen. Zach was dressed in a brilliant, white, flowing gown. Suddenly Joseph was afraid to look at him as he drew near.

Joseph tried to back away from Zach's approach and, as he did so, he became aware of his own surroundings which were much different than where Zach Miles stood. Joseph looked down at his own feet and realized he was standing on dry, cracked ground with dead and dying plants sparsely strewn over the land. Around his feet were fierce looking snakes with huge heads and massive, dripping fangs. Joseph tried to scream, but nothing came out. He took a step backwards and tripped over a broken skull that looked to be human.

Falling to the ground, Joseph was suddenly aware of the red and orange sky above him. The air was thick and brownish-yellow with the pungent smell of sulfur and rotting flesh. Joseph looked in Zach's direction and suddenly lost his ability to breathe as he witnessed what appeared to be millions upon millions of people, all dressed in dazzlingly white robes standing behind the most remarkable-looking Man.

Joseph was terrified to look at the beautiful Man, but he could not take his eyes off Him. The Man had absolutely white hair, and His eyes shone like the sun. His face was radiant as if its owner held all the powers of the universe in His grip. The sash He wore around His waist glistened as pure gold. The Man raised His arms into an outstretched position. Joseph could clearly see the large scars on His palms.

"Jesus!" he whispered in awe.

Gradually Jesus turned away from Joseph and back towards the massive crowd of people who were standing behind Him. As Jesus turned, a darkened cloud began to engulf Joseph until he could no longer see Christ or the multitudes that stood with Him.

The separation was unbearable; Joseph felt pain throughout his body. The anguish was beyond anything he could ever imagine.

Writhing from his torture, Joseph screamed, and suddenly he found himself lying on the living room sofa in Zach's apartment. Covered in sweat, he lifted himself from the couch and walked weakly into the bathroom.

Turning the light switch on, he caught a horrible glimpse of his face in the mirror. Tears filled his eyes as he sat down on the edge of the bathtub. "Oh, Lord! Dear God, please help me!" This had been his cry and his prayer for the last three days, but to no avail. He was now convinced that no answer was to come. Joseph knew his Bible well enough to understand what had happened just a few days ago, and he was horrified by what he knew was soon to come next.

Joseph had been inside Zach's Chicago apartment for three days and nights without so much as a piece of bread or even a glass of milk. With the exception of a few sips of tap water, he was on a complete and total fast. It wasn't that Joseph was fasting out of fellowship with God. On the contrary, he found himself so grieved and separated from God that he simply could not eat for the sorrow he felt.

He had not slept more than a handful of hours in the last three days. Each time he fainted away out of exhaustion, he would have the same terrifying dream, and it always ended with him being tortured beyond all description. Joseph moved back to the couch, picked up his Bible once more, and turned to the book of Revelation. How many times had he read this particular book during the last few relentless days? He was desperate to find a solution to his being left behind during the Rapture.

Once again Joseph reached the point in Revelation where Saint John described those martyred by being beheaded. He described them as *The Faithful Remnant* that did not take the mark of the beast, 666. "Okay!" Joseph shouted aloud. "I have not taken the mark of the beast, and if I have to die to enter Heaven, then so be it!" Joseph closed the Bible and laid it gently on his lap. With his head lifted to God, he spoke, "Father, forgive my failures and my lack of faith. Lord, may Your will be done with the remainder of my pitiful life. Give me strength to overcome Satan and, Father, guide my path." Joseph closed his eyes and whispered, "Zach, my friend, I will join you someday soon."

Suddenly he had an incredible sensation of love and warmth all around his body. "Joseph!" spoke a soft, yet powerful voice. "You have chosen a difficult path. It will not be easy for you. Your suffering will be great." Joseph fell to the carpet face down trembling with fear.

"Joseph," said the Lord. "The world is dead in sin. There is little hope, but for the few who will stand against evil, I will show mercy." Joseph wept uncontrollably as the Lord spoke to his mind.

"Soon I will be an abomination to this corrupt world. Those who speak of Me or read My Word will be slain. Use My Truths to comfort you, and keep them alive until the final battle is won. You will be My disciple in this grievous time. Hide My Words in your heart, for they will comfort and aid you in your times of distress. "Now go!" said the Lord. "Go to meet your brother, for I will use him also. Take him to Rome with you, back to the Vatican for a time. Follow your heart, Joseph, for it is all you have left."

Joseph lay on the carpet weeping and praising God for nearly an hour. Finally God's peace gave him the rest he had gone so long without.

Joseph awoke after nearly 12 hours of dreamless sleep. Feeling weak and groggy, he decided he needed some food to strengthen his body. He made himself a cheese omelet and poured a tall glass of what turned out to be very sour milk.

After breakfast Joseph attempted to call his family in Wisconsin for the first time since the Rapture. His father had passed away a few years back, but his mother—a lovely, God-fearing woman—still lived in his small hometown of Appleton. So did his brother, Peter, the doctor.

Joseph's brother, Peter, was 44 years old—three years older than he. Peter was a physician in Appleton, and until he and his wife's divorce, Joseph was certain that Peter had been his parents' pride and joy. Oh, sure, they were proud of Joseph too. After all, he was a priest, but Peter was the firstborn and a total success at everything he put his mind to. Peter's problem was he so often focused on his job that he forgot the little, but important things that make for a good marriage. Over the years this just seemed to drive his wife, Melissa, further away from him, and without any children to keep the couple together, their marriage just simply eroded past repair.

It was shortly after Peter's divorce that his father died of a sudden heart attack. Two weeks later he moved out of his apartment and into his mother's home where he could be close enough to take care of her.

Joseph tried dialing the number for a third time, but the line seemed to be full of static. Unknown to Joseph most phone systems had been severely disrupted due to the earthquake, and those that hadn't were simply overloaded by people in search of their loved ones.

Joseph sat back on the sofa as he hung up the phone. On the other side of the room, a small flash of silver caught his eye. At this he stood and walked across the carpet towards the kitchen counter, and reaching out his hand he picked up a small key ring containing two silver keys and a small plastic frame. The weary ex-priest turned the little frame over, revealing a picture of Valerie and Timothy. Joseph smiled and spoke aloud, "Well, Zach, you have your family back for good now."

Chapter 3: The White Horse—A False Trinity

Day 6: It had been less than a week since the Rapture, and the world was still in horrible chaos. The death toll rose by hundreds of thousands each day. Many of them were now the result of suicide as well as from injuries sustained by the gigantic earthquake. The major systems of the world were rapidly collapsing, and if someone did not assume control quickly, the world would not survive.

Basic systems such as water, sewer, transportation, and medical care were in a shambles. Three of the world's leaders had been assassinated in a single day, and another had taken his own life.

The biggest problem the world faced at this very moment—even worse than the water shortage—was figuring out what to do with the millions of dead bodies. There just wasn't enough time, manpower, or available locations to bury all the dead. Many countries had taken to burning corpses for fear of cholera and other diseases that typically followed mass deaths from disasters.

The hardest hit countries tended to be those which also had the densest populations such as Japan, India, and China, but Europe and America were not far behind in total carnage and chaos.

******

On the horizon a few streaks of red and orange light could still be seen as Carlo Ventini, the European agricultural minister, and his personal secretary, Simon Koch, pulled their Mercedes into the parking lot of the oldest cemetery in Rome. Both men exited their car without a word. Simon followed Carlo closely as he walked through the broken iron gate that separated the parking lot from the graveyard. The men walked past numerous statues of angels and many large granite and marble headstones.

Finally as they reached the back of the cemetery near the tree line, Carlo stopped. Simon moved up beside him and observed Carlo staring directly at a small headstone. Simon gazed off to his left at another gray headstone that was obviously very old. He could not read the name chiseled into the marble face. It was completely worn away by hundreds of years of rain. The stone was cracked down the middle, and the left edge was gone. All that Simon could discern from the stone were three small numbers in the upper, right-hand corner. They were faded and worn but, unlike the name, they seemed to be chiseled much deeper. The three little numbers read 665.

Simon looked to his right to see Carlo bending over the headstone in front of him. Carlo began to pull the weeds away from the little marker, and with the side of his hand he wiped away the crusty mud and debris. Finally with one deep breath Carlo blew across the face of the granite stone, unveiling the name etched thereon. Simon read the name as it revealed itself—*Car...Carlo...Carlo Ven...Carlo Ventini.*

Simon was stunned, but there it was clearly illuminated by the few remaining streaks of sunlight. The stone simply read *Carlo Ventini.* There was no date of birth or death. Simon continued to stare at the marker as Carlo stood, revealing the entire headstone. Simon observed the three small numbers carved into the right-hand corner: 666. He turned to look at Carlo, and as he did this the ground beneath his feet began to tremble as the last rays of sun were lost beneath the horizon.

Simon was frightened by the quake and completely unaware of the hideous grin that spread across Carlo's face. He and Carlo suddenly found themselves surrounded by thousands of evil and grotesque-looking creatures. The ground shook even more violently until finally it cracked wide open before the men and creatures. Fire leaped out of the fissure as smoke bellowed up. Carlo fell to his knees with his face to the ground. Simon, still unsure of what exactly was about to happen next, followed Carlo's lead and fell to the ground beside him. The shaking began to subside until finally it quit completely.

Turning his head slightly and looking out of the corner of his eye, Simon observed all of the evil little creatures lying flat on their stomachs. Suddenly the air was filled with an eerie sound like the call of a rutting mule deer. The noise hurt Simon's ears so much that he had to put his hands over them to diminish the pain.

"The time has come," spoke a thundering voice. Simon could hear creepy giggles coming from the monstrous creatures that lay all around him. "My hour is at hand!" the voice boomed.

"Yes, Father. Now is our time!" returned Carlo.

Simon turned to look at Carlo as he spoke. Simon Koch had been a follower of Satan since his youth when he was first confronted by a powerful demon who had promised him great power and wealth if he would serve the *Lord of the Underworld.* Being a person who never seemed to have enough and who seemed to be disliked by everyone, including his own devoutly Jewish parents, Simon saw this offer as his opportunity to show the world how great and powerful he truly was. Although Simon had never before this day heard the voice of Satan, he had on many occasions prayed to him and followed the direction of Satan's demons. In fact, it was these demons who led Simon directly to Carlo.

From the beginning, Simon liked Carlo. In fact, he was in love with him, yet he kept that bit of information to himself. Simon knew that Carlo was important to Satan and that he was powerful. But it wasn't until this very moment that he realized Carlo was, in fact, Satan's chosen one...the one selected to rule the world...to deceive the world. He was the Antichrist.

"Yes," said Satan. "We will defeat that Carpenter, that illegitimate Son. I will be worshiped in heaven and on earth. My power will be the greatest. I cannot be defeated! Stand to your feet both of you."

Carlo stood quickly. Simon was a bit slower to move, but eventually he found himself standing in awe next to Carlo. "Today," Satan said, "I will form my trinity. Carlo, you are my Son and rule over the earth. Simon, you will be my prophet, and I will speak through you, and you will assist my Son." Simon felt a surge of power that made his head dizzy. He felt euphoric and was in ecstasy.

"There is much to do. I will make your names known to all people. Carlo, you will be a god to them, and you will rule over them until I come to take my permanent place."

"Now go! I will reveal my plans to you. There are still a few believers and followers of that false prophet, Jesus. They must be destroyed!"

As Satan spoke the name of Jesus, the hideous creatures, still on their stomachs, shrieked with fear. This did not go unnoticed by Simon. "Go and seek them out as we prepare to conquer the world."

Chapter 4: The Disciples

Day 10: Tommy stood on the balcony of the Best Western Hotel as the sun rose above the Pacific Ocean. He and Tina had spent the last week at this hotel 70 miles inland and north of Long Beach. *So much death,* Tommy thought as he stared at the early morning sky. The tidal waves and earthquakes had nearly destroyed all of southern California. Millions were either dead or had disappeared.

The city was in ruins, and repairs were impossible due to the lack of stability of the buildings and the ground itself, for that matter. The major cities were full of looters, and the state and military police were hardly in a position to risk the lives of the few remaining workers they had just to prevent the theft of merchandise or the robbing of a destroyed bank.

Tommy walked back into the room through the sliding glass door and towards the small kitchenette area where he poured two cups of coffee. He set both cups down on the nightstand and reclined on his mattress. The bed looked as if nobody had even slept in it, or at least not for very long. Tommy stared across to the other bed where Tina lay sleeping.

He looked at her for quite some time as she stirred in her sleep. She was obviously having another one of those dreams—the ones that woke her up nightly covered with sweat and crying from fear. Each time she would wake up and realize that the tidal wave had not caught up to her, nor was she drowning.

"What do we do now?" Tommy asked as he looked up. "God, I don't even know who You are!" Tears began to fill Tommy's eyes. All of this death and tragedy was just too much to bear. He looked again towards Tina. She was no longer stirring but was sleeping peacefully.

Suddenly Tommy felt a presence in the small hotel room. He stood in the center of the room and turned 360 degrees, but saw nothing.

"Is someone here?" he asked fearfully.

The room took on an amber glow. "Fear not!" said a soft voice.

"Who are you, and what's going on?" a terrified Tommy inquired. His legs shook so much that he had to sit down in the middle of the floor.

"Be still," said the voice, "and I will tell you what you need to know."

"I am the Lord, your God! Although you have not known Me, I have always known you. This world is coming to a swift and just end. It will not be long before My wrath is to be poured out. But for the sake of the few who will remain faithful to Me, I will be patient to delay My destruction until they are safely gathered."

"What do You want from me, Lord? I have not been faithful to You," said Tommy as he sobbed bitterly.

"You will be faithful to Me, and you will help to lead many to Me before the end comes. I have chosen you even though you did not choose Me. I have found you to be a righteous man. You have shown that by taking care of your sister your entire life. You will serve Me well," said the Lord.

"What do I need to do?" Tommy asked.

"You must stay here and prepare. I will come to you and guide you when the time is right."

"What about my sister?" Tommy was apprehensive.

"She will stay with you, but her heart is not the same as yours. You must be careful not to stumble."

******

The waters were still very turbulent, especially in the Yellow Sea. The 10-foot swells continued to torture the side of Izuho Saeki's 30-foot fishing boat. After the disaster in Okinawa, Izuho had no place to live, so he took the life insurance money that came to him after his mother and sister died and bought a boat. He had been very lucky, once again, to avoid a tidal wave. The recent disastrous earthquake had caused many deadly waves around the world, but somehow he always seemed to be south or west of each monster Tsunami.

Izuho had nowhere in particular to go. He just couldn't stand to be around all the misery in Japan, and the southern part of the island was off limits due to radiation fallout.

Fighting 10-foot waves continuously was a fair tradeoff as far as he was concerned.

The sun was just beginning to rise over the stern of the boat as Izuho trailed off at only seven knots. "Izuho," said a comforting voice. Izuho looked over his shoulder. *I'm hearing things,* he thought. *Maybe it's the wind.* With the waves crashing into the side of his boat it was easy to believe that the noise of wind and water could sound like just about anything.

"Izuho!" said the voice again. This time it was clearer to Izuho. Suddenly the wind and waves began to settle down until there was merely a light breeze and the water was as flat as glass. Izuho turned off the boat's motor and drifted along for a few minutes.

Above the bow of the boat Izuho began to see a golden light growing brighter and brighter until he could no longer look at it without feeling pain. Izuho held his hand over his brow to shelter his eyes.

"Who are you?" he asked timidly.

"I am your God. The Almighty God!" said the voice.

"Are you Jesus?" Izuho asked in fear.

"I am!" said the powerful voice.

"Are you the god who saved me from the tidal wave?" he asked cautiously.

"I am the only God!" boomed the voice.

Izuho fell to his knees and bowed his head. "I am not worthy," he whispered.

"Nevertheless," said the Lord, "I have chosen you."

"Chosen me? What can I do?" a trembling, young Izuho asked.

"You will be My disciple to this part of the world. You will help to lead the lost back to Me before the evil one devours them. You have a good heart and the courage necessary. Your task will be difficult. You will be rejected and assaulted, but your courage will lead many to Me before the end comes."

Izuho began to cry as God spoke to him. "Dear Lord, how? Tell me how will I lead people to You. Where should I go?"

"For a short while you must go back to Japan. I will send you helpers. Now go!"

The light faded as the wind began to howl. Shortly after that the waves began to pound the side of Izuho's boat again as he made a 180-degree turn towards Japan.

******

Stan could not take another minute cooped up in the small shelter. His children were fast asleep. With that in mind, Stan took Ruby by the hand and led her out of the huge tent.

It was a hot and dark evening. This was typical for Australia this time of the year.

The world may have changed forever, Stan thought as he stared up at the night's sky, *but the stars still look the same.* Stan had always planned on living on one of those stars in an imperishable body, as promised by his former church. After the events of the last week, he no longer believed any of that. In fact, both Stan and Ruby were horribly and sadly aware of the deception that had gripped them for so long. Ruby cried herself to sleep nightly, as did Stan, but he managed to keep this a secret from his family, or so he thought.

"It's not about us," said Ruby flatly. "We had our chance, but look what we've done to our children," she said through her stinging tears. "They have been deceived because of us, and now what will happen to them?"

Two of the Evans' children had been killed in a raging fire some weeks back. Both Ruby and Stan understood that all of the crying in the world would not change the fact that those two boys were also deceived and never knew Jesus as the true Son of God. They were lost, and the pain was too much to bear.

"We cannot help those two," said Stan one evening as he held and rocked Ruby in consolation. "We still have six children left—and each other. Maybe there is still time." Stan didn't really believe this. He was sure that he had led his family down a path of eternal damnation. He felt guilt beyond expression, but he had to continue on for his family's sake.

"God, if I could only do it over again," he prayed. "Please, Lord, for my children's sake, help us! Give us another chance." Stan prayed this with all his heart and soul.

Ruby, on the other hand, tended to bury her nose in the Bible. She was sure there had to be a loophole in there somewhere. She could still remember something she had heard or been taught from her childhood, but she wasn't sure. *Those coming out of the tribulation...* This phrase continued to run through her mind. Ruby prayed, asking God to help her prepare her family for what was yet to come.

Stan and Ruby walked along silently hand in hand. There was no need to speak. It was clear what was on both of their minds. They needed a miracle. They needed guidance and direction for their family to survive what was coming.

A cool breeze blew lightly across Ruby's cheek. She stopped in her tracks and stared out into the night sky. Her abrupt stop confused Stan. "What is it?" he asked.

"I don't know, but something—someone—is here!" she said with fear.

The wind stilled as a soft white glow began to engulf them. Terrified, Ruby and Stan clutched each other tightly. This was the moment they had feared. The punishment they both knew was coming was now here. "Do not fear," said a gentle voice. "I have heard your repentant cries."

Ruby could not stand, and as her legs gave way, Stan led her gently to the ground. "I have searched your hearts," said the Lord. "You have been misled by a deceiving angel of light. You must now follow your heart and seek Me with all of your soul. I will use you to overcome Satan, to lead men back to Me before My wrath is turned loose. Your tasks will be hard and hurtful! You will suffer greatly, but for the faithful there is a paradise prepared for eternity. Just as Abraham obeyed Me, you must do the same. Now leave this place and take your family to Sydney."

"Lord," Stan said. "What do you want us to do?"

"I will bring others to you that will help you. Now see to it that you are no longer deceived by the Devil."

******

Jasmine and Elisha had been walking for days through the knee deep—and sometimes waist deep—sand. Finally they had successfully carved a path through the Judean Mountains and down into the desert of Beersheba. They were now wandering through the same land that Hagar and Ishmael had nearly died in, and like He did for Ishmael and Hagar, God provided for Jasmine and Elisha. They continued to find water sources along their journey.

Although it had been weeks since the sandstorm and nearly a week since the earthquake, the people of this region were still very much trapped in their small towns. Elisha wondered if he and Jasmine would ever see a living person along their travels.

Jasmine followed some 10 feet behind Elisha as he pushed his way towards a small stand of date palms. Although the sun was directly over-head, the breeze at their backs made the heat bearable. Elisha stood star-ing up at the tall palm tree as Jasmine approached. She stood beside him and looked up to see what he was staring at. Jasmine's mouth began to water as she gazed at a large clump of ripe dates some 20 feet up the smooth-barked tree.

"Well, how are you going to get those down?" she asked.

Elisha had to laugh. After a month with Jasmine, he was really begin-ning to appreciate her negative humor. "How hungry are you?" he asked without looking at Jasmine.

"I'm starved!" she said impatiently.

"Good!" said Elisha. "Then you won't mind giving me your pants."

"My pants! What for?" she asked.

After a little persuasion, Jasmine finally stood behind one of the palm trees and handed out a small pair of Levi's to Elisha. "I want these back!" she said harshly.

"No problem," he giggled.

Elisha stood next to the tree and, with his right hand, he slung Jasmine's pants around the trunk of the tree. Slowly, like a caterpillar, Elisha worked his way up the tree until he reached the clump of dates. With one hand he pulled at the fruit, but it would not let go of the tree. Again and again he tugged at the bunch of dates until he was nearly exhausted.

"Hurry up!" Jasmine begged. "I want my pants back!" Elisha wrapped his legs around the tree's trunk as tight as he could and then dropped Jasmine's Levi's. With both hands he reached out to the fruit and pulled with all of his might. This plan was not well conceived from the beginning, and Elisha had not even taken the time to consider the weight of this large bunch of dates. He was about to learn the power of gravity.

Minutes later Jasmine giggled quietly to herself as she leaned back against the tree eating a large, ripe, delicious date. Elisha didn't think it was very funny. "I could have broken my neck, you know." He looked for some sympathy from the little Palestinian rebel.

"You look fine to me," she smiled nonchalantly. Thanks to the sandy landing, Elisha was unhurt—all except his pride, of course.

"How long until we get to Sederot?" asked Jasmine inquisitively.

"I'm not sure. I think it's about 40 miles southeast of here," said Elisha, "and at the rate we're moving, that will take us four or five days unless we run into somebody with a Jeep or something."

Elisha and Jasmine decided to spend the night right where they lay. After nearly a week of struggling through the sand and hills with very little rest, it seemed reasonable to them that they should take the time to recuperate. As the night began to close in on the two of them, they moved closer together to keep each other warm. They had developed this routine while they were in the cave, and now it just seemed like the natural thing to do.

In truth, both of them looked forward to this intimacy. Neither of them spoke it, but it was obvious that these two young adults had fallen in love with each other. This was a new emotion for them both, and they were not sure of what to think about it.

Jasmine yawned as she nestled in closer to Elisha. "What do you think God wants the two of us to do?" she asked with a tired voice.

Up to this point they hadn't spent any time talking about God. Nei-

ther of them was sure how to deal with the fact that they had both neglected the truth of Jesus Christ.

They didn't know who He really was and what it meant to follow
after Him and especially what it meant not to follow after Him. Neither
Elisha nor Jasmine had any idea of the Rapture that had already occurred.
All they knew was that Jesus was coming back, and they somehow needed
to get ready for His return.

"I don't know, but I'm sure God will tell us eventually," said Elisha in
a gentle and kind voice. He lifted his arm and draped it over Jasmine's
shoulder as she fell asleep on his chest.

In the morning, while the early rays of light skimmed across the desert
sky, Elisha awoke to see that Jasmine was nowhere in sight. He stood to
look around, and as he did so he felt the effects of falling 20 feet out of
the palm tree. His back and behind smarted terribly.

Elisha could see the silhouette of Jasmine as she walked down a
small sand dune towards their camp. "Finally wake up?" she asked brightly.

"Yeah, I guess so," he said painfully as he tried to stretch his back.

"Well, we'd better get going," she suggested.

"Okay, you gather up some of these dates while I go and find a sand
hill of my own."

Elisha traipsed off towards a small dune to find relief while Jasmine
piled as many dates as she could into her coat pockets.

"Are you ready?" Elisha asked as he approached the oasis.

"Yes, but first put these in your pockets," she said as she held out two
hands full of large dates.

The sun was barely high enough to provide sufficient light to guide
their way, yet the two of them marched out into the desert just the same.
They had not been walking for even 30 minutes when the wind started to
pick up. The sand began to blow back into their faces, stinging their un-
protected eyes. Elisha could hardly see sufficiently to guide Jasmine along
the desert's floor.

"I can't see!" said Jasmine desperately.

Elisha took hold of Jasmine's hand. "Close your eyes and cover your
face, and don't let go of my hand whatever you do!" Elisha could make

out a small rock formation to his right. It was about a quarter of a mile away, but it was their only hope of shelter. Elisha's nose and mouth were full of sand, and breathing became very difficult. Protecting his eyes as best he could, Elisha struggled as he led Jasmine towards the rock ledge.

Finally, just as the wind and sand were intensifying to an unbearable level, Jasmine and Elisha reached the rock pile. The way these rocks stuck out high about the sand made them look like the world's largest set of steak knives. Five rocks all in a row stood at a 45 degree angle with small gaps between each of them. Elisha headed directly towards the center of the rock formation. There was just enough room for Jasmine and him to sidestep their way in between the rocks. As soon as they entered the formation, the wind disappeared and the sand discontinued its assault.

Jasmine took one look at Elisha and then another. Finally she had to laugh. Elisha's eyes and nose were nearly closed off by the sand. Elisha coughed as he tried to clear his mouth of the sand. He began to choke violently. At that point Jasmine was no longer laughing. Instead she was knocking the sand from Elisha's face with both her hands without regard to how hard she was wiping. Elisha wasn't sure what was worse—the coughing, the burning eyes, or Jasmine's slaps on his face. He grabbed her hand. "I'm okay!" he said.

Jasmine had a look of concern on her face. "Are you sure?" she asked out of genuine kindness.

"Yes, I'm fine!" he said softly.

"What do we do now?" Jasmine asked.

"Wait," Elisha answered flatly.

The two of them were wedged between the rocks for hours. Every once in a while Elisha would step out to check the weather conditions, but they had not improved in the least. Jasmine sat crouched against the rock, a look of boredom covering her face. "I hope we don't have to spend the night here," she said in a testy voice.

Unexpectedly there was a brilliant flash of light between the two rocks. Jasmine stood and moved closer to Elisha. Oddly enough he did not feel any fear; in fact, he was hoping and praying that God would send someone to help them. The light grew, faintly revealing the outline of a man—a very large man. Finally the light became an aura. They could now clearly see a large, handsome black man who seemed to tower over them both.

"Fear not!" said the man in a gentle but firm voice. "I have been sent to you by our Father in Heaven. You must not go to Sederot. You must go to Bethlehem."

Elisha found the courage to speak. "Bethlehem? But that must be 80 miles from here! We'll die if we try to walk there."

Jasmine looked at Elisha approvingly. *Enough is enough!* she thought. "I want to go home!" she said aloud.

"Child, you have no home," said Philip, the angel. "The Lord Jesus Christ has come back." Elisha and Jasmine were both made afraid by this comment, even though they really didn't understand yet what Philip was telling them. "Jesus has taken the faithful with Him, and He will not return until the final battle is prepared."

Jasmine slid back against the rock. "Does this mean that we don't get to go to Heaven?" she asked with tears in her eyes.

"No," answered the angel kindly. "It means that you have to wait until God comes for you."

"Then why can't we go home?" Jasmine asked.

"Child!" said Philip. "You have no home. Neither of you has a home. The earthquake has destroyed your houses and killed your families." Philip's proclamation stole the breath from Elisha and Jasmine. Their pain and sorrow was overwhelming.

"The Lord has chosen you two for a special purpose."

"What purpose?" Jasmine cried. "Why didn't He save my mother and brothers?"

"Only God knows this Little One, but His ways are perfect. You must accept this."

"What does God want from us?" a teary-eyed Elisha asked. "Until four weeks ago we didn't even know that Jesus was the Son of God!"

"The Lord has selected the two of you because of your pure hearts. You will be disciples to His chosen people, the Jewish nation," said Philip.

"What can we do?" Jasmine asked. "We're just children!"

"You must have the faith of a child to enter His kingdom. Out of the mouths of children will God's word be spoken."

"Why Bethlehem?" inquired Elisha.

"This is where you must start," Philip proclaimed. "This is where it all began for Jesus as a man, and this is where it will begin for you two as disciples."

"But what are disciples?" Jasmine asked. "We don't know anything about Jesus except that He is real and He is God."

"That's all you need to know," said the angel. "A disciple must stand up and proclaim the truth. People must then choose to believe or reject the truth."

Philip stepped closer to Elisha and Jasmine and his eyes intensified greatly. "Satan is looking for the two of you. He wants to destroy you before you can lead others to God. He will come after you. He will try to deceive and kill you!"

"Will you protect us?" Jasmine asked in fear.

"If God allows it," said Philip. "Draw your strength from God and each other. Trust nothing else." The light around Philip brightened until Elisha and Jasmine were also engulfed. The sensation was one of peace and love.

******

Elisha awoke first and began to stand. "Where are we?" he spoke aloud as he looked down from a hilltop into a small sandy valley. Elisha could see people moving around in the streets. He could see bulldozers pushing mountains of sand along the edge of the small city.

Jasmine stood next to Elisha. "Bethlehem, I assume?" she said in a witty way.

Jasmine was a person who could quickly adjust to the fascinating and the fantastic. Elisha was a little more perplexed and cautious.

"Now what do we do?" Jasmine inquired.

Elisha turned towards her and stared into her young and beautiful dark eyes. "We become disciples."

******

Calvin Fraser lay atop the covers of his bed drifting in and out of a light sleep. His cell was dark and hot. Over the course of the last week Calvin had suffered great mental anguish to the point of exhaustion.

For many days now he had been searching for understanding. He knew, just like the rest of the world, that something extraordinary had occurred. In fact, he had witnessed with his own eyes the disappearance of another prisoner in the cell not 10 feet away from his own cell. All that remained in the empty cell was a prison uniform and an old Bible that the prisoner had been reading aloud before he disappeared. When the guard came to investigate, Calvin asked him if he could have the vanished prisoner's Bible. "Well, I guess he won't need it anymore," said the guard in a sad and defeated voice.

Calvin had been reading the old Bible night and day with very few interruptions. The one thing about prison is that there are very few interruptions. He could not fully understand the book of Revelation, but he was certain that the answer to the most recent mystery was in there somewhere. Out of frustration Calvin gave up on the book of Revelation and began to fan his way through the Bible one book at a time. Eventually he found himself in 1 John. More specifically, he found himself reading 1 John 5:5. *"Who is it that overcomes the world? Only he who believes that Jesus is the Son of God."* Calvin put the Bible down on the floor beside his bed and reclined against his pillow. "Jesus, I know that You are the Son of God," he said with a whisper.

******

It had been two days since Calvin stumbled across 1 John 5:5, and yet he could not get the verse out of his mind. *"Who is it that overcomes the world?"* This thought echoed through his head constantly. "'Only he who believes that Jesus is the Son of God,'" he would reply aloud out of frustration.

Calvin tried to get the question out of his mind by reading other books of the Bible. However, again and again he would find his thoughts drifting back to 1 John 5:5. *"Who is it that overcomes the world?"* his mind would scream until he finally had no choice but to say aloud, "'Only he who believes that Jesus is the Son of God!'"

With frustration Calvin threw the old leather book across his cell, smacking it hard against the brick wall and dislodging a page of the Bible as he did. He rolled in on his bunk facing the wall, opposite the book that caused him so much grief. "I said that I believe!" he grumbled. "What more do You want?"

Calvin drifted away into a much needed sleep. Abruptly he found himself standing on a rock ledge overlooking a long, narrow valley. The sky overhead was black and smoky, and except for a red glow in the center of the sky, there was no visual sign of the sun. Calvin stared down into the valley, and what he saw terrified him to the point that his knees buckled, sending him falling forward down a steep, rocky path. He landed with a splash, and after catching his breath, he attempted to stand, but for some reason it took considerably more effort than he had expected. Calvin used his hand to push himself up, but what he was pushing against was not solid. At first it looked solid. Soon, however, it registered in Calvin's mind that what he was pushing against was actually liquid or partially so.

"What is this?" he said aloud. Calvin finally struggled his way onto his feet. As he stepped forward, he found himself wading knee deep in a thick, slimy liquid. He walked slowly forward towards the center of the valley. The orange glow of an intense fire grew as he approached.

Finally Calvin reached the edge of his destination. By this time the slimy fluid was nearly waist deep. He had to refocus his eyes against the intensely bright light of the fire. Calvin still wasn't sure what its source was. As he moved on again, something bumped into his left thigh. Looking, down Calvin pushed the object away with his hand, revealing the torso and head of a young man. It was a grotesque sight, causing him to fall backwards into the stiff liquid. Calvin settled down in the fluid up to his chin. As he stared at the pitiful remains of the young man, another body floated into his view. This body was missing its head and one of its arms. What remained, however, was obviously female. In the distance Calvin could now see hundreds—no thousands, maybe millions—of dead bodies.

Calvin stood and pushed his way through the many corpses that floated in front of him. For some reason he was compelled to continue toward the source of the fire. The closer he came to the bright glow, the more the light reflected off the liquid. At first the fire made the slimy goop look black, but as he drew closer the color changed from black to a shiny white to a burnt orange color. As Calvin stepped forward to the edge of the fire, the light revealed the true color of the liquid. It was red—blood red. In fact, it was blood. Calvin felt terribly nauseated as he became aware of the fact that he was wading waist deep in human blood.

As Calvin moved to the fire's edge, he found a large, jagged rock sticking out above the blood pool. He pushed against the decapitated and mutilated bodies until he finally made his way to the rock and climbed aboard, slipping twice as he tried to get out of the slimy death.

Calvin turned and faced the fire. From where he stood he realized that the fire was in a huge circle, and oddly enough the fire was not burning up towards the sky. In fact, just the opposite was happening. The fire was burning inward towards the center of the circle. As Calvin continued to study the flame, he realized that the center of it was hollow. The fire rushed in all around the edge in a perfect circle, but the center was void— completely empty. It frightened Calvin to look into the heart of the inferno. He felt as if he was being swept into it, and he was terrified!

As he watched, the current surrounding the blaze pulled the dead bodies towards itself. Body parts and complete corpses went hurling into the center of the ring of fire. It was like a gusher only it was going down instead of up. Suddenly he became aware of the sound of screams and moans. He leaned forward to try and see into the center of the circle, and as he did so he slipped off the rock.

Calvin screamed as the pull of the fire began to drag him towards the horrible black empty center. The pain he felt was tremendous. The flames burned his flesh. He tried to climb over the multitude of bodies to get away from the blackness.

Calvin cried out, "Lord, help me, please!" The weight of the corpses piling up from behind began to push him towards the abyss. *That black empty center is eternal death,* he told himself. "God, I don't want to go there. Help me!"

Calvin woke up screaming and covered with sweat. He swung his legs over the side of his bed and leaned his body forward. His hands were shaking, and he was still sobbing even though he was unaware of this.

Though his cell was dark, the dim light of the hall illuminated the small piece of paper that had so rudely and abruptly been torn from the old Bible. Calvin stood weakly and walked over to the book. He picked it up and carefully set it on the shelf. Next he bent down and picked up the dislodged page. Calvin held the page up to his face. The light struck the scripture revealing Matthew 28:19-20. "'Therefore,'" Calvin read aloud, "'go and make disciples of all nations, baptizing them in the name of the Father and of the Son and of the Holy Spirit, and teaching them to obey everything I have commanded you. And surely I am with you always, to the very end of the age.'"

He stared at the verse and finally it all started to make sense. Calvin had seen Hell. He knew that people were going to spend an unimaginable eternity in that terrible place.

"Who is it that overcomes the world?" This thought echoed in his mind once again, but this time he was at peace with the verse. "'Only he who believes that Jesus is the Son of God,'" he told himself as his tears glistened in the dim light. "Only he who believes."

Calvin held onto the page of text as he sat back on his bed. "Lord, I believe in You!" he cried. "If You have a purpose for me, if You want me to tell nations about You, so be it! God, I want to follow after You, but what should I do?"

Calvin turned around and knelt by the side of his bunk. He prayed silently for quite a while before being startled by a warm, soft glow illuminating his cell. Calvin turned around to see the source of the light while still on his knees. The feeling around him was one of peace and great joy. "Who are you?" Calvin asked fearfully.

"I am your God," a loving voice responded. "You are now ready to serve Me. I will use you to disciple many before the end comes."

"Lord!" said Calvin. "How can I be of any use locked in this place?"

"This is where you will start My work, but this is not where you will end it."

The glow began to fade before Calvin could ask another question. Calvin buried his face in his hands and wept for joy.

Chapter 5: The Asteroid

Day 14: Hector Roundtree stared at the chart for the third time. Again his calculations bore out the trajectory of the star-like mass moving at a tremendous speed through the Kuiper Asteroid Belt. Hector had been trying to coordinate observation of this dense little asteroid's movement with the help of the Arecibo radar site as well as his own Goldstone facility in New Mexico and his sister Goldstone radar facility in California.

Hector plugged in another disc and quickly clicked the enter key. A few seconds later he ejected the disc and attached a small label. On this he wrote: "ED14, Possible S-class or Full metallic, Non-threatening orbit." He slid the disc into a folder and slipped the folder into a large metal filing cabinet. Sitting back in his chair he let out a long sigh and rubbed his tired eyes. *How long has it been since I slept?* he wondered. *How long has it been since the world fell apart?*

Working at the observatory was at least a way to avoid the reality of the last couple of weeks. However, now that he had finally cataloged the asteroid that he had been working on for six months, there was nothing left to keep him distracted.

Hector Roundtree was a Navajo Indian who had been raised by his mother and older sister on a small reservation in New Mexico just off Highway 10. A drunk driver had killed Hector's father when he was only three weeks old, leaving him as the only living Roundtree male from his tribe.

Hector's mother and big sister were stern but loving. They watched every move he made until the day he finally went off to college to become an astronomer. Hector had always loved the stars. Many times as a child he would sneak outside and lay on the cool grass, flat on his back, while staring out into the dark and warm New Mexico sky. He had heard all the legends about what the stars really were and where they were supposed to have come from. He knew both the Indian and Christian versions of the story, but he believed neither of them.

Now this 23-year-old scientist sat back in his chair to ponder a new mystery. *Where did they go?* Could everything Hector thought he knew to be true, be all wrong? He saw his mother and sister disappear from the dinner table. He knew that they were not the only ones to go. His life was spent with his mother and sister preaching Jesus to him until he was fed up with all of the stories they told.

"I can't believe what I can't see," he had told his sister one day after a 30-minute lecture on the need for him to go to church.

******

Hector had dozed off in his chair for a few hours as the sun began its brief climb into the morning sky. Suddenly a loud buzzing noise nearly caused him to fall out of his reclined position. He turned around to see an early detection alarm going off on his main console. Hector hit the button, which killed the deafening blare of the alarm. "What do we have here?" he asked aloud as he scooted his chair closer to his instruments. His infrared reading was off the chart.

Hector tried to maneuver his radar to a position that would give him a better chance of detecting this anomaly, but the signal-to-noise ratio was terrible, and he couldn't get a good fix. Finally, after many attempts, he had a true location and began to scan the sky.

"Whoa!" said Hector as he looked at the image on the screen. He had seen solar storms before, but this one was spectacular. The solar flares, as they were called, just seemed to leap off the surface of the sun as they reached into the deep black space.

Hector tried to link the Hubble telescope and the Galileo to enhance the image. "This is going to create a magnetic storm," he said aloud. Three seconds later Hector lost communications with both telescopes.

Goldstone's radar was the most powerful Xband in the world, but at the moment the parabolic reflector was paralyzed by the magnetic disruptions. Hector tried to contact the observatory in Haleakala, Maui, but the phone was dead. He had no way of knowing if Haleakala was even still alive after the last earthquake and subsequent tidal waves. "All right," said Hector. "I'll just have to wait this out." He made a brief note in his ledger and then switched off his telescope.

******

In the Kuiper Asteroid Belt in view of the Galileo spacecraft, which unfortunately had been temporarily disabled by the magnetic storm, was a small but extremely dense asteroid of the Aten type. Aten-type asteroids are closely monitored by the NEAT (Near Earth Asteroid Tracking) system. This was a joint decision between NASA and the local scientific community.

Since these particular orbits provide the least amount of reaction time, in the unlikely event that a killer asteroid of sufficient mass and velocity was to get bumped into a collision trajectory with Earth, the NEAT system would alert NASA to the impending asteroid.

As this metallic Aten-type asteroid hurled through space completely unobserved, it was rudely redirected by a C-class, low-density asteroid. The impact of the collision destroyed the larger, star-like projectile due to its composition of silicate and frozen water. The smaller but much denser asteroid spun into a new orbit which now would take it directly into the path of Hector's newly discovered S-class asteroid ED14. This impending impact would be hidden in space along with the other 90 percent of undiscovered asteroids.

The results of this collision would not be felt for over three years. The new destination for ED14, the non-threatening asteroid, was now Mother Earth. If a 50-meter-diameter asteroid could destroy the Tunguska Wilderness of Siberia with the explosive power of millions of megatons of TNT, what could an extremely dense, six-mile-wide asteroid do to the planet?

Chapter 6: Brothers United

Joseph turned off Wisconsin Avenue and onto Bell Street. He didn't remember this street being as dark as it was at this moment. Of course, he hadn't been home for over a year. Soon though, Joseph began to realize that the lighting in this entire neighborhood was out. *Perhaps this is a result of the earthquake,* he told himself. Nevertheless, Zach Miles' car had good headlights, and Joseph knew the way.

Two blocks later Joseph turned the car into a dark driveway and parked beside an old Chevy pickup truck. Joseph sat in the driver's seat for a few minutes while he stared at the front porch of this familiar old house. "So many memories," he said softly. The moon's light temporarily illuminated Joseph's childhood home as the clouds drifted by.

How much time had he and his big brother, Peter, spent sitting on that porch during those warm summer evenings listening to their father tell them stories from his youth? Joseph especially liked the stories his dad told them about the time he spent in the Navy during WWII.

Slowly Joseph climbed out of the car and shut the door. As he walked past the blue truck, he stopped and looked into the cab. It was really too dark to see much, but he could make out an empty soda can and a candy wrapper. Joseph had to laugh. Peter may have been good at taking care of others, but he certainly didn't give much thought to his own health. Joseph patted the hood of the old truck as he walked past. *Some things never change,* he told himself.

The porch entrance was dark, as was the living room—or at least it seemed that way to Joseph as he tried to peek through the front bay window. He turned the doorknob slowly, and to his surprise the door slid open with just the lightest squeak. Joseph stepped in leaving the door open behind him to let a little of the moon's light into the dark room. This didn't help much, but it was better than the pitch-black alternative.

Joseph stood silently listening for any signs of life. He really hadn't expected to hear anything. He was sure that his mother would have joined his father in Heaven after the Rapture. After all, she was a wonderful servant of the Lord.

Joseph really didn't expect Peter to be there either. He knew that his big brother would probably be spending all of his time at the Neenah Hospital. "He will probably eat and sleep there now that Mom has gone to Heaven," he told himself.

Something caught Joseph's eye down at the end of the narrow hall. Two small orange creatures danced slowly against the far wall. It took Joseph's mind a few seconds to realize that these creatures were actually shadows cast by some unknown light source. He also heard the scraping sound of a chair leg as if it was being pushed or dragged across the wooden floor. Joseph took a couple of cautious steps towards the sound. *It's coming from the kitchen,* he thought. With so much vandalism going on, it was possible that somebody was trying to rob his mother's house.

Suddenly the orange dancing creatures disappeared from the wall. Joseph stopped and froze where he stood. The moonlight behind him illuminated the outline of a person stepping into the hallway from the kitchen.

"Who are you?" said a voice with a slight northern accent.

Joseph blew a sigh of relief through his tightly clenched lips as he recognized the voice. "Peter, it's me—Joseph!"

"Joseph, it can't be you! You're in Heaven with Mom," said the frightened big brother. "All of the Christians went to Heaven, didn't they?"

Joseph fished his cigarette lighter out of his pants pocket. He hadn't smoked for days, and he probably never would again, but he still had his old familiar lighter. Joseph lit it and held it up to his face.

"It's me, Peter. Really, it's me!" Joseph waved the Zippo back and forth so Peter could get a good look at his face.

Peter stepped forward cautiously. "It really is you!" he said. "But why—why aren't you in Heaven? Didn't the Rapture really happen?"

Peter was totally confused.

For a week now he had been certain that his mother and Joseph were enjoying eternity in Heaven with his father, Jesus, and the rest of the Christians while he spent night and day at the hospital taking care of attempted suicide victims, wounded vandals, and numerous motor vehicle accident victims.

"Yes!" said Joseph. "The Rapture really did happen, but I didn't go."

Peter looked at Joseph with a confused and worried look on his face. "Why not?" Peter asked suspiciously. "You're a priest for crying out loud!"

Joseph stepped up to Peter and extended his hand. Peter stared at Joseph's hand, examining it to determine if it was real or just a hallucination. *After all,* he thought, *I haven't slept for more than a few hours this entire week.*

"I'm real," said Joseph as if he was reading Peter's mind.

Peter shook his little brother's hand and then pulled him in and hugged him tightly.

Peter began to cry aloud. "I thought I'd never see you again." He hugged Joseph even tighter until Joseph thought Peter was going to break his ribs.

"It's good to see you too!" said Joseph as he gasped for air.

Peter loosened his grip. *Just in the nick of time,* Joseph thought. *Another minute and I'd have passed out.*

"Come on in here," said Peter as he led Joseph into the kitchen. On the table were two medium-sized candles.

"The orange dancers," whispered Joseph.

"What?" Peter asked.

Joseph smiled. "Nothing."

Joseph looked at his older brother as the candles bathed him in soft light. Peter looked tired to him. Joseph imagined that he probably looked warn out to Peter as well.

Peter was taller than Joseph, but they weighed about the same. Joseph was stocky and well built. Peter was slender with the shape of a runner, which he definitely was not. The brothers looked quite a bit alike. Peter's hair was curlier, but it was just as dark as Joseph's with a bit of gray thrown in. Both men also had broad, handsome smiles and dark, soft eyes.

Joseph pulled out one of the wooden chairs and set his tired body down. Peter sat down next to him. "Why are you here, Joseph?" Peter asked cautiously.

Joseph stared at the old wooden table. He rubbed his hand across the walnut finish. "Dad made this, didn't he?"

"What?" Peter said. "Yes, he made the table, but what are you doing here? Why aren't you in Heaven?"

Joseph looked up at Peter's tired and worried face. For as long as he could remember his big brother had been a caregiver. Peter had always been his mom and dad's big helper. He sheltered and protected Joseph as he grew up. When Joseph would get into trouble, Peter would get him out of it. Occasionally Peter would have to knock some sense into Joseph to keep him on track, but in general he was gentle and caring. After their dad died, Peter was quick to assume the responsibility of taking care of their mother. It was a natural fit for him to select medicine as his choice of careers.

Peter waited patiently for Joseph to explain himself.

"I'm not in Heaven," said Joseph, "because I didn't believe!"

Joseph paused and looked at Peter. It was obvious that his big brother was still confused. *His preconceived notions about me are going to be hard to break,* Joseph thought to himself.

"You didn't believe what?" Peter inquired.

He needs more clarification, Joseph thought. "I wasn't sure what I believed. All I knew was that I didn't feel God in my life. I didn't have a personal relationship with Jesus. All I had were doubts."

"But you're a priest!" said Peter. The way he said it caused Joseph to laugh out loud.

"I may be a priest," said Joseph, "but I am also a man—a weak man!"

"So let me get this straight!" said Peter. "You didn't go to Heaven because you didn't believe, but you are a priest, right?"

"That's just about it," said Joseph softly. He felt a little ashamed all of a sudden.

He didn't realize until this moment how important Peter's opinion of him was.

"Well, that's just stupid!" said Peter. "Now what are you going to do?"

Joseph patted Peter's hand. "You mean what are we going to do?"

Joseph proceeded to tell his brother about his visit from the Lord. Peter was suspicious and skeptical. Joseph decided to back up and tell Peter the entire story involving Zach Miles, including the funeral. "I didn't know what to do!" said an emotional Joseph. "I thought God had abandoned me forever, but finally I surrendered my miserable life to Jesus, and then He came to me."

"Tell me again what God said," Peter requested.

"He told me that I had chosen a hard path and that it was going to be difficult and painful, but He would help me. His words would lead me. And I—no—we would lead others back to Christ before the wrath of God was poured out."

"What did He say about me?" Peter inquired.

"He said for me to find you and to bring you back to Rome with me."

"Rome!" said Peter. "What for? What will we do in Rome?"

"I don't know exactly, but it has something to do with me going back to work at the Vatican," said Joseph.

Peter stood and walked to the kitchen window. The moon was clear and bright. Through the trees Peter could see the beginning of what was sure to be a beautiful sunrise. He looked at his watch and then towards Joseph. I need to get to work," he said. Joseph nodded lightly. He knew that the doctor needed time to absorb all that he had heard. "There's peanut butter and crackers in the cupboard and warm soda in the refrigerator," said Peter. "I'll get back when I can."

******

Peter worked all through the morning and into the afternoon. Patient after patient came into his emergency room with injuries ranging from the trivial to the terrible. Dr. Bastoni was like a man in a trance. He stitched and patched, injected medicines, and even performed CPR when necessary. But the whole while his thoughts were on the story Joseph had told him. *God knows me,* he thought. *He wants me to go to Rome, but why?*

Finally the emergency room was under control—at least for the moment. *I'm hungry,* Peter told himself. He decided to try a little of the cafeteria food. It was never very good, but it beat option two—a candy bar and a soda pop. Peter put his stethoscope and pager on the table as he sat down to a large bowl of macaroni and cheese. He ate the tasteless food with little enthusiasm. "I can't go to Rome!" he said aloud. "I'm not even a Christian. Why would God want me to do anything?" Peter stared blankly at his empty plate. He was so confused. *Joseph didn't go to Heaven? How is that possible?* Peter was startled by the sound of his pager. He picked it up and looked at the number. Dr. Bastoni grabbed his stethoscope and headed quickly back to the emergency room.

"We've got a gunshot to the abdomen," said a young nurse as Peter hurried into the room.

The patient was an elderly black man of around 65 years of age. "Sir, can you tell us what happened?" Peter asked as he began to inspect the wound.

"Two kids broke into my liquor store, but they didn't have to shoot me!" said the man. "I told them I didn't have any money." The man grabbed Peter's arm with his bloodstained hand. "It doesn't matter," the man whispered. "I asked God to forgive me. I want to go to Heaven and be with my wife and daughter. I asked God to forgive me—" said the dying man as he gasped for breath.

The EKG monitor began to blare out its alarm. Peter stared into a shotgun wound that could never be repaired.

"Time of death?" he asked.

"2:15 p.m.," said the young nurse. Peter had to pull the old man's grip loose from his scrubs. He covered the man with a white blanket and whispered, "Now you're home."

Dr. Bastoni set his pager on the surgical tray along with his stethoscope. "Call Dr. Martin," he said to the nurse. "Tell him you need a doctor for the ER."

"Where are you going?" the nurse asked inquisitively.

"To Rome," said Peter softly. "I'm going to Rome." Peter turned and walked out of the room as the dumbfounded nurse watched him go.

Chapter 7: The Sacrifice

Day 90: It was the early part of October—a whole three months since the disappearance of Christians from around the world. Carlo Ventini sat under the shade of a large elm tree at the edge of a beautiful deck overlooking the Adriatic Sea. Carlo's summerhouse in Pescara was anything but modest, with over 20 separate rooms, all exquisitely furnished.

Pescara was approximately 100 miles east of Rome, a pleasant two-hour drive. Carlo enjoyed Rome, but from time to time it was nice to escape all the activity of the big city in favor of the seclusion of his coastal mansion. Things were really going well for Carlo. The world was in a sad and desperate state. *They're almost ready for a world leader to save their miserable hides.* He chuckled at the thought.

Simon Koch followed a servant out onto the deck. His stomach was tightened into knots and his hands gripped the latest agricultural reports from around the world. Carlo waved the servant away.

Simon stood in front of Carlo trembling with fear. "Sit down, Simon, before you fall down," said Carlo. "Do you have the reports?"

"Yes," said Simon still gripping the files tightly.

"Well," said Carlo impatiently, "what do they say?"

Simon's voice trembled as he spoke. "Europe—" he said as he cleared his throat. "Europe has maybe a 90-day supply of perishable food products and maybe six months of canned supplies."

"Who will run out first?" Carlo asked.

"Russia and then all of the Baltic countries soon after," said Simon.

"Continue," said Carlo casually.

"The continent of Africa will not survive past Christmas," said Simon thoughtlessly. Carlo glared at Simon. Just the mention of Christmas made his blood boil. "I mean past December," said a frightened Simon. "Asia Minor will not last much longer than that. They have been under trade sanctions from the United States for years, so they were already in trouble." Simon loosened his grip on the two remaining files.

"So what's the bad news?" Carlo asked impatiently.

"Asia," said Simon, "has not been hurt as badly as we had hoped. Even though Japan and Taiwan have been pretty much wiped out, Mainland China is still producing enough food to feed the billions of people living there." Carlo looked nonplussed by the news. Maybe Simon had been worried for no reason.

"Is that it?" Carlo asked.

Simon slid the last file onto the table, "No," he said. Carlo stared at the file. The label read *North America*. "It looks pretty bad for Central and South America, and Australia is definitely in big trouble, but—" said Simon as he looked up at Carlo.

Carlo's eyes captured Simon's causing him to visibly tremble. He smiled at this show of fear. "But what?" Carlo growled.

"It seems that the United States has years of preserved foods and canned foods stockpiled. They can easily feed every American for at least the next two years."

Simon watched Carlo Ventini's face closely for his reaction. Carlo rose quickly from his chair, startling Simon greatly. "We will have to seek the advice of my Father on these issues." Carlo turned and walked across the deck back towards his spectacular home. Simon gathered up his files and moved rapidly to get ahead of Carlo in time to open the sliding glass door for him.

Carlo walked past two of his evil-looking servants and headed directly towards the staircase. Simon followed along as Carlo headed down the stairs. Carlo walked through a cold, dimly lit hallway towards a large, ominous-looking wooden door. Simon stopped and waited as Carlo typed on the keypad, then gave the heavy door a solid push open. Simon had not been in this room before. His knees shook with fear.

Inside the room was dark, but for some reason Simon could easily see to make out all of the items in the room. Somehow the darkness was illuminating. The smell of the room was barely tolerable. It was the smell of rotting flesh—the odor of death. On the far wall was a large bronze pentagram with a goat's head in its center. Below the pentagram were two large candelabras containing 13 candles in each holder. Carlo walked forward and fished a lighter out of his pocket. He lit the first candle and then pulled it from the holder. With the lit candle in hand, he proceeded to light the rest of the wicks.

"Shut the door," said Carlo calmly. Simon turned to close the door, but before he could, it shut all by itself. This greatly startled Simon. He turned to look at Carlo as if to get an explanation of what just happened.

Suddenly he became aware of a large, black marble table in the middle of the room. *Was that there before?* he wondered. Carlo moved one of the candelabras over to the large table and set it down. The candlelight revealed numerous symbols carved into the top of the table. *It's some kind of writing. What does it say?* Simon wondered.

Unexpectedly the door behind Simon reopened and two wicked-looking servants walked in dragging a large, black plastic bag obviously heavily weighted down with something inside.

"Put it on the table," said Carlo. The two men hoisted the bag onto the table and began to remove the plastic. "That will be all," said Carlo. The men stopped what they were doing and walked quickly out of the room. Carlo took off his shoes and placed them neatly on a nearby shelf. Simon followed suit mindlessly. Carlo stepped back to the table and slowly began to unwrap the plastic. Simon watched carefully.

Soon Carlo revealed a young girl of maybe 16 years of age. The girl's mouth was taped shut, and she had a piece of white cloth tied tightly around her head covering her eyes. Carlo inserted his index finger under the blindfold and pulled the cloth off. Simon was amazed to see that the young girl was alive. Her frightened, young blue eyes glistened as tears rolled down her face.

Moving towards a tall, narrow closet, Carlo pulled out a long black robe and threw it towards Simon. Next he put on a similar robe and tied the sash tightly around his waist. Simon struggled to put the robe on as he watched Carlo closely for his next move. Carlo opened a small cupboard and pulled out a large, brass basin. Then, moving toward the young woman, he set the basin down with a loud clang. The terrified girl stared at the bowl from the corner of her eye. Around the outside edge of the basin a series of symbols and another pentagram were etched. The goat's head in the center of the pentagram appeared to be encrusted with a dark substance. The young girl quickly realized that she was looking at the remains of dried blood. She tried to scream, but the tape that covered her mouth prevented any sound from escaping.

Simon was frightened but also very excited. He had an idea of what was about to happen. He had never killed or even seen another person die, but the idea fascinated him. He began to get excited both mentally and physically. He wondered if Carlo would remove all of the young girl's clothing and if they were going to abuse her sexually before they sacrificed her. He hoped so.

Carlo reached into the basin and removed a black leather case. He set the case down in front of the girl's face and opened the container revealing numerous stainless steel instruments. Carlo lifted one of the instruments and held it up to the candle as if to examine it for effectiveness. The knife was scalpel-like, but longer. It was razor sharp, broad, and flat. The young girl began to rock her head back and forth. The look in her eyes was one of unimaginable fear.

Carlo smiled at the girl and then he looked up towards the ceiling of the room. The young girl's eyes followed his up and were startled to see a mirror affixed to the ceiling. The poor child stared at herself lying on the marble table, partially clothed in plastic with a broad piece of tape across her mouth. She knew she was going to die. She didn't know exactly why, but she knew that her time had come.

Her parents had raised her in a Christian home, and the whole family had been very involved in their church. She knew right from wrong but had chosen to walk away from her Christian upbringing and get involved in a life of drugs and drinking. The drugs certainly pushed her away from her family and her church, but she could never have imagined drugs leading to this kind of death. Her family has disappeared during the Rapture, and she had been left to survive on her own. She had been walking the streets until this morning when she was picked up by a strange man she did not know who promised her a place to stay and drugs to satisfy her addiction. *Oh, God! Why did I go with him?* she wondered desperately.

Moving next to Carlo, Simon stared at the little girl with a horrid grin on his face. She saw in his eyes that he was a lustful and evil person. Carlo began to chant in some language that Simon did not understand. Next Carlo ran his hand down the symbols stenciled into the side of the brass basin—the same symbols as those under the young girl. "You are the true morning star, the everlasting god and king of kings. You were created above your creator as ruler of this world," Carlo spoke with passion.

The young girl stared at the two wicked men as they spoke the meaning of the cryptic symbols. She closed her eyes and began to pray earnestly. *Jesus!* She cried out in her mind. *I want my mother and father. I am scared! God forgive my sins. Please let me live with You in Heaven.* The room shook as a cloud of pungent smoke appeared. Soon the presence of Satan was in the room.

"Kill her! Why did you wait? Kill her!" Satan bellowed. Carlo lifted the knife and placed it against the young girl's throat.

The poor child looked into the mirror on the ceiling just long enough to see her own throat burst wide open and blood begin to spurt out. Simon watched as her eyes rolled back into her head and her body convulsed. Carlo lifted the basin and tilted it to catch some of the blood as it gushed forth. Simon giggled as the child went limp and died.

"Father!' said Carlo. "This sacrifice is to you for your glory and greatness."

The boom of Satan's voice shook the room again as he roared, "You have cost me her soul! That pretend Son of God has taken her!"

Now Carlo trembled with fear as Satan spoke.

I hope he does not need another sacrifice, Simon thought. *I'm the only other person in the room.*

"Father!" said Carlo. "I have need of your help. Our famine is not complete."

"Do not concern yourself, my Son," said Satan. "I will take food out of the mouths of children before their very eyes. Now begin to prepare your food for shipment to the world."

Carlo and Simon worshiped Satan with chants and prayers for another hour before they finally left the dark, ominous room. Simon peered back one last time at the young girl lying motionless on the table as he shut the ancient door. "I hope you rot in Heaven!" he giggled as he looked at the poor, slain child.

Chapter 8: A Fiery Red Horse called War

December 25, Day 15: It had been a stalemate for India and Pakistan since the Kargil War of so many years ago. The lines of control had continually changed hands. Recently, however, in the year that followed the disappearance of so many people, the Pakistani Inter-Service Intelligence had been monitoring some secretive Indian activities. It seems that in the cities of Jammu and Kashmir, India's military was busy trying not to look busy. Something was up, and the Pakistani government knew it.

The personality clash between both governments was an old one. There was a constant effort in New Delhi to stay abreast of all of Pakistan's military activities. The same held true for Islamabad. The Pakistani government spent a great deal of time and sacrificed many good men and women to get all of the latest surveillance information on India's military activities.

There was a lot of history between these two warring factions. It was amazing that after so many years they had never resolved their issues. This was primarily because their issues were based on religious differences.

The Hindus and the Muslims just didn't get along at all. In addition, there was a lot of military bravado being constantly displayed on both sides, starting at the highest levels in the military and rolling down to their troops.

Recently tension had been at a maximum between the two countries. Both sides were flexing their muscles in feeble attempts to intimidate one another. Things had escalated to the point that both countries were on full nuclear alert.

Normally about this time each country would rely on America and Russia to defuse things, allowing both sides to save face and avoid appearing as if they had backed down. Presently, however, neither Russians nor Americans were paying much attention to India or Pakistan. They had problems of their own. Times had been hard, and both countries were trying to maintain governments of their own. The threat of revolution was very real. Besides, there were at least 30 additional countries arguing and fighting at the present time. Who could keep track?

******

Pakistan was first to strike. It was December—nearly six months since the Rapture. While the world struggled along with issues of crime, violence, hunger, and war, the Pakistani military eased one of their few nuclear-capable submarines in near the Arabian shoreline no more than 50 miles off the coast of Bombay.

The captain of the submarine was a bold and crafty submariner with over 20 years of experience. Captain Pervez Malik was also a devout Muslim who still believed that a soldier's death was the only true way to honor his god.

Captain Malik had orders to sit on the bottom of the ocean and wait. He had played this game many times, but today was different. Unknown to everyone in command, Captain Pervez Malik had recently discovered, with the help of his personal physician, that he was soon going to die from liver cancer. *A soldier's death is the only death for me,* he told himself the day he got his new orders to take his sub in close to India.

"Weapons check," said Pervez. "All hands to battle stations!" Captain Malik was proud of his officers and crew. They were well trained and followed his directions to the letter.

"All weapons are armed and ready," said the executive officer. He was expecting the captain to tell the crew to stand down and disarm all firing systems.

"Blow ballast tanks," said the captain. At this command every eye in the control room turned towards the captain.

"Captain, they will detect us, and we are within a 50-mile range. They will see this as an act of war," said the executive officer.

"You have your orders," said Pervez. "Weapons status check?"

"Armed and ready, Sir. They only need your executive key and code," said the executive officer.

The submarine rose swiftly off the 300-foot ocean floor. Captain Malik inserted his personal key into the weapons arming device and then began to authenticate the activation code.

"Sir, you do not have authorization to launch your weapons," said the executive officer.

"I have God's authority!" he said curtly. At this the executive officer attempted to draw his sidearm, but before he could remove it, Captain Malik shot him right through the heart.

"Now you, too, have died in battle. Praise be to Allah!"

As luck would have it, the submarine emerged not a quarter mile away from an Indian patrol ship.

"Sir, we have a contact emerging directly aft at only 500 yards!" the excited sonar man yelled from the bridge of the patrol ship.

"What?" said the captain. "Who is it? Make contact now! Go to full alert!" the Indian vessel's captain shouted.

The captain and his executive officer stood on the bridge of their patrol ship helpless as they watched the amazing sight of three consecutive nuclear missiles flying directly towards their mother country. Fifteen seconds later the ship blew Captain Malik's submarine apart. Quickly the sub and all hands sank to the bottom of the ocean without ever knowing the damage they did to India. Captain Malik died in battle just as he had planned.

A handful of seconds later three of India's major cities were turned to rubble. Literally millions died instantly, but not before India had an opportunity to return fire on Pakistan, which they did with every nuclear weapon in their arsenal—a couple of which blew up in the air as their cracked rocket motor propellants created a massive, above-ground set of explosions. The air was now full of deadly radiation heading in every direction from China to Russia.

******

In the Mediterranean Sea the small island of Cyprus was in a major turmoil as another coup was taking place. The Greek government had been watching the Turkish military carefully for the last six months due to the many threats that the Turks had made to the Cypriots.

From times of old the Turks had established claims to the island, but over the centuries Greece had emerged as the stronger of the two countries and had claimed Cyprus as its own. In fact, the Greeks had acquired for themselves virtually every island in the Ionian Sea, the Sea of Crete, the Aegean Sea, and even reaching into the Mediterranean Sea.

Times were changing and Cyprus was ripe for the picking as one of the few countries left in the world that still had an agricultural system intact. Cyprus was miraculously unscathed by the earthquakes and tidal waves. Its supply of pine and range grass, along with fruit and vegetables, was very attractive to Turkey.

Additionally Cyprus was rich in minerals, especially copper. Turkey's government could use this revenue to help pay for the food they needed to purchase each month.

The major portion of the attack on Cyprus came from the Karpaz Peninsula. The Turkish military had a brilliant plan. They entered the Mediterranean Sea from western Syria dressed as men and women vacationers. They even crossed the sea on an Italian Carnival cruise liner. Although the world was in turmoil, there were still those wealthy enough to vacation.

The Turkish soldiers traveled through the Troodos Mountain Range by nightfall and made it to Nicosia, the capital of Cyprus, at dawn. The majority of the Cypriot people were still asleep when their entire government was captured and quickly assassinated.

Undoubtedly Greece would retaliate on Turkey as soon as they figured out what had happened, but for now Turkey was once again in control of Cyprus and, after all, possession is nine tenths of the law. Isn't it?

******

In Lhasa, the Chinese government was on a huge campaign to find and exterminate every Tibetan it could find. This was not a particularly new activity for the government. They had been torturing monks and nuns for centuries, but now it seemed that they, along with nearly every other country on the planet, were looking for ways to reduce the number of mouths to feed. They all seemed to leverage old hatreds and feuds as an excuse to annihilate one another.

Communist China had never really supported religious freedoms of any kind. Buddhist, Hindu, Muslim, or Christian—it really didn't matter to them. They saw all religion as subversive.

Tibet had attempted to become an independent, self-governing country for some time. This was a real thorn in the side of the Chinese government, and now that the Dalai Lama had fled his own country, the door was wide open to the Chinese military. The word was that the Dalai Lama had moved to India. Unfortunately for him, a nuclear explosion destroyed the city of his self-imposed exile. Many would die over the next few months as the Chinese government implemented their zero-tolerance plans—a genocide campaign designed initially to extinguish all non-government supported religions.

******

"There are also major battles emerging in Columbia and Brazil," said Simon as he read from a report, "as well as Bolivia, Chile, Russia, Afghanistan, and many of the Baltic countries.

"Who's not at war?" Carlo asked with a smile.

"The U.S.A.," said Simon, "but that will change soon if Iraq and Syria attack Israel. Africa has 16 separate tribal battles going simultaneously. Ireland has made some loud threats to the United Kingdom and has also threatened Scotland to join their cause or else prepare for war."

Carlo was pleased with the state of the world. Once again human nature was predictable and playing right into his hands. "We will find a

way to bring peace to all these countries, and we will stop all this violence," he said.

"Why?" Simon asked.

"Because I am a man of peace!" Carlo grinned.

Chapter 9: A Black Horse Called Famine

Day 315, May: Joseph and Peter had been in Rome for the last 10 months. Joseph was back at the Vatican doing his usual tasks—translating documents and sending out the church news in a small newspaper written in Latin text called *Deacon's Horn*. In the past this paper had been written primarily by Joseph with the help of two other priests, both of whom had gone to Heaven during the Rapture. Joseph now had the sole responsibility for writing and editing this paper.

To Joseph's surprise, things really hadn't changed all that much back at the Vatican. Many of the priests and cardinals had disappeared 10 months ago like so many others around the world. In fact, even the Pope had disappeared. But for the most part everything was just as it had been before. The same tasks and rituals continued to play themselves out daily.

Today was an exciting day at the Vatican, although not for Joseph. Today the Catholic Church would have a new Pope. The white smoke had been coming from the chimney of the closed chamber for some time now, signaling that the leaders of the Catholic Church had made a decision. After nearly a year of thrashing since the last Pope had so mysteriously disappeared, they had finally picked the man who would connect them to God and head their church.

To Joseph the man elected would be no real surprise. *It really doesn't matter,* he told himself. *None of these men will be God's selection. None of these men even know God. This is just an exercise in piety. They need to keep their government alive for their own sake.*

It was the same for all religious groups worldwide. The truly saved

Christians had been Raptured. Now as each church tried to reorganize and reform its respective government, all they had to choose from in most cases were the ungodly. Certainly some men and women had understood the significance of the Rapture just as Joseph had, and they would be working to make amends, but some power-hungry man or woman would undoubtedly be elected to govern each church.

The winner, Joseph thought, *will be Archbishop Lewis.* Joseph knew this man had ambitions. He had seen firsthand that Lewis was a smooth talker and very well liked among his peers. Archbishop Lewis had always made Joseph a little nervous whenever he came around. There was something about him—something just under the surface that seemed very wrong to Joseph—the way Carl Perkins had made him feel—yet worse, much worse. Now that the Rapture had occurred, Joseph was certain that whoever led the Catholic Church next would be working for the other guy—Satan.

Joseph was becoming a little impatient. He had been obedient to God and had brought Peter and himself back to Rome. He even went back to work as a priest, though he knew it was merely a pretense. He was no longer Catholic. He was no longer any particular religion. He was simply a born-again believer masquerading as a priest until God made His next move, which he hoped would be soon.

Peter spent the first few months just sitting around Joseph's small apartment. He explored the city from time to time, but Rome was a big place—too big for a loner like Peter, a guy from the small town of Appleton, Wisconsin.

Joseph knew that Peter was going stir-crazy sitting home all day. The two brothers were starting to bicker with each other even over the smallest things. *Something has to be done soon,* Joseph thought, *before Peter takes a notion to go back home.*

"Why don't you get a job?" said Joseph one morning over breakfast. Peter stared at his little brother. For some reason he had not considered working again—as least not as a physician. He assumed that when he laid down his stethoscope to follow God, his days of practicing medicine were over.

Peter looked carefully at Joseph. "Do you think it's okay with God?"

he asked.

Joseph had to keep himself from laughing. Peter's question was so sincere. "Well, if it's not, then I guess God will let you know," said Joseph.

"What kind of job should I get?" Peter asked.

"What are you good at?" Joseph laughed. Peter stared at his little brother. He was slightly annoyed. "I'm just kidding!" said Joseph. "Go be a doctor. I hear you're pretty good at that." Joseph smiled.

From that day on Peter worked at a medical clinic not more than a mile from Joseph's apartment. The job was not always very exciting, but since he couldn't speak Italian and because he was not licensed to practice in Rome unsupervised, he just couldn't get a job at any of the bigger hospitals.

For months Peter had been working under a clinical nurse named Yvette Lewis. She was a beautiful, single 35-year-old woman. Her hair was a very dark red, and her eyes were a bright emerald green. She was nearly as tall as Peter and very shapely. It was not a coincidence that her last name, Lewis, was the same as the new Pope, Archbishop Lewis. In fact, she was his daughter, but she didn't know that. All she knew was that the new Pope was her father's brother, her uncle.

Her father had been a machinist for 23 years before an unfortunate accident took his life. He had been a good father who, like his daughter, had no idea that he was not Yvette's biological parent.

Yvette's father's death was a bit peculiar. It seems that he was found with his head crushed in like a tin can. The word from his employer was that he was careless while moving a large train wheel from one location to another. The one-ton wheel apparently had begun to swing out of control, smacking Yvette's father firmly in the back of his head and spilling his brains.

The reality was a little different. Yvette's father had been suspicious that his beautiful wife was less than faithful. One day he slipped home early and caught her in the act of having sex with his own brother, Archbishop Lewis. The two men fought until Archbishop Lewis swung a large brass lamp at his brother, killing him instantly. The Archbishop had connections, and they helped to get the body back on the job site and stage the accident.

After many months of working with Yvette, Peter was starting to feel attracted to her. Oh, sure, she was 10 years younger and it bothered him that he had to take direction from a nurse, but he couldn't help but feel attracted to her. She was so kind to the patients and so friendly to all she met. Her laughter just seemed to bring out the best in Peter. *I wonder if she likes me,* Peter thought. *I think I'll ask her over for dinner—that is, if we have any food left to eat.*

******

The world was really starting to feel the effects of so many disasters. People were beginning to go hungry more often than not. In places like Africa people were literally dying daily by the tens of thousands from starvation. This was not particularly new to Africa, but in the past other countries had at least tried to help by sending food. That was no longer the case. If people had food, they hid it and guarded it with their very lives.

The cost of food was astronomical. Governments from around the world tried to freeze prices to avoid rioting and violence. They even encouraged the black market as a source of competition to keep costs down, but in the end there was simply more demand than supply which meant that buying food was outside the means of most people. So as a method of survival, people were stealing and killing to get or to keep what food they had. The U.S. government had instituted a curfew and was patrolling the streets with regular and reserve military forces. *Shoot to kill,* was their motto. *It's one less mouth to feed.*

Each warehouse facility in the United States containing government stores of food was being heavily guarded around the clock. A system of food distribution was being developed to try and get the food into each community and into the mouths of the hungry. Previous attempts to move shipments of food had ended in disaster.

Two C-5 aircrafts had been loaded with thousands of pounds of food.

One shipment was supposed to be flown to the West Coast and the other to the East Coast, but neither made their destination. The C-5 heading west lost power over the Rockies and augured into a mountainside. The next flight flew over New York right on schedule, but unfortunately it kept on flying east until it had to be shot down over the Atlantic ocean by a United States fighter pilot. The pilot and copilot of the cargo plane claimed over the radio that they were not in control of their aircraft, but that seemed absurd to the American government so they blew the plane from the sky.

Oh, sure, these were only two small shipments. There was still enough food stored in warehouses throughout the United States to last for a couple of years at least. Unfortunately for the Americans a lot of their food preserves were pre-World War II, and even though they were sealed in tin cans, they would not be edible. The vacuum seal processing back then just wasn't sufficient to prevent the food from virtually petrifying over the last 50 years or so.

It also would soon become evident that there were some major accounting errors in calculating the stockpiles of America's emergency food supplies. The United States would soon have a new awareness that they had much less food than they had figured, and their supply of fresh, perishable food was all but gone already.

Had it not been for the food distributions coming out of Europe from Carlo's marvelous Agripods, the death rate from starvation would have been staggering. Because of these Agripods, the world had so far avoided a total and complete disaster. However, if anything happened to these food supplies, many would die.

******

Weeks earlier in California a dozen men met with the European agricultural minister, Mr. Carlo Ventini. These men had been working alongside of Carlo for some time now. They had plans—big plans—and now it was time to implement Phase One. Each man there represented a co-op of food growers and distributors from around the states, and each man had sworn his allegiance to Carlo. In return he promised them power and wealth beyond their wildest imaginations.

"Okay," said Carlo. "You know your assignments. Don't disappoint me!" As he said this to the men, he looked towards an empty chair. All eyes followed his. The chair had belonged to the owner of a large food packaging and distributing business. But after the man's wife and children disappeared in the Rapture, he had become uncooperative with the rest of these men and in particular with Carlo.

This gave Simon Koch his first opportunity to kill. He relished this chance, and having seen Carlo slit the throat of the young girl a short time back, he yearned for an opportunity to do the same to someone else. The rich canned food supplier was a nice first kill for Simon. It was much easier than he had imagined. Representing Carlo Ventini, he simply walked into the man's mansion. It was obvious that the man was nervous and maybe even afraid of Simon. Simon hoped that he was afraid, because it made it all the more enjoyable.

After a short amount of small talk, Simon excused himself to use the restroom. There he attached the silencer to the end of his large handgun and tucked the weapon inside his coat pocket. As he re-entered the living room, the heavy businessman sat with his back to Simon. His head was in plain view—a very easy target even for a beginner like Simon Koch. "Tempting!" Simon whispered to himself. But he didn't just want to kill this man. He wanted to see his fear. Simon wanted to look into the man's eyes as he died.

"Mr. Ventini is very concerned with your lack of response to his calls," said Simon flatly. The man swallowed hard, but before he could speak, Simon continued. "Mr. Ventini doesn't think you support his cause any longer." Simon sneered as the man squirmed in his plush seat.

"What we are doing is wrong," said the man weakly. "People are going to die because of us."

Simon nodded and grinned. "Yes, they are. Isn't it great? But do you know what? You won't be here to see any of it!" At that Simon giggled hysterically.

The man began to stand, but before he could get his big body out of the chair, Simon pulled out his large black gun. "Goodbye, Fatso!" said Simon as he pointed the gun and pulled the trigger. The man slumped forward and toppled out of the chair onto the wool rug.

Simon tried to use his foot to turn the man over. He had intentionally shot him in the stomach because he thought the man would die much slower that way. It would give him a chance to watch the entire process. Unfortunately for Simon the bullet of the large gun was just too powerful and his shot was a little too accurate. When he turned the man over, he was already as dead as could be. "Next time I'll use a smaller gun," he said with a smile, "or maybe even a knife like Carlo."

******

Joseph sat in his small office staring out of his window. Not much of a view, but it gave him something to look at. The phone rang and Joseph picked it up. "Joseph—um—Father Bastoni. May I help you?"

"Hey, Joe, it's me!"

Joseph relaxed. "Hey, Peter, what's up?"

Peter made small talk for a while until he finally got around to his reason for calling. "I'd like to invite someone over for dinner, okay?"

"That's all right with me," said Joseph. "Who is it?"

"Yvette—the nurse I told you about," said Peter with a little hesitation in his voice.

"Sure, I'd love to meet her," said Joseph, "but we don't have much to eat. I hope she doesn't mind."

"I'm sure she won't," said Peter.

"You haven't asked her yet, have you?" Joseph inquired.

"Not yet," said Peter, "but I'm getting to it!" He hung up the phone and walked back into the suture room where an elderly lady sat waiting to have her thumb sown back together after accidentally carving it with a steak knife. Yvette was cleaning the wound as Peter grabbed a suture kit and moved in beside her. Peter tried to make small talk with the woman, but it was apparent that she spoke no English at all.

When the thumb was anesthetized good and numb, Peter started a neat little row of small sutures. Yvette observed carefully.

"If you're not busy tonight," said Peter without looking up, "maybe you'd like to come over for dinner. You can meet my brother, the priest."

"Are you asking me on a date?" Yvette asked brightly.

Peter looked at the old woman. She appeared to be listening intently to their conversation. The woman smiled at Peter.

"Does she speak English?" he asked without taking his eyes off the woman.

"Not a bit!" said Yvette.

"Hmm," said Peter. "I could almost swear that—"

Yvette interjected, "For some things it is not necessary to speak the same language." She smiled. "What are we having for dinner?"

"You'll come then?" Peter asked.

"Sure, I'd like to meet your brother. So what are we having for dinner?" she asked laughingly.

"Potluck!" said Peter as he shook his head disappointedly.

******

Carlo walked slowly through one of the Agripods. The building was huge and multistoried. Everywhere the eye could see were vegetables, grains, and fruit trees, all of them nearly bursting with abundance. Simon walked ahead of Carlo and picked a large, near-ripe peach from one of the many trees.

The security measures around the nursery were like that of Los Alamos nuclear facility only a lot better. There were cameras in every corridor, coded entries to each level, and a series of security checkpoints just to enter the building. The entire compound was like a reinforced military base with armed soldiers everywhere. This additional security was gladly paid for by the Vatican which had been promised an ample supply of food for each of its millions of members worldwide.

Carlo had also promised the European community a large royalty and the freshest portion of each crop. In return the European transportation facilities would be at Carlo's disposal, and if he needed any additional security beyond what the Vatican had provided, all Carlo would have to do was ask. *Soon,* he thought, *I won't even have to ask. I'll command.*

"When will the next shipments go out?" Carlo asked as he passed by a greedy Simon who was now eating from a pear tree.

"Today," mumbled Simon through a mouthful of fresh fruit. "Fifty of our facilities worldwide will make their next set of deliveries today. Each day after that 50 more facilities will make delivery until all 5,000 Agripods are on a 100-day rotation for fruit and grain and a 60-day rotation for fresh vegetables."

Carlo's mood was jovial. He even smiled at Simon approvingly. Simon couldn't help but love Carlo. After all, he was everything Simon wished he could be.

"Where are these shipments going?" Carlo inquired.

"Africa and Australia are in the worst shape followed by Russia and the rest of Europe," said Simon.

Carlo mulled this over. "Yes, it looks very good for us to continue to feed Africa. Let's get photographers and our news staff over there right away. In fact, let's get reporters in every country right away so that as we deliver food to the starving children and senior citizens, they can report it live.

Simon smiled in agreement.

"As for Russia, make them wait," said Carlo. "Feed our countrymen first including England."

Simon was a bit confused. "But why would we not feed Russia next? They're starving!"

Carlo raised his hand in front of Simon's face ending the conversation.

Simon couldn't care less whether or not every Russian mother and daughter died of starvation, but he and Carlo had had a plan, and now for some reason Carlo had changed his mind.

"Who is our point of contact for distribution of food to the Catholic Church?" Carlo asked.

"Joseph Bastoni." said Simon in a somewhat defeated voice.

"Quit pouting! And get me an appointment with Father Bastoni,"

Carlo grinned. "I assume he didn't go you-know-where with the rest of those nasty Christians."

"No," said a hurt Simon. "He's still among us."

Carlo nodded approvingly. *This has been a good day,* he thought to himself.

Chapter 10: A Harvest of Souls

Calvin stood atop the dining room table for the second day in a row. "Jesus is coming soon, so you'd better get ready!" he said. This was the same message he had shared yesterday; however, he hoped that it would go a little better this time.

The first time Calvin stood and proclaimed Jesus to his fellow inmates he was laughed at and verbally assaulted until one of the security guards finally had to intervene on his behalf.

Calvin was not dissuaded, however, and until the security guards actually forbade it, he had every intention of continuing his campaign. "Jesus loves you!" he said boldly as the men around him sat eating a dismal breakfast of scrambled powdered eggs and pressed ham. The morning light was barely shining through the large glass windows lining the side of the cafeteria. "And He wants you to know that the end is coming soon," Calvin stated with conviction.

In the corner of the room at a small table sat two security officers. One was short but extremely stocky with fire-red hair. The other was a tall, lean black man of no more than 30 years of age.

"Should I stop him?" the young guard asked.

"No," said the stocky middle-aged man. "Let him alone."

The young guard was a little surprised by the older man's tolerance. "You think its okay for him to get these guys all worked up?" the man asked.

"No, but I think we ought to listen to what he has to say. Now be quiet!" said the man irritably. The young man obviously did not like the answer he got, but he bowed to the seniority of the older guard.

One of the inmates threw a cold piece of toast at Calvin as many others laughed at him. Calvin ignored the inmate's rudeness and continued to preach. "Don't you understand what has happened to our world? Don't you know about the people that Jesus took to Heaven?"

At a nearby table sat an extremely big and tough looking black man who had been in Leavenworth since 1975. He was a Vietnam veteran who took it upon himself to stab and kill his own squad leader.

The story was that Sergeant Cory Parker was a dedicated Army soldier with three years of service to his country, two of which were spent in Vietnam fighting for what he thought was a worthy cause. At least in the beginning it had seemed like a worthy cause, but over time Sergeant Parker began to change his opinion of the war.

Many of the soldiers in his platoon were nothing but young kids with little opportunity. Many were minorities, some were delinquents forced into service by the courts, and some were just unfortunate white kids whose parents didn't have enough money to send them safely away to college.

During the Vietnam War the military developed a bad habit of training their squadron leaders in combat situations. These leaders were young lieutenants and ROTC mostly with no prior military experience. Many of these fresh officers were wise enough to follow the advice of their sergeants, yet some out of their own arrogance refused to heed the warnings of the more experienced men. It was one such lieutenant who was briefly assigned to Cory Parker's outfit that inevitably led Cory down a path of destruction.

After two tours in Vietnam, Sergeant Parker had seen all of the senseless death he could tolerate. When his previous platoon leader was promoted and moved out of his squadron, the Army quickly replaced him with a cocky, young ROTC officer straight from the cornfields of Indiana's Purdue University.

In the first week of the young officer's tour in Vietnam he repeatedly ignored advice and warnings from Sergeant Parker and other non-commissioned officers. Eventually the overconfident and thoughtless officer began to get young men killed. Finally, after several attempts to reason with the lieutenant, Sergeant Parker made what he believed to be the most rational decision. He had tried to share his concerns with other officers in his company to no avail. It was obvious that this inexperienced officer was going to get many men killed before he got his next promotion.

One evening after a long, eventful patrol where three young soldiers were killed, Sergeant Parker had his opportunity. While most of the men were napping under the shade of a large group of trees, the reckless lieutenant slipped away to empty his bladder. Sergeant Parker followed at a distance as the officer slid in between two large trees.

From behind Parker approached quietly. Just a few paces away he drew his field knife and tightly gripped the handle. Sergeant Parker slid his knife forcefully into the officer's ribs while placing his other hand firmly over the young man's mouth. "You won't get anybody else killed after today," said Cory Parker.

A couple of soldiers saw Sergeant Parker walking slowly back from the two tall trees. From that moment on Parker knew he would be found out which, of course, he was—only minutes later.

Sergeant Parker's lawyer managed to get him a life sentence instead of the death penalty. Combat fatigue was his plea, and it was sufficient. Cory would live out the remainder of his life in a military prison in Kansas.

Calvin continued to speak boldly. "It's not too late. You can still receive forgiveness, and where there is life, there also is hope." The crowd really began to insult Calvin as he spoke. The red-headed guard was beginning to believe he had made a mistake in letting him preach.

Suddenly Cory Parker stood and walked towards Calvin. "Oh, man!" said the thin black guard. "Now we got trouble!"

Cory was nearly as tall as Calvin even though Calvin was standing on a table. The big man looked Calvin straight in the eyes. Calvin swallowed hard. He knew about this giant. He knew that every prisoner steered clear of the Vietnam veteran.

Suddenly Cory smiled and winked at Calvin. Calvin was stunned. Sergeant Parker turned and looked at the inmates as they jeered him to rip the preacher apart.

Both guards stood and released the safeties on their guns. "I told you we should have stopped this," said the young black man.

Cory spoke up. "Let him speak! What is the matter with you? Can't you see that he is right?" All of the inmates quickly became silent as Cory continued. "Do you think aliens took all of those people away? Don't you see he is right?"

******

From that day on Calvin preached and read to the inmates from the Gideon Bible given to him by a security guard. Calvin was so successful preaching that he had nearly all of the security guards participating in Bible study along with the prisoners. Daily men came forward to give their hearts to Jesus. The first one to accept Christ was Sergeant Cory Parker.

Chapter 11: Ultimatums

It was late in the evening when Simon called Joseph at his home to set up an appointment for the agricultural minister and his assistant. Just the sound of Simon's voice made Joseph's skin crawl. "10:00 a.m. is fine with me," said Joseph. "See you then. Thanks, and goodnight, Mr. Koch."

Peter could tell by the look on Joseph's face that he was troubled about something. "Who was that?" he asked.

"The assistant to Carlo Ventini, Europe's agricultural minister."

"What's the matter?" Peter inquired.

"I don't know for sure," said Joseph as he shook his head. "But something isn't quite right with either of these guys."

Peter was about to ask for more clarification when the doorbell rang. Joseph opened the door to the beautiful sight of Yvette with a loaf of bread in her hands. "Peter said it was potluck, so here's my contribution."

The friendly nurse practitioner smiled brightly. Joseph was awestruck from the moment Yvette walked into the room. It had been many years since he had felt this way about a woman. He tried to put the brakes on his emotions when suddenly a thought occurred to him. *I'm not really a priest anymore. I can enjoy the company of a woman without fear of falling away from the Church.*

Peter introduced Yvette as his assistant down at the clinic. Yvette smiled and more clearly introduced herself as Yvette Lewis. Joseph shook her hand. Just the touch of her skin made his heart pound. He had only felt this emotion with a woman once before in his life and that was many years ago when he was a college student. In fact, she was one of the reasons he became a priest. His heart had been broken at a young age, but now apparently Joseph's heart was functioning perfectly.

"Ms. Lewis," said Joseph with a smile as he released her hand, "Any relationship to Archbishop Lewis—or should I say Pope Peter John, the First?"

"Yes!" Yvette said with a nod. "He's my uncle."

At first Joseph thought the striking Italian nurse was just kidding, but soon Yvette began to elaborate on her family genealogy. Joseph was speechless. "Small world isn't it?" said Yvette with a wink and a smile for Joseph.

******

Joseph, Peter, and Yvette had a pleasant evening. The conversations had been kept to simple subjects like college life, family, and childish escapades. However, as the evening drew to a close, Yvette began to ask Joseph questions about what led him to become a priest. Instead of answering her questions directly, Joseph decided to ask a question of his own. He turned towards Yvette and stared into her green, sparkling eyes. She was so lovely. Joseph couldn't help but envy his brother and also approve of his taste in women. "Many months ago," Joseph started carefully, "people from all around the world disappeared." Yvette followed along as Joseph spoke. "Where do you think they went?" he flatly asked.

Yvette squirmed in her chair. This was a question that she had asked herself a thousand times. In her heart she knew the truth, but to believe it meant she would have to reevaluate her own world. In particular, if Christ has taken the true Christians to Heaven, then why was her uncle—the Pope—still here? Why was her mother still here? And why was she still here? The answer had been too painful for her to tolerate.

"I don't know. I'm not sure," Yvette said cautiously. Joseph could tell by the look in her eyes that she was not telling the whole truth. He decided to take a chance, and in light of the fact that Yvette's uncle was the new Pope, it was a really big and potentially dangerous chance.

"Do you reject the possibility that Christ has taken these people to Heaven to be with Him and the possibility that we are now entering into seven years of tribulation?"

Peter was stunned by Joseph's boldness, but he was impressed by his little brother's ability to lead this conversation. *I hope he knows what he is doing,* Peter thought.

Yvette was also surprised by Joseph's candor. "Well, if Christ did take all of the missing people to Heaven, then why didn't He take you? You're a priest," she said.

Joseph shook his head. "No, Yvette, I am not a priest." Yvette looked very confused. "Even when I was a priest—" Joseph decided against finishing this sentence.

"Yvette," said Joseph as he held out his hand to her. She took it cautiously. "Do you really think that all of these people were taken away by aliens? Or that God was somehow punishing them? Virtually every child in the world below 12 years of age has disappeared." Yvette didn't know how to respond. She just sat there staring at both Joseph and Peter.

Finally she spoke, and her voice wavered as she did. "No, I don't believe aliens came and took the people away. I guess I don't even believe that God was punishing them for something they did. After all, how could so many children have done something that bad? But," Yvette continued, "what about me? What about my family, my uncle? And what about you—why didn't God take any of us?"

Joseph patted her hand. It was obvious that this conversation was difficult for her. Joseph understood why. In fact, he had felt the same way at one time in his own life. He used to follow all of the rules set forth by the church as well. But all of this only led to emptiness and loneliness. "I can't speak for anyone but myself," said Joseph. "I know that I did not have a personal relationship with Jesus. All I had was rules and traditions."

Yvette nodded. "Why did you say you weren't a priest anymore?"

Peter looked at Joseph to see what would come next. Joseph told Yvette the entire story about the program that Zach Miles had produced, about the funeral, and finally, about his visit from God. "So you see, we are waiting for God to tell us what to do next, and I have a feeling that He will very soon," said Joseph.

As Peter sat back to listen and watch the interactions between Yvette and Joseph, it became clear to him that they were a better fit than he and Yvette. At first this bothered him to the point of jealousy, but when he really started to think about his little brother finally having a chance at a close relationship with another woman, he found peace from within.

After Yvette left Joseph went into the kitchen and began to wash the dinner plates. Peter stepped in next to him with a towel and began to dry each plate as Joseph handed them over. "She's a nice girl, don't you think?" said Peter. Joseph didn't look up as Peter spoke. He felt a little shame over the fact that he was so attracted to Peter's friend.

"You two look good together," said Peter. This statement got a rise out of Joseph as he lifted his eyes towards Peter. "You know, little brother, I was thinking that I am not really cut out for a relationship right now. Besides, I think Yvette likes you."

Joseph began to blush at the thought. "I don't know, Peter. I really don't know."

Peter wiped off the last plate and dropped the towel on the counter. "You're not a priest anymore, you know. It's okay for you to have a little happiness. Besides, I suspect that our time here is getting short."

Joseph nodded, "I've felt that way all day."

Peter looked at Joseph inquisitively. "Do you think that maybe God has brought Yvette to us for a reason?"

Joseph had not really considered it. He was surprised by his brother's new belief in the providence of God. "Maybe," said Joseph.

******

Alexis Kurpov sat in the airport waiting not so patiently for Mr. Ventini's personal plane to land. It was a hot, dry day in Moscow and the weather only increased the irritability of all of Moscow's hungry citizens. The Gulfstream taxied slowly as Alexis watched. "I've got to get me one of those," he said aloud.

Alexis Kurpov was a complicated man. In his lifetime he had worked for the Russian government as their manager of a top-secret defense agency whose sole purpose was to develop global threats such as biological, viral, and chemical agents. It was a nasty job and not one that Alexis truly enjoyed. He had also at one time in his life worked for the Russian Orthodox Church, primarily as a military advisor to the Reverend Bishops and Patriarchs of the church.

This was an interesting job for him. He found it incredible how much paranoia existed inside the church. *After so many years of government rule, who could blame them?* he thought. Alexis' job inside the Orthodox Church was to help it prepare for world domination. Under Communism it was the church's belief that someday it would be the ruling religion worldwide, so it was thought necessary to develop tools of defense lest any other church try to emerge. If a new church were to spring up, the Orthodox Church would be ready to stomp them into the mud—in a loving sort of way, of course.

Alexis met Simon first as he exited the staircase. "Mr. Ventini!" said Alexis as he extended his hand.

Simon giggled foolishly. "No, Mr. Kurpov. I'm Simon Koch, Mr. Ventini's aide."

Both men turned as Carlo made his way up the stairs. Carlo smiled brightly at Alexis. It was a frightening smile, causing Alexis to swallow hard.

"Mr. Kurpov," said Carlo. "Good to meet you!"

Alexis shook Carlo's hand cautiously. *This guy's a little strange,* he thought. "Please call me Alexis," he said to Carlo.

"Yes," said the agricultural minister. "Enough of the formalities. Call me Carlo."

"I have a car waiting," said Alexis.

"Lead the way," answered Simon.

All three men sat in the back of the limousine as they drove north. Alexis sat on a large, black leather seat directly across from Carlo and Simon. "Would you like a drink?" Alexis asked as he opened the door to the wet bar.

"What is it that you enjoy to drink most, Mr. Kurpov?" Carlo asked with a smile.

"Vodka, of course!" said Alexis.

"Yes, that would be nice!" said Simon.

"We'll just have water," Carlo said with an eerie grin.

"Suit yourselves." He handed both men two small glasses of water. At this Simon looked very disappointed. Alexis poured himself three fingers full of Absolute. "Russians don't drink water," he said flatly.

Alexis took a large gulp and then set the glass down. He needed that. After all, it was already past noon, and he had not drunk a thing yet. "So, Carlo, what is it exactly that I can do for you?" Alexis inquired.

"No!" said Carlo. "You've got it wrong. It's what can I do for you." Again as Carlo spoke Alexis began to feel nervous. He picked up his glass and took another long belt. Simon licked his lips as he watched the vodka go down.

"All right then, Mr. Ventini, what is it that you can do for me?"

Carlo could tell that Alexis was trying to appear tough and professional, but Carlo knew that he was intimidated.

"I can give you the world," said Carlo with a grin.

"And what would I do with the world?" asked Alexis as he looked over to Simon.

"A lot!" said Simon.

These guys are crazy! What have I gotten myself into? he wondered.

Carlo pointed to the glass separating the driver from the passengers. "Is that glass soundproof?"

"Of course!" said Alexis. This was a true statement, but Alexis neglected to mention that the passenger compartment was bugged and the entire conversation was being recorded from the second he opened the mini-bar. Alexis was a cautious man.

"How's the Russian food supply holding up these days?" Carlo asked.

Alexis understood that the agricultural minister already knew the answer to this question. "Not so good," he said in his heavy native accent.

Simon smiled at his response.

"How would you like to change that?" Carlo asked.

"You could be the hero of your country!" Simon chirped.

"We have heard that you have been providing food to most of the world. We have also heard that you are not charging unreasonable prices like the open market," said Alexis. "Why do you come to me for this? Why not go directly to our own agricultural minister?"

"I thought you'd never ask!" Carlo said. "You see," he continued, "I really don't like Russians, and I really don't care if you starve to death." Alexis listened in amazement as Carlo spoke. His tone of voice combined with the horrid look in his eyes frightened Alexis. Simon let out a little giggle as Carlo spoke. "But!" said Carlo, "I hate the Chinese even more than I hate the Russians."

"Why are you telling me all of this?" Alexis asked.

Just then the limousine pulled into the city of Tver and slowed as it approached the afternoon traffic. Carlo looked out the side window into the streets of the city. "Look around you," he said. "These are your people, and unless they get food soon, they will not survive the winter. You would help them if you could, correct?"

Alexis did not answer the question.

"Correct?" Carlo asked with sharpness that Alexis could not ignore.

"Yes! I would help them if I could," he whispered.

"Well, you can!" said Simon. Carlo looked at him disapprovingly. Simon looked down, dejected.

"Mr. Kurpov, what do you know about LH217?" Carlo asked.

This question got Alexis' full attention. He stared at both Carlo and Simon carefully. "I don't know what you are talking about," he said.

"Come now," said Carlo, "you must remember all of the hard work your team did to develop a biological weapon capable of destroying the DNA of nearly all plant life it comes into contact with."

"That was many years ago," said Alexis. "All of that research has been destroyed in an agreement with the West."

"All of it?" Carlo asked suspiciously.

"Yes, all of it!" said Alexis.

"Well, Mr. Kurpov, I think you are lying and, for your sake, I hope so!"

The limousine pulled into a long driveway leading down to a big two-story house a little smaller than a mansion but still quite large and striking.

"Shall we have some lunch and talk this over a little more?" Carlo asked.

"Yes, of course!" said a nervous Alexis. He knew that he was in over his head. *How is it possible that they know about LH217?* Alexis asked himself. He had only kept a small quantity of the deadly chemical as an insurance policy. The Russian government had a nasty habit of eliminating not only the incriminating evidence of illegal activity, but also the inventors and anyone else who had relevant knowledge. Alexis knew the system well. He had seen a lot of good men—good scientists—disappear from their homes in the middle of the night. That's why he decided to keep some of the LH217—as a bargaining chip if need be. However, he never expected anyone from outside his own government to come asking about this particular deadly biological agent.

Alexis' home was decorated with relics from an older Russia. He had swords on his mantle above the fireplace. Large tapestries covered his marble floor at the entrance to the house. There was even a set of full armor in the hallway outside of his private library. All in all his entire home was very stylish, showing his obvious patriotism towards his country.

Alexis spoke briefly in Russian to one of his servants and then turned back towards Carlo and Simon. "Let's adjourn to my study for a drink while lunch is being prepared."

Carlo turned to Simon, whispered something into his ear, and then smiled at Alexis as they walked into the study. Simon stood at the arched doorway to the room. "Excuse me while I use your restroom," Simon said. Alexis turned to guide Simon, but with a wave of his hand Simon said, "Just point the way and I'll find it."

"Third door on the left. You can't miss it."

Simon left the room, shutting the door behind him. The sound of the solid oak door closing made Alexis a little jumpy. He had no desire to be locked into a room alone with Carlo.

"So, Mr. Kurpov, it seems that you've done well for yourself."

"I can't complain," said Alexis.

"Yes," said Carlo. "Complaining in Russia can be a very dangerous habit."

"Would you like a drink?" Alexis asked.

"No, but help yourself!" said Carlo. Alexis' hand shook as he poured himself another glass of vodka—only this time he used a tall glass. "Now about LH217," said Carlo. "I assume you have enough of this nasty little chemical to destroy the majority of the crops throughout China."

Alexis did not know what to say, so he drank instead.

Simon slid out the front door and over to the limousine where the driver stood smoking a cigarette. Simon extended a hand as if to ask for a smoke of his own. The driver bent over into the front seat of the car to retrieve his pack of cigarettes. As he did so Simon pulled his revolver from his coat pocket, and with the butt end he smacked the back of the driver's head as hard as he could. The sound was grotesque—like a rock smashing a cantaloupe.

The driver slumped over the steering wheel, sounding the horn loudly. Simon pulled him off quickly and then looked around to see if anyone had been alerted. Next Simon picked up the man's lit cigarette and began to puff on it as he made his way into the back seat. He moved his hand along the edge of the wet bar until he found a wire; then he traced the wire under the passenger seat. He pulled the seat cover off to reveal a large recorder with two small reels of tape. Simon removed the reels and slid them into his coat pocket opposite his handgun. He then picked up the bottle of vodka and removed the crystal stopper. Tilting the bottle, Simon took a long, greedy drink, allowing the vodka to run down his chin.

******

"Here's the deal," said Carlo as he sat back in one of Alexis' large leather chairs. "You administer the necessary amount of LH217 to destroy China's crops, and I will make you a Russian hero and a very rich man." About this time Simon walked back into the room with a large silly grin on his face. The sense of pride he felt for a job well done mixed with a large quantity of vodka made him giddy.

"What makes you think that there is such a thing as LH217? And even if there is, what makes you think I have any?" Alexis asked as calmly as he could.

Simon began to describe the deadly chemical to Alexis, slurring his voice a little as he did. Carlo noticed this but decided to shrug it off. "LH217 kills all plant life it comes into contact with by altering the plant's DNA so that it cannot absorb water. The agent can be delivered by air or water, and it spreads from plant to plant as it is carried along by insects and by the wind or rain."

Alexis stood and refilled his glass. "Why do you want to do this?" he asked with his back to Simon and Carlo.

"Does it really matter?" Carlo asked.

"People will starve," said Alexis, "and it will take years before plant life can re-grow." Alexis caught himself. *Now I've done it,* he thought. There was no longer any reason to try and hide the reality that LH217 did, in fact, exist.

"People will die in Russia if you don't help them," said Carlo, "and I promise you nobody in China will starve to death. I will personally see to that."

Alexis turned and looked at Carlo and then towards Simon who was now playing with the reel of tape that he had taken out of the limousine.

Alexis knew that he was over his head with these two guys. "And if I do this, then what?"

Carlo smiled brightly. "Russia will eat, and you will be a hero—a rich hero."

"And if I don't do it?" Alexis inquired nervously.

"Then you will be dead and all Russians will starve!" said Carlo.

Alexis swallowed hard as he took another long drink from his glass. "When do you want it done and where?"

"Now you're talking!" said Simon.

"What is the confinement area of LH217?" Carlo asked.

"It will spread as far as the wind carries it—typically as much as 1,500 miles in every direction," said Alexis without much enthusiasm.

"How long will it remain virulent?" Simon inquired.

"About a week. It depends. If it is too hot, it will neutralize more quickly," said Alexis.

Simon walked over to the large world globe sitting neatly on a stand in the corner of the study. "We will need three separate drops to ensure that we cover all of China," said Simon.

"I don't think I have that much of the weapon available," said Alexis trying not to show he was lying.

Carlo walked over to the globe and peered closely at the country of China. Simon nearly toppled over as he bent down to examine the globe more closely. Carlo caught him by the back of his collar. His angry look told Simon all he needed to know.

"Sichuan," said Carlo as he traced his finger along the globe, "Qinghai, and Shanxi should give us sufficient coverage without endangering much of Mongolia or what's left of India."

Alexis stared at the two crazy men. He was having second thoughts. "I don't have enough of the chemicals," he said.

Carlo walked over to where Alexis stood. "I think that you do, Mr. Kurpov. In fact, I'll bet your life on it," Carlo grinned.

About that time there was a knock at the door. "Enter!" said Alexis.

It was the maid. "Lunch is ready, Sir." Alongside her was the chauffeur holding an icepack to the back of his head.

"Yes, fine. We'll be right in."

Simon sneered at the chauffeur as the maid closed the study door.

"I don't have it here," said Alexis spontaneously.

"I think you do," said Carlo flatly.

"Fine then. After lunch we will take a look at it," said Alexis. He was wondering if there was some possible way out of this mess.

"We'll look at it now!" said Carlo sternly, not to be ignored.

Alexis led the two men down to the basement and walked directly to a fuse panel. Alexis turned two screws on the panel box and suddenly the panel face fell forward, revealing a hidden safe. "Nice!" said Simon.

Alexis' hands shook as he turned the tumbler clockwise and then counter-clockwise. He pulled the steel handle and opened the small black door. Finally he reached in and pulled out a long, thin metal box that had three breakaway tabs crimped to the lid and a large padlock covering the hasp. Alexis fished a set of keys from his pocket and inserted a small, fat, brass key into the lock. He then pulled against the lid until the security tabs broke under the stress.

The light in the room was dim, but it was still possible for Simon and Carlo to see the lime green liquid through the small, clear glass bottles. There were some 12 bottles in all.

"How much area will each bottle cover?" Simon asked.

"It depends," said Alexis.

Carlo was getting tired of Alexis' conservative answers. "How much?" he asked impatiently.

"About 1,000 miles," Alexis blurted.

"You are going to be a rich man," said Carlo.

"I don't want your money, Mr. Ventini. I will do this to save my country, but I will not be paid to destroy the lives of so many."

"Admirable," said Carlo. "Russia will always remember you as the man who brought them food when they were starving."

******

One week later six bottles of a deadly, lime green biological agent were dumped on China—two bottles per each pre-selected site. The first drop was in the local irrigation water supply in Sichuan. The density of LH217 was such that it sat atop the water as if it were nothing more than a bit of algae. The next four bottles were all dropped from the air at a very low altitude. They were instantly picked up by a moderate 12 mile-per-hour breeze and whisked away towards the farmlands of China.

In a mere 40 days after several attempts at stopping the horrible and unexplainable plague that had totally devastated all plant life, the Chinese government was defeated. China had no choice but to ask the European government—in particular, Carlo Ventini, for help in feeding her people—all 2 billion of them.

Chapter 12: Good News Bad News

Day 585, February: It was another freezing day in Chicago. For the 17th day in a row the temperature dipped below minus 20 degrees. Many had died from the cold weather throughout the Midwest—especially the old and the poor, neither of which could afford the gas and electricity costs to stay warm. Scott sat looking out of his high-rise office window. It had been nearly a year and a half since the Rapture and still it was hard for him to get enthusiastic about anything. He even contemplated suicide, but for some reason he held out hope that God had a plan for his life.

Since that frightening day when the world shook, all Scott ever did was sit in his office going through the motions. Many people had overcome those events and moved on with their lives. They just didn't seem to need an answer to the second biggest mystery in human history—the first being where did man come from in the first place—and the second—where did many of them recently disappear to?

Scott was like most Americans—he had heard the truth about the Rapture—but he was different from most because he believed it.

Scott was startled from his daydream by a knock at his office door. "Come in," he said softly. Everything Scott did lately was gently done. He no longer had the fire to be impromptu and brash. Scott had grown up considerably in eight short months. Zach Miles would have been proud of him.

Ruth Jefferson, Scott's star reporter, entered his office with a kind smile. Ruth was a tall, slender black woman who looked a little like the actress, Grace Jones, but prettier. In her youth Ruth had been Miss Illinois and was runner up for Miss America. She was extremely talented and charismatic. However, Ruth never seemed to let her talent or success affect her self-image. She was always bright and cheerful yet humble and kind.

For some reason Ruth had never married, and now that she was near 40, it looked like she never would. She was the daughter of a farmer and part-time minister from Lincoln County, Illinois. Her mother and father had nine children, three of which her mother had before marrying Ruth's father.

It was a pleasant childhood, and for a blended family, the Jefferson's did quite well at maintaining harmony and happiness. Ruth had so many brothers and sisters, as well as nieces and nephews, that she just never seemed to need a family of her own. After the Rapture many of Ruth's family members disappeared, including her mother and father. A few of her brothers and sisters still remained, but for some reason none of the children could manage to spend any time together. Ruth figured it was guilt. All of the Jefferson children had been raised Christian, and they all knew well what had happened, so seeing each other just made it worse.

Ruth had asked God to forgive her for walking away from Jesus and living a worldly life for herself. She was determined to go to Heaven to be with her family and with Jesus, but first, she reasoned, she would have to endure what was soon to come. She would have to remain strong and committed to Christ. Daily she presented the news so she knew exactly what condition the world was in. She saw the signs of the times, and she was capable of following along in her Bible. Ruth knew that there would likely be a sequence of events leading up to the *Battle of Armageddon* and eventually the second coming of Christ.

So far Ruth had seen famine and war engulf the world. She had reported on a gregarious agricultural minister from Europe who had become a world hero by providing enough food for every country to survive the famine. Presently she was preparing a news piece on how the world was working collectively to rebuild each nation's economy, including massive repairs on homes, highways, and businesses. The busier the people were, the less time they had to dwell on the past.

Scott smiled back at Ruth. "Come in," he said. Ruth sat down in front of Scott and kicked her feet up on his desk. Ruth was naturally a very relaxed person. "What's up?" Scott asked in a semi-interested tone.

"A lot!" said Ruth. "But I guess you wouldn't know that since you never leave this tomb anymore."

Scott slumped back in his chair and stared up at the artificial ceiling. "I've been busy," he said without looking at Ruth.

"No, Mr. Producer," said Ruth softly. "You've been hiding."

Scott leaned forward toward Ruth as if to say something derogatory, but instead he merely said, "You wouldn't understand."

"Try me!" said Ruth.

Scott wasn't sure where to begin, so he started in the middle. "When will it be over?" he asked. It was a profound question that Ruth had asked herself many times, although she chose to play dumb this time.

"When will what be over?" she asked.

"Never mind!" said Scott. "You won't understand."

"Maybe not, but give it a try anyway." Ruth smiled reassuringly.

Scott had stolen Ruth away from another news station in one of his first acts as the station's producer. From the beginning these two seemed to get along almost as if they were brother and sister. Ruth understood Scott's ambitions, and she seemed to be able to look past all of his youthful and thoughtless ways. Scott in turn had always relied on Ruth's judgment when making tough decisions, but lately they hadn't spent much time together.

"Did you see the show on prophecy that Zach Miles did before he—"

Ruth nodded, sparing Scott the need to elaborate on Zach's horrible death.

"Well, I was at the funeral," said Scott. Ruth already knew all of this, but she thought it best to let Scott get it out of his system. *Maybe he needs this to clear his mind,* she thought.

Scott drew an accurate picture for Ruth of the entire graveside scene up to the point that the earth began to shake. Then he stopped and stared into Ruth's dark, beautiful eyes. "I know where they've all gone," he said as if he held a great mystery in his hand.

"Where?" asked Ruth as if she didn't already know.

Scott stood and walked to the large glass window. Looking out from the 17th floor with his back to Ruth, he spoke quietly. "Do you know how many times I've considered jumping out of this window?"

Ruth walked over to Scott and put her arm around his shoulder. "Probably no more than I have," she said in a whisper as she stared out into the dark, cold sky.

Scott turned and put his arms around Ruth. Suddenly he began to cry. "They've all gone to Heaven," he sobbed.

"Yes, I know," said Ruth sympathetically. Then she pushed Scott away and shook him. "But you listen to me, Mr. Producer—we haven't lost yet. We have a hard road ahead of us, but there is hope."

Scott smiled weakly through his tears. "Do you really think so?" he asked.

"Sit down, Scott. Let's talk." Both Ruth and Scott sat on the small couch facing each other.

"When I was a child, my father used to read me stories from the Bible. In fact, my father was a minister." Scott was surprised that he never knew this before. "Dad used to read me all of the great stories from the New and Old Testament. He also used to read to me from the book of Revelation. This book used to scare us children, and Mama didn't want Daddy to read it to us, but he said that we needed to know so that we would not be deceived by the Devil."

Scott listened carefully as Ruth described for him the events that were foretold in the book of Revelation. "You see," said Ruth, "you and I already know that the Rapture has occurred, and what we have seen recently is a world famine and a tremendous number of natural disasters and war across the planet. What is still to come is somewhat confusing, but the one thing I know for sure is that somewhere in this world the Antichrist is already at work. He will soon rule the world, and when he does, he will make everyone serve him. All will have to take some kind of mark proving their allegiance to him. Nobody will be able to buy, sell, or eat if—" Ruth stopped midsentence as fear overcame her temporarily.

"What is it?" Scott asked.

Ruth stood and began to turn in a slow circle as if she were miles away deep in thought. "Do you have a Bible?" she asked.

"Yes," said Scott as he walked over to his bookshelf. He pulled out the same black leather Bible that he had shared with Zach over a year and a half ago. Scott handed the Bible to Ruth. She began to scan the pages in the back of the book.

"Revelation 13:11-12," said Ruth. "'Then he saw another beast coming out of the earth. He had two horns like a lamb, but he spoke like a dragon. He exercised all the authority of the first beast on his behalf and made the earth and its inhabitants worship the first beast whose fatal wound had been healed.'" Ruth closed the Bible and looked to the ceiling as if to pray for understanding.

"What does it mean?" Scott inquired.

"Do you understand the trinity of God?" Ruth asked.

"You mean the Father, Son, and Holy Spirit?" said Scott, a little unsure.

"That's right," agreed Ruth. "Well, Satan is a copycat. He will form his own trinity adding to himself a False Prophet and the Antichrist. You see, Scott," Ruth continued, "the lamb with two horns is the False Prophet whose job it is to build up the Antichrist so the world would believe in him."

"Who is the Antichrist?" Scott asked fearfully.

"Nobody knows for sure, but I have a good idea!" said Ruth.

"Who?" Scott asked.

"Carlo Ventini," answered Ruth.

"Carlo Ventini!" said Scott. "But he is saving the world from starving. He has been good to every country."

"Maybe too good!" said Ruth.

"How will we know for sure?" Scott asked inquisitively.

"If he is the Antichrist, then soon he will be wounded fatally, but he will rise up again, and then he will proclaim himself as god and the people will let him rule the world."

"So we have to wait then," said Scott.

Ruth stared at Scott closely. "The tribulation is only seven years from start to finish, and it has already been over 18 months since the Rapture."

"What does that mean?" Scott asked.

"It means," said Ruth, "that the Antichrist does not have much time to deceive and destroy the world. It won't be long before we know for sure who he is."

Ruth and Scott sat down and opened the Bible to the book of Revelation and began to study. They had a lot to learn and not much time to learn it. It was a safe bet that soon they would have to choose to serve the Antichrist or else run for their lives.

Chapter 13: A Meeting of the Minds

Day 730, July: It was a horribly hot day and in California people were living on very little water and even less power. Rolling blackouts had become a daily event. Tommy and Tina had spent nearly two years in their small, inconspicuous motel. The heat was stifling, and Tommy had all but given up. It seemed as if God had forgotten them. It was bad enough for Tommy to have to sit on his hands and wait patiently for what was next to come, but Tina made things even worse. She was so impatient. "Maybe God really didn't talk to you. Maybe you imagined it," she would say irritably.

Tommy persevered, however, and eventually he began to see God's plan emerge. One particular morning he left the motel room early while Tina was still asleep. He had decided to walk to the neighborhood grocery store to pick up a few items that he and Tina needed. As he entered the store, his eyes caught sight of the morning newspaper displayed in the newsstand. *"Scientist Convention coming to L.A. this Friday."* Fishing around in his pocket, he found 50 cents to buy the paper.

An hour later Tommy found himself back in his small motel room. Quietly he put the groceries away while Tina snored softly. Finally Tommy made his way out onto the balcony where he sat on a lawn chair and began to read the paper. The sun was breaking through the tree limbs, casting an intolerable glare. He repositioned his chair, reducing the sun's effect, and finally began to read the article that had captured his attention. The first line read: *"U.S.A. calls for scientific convention."* Tommy read on. *"The President of the United States has asked that scientists from all disci-plines unite to discuss the events of these last couple of years. The President's goals are outlined in three distinct parts: first we need a consensus on what happened to all of the people that disappeared."* Tommy scoured the newspaper carefully. *"Next it is imperative that we as a technological society find a solution to our present food shortage. And finally we need an assessment on any further risk of natural disaster, plague, or famine."*

"Tommy," said a soft voice from within the room. Tommy grabbed his paper and reentered his motel room.

"Good morning, Tina. Wait until you hear this!" said Tommy excit-edly as he sat on the edge of Tina's bed.

"What do you have there?" she asked.

"Direction for us, I think." Tommy smiled.

Tina propped herself up on her pillow as Tommy began to read the article to her. "'—I am calling on scientists of all disciplines to work and share research together to find some much needed answers and direction for this nation and for the world in general—'"

"That's from the President himself!" said Tommy enthusiastically.

Tina really didn't see the significance of this particular meeting. "How can this article have anything to do with the plans that you say God has for us?"

"Don't you see?" Tommy asked. "God told me that He would bring others to us for some greater purpose. This meeting must be where we go to meet some of these other people."

It was all pretty circumstantial to Tina. She wasn't buying Tommy's interpretation of the morning news. *But then again, what would be the harm?* she thought. *Anything is better than being cooped up in here.*

******

Tommy entered the L.A. Convention Center a good five feet ahead of Tina. It was as if she was passively resisting the idea. "Come on, Tina! I don't want to miss any of the introductions."

Gazing at her watch, Tina grumbled under her breath, "The stupid thing doesn't even start for 90 minutes."

Tommy had pre-registered Tina and himself the same day that he read the article. He thought it advisable to ensure that he and Tina would get reasonable seating. Upon entering the convention center, Tommy followed the signs overhead. ABC read one. GHI read another. Both Tina and Tommy stood and waited until they received their nametags which also included their table number.

As Tommy sat back and observed, the place was filling up fast. From time to time he and Tina would see a renowned scientist of whom they had heard though not known personally. Eventually the time came for the host to begin the convention. This part was a mystery to Tommy. He had no idea who the host was to be.

The U.S. Secretary of Agriculture stepped out onto the platform. "Good evening, ladies and gentlemen, I am glad that you could attend. Our nation needs your full support."

Pretty impressive, Tommy thought, *to have a member of the President's own cabinet preside over this historic meeting.*

"I am honored to be among so many great minds," said the speaker. "I am doubly honored and proud to introduce our special guest speaker for this occasion, Mr. Simon Koch. As you all know, Mr. Koch, previous to being appointed Assistant United European Leader, was the Assistant Agricultural Secretary and one of the main reasons that we are not starving to death today."

Simon strolled up to the podium amidst cheers and a loud standing ovation. Even Tina and Tommy stood to salute the man who had so graciously helped to save the starving masses around the globe. Simon wore a greedy expression. He loved the adoration. *Now it comes to pass,* he told himself. Just like he was told many years ago when he chose to serve Satan. Simon motioned the group of scientists to take their seats, but this gesture only brought more adulation upon Simon. He was in ecstasy. Oh, how he loved the praise.

Finally after five minutes of roaring the crowd reseated themselves and began to listen as Simon spoke. "Over two years ago Carlo Ventini had a vision, and in this vision he saw a terrible disaster strike the earth.

It was a horrid, unimaginable scene—mothers holding crying children as they wasted away in starvation. It was this vision that led Carlo and I to begin to develop our genetically engineered plants and Agripod Growth Centers. So you see," said an overly sympathetic Simon, "as soon as I heard about this monumental meeting, I told Carlo—excuse me—Mr. Ventini," said Simon with a smile, "that I just had to go to Los Angeles and give you some words of encouragement as you explore possibilities for a new and better future."

In reality, Carlo had sent Simon to L.A. to observe and report back. So far the United States had not cooperated much with Carlo's plans. Oh, sure, he knew that soon all of this would be unimportant, but he also knew that the insight of a single scientist could spread across the globe faster than a plague, and so many of the best minds all meeting at the same time caused Carlo even greater concern.

Simon hadn't wanted to go because he hated scientists. "Just a bunch of smug know-it-all's," he said aloud.

"Yes, well, maybe these know-it-all's will turn out to be a bother for us, so I want you to watch them closely," said a short-tempered Carlo.

Tommy listened carefully as Simon spoke. His heart was full of admiration for the man. He had always wanted to help save the world too. That was one of the reasons he became a volcanologist. A volcanic eruption could be devastating, so he wanted to help invent an early warning system that would give people adequate time to evacuate their villages and homes to avoid injury or death.

Tommy looked briefly over to Tina who seemed to be even more fascinated with Simon than he was. Suddenly in the middle of the room a voice rang out. It was a woman's voice. Tommy had trouble locating the person attached to the voice at first because there were so many people in the room.

"Mr. Koch, can you tell us why you and Mr. Ventini have not shared your genetic harvesting secrets with the world? Don't you think that it is time each country is responsible for mass production of their own crops?"

Finally Tommy located the table the questions were coming from. The woman speaking was dressed in a business suit, but even from across the room Tommy could tell that the young woman was not the business suit type. She appeared from a distance to be very nice looking and shapely. It was for sure that she was very daring and bold.

Simon was caught off guard by the question but quickly regained his composure. "What is your name, may I ask?"

"Sara Allen—Dr. Sara Allen," said the young lady.

"Well, Ms. Allen, you have asked a very good question." Simon desperately searched his mind for a plausible answer. "Ms. Allen, Carlo and I believe that our new genetically engineered plants should be shared with the world, and we would very much like to get out of the crop distribution business," he said with a laugh and a sigh which in turn brought a laugh from the audience.

"Ms. Allen, do you know how many people in our world would like to exploit our secrets to make a profit or how many nuts would like to alter our genetic codes to destroy any hope of raising enough food to feed the poor children?"

Sara Allen began to get angry looks from people sitting throughout the room. Simon had achieved the effect that he had hoped for.

"In summary, Ms. Allen, one of the reasons I have come so far to be here with all of you good people is my hope that you will come up with a workable solution to our food dilemma. I hope we can find a quick resolution," said Simon earnestly.

"Sit down, Lady!" yelled someone in the crowd.

"Yeah, sit down!" said many others.

"One last question, Mr. Koch," said the brave, young doctor. "What do you know about a chemical that modifies DNA, preventing plants from absorbing water?"

Simon was startled. He looked angrily towards Sara. "I don't know anything," said Simon. He had temporarily lost his ability to reason. "Ms. Allen, may I ask you what your particular doctorate is in?"

"Yes, Mr. Koch, my background is in creation science." Sara spoke boldly, but inside she was nervous and frightened.

Simon laughed loudly. "I didn't know there was a science dedicated to mythology," he said smugly. This brought down the house with laughter. Dr. Allen quickly reseated herself.

Tommy was intrigued by the boldness of the young woman. He was a proponent of Simon and Carlo, but he admired Sara's nerve. *I need to meet this woman,* he thought to himself.

The convention was scheduled to run three consecutive days, but after the first day it seemed as if Tina just didn't have the stamina or interest to make all three days. In fact, it was obvious after the first night that Tina would probably not choose to return. After two years of being cooped up together, Tommy really didn't mind leaving her behind at the motel. This would also give him an opportunity to meet the bold young lady who had spoken up the night before.

******

Day two of the convention started with several different presentations by many renowned scientists. The discussion first centered on the effects of the last few years of disasters. The speaker was an elderly man who was obviously uncomfortable with the topic at hand. His name was Dedrick Bishopf, an immigrant from Germany.

Dr. Bishopf was a small child when his father accepted a position with the U.S. Defense Department. He, too, was a scientist and a Jew. The Bishopfs were an affluent family, but in 1938 things began to change for Jews living in Munich. It was fortunate for Dedrick that his father saw the signs.

"My staff has compiled an extensive list of the effects of the last series of disasters. It is broken out by region, so if you will bear with me, I will briefly cover each area in succinct detail."

Dr. Bishopf's voice cracked as he spoke. *What am I doing here?* he wondered. He understood fully the effects of these disasters, especially the huge weather changes that had devastated the entire world's agricultural system, limiting crops to a very few—an amount that was insufficient to feed the billions of hungry people. What he didn't understand was how all this was possible, but today he was expected by many to have all of the answers. Dedrick moved from slide to slide illustrating the horrid condition of each country with the U.S. Secretary and Simon Koch behind him looking on.

The room was deadly silent as the professor spoke. Everyone in the room was stunned by the horror they observed. Tommy knew about most of these disasters—especially the volcanoes and tidal waves—but the floods, snow, droughts, fire, nuclear disasters, and effects of war were overwhelming.

While Dr. Bishopf continued to speak, Tommy began to slowly search the audience for Sara Allen. Finally he found her standing up against the far wall of the convention center. *I guess she is an outcast now,* he thought. Tommy watched Sara as she followed along with Dedrick. Each time he would put up a new slide showing the sad state of a particular location, Sara would turn towards Simon Koch. Eventually Tommy found himself doing the same thing. "The drought in Africa," said Dedrick as he put the slide on the screen. "Thirty million have died from famine and disease."

Tommy watched Simon's face closely. His expression changed temporarily. *I think he is almost smiling,* Tommy thought.

Tommy followed along with Simon for the next hour or so. "In conclusion," said Dr. Bishopf, "we believe that these disasters are the result of evolution—more precisely the evolution of our planet. It is statistically improbable that each of these events could happen again. We unfortunately have the responsibility of living through and rebuilding as a result of these disasters."

This was the conclusion that his team came up with. It was also the closure that the world wanted to accept. However, it was not the conclusion that the professor himself was willing to accept. *The real probability is that it is statistically impossible for each of these events to happen unrelated to some greater cause,* he thought to himself.

Dedrick had a traditional Jewish upbringing, but like his father he never really gave it much priority in his life. It was plausible that there was a God, but Dedrick couldn't prove it scientifically, so he chose to ignore it.

During the first break Tommy wandered over to where Sara had been standing. She was no longer there. "Darn!" said Tommy aloud. He began to look around the convention center. It was impossible to find her now because everyone was up and moving around. *I'll just stay here by the wall, and maybe she'll come back,* Tommy decided.

He didn't have long to wait. Sara came strolling back to the wall with a soda in hand. Tommy looked up at her as she approached. She really was as beautiful as he had thought.

Sara's eyes met Tommy's and fixed in a mutual stare. With a little smile Tommy said, "Hello."

Sara was a bit surprised. She had come to the conclusion that every person in this convention center hated her.

"Hi," said Sara shyly.

"Do you mind if I share your wall?" he said with a charming grin.

"Have you been banished too?" Sara asked. They both laughed at this.

"My name is Tommy Glover, and if I am correct, you are Dr. Allen."

Sara smiled brightly. "I think everybody in here knows my name by now!"

"That's probably true." said Tommy. "Listen, can I ask you a question?"

"Maybe. It depends on the question," said Sara as she composed herself.

"Fair enough!" nodded Tommy. "It seems like maybe you do not trust Mr. Koch. It seems as if you have some suspicions about his motives. Am I correct?" he asked.

Sara looked at Tommy carefully. Recently she had become a bit paranoid around her peers and not just at this convention. Tommy gave her a kind look, and she decided to trust him. "Did you see all of those disasters that Dr. Bishopf was talking about?" Sara asked.

Tommy nodded attentively.

"Do you think these are all a coincidence—part of the evolution of our planet?" Sara inquired and then awaited Tommy's reply.

It was an easy question for him to answer. He was one of the few fortunate ones to actually hear from God Himself, so he knew beyond a shadow of a doubt that these events were divinely inspired. "No!" said

Tommy. "These disasters have a purpose." Sara was surprised by his answer. "But what does that have to do with Simon Koch?" Tommy asked.

"If you had been watching him like I was, you would have seen that he was obviously happy with each of these disasters," said Sara

Tommy nodded. "I saw him." Again Sara was surprised by Tommy's answer. "What do you think it means?" he asked.

"What kind of a scientist are you?" Sara asked.

"Volcanologist," said Tommy. "And you are a creation scientist, right?"

"You pay attention well!" said Sara. "Tommy, do you know what a creation scientist does?"

"Not really," said Tommy.

"I look for proofs of God in the design of our planet and universe. It is a counter proposal to traditional evolutionists."

Tommy looked at Sara carefully. "But what does that have to do with Simon Koch?"

"Why did you say that these disasters have a purpose?" Sara asked.

Tommy was a little uncertain as to what to say. If he told Sara about the conversation with God, she might think he was nuts, but if he didn't tell her, then how would he ever find others like him—others serving God?

"God told me," said Tommy in a whisper.

"What?" Sara asked as she looked at Tommy suspiciously.

"It's true!" said Tommy. "God told me about two years ago, and I've just been waiting for Him to bring other people to me."

"Are you a Christian?" Sara asked.

"I wasn't raised that way. I never gave God any real thought, but apparently He knows me, because long ago He came to me and told me that He had a plan for my life."

"What plan?" Sara asked.

"I am going to be a disciple, and I am going to help lead people— probably scientists and others—to Jesus before the end comes."

Sara smiled cheerfully. "I believe you. I really do!"

"I'm glad!" said Tommy. "I was afraid you wouldn't."

"The reason I am suspicious about Mr. Koch is because he and Carlo

Ventini—the man he works for—hold the lives of billions of people in their hands. They are the only ones capable of feeding the world. I've seen Mr. Koch on the news, and I've watched him closely. Something is wrong with him. I think maybe he and Mr. Ventini—" Sara paused.

"What is it?" Tommy asked.

"I think they are evil," she whispered. "Maybe very evil!"

"The Antichrist?" asked Tommy.

Sara nodded slowly.

Both Sara and Tommy were startled as Simon Koch and the U.S. Secretary walked by them on their way back to their seats of honor. "Ms. Allen," said Simon with a conceited smile on his face. "Won't they let you sit at your table today?" Simon looked past Tommy and walked off laughing.

******

On the third day Tommy and Sara found themselves back at their familiar wall slightly removed from the main audience, only this time they were not alone. Dr. Bishopf stood leaning against the wall only a few feet away.

"You are a brave woman," said Dedrick in passing as Sara stood close to Tommy.

Sara smiled at Dr. Bishopf and spoke softly, "I didn't feel very brave."

Dedrick laughed. "Understandable considering the company, but it was brave just the same."

"Thank you, Sir," said Sara.

"And who might you be, young man?" Dedrick asked.

"I'm Tommy Glover—a big fan of yours!" said Tommy as he stuck out his hand. Dr. Bishopf shook it firmly.

"Are you a creation scientist as well?" Dedrick asked.

Tommy laughed. "No, Sir, I am a volcanologist."

"Oh, so you are a brave person as well!" said Dedrick. "Why are you two here?" Dedrick asked. Neither Sara nor Tommy really knew the answer to that particular question.

"To try and understand, I guess," said Tommy. Dedrick suspected there was a little more to what Tommy was saying, but it could wait until they got to know each other a little better.

Dedrick, Sara, and Tommy spent the last day of the convention together listening carefully as each guest speaker gave his or her version of the state of the world. They heard each theory play itself out until finally came the question of what was next for planet earth.

Simon answered this question for the audience of scientists. "We cannot go back—only forward," he said. Simon paused and waited for a response from the audience, but none came. "We in this room have the awesome responsibility of reshaping our future. We will determine together the course that lies ahead for all of mankind. It is time to unite and to use all of our global technology to master our planet. We can no longer allow our world to dictate our future."

Simon paused again, but this time he received a standing ovation from the audience. "Thank you. Please be seated," said Simon as he dined on the attention and fame. "Mr. Ventini and I have been working on solutions to many of our common plaguing issues. We would like to unveil much of this over the next few weeks. We strongly recommend that you elect a leader from your scientific community to act as your focal point.

"Carlo and I will ask for scientists from each nation to represent their respective countries, and together we will ensure a cohesive team effort as we transition into a new and brighter world." Again the audience stood and cheered loudly. *Maybe I have underestimated these scientists,* Simon told himself. *They're not that bad after all.*

Dedrick listened carefully as Simon spoke the closing words. *I wonder,* he thought, *if this was the way Hitler closed his speeches?*

"What do you think of all of this?" Dedrick inquired of Sara and Tommy.

Tommy spoke up first. "It's not real," he said. Sara watched Tommy as he searched for a way to tell Dr. Bishopf the truth about God. "There is a purpose in all of this, Dr. Bishopf. Excuse me, Sir, but your conclusions about the earth simply evolving are not correct."

Dedrick admired the young man's courage.

"What do you think has happened to our world, young man?"

Tommy looked to Sara for strength. "The end is coming. God is returning for his people, and destruction is coming to the world," said Tommy as boldly as he could.

"How do you know this to be true?" Dedrick asked.

Tommy looked into the old man's eyes and spoke with conviction. "God told me!"

Dedrick stared back at Tommy for a long time as if to decide once and for all what he had already known to be true. "I believe you," he said sadly.

Dedrick pulled out his wallet and fished out a small business card. He handed the card to Tommy. "I think we will meet again. Here is my number in case you need me."

Tommy took the card from Dedrick and stared at it as Dr. Bishopf smiled at Sara and walked off.

******

The convention was finally over, and Tommy really wanted to bring Sara home to meet Tina. He had not mentioned Sara to his sister because he was afraid that this would upset her, and recently it didn't take much to make Tina angry. Just the night before he had tried to tell her about his suspicions that Simon Koch was an evil man. Tina quickly became defensive. "Evil—he has saved the world! What is wrong with you?"

"Tina, don't forget that God has told us that the end is coming and that evil is already out there to deceive us."

Tina was fed up with Tommy's conversations about God. "If God really talked to you, then why are we still here? Why didn't He talk to me? Simon is a hero to the world, and you are the one who is being deceived."

After hearing Tina's convictions, Tommy wasn't sure it was a good idea to bring Sara around. Tina and Tommy had never spent time with other men and women. They relied entirely on each other for support.

Tommy was also certain that Sara would have more to say about Simon and Carlo. He knew Tina was going to be a very unhappy person.

Unhappy or not, this is the beginning that God has promised me. Tina is just going to have to deal with it, Tommy thought.

Chapter 14: The Visitation

Day 750, July: Nobody was out and about. The heat of summer was staggering—nearly 110 degrees daily. This had been going on for the last 45 days. It had been more than two years since that fatal day when the earth shook uncontrollably for over five minutes. Joseph and Peter had been living in Rome for the last 24 months. They were going through the motions, firmly convinced that God would lead them. "In God's time!" said Joseph to Peter. "We have to be patient and trust in Him."

Joseph sat at his desk reviewing the rate of food consumption in each of the Catholic Church communities around the world. What was it that Carlo had said to Joseph on that morning many months back when he, Simon Koch, and Carlo Ventini met to discuss food distribution to all of the Catholic Churches around the world? "Feed them well," Carlo had said smiling brightly. Joseph could still remember that morning when Carlo came to call.

It was such a fine, sunny day that Joseph had decided to jog to work. Taking a detour from his usual jogging route, he rounded Peter's clinic in hopes of capturing a glimpse of Yvette. She was still on his mind after last night's visit.

The niece of our new Pope. How ironic! he thought to himself as he jogged by. Unfortunately for Joseph, Yvette was nowhere to be seen. *Maybe tomorrow,* he thought, *if I'm not too sore to jog again.*

Joseph rounded the corner of the last set of buildings and entered his own courtyard. To his pleasant surprise Yvette was sitting on the steps of his office building.

Joseph approached Yvette with his curly hair dripping with perspiration. With a smile Joseph said, "What brings a nice girl like you into this neighborhood?" They both laughed heartily at the comment.

"I came to talk to you," said Yvette.

Joseph unlocked the front door of the old building and led Yvette up to the second floor and into his small office. "Have a seat," said Joseph. "Would you like me to make some coffee?"

"No, thanks. That's not necessary," said Yvette. "I really don't have much time."

"What's on your mind?" Joseph asked calmly.

Yvette smiled as he spoke. *He would make a great psychiatrist,* she told herself. "I was thinking about last night—I mean—what we talked about." Yvette was a little uncomfortable with this subject.

"Yes, what about it?" said Joseph.

Yvette just sat there not knowing what to say next. It wasn't just the topic from last night that had brought Yvette to Joseph this morning. It was much more than that. Yvette was very confused. She had feelings for Peter, but she also had feelings for Joseph. Her thoughts for Joseph made her uncomfortable—as if she were cheating on Peter. At the same time she couldn't help the way she felt about Joseph, yet this caused her grief because he was a priest. However, Joseph had told her he really wasn't a priest anymore which meant that he was just a man—a handsome, single man. The whole thing was confusing—too much so for Yvette. She needed help from Joseph to figure it out.

Joseph was a very perceptive person. He knew that Yvette had not come all the way down to his office just to continue last night's discussion even though there was still much to be said. Joseph figured—hoped— that she was here, because she needed to see him again. He decided to take a chance and put this thought to the test.

"I am really glad to see you. I've been thinking a lot about you," said Joseph. *If that isn't plain as day,* he thought to himself.

"Thinking what?" Yvette asked. She was going to make Joseph come right out and say it.

"Oh, well, you know—stuff! I mean good stuf—like you are pretty and nice and stuff." Joseph was making a fool out of himself in a hurry. He hoped it was not just a big waste of his time. He really had no practice at this sort of thing, and he felt foolish.

Yvette smiled a lovely, bright smile. "Me too," she whispered.

"So why did you come down here? And how did you know where my office was, anyway?" Joseph asked lightly.

"Oh, that's easy!" said Yvette. "Peter told me many times that you worked down here and, well, my uncle—"

"The Pope," Joseph interjected.

"Right—the Pope used to bring me here all the time when I was a little girl."

"Okay," said Joseph. "We've got that figured out. So why did you come here, Yvette?"

"I wanted to see you, I guess," Yvette whispered. "To see if you were real or if last night was just some kind of weird dream." Joseph enjoyed listening to Yvette speak. She had such a lovely accent, and it was cute the way she tried to pronounce some of the more unusual English words, such as weird.

"Well, as you can see, I am real—a little sweaty, but real," said Joseph with a boyish grin.

Yvette held out her hand to Joseph. He took it gently into his own powerful hand. "Are you sure that you are not a priest anymore?" Yvette asked cautiously.

Joseph laughed loudly. "I'm positive!" he said.

"Then I guess it's okay," said Yvette.

"What's okay?" Joseph asked. Now it was his turn to make her speak plainly.

"Okay that I like you," the beautiful Yvette smiled shyly.

******

That had been approximately one year ago, and now Joseph and Yvette saw each other daily. Their relationship was extremely respectful and Godly. Not that the passion wasn't there—it was just that it was under control. Joseph entertained thoughts of marriage. He knew that he and Yvette would never be intimate unless they were married in the eyes of

God, but for some reason, he never felt a release from God authorizing this union. Joseph rationalized that he and Yvette had less than seven years before the world came to an end and two of those seven years had already gone by, but still it was five years that he and she could be united as one. Unfortunately for Joseph, he knew that it was much more likely that he would have to die in opposition to the Antichrist, lest he take the mark of the beast and spend eternity in Hell.

******

Joseph was barely showered and dressed when Simon and Carlo came to visit him at the Vatican. It was his first formal meeting with these two guys. Oh, sure, they had met and even had dinner on one other occasion when Zach Miles had come to town. However, they had never really sat down to discuss Carlo's plans for food distribution throughout the world.

The meeting started out politely enough with both Carlo and Simon treating Joseph like a real priest in a particularly important position. Of course, none of this was true, and all three men knew it.

Joseph was preparing huge lists of names. He had been asked to compile a complete listing of all Catholic memberships, both new and old, from around the world. It seemed that since the Rapture church membership had grown considerably. People were hungry to know the truth about what had happened to the many that disappeared. In fact, millions had been Raptured from both within the Catholic community and elsewhere, but millions more had been left behind.

"My, my! There sure are a lot of God-fearing people on these lists," said Simon.

Carlo and Simon both smiled as Carlo patted the four-foot pile of Catholic memberships. "You've been very helpful, Father Bastoni," said Carlo. "How can I repay you?"

Joseph didn't really understand the question. *Isn't it you that is helping all of us by feeding the world?* he thought to himself. "I haven't done anything worthy of your praise," said Joseph.

"Oh, no!" said Simon. "You've done much more than you'll ever know." This statement from Simon caused Joseph to cringe a little. He didn't trust these guys. They were up to something, but for the life of Joseph, he could not figure out what. It all looked legitimate, but it felt wrong to him. They felt wrong.

******

This first meeting had taken place nearly a year ago and a lot had happened since then. *Focus on your job, dummy,* Joseph told himself. He did not enjoy the mundane task. He understood the importance of ensuring that every church community got its necessary ration of food each month, but the task was tedious all the same.

There was a heavy knock at his office door, startling Joseph. "Come in, please," said Joseph.

Dr. Bastoni walked in with a large white bag. "Hungry?" Peter grinned.

"Anything is better than doing this," Joseph sighed.

Peter set the bag on Joseph's desk and pulled up a chair.

"Smells good!" said Joseph.

Peter pulled out a large calazone and divided it into halves. This would be a treat for both men. There wasn't a lot of meat available nowadays because so many animals had starved to death due to the many droughts, fires, floods, and plagues. What meat was available was extremely expensive. "How much did this baby cost you?" Joseph inquired.

"Don't ask!" said Peter. "Just eat it and enjoy." He didn't have to say that twice. Joseph was already halfway through his piece of the sausage-stuffed calazone.

"What brings you here?" Joseph asked with a mouthful of food.

"Your Fiat!" laughed Peter.

Joseph laughed as well. "I know that, but why are you here?"

Peter put his calazone down and looked at Joseph. "I'm not sure, but I felt the need to come."

Both men finished eating and sat back in their chairs to relax. "How's Yvette doing today?" Joseph asked.

"A little grumpy for some reason," said Peter.

Hmm, Joseph thought. *I wonder why.*

Suddenly Joseph's office was flooded with a soft white light. A little breeze blew across the faces of both men. Joseph felt great joy instantly, but Peter was frightened and began to stand. "Its okay, Peter," said Joseph softly.

"Be at peace," said a soothing yet powerful voice. About that time the door to Joseph's office opened and Yvette walked in.

The glow of the room startled her, but not nearly as much as the presence of God. Yvette began to tremble so much that she fell to her knees. Joseph wanted to help her, but he was also frozen where he sat.

"You must prepare," said the Lord. "The time has come, and soon the world will be completely deceived. You must begin to warn the world against the Antichrist and against taking his mark."

"Lord," said Joseph, "who is the Antichrist? And how can I warn the world about him?"

"Today, Joseph, you will see and know the evil Son of Satan." Joseph shivered with fear at the thought. "Fear not, greater am I than he. For a time, My Words will protect you all from harm."

Peter was afraid to open his eyes. He could not believe what was happening here. God was actually taking the time to talk with them and to guide them. If Peter had really considered this, he would have understood that God was always available for us to talk with.

"Lord," said Joseph. "What do I tell the people, and how will they believe me?"

"Tell them the truth, and let the truth of My Words convince those that are willing. Joseph," said the Lord, "you must do this in secret, for the religious leaders of this world are corrupt."

"Peter and Yvette, you must seek out others like yourselves. You must prepare for sickness and plagues. Now take heart, for everything that was written will come to pass."

The light in the room began to fade and Joseph had a sense of sorrow as the Lord departed, but being in His presence revitalized Joseph. It was where he wanted to stay forever.

Yvette, Joseph, and Peter hugged and cried. Finally they agreed to get together this evening for supper and a further discussion of what the Lord had said to them. *But at least we finally have some more direction,* Joseph thought to himself after Peter and Yvette left.

Joseph looked at his calendar: August 14. *Two years and one month since the Rapture,* he thought, *and today I will meet the Antichrist. How and where will I meet him?* he wondered.

As Joseph read over the appointments for the day, Simon Koch's name was listed for a 1:00 p.m. meeting. Joseph had nearly forgotten that he was supposed to meet Simon today. He needed to have all the food ration slips ready to hand over. Joseph looked at his watch, and it was already 1:00 p.m. on the nose.

Could Simon be the Antichrist? he wondered as he looked up at his office door. Joseph was frightened, but he tried to maintain his composure. He was nearly certain that in just a minute or so the most evil person on earth was about to walk through his door. He had always thought of Simon and Carlo as odd, but he had never feared either of these men until now.

There were two solid raps on Joseph's office door. He wanted to stand and open the door, but his legs refused to oblige him. In a weak and wavering voice Joseph simply said, "Come in, please." Simon entered the room first with Carlo two steps behind. Joseph had not expected to see the new European leader today. His appointment was with Simon alone. *Maybe,* Joseph thought, *Carlo is the Antichrist instead of Simon. How will I know?* he wondered.

"Good afternoon, Father Bastoni!" said Simon cheerfully. Joseph was finally able to will his legs to stand. He shook hands with Simon and then waited for Carlo to approach. As Carlo moved towards Joseph's desk, he suddenly stopped. Both Simon and Joseph observed Carlo carefully. They were amazed as Carlo began to scan the room cautiously in much the same way a bird dog stalks his prey.

Simon got a terrified look on his face. He felt that something was very wrong. Something in the air wasn't right, and his leader, Carlo, was acting very peculiar. Suddenly Carlo began to clutch his stomach in pain. Soon after he put his hands over his mouth and ran from the room in search of the nearest toilet.

With an angry look on his face, Simon looked at Joseph and then ran out after Carlo.

It was the residual presence of God in my office that made him sick! Joseph thought.

"Lord," said Joseph softly. "Thank you for revealing to me that Carlo Ventini is the Antichrist. Now, Lord, help me to overcome my fear." Joseph reflected, *and that would make Simon the False Prophet if I am not mistaken.*

A few minutes later both Simon and Carlo reentered Joseph's office. Simon was very protective of Carlo as he walked him to a nearby chair. He looked scornfully at Joseph. "Could you please open your window?" Simon asked.

"Of course!" said Joseph as he walked over to the window.

Carlo began to improve in just a few minutes. "Have you had any visitors today?" he asked suspiciously.

"My brother and another friend of mine visited me at lunchtime," he said. Joseph had no intention of telling either man about the Lord's visit, although Joseph was sure that Carlo could sense the presence of God in the room.

The real question was whether or not Carlo and Simon perceived that Joseph was really working for the Lord and not for their particular cause. They would have to watch Joseph a little more closely. Sure, he didn't go in the Rapture, so he was probably far from God and totally unaware that Carlo was using him, but you never know—and maybe he had found God after all.

******

Joseph, Peter, and Yvette met at Joseph's apartment for dinner. The three of them sat and prayed to God for wisdom and guidance for what they were about to do. "Lord, we thank You for choosing us to do Your will. Lord, guide us and help us to lead people to You before they are devoured by the Devil."

"God said that we need to prepare for a plague," said Peter softly. "What kind of plague, and how do we prepare?"

"He said that we need to get others in the medical profession to join us as well," interjected Yvette. "How do we do all of this, and how will you warn the world, Joseph?"

Joseph took Yvette's fragile hand in his. "Fear is from the devil. God would not have us do any of this if He didn't think we could." Joseph looked to his older brother. "God will give you the wisdom to fight this plague, and He will bring others in to help us. As for me, I think I already know what God wants me to do." Yvette looked at Joseph for clarification. "I think He wants me to use *Deacon's Horn.*"

"Use what?" Yvette asked.

Peter didn't have to ask. He had seen many of these newspapers around the apartment. He knew it was part of Joseph's job to write this paper. "They'll trace it back to you, Joseph. If Carlo and Simon are what you say, then you are too close to them and they will trace it back to you," said Peter.

Yvette had no idea what these two brothers were talking about. "Maybe not," said Joseph. "Maybe there is a way to keep the messages a secret until a specific time has passed and we have planned our escape."

"What are you two talking about?" an irritated Yvette asked. Joseph stood and walked into the kitchen. Quickly he returned with a thin newspaper in his hand. "What is that?" she asked.

"*Deacon's Horn!*" said Joseph with a smile.

Chapter 15: Two Young Witnesses

D ay 820, October: Elisha and Jasmine had been in Bethlehem for about two and a half years, most of which they spent witnessing by day to whoever would listen to them, and by night they slept in alleys behind the downtown businesses. They were hungry and dirty continually. In addition to this misery, the heat and drought in Jerusalem was unbearable. Since the sandstorm and subsequent earthquake, numerous children found themselves homeless and without parents to tell them that everything was going to be all right.

Daily Elisha and Jasmine would go on their usual hunt for food, looking in trash bins in the backs of dimly lit alleyways. The pickings were extremely slim. Most people found creative ways to use nearly every portion of their food rations, and some young, starving child quickly scavenged whatever was thrown out, making the hunt for food a competitive and dangerous one.

One day Elisha found himself crawling around a small dumpster just behind Benjamin Cohen's kosher deli. Benjamin was a kind old man. In fact, he intentionally deposited small cuts of good meat, neatly wrapped, on the top of his trashcan each evening. He knew that some poor starving child would find it and eat well—at least for the night.

Benjamin had been seeing Jasmine and Elisha prowling around his trash looking for food months earlier. From the second story window above his shop he would often watch the two youngsters seated beside each other late in the evening trying to stay warm as they ate the small scraps of food Benjamin had deposited earlier. Benjamin was so moved by the love and tenderness these two showed each other that he began to leave them double portions of food nightly on his back porch.

One evening after Benjamin had closed his shop he spotted another teenager going through his garbage. Benjamin had not seen this particular boy before. He wondered what Elisha and Jasmine would do when they saw this child invading their territory. He was sure that Jasmine and Elisha were likely relying on this food as their primary source of nutrition. He imagined that the two would fight to protect the food supply.

Benjamin did not have very long to wait before the starving teens showed up. Jasmine was the first to spot the boy in the trashcan. She quickly looked over to the back doorstep where Benjamin had been placing their food each night. Jasmine spotted two neatly wrapped white packages. *He hasn't found it yet,* Jasmine thought.

"Hello!" said Elisha. This startled the boy and stopped his rummaging.

"I was here first!" said the child as boldly as he could.

"What is your name?" Elisha asked.

"None of your business!" said the boy who was probably only 13 years of age.

Pretty bold talk for a boy who was an easy five or more years younger than Elisha was. "All right then I'll just have to make up my own name for you." The boy stopped and stared at Elisha and then over at Jasmine.

"What does she have in her hands?" the frightened boy asked.

Elisha couldn't help but laugh. The young boy was trying so hard to be tough, yet as he stood barely visible from within the dumpster pointing at Jasmine, the scene was suddenly humorous. "I think I'll call you Samson because you are obviously very strong and powerful!" said Elisha with a smile. "Now if you are hungry, climb out of that garbage and share our food."

Jasmine was a little put out by Elisha offering some of their precious food to a rude little boy, but she also understood what it felt like to be alone and hungry.

Benjamin had been watching this encounter closely from his bedroom window. He was astounded to see the three children sit down side by side and begin to share the thin slices of salami and smoked chicken. The kindness that he had shown these two children was now being passed on to a third needy child.

"So, Samson, where do you live?" asked Elisha as he smiled and winked at Jasmine.

"Around!" said the tough little boy. "And my name isn't Samson. It's David."

"Even better," said Elisha as he handed the boy another piece of chicken under Jasmine's intense watchfulness.

Suddenly the back door to the deli swung wide open, terrifying all three children. Jasmine clutched the white paper and its contents while Elisha stood and turned towards Benjamin. David leapt to his feet and began to run.

"No! Don't go! Stop!" said Benjamin, but by this time David had rounded the corner and was out of sight.

Jasmine stood next to Elisha as bravely as she could. Her desire was to run away just like David had done, but for some reason Elisha wasn't moving and there was no way Jasmine would ever leave him behind. "My name is Benjamin Cohen, and this is my store."

Elisha stared at the old man carefully. *He's been feeding us intentionally, and unless he plans on eating us, I'd say he is trying to help us,* Elisha thought silently.

Elisha stuck out his hand in a friendly manner. "Elisha Kaufman— and this is Jasmine Hamar." Benjamin shook Elisha's hand and smiled at Jasmine.

"Come into my house, please!" said Benjamin as he led the way. Jasmine was not sure that this was a good idea, but Elisha was already heading in, so she followed behind slowly.

Benjamin and Elisha hit it off together within minutes; however, Jasmine was a bit of a mystery to Benjamin. It was obvious that she was Palestinian. Why she was traveling with a Jewish boy—in Bethlehem of all places—would require some explanation for sure.

From that day on Benjamin made room in his home for Elisha and

Jasmine. Three days later—out of sheer hunger—David came snooping around in the middle of the evening. Benjamin saw him from his second story window. "He's back!" Benjamin yelled. "Go get him, Elisha, and bring him in."

Elisha went out the front entrance to the deli and made his way around to the alley. David was busy digging out meat crumbs and eating them as if he were starving which, of course, he was. He hadn't even noticed when Elisha walked up to the dumpster.

"Hello, David," said Elisha. David was startled so greatly he nearly fell out of the trashcan. "It's all right, David. It's me, Elisha."

"I guess that man didn't catch you either," said David as he looked around for Jasmine. "Got the girl though, I see," he said, trying to pretend that he was composed.

Jasmine and Benjamin watched from the window.

"You don't have to be hungry anymore."

"What do you mean?" David asked.

"I mean that you can live here with us." David was confused and distressed. It didn't seem reasonable that Elisha and Jasmine were living in this deli. It was strange to believe that anyone would care for him enough to take him into their home.

David had been surviving alone for a couple of years. He was a runaway from a neighborhood orphanage. "Its okay, David. He is a good man. It's safe here!" Benjamin could tell that David was resistant to the idea, so he sent Jasmine out to reinforce what Elisha was saying.

"David, this place is safe for us. We have food and warm beds to sleep in," said Jasmine in a much softer voice than Elisha had ever heard her use before. "He won't hurt you." David stared at the back door where Benjamin now stood.

"Its okay, Son. You can stay with us! Come in, won't you?" said the old man.

******

The three children had been living with Benjamin for nearly six months now. Elisha had shared with Benjamin and David everything that happened in the sandstorm and how God had saved them. It was a bit trickier to explain to Benjamin about the Return of Jesus. In fact, not even Jasmine or Elisha were aware that the Rapture had even taken place until Philip, the angel, told them just before they came into Bethlehem from the desert.

"We have a purpose given to us by God," Elisha told Benjamin one evening as the other two children sat by listening. "God wants us to tell the Jews—"

"And Palestinians!" interjected Jasmine.

"Yes," Elisha smiled, "and the Palestinians—and anyone else who will listen. God told us that the end of the world is soon to come and that we have to spread the Word so people can know the Truth and can choose."

Benjamin was so impressed with Jasmine and Elisha's story that he began to believe that they were telling the truth. This meant that he had to seriously reconsider his own faith. Sure, it was the same God, but to finally recognize Jesus as Lord was another matter altogether. Eventually through prayer Benjamin began to have a peace about accepting Jesus as God's only Son.

Although they had not received any further guidance from God yet, all three children and Benjamin began to comb the neighborhoods of Bethlehem proclaiming the Return of Jesus Christ. This effort was a volatile one, for sure. Many of Benjamin's neighbors accused him of betraying God. Additionally they accused him of being senile. However, over time Benjamin and the children began to develop a large number of followers.

Elisha and Jasmine repeated often their tale of how the Lord had saved them and transported them to Bethlehem. Their testimony converted many.

Small groups met nightly at Benjamin's house for a Bible study. This effort was nearly comical in the beginning since none of the new followers had any idea how to read and interpret the New Testament. In fact, they found it difficult enough just to find Bibles for each member. Through their perseverance, however, all soon became true followers of Christ.

The word was beginning to spread to surrounding regions, but in Elisha's heart he knew this was not enough. He understood time was short and that the Lord had more planned. He would have to wait on God for guidance as to what to do next, but for now he was content to tell his story to whoever would listen.

******

Carlo stood and walked to the large, plate-glass window overlooking the Adriatic Sea. He loved his Pescara mansion. It had been months since he was able to vacation there. Carlo had been an extremely busy man, traveling to virtually every country in the world, surveying devastation and starvation firsthand, consoling the peoples of each country while they exalted him as their hero and savior.

Eight months earlier all the major European communities had met to discuss their future. They were in agreement that their particular famine was not nearly as severe as most countries, primarily due to Carlo Ventini's efforts. In fact, the export of European food had really improved their economy. It was starting to look like Europe was once again going to be the dominant economic power in the world.

"How can we take advantage of this good fortune that Carlo has brought us?" the Prime Minister of England asked. This was the theme at this historic first meeting. Presidents, kings, and prime ministers from various countries all agreed with the point of the convention.

Many of the smaller European countries were not invited to this session due to a request from Carlo. "It is important to get their input," he told the leaders from each of the 13 major countries, "but we have much more at stake than they, and we are responsible for the health and well-being of their nations."

In the many weeks prior to this eventful meeting Simon Koch had personally visited each leader from every major country. In each case he planted a seed and assessed the resistance to his ideas. The seed was simple: "Let's unify and become one large European government. Each of you leaders will still rule your own country, but the defense and economic leadership will come from a single branch of government," said Simon persuasively.

At first most leaders shied away from the concept of a single government. It was a little too communistic for them, but after several visits and additional explanation Simon convinced them that it was not a communist government. "In fact," he said, "it is really a democratic and capitalistic government just like that of the United States."

******

It had been eight months since Carlo had been elevated to President of the European Federation of Countries. The vote was a majority—10 in favor and 3 opposed. Carlo had plans for those three countries, but that would have to wait until he assumed an even higher office as the world leader.

Carlo did not have much interest in the administration of his new office. He left all of the details to Simon who had hand selected Carlo's cabinet. Simon was careful to try and please each country with equal participation. He selected key government officials from each nation and elevated them to their new positions.

The consensus of the first meeting with each nation was that officers would be selected based upon years of experience and ability. They also agreed that they would limit the terms of office to four years and that all future positions would be filled by a majority vote.

As Carlo stood looking out his bay window, he thought about what was soon to come to him, and he cringed with fear. "Father," he said in a whimpering voice, "I don't want to die!"

Simon could sense Carlo's mood change. "Is there anything I can do for you?" he asked.

The tears burned Carlo's eyes as he turned towards Simon. "Maybe!" he said with an eerie smile that frightened Simon. Carlo clapped his hands twice, and one of his creepy servants walked into the room. Carlo whispered into the man's ear. He nodded and walked out of the room.

"Let's go and see my Father," said Carlo. At this Simon was both scared and exhilarated. He followed Carlo closely down the stairs and into their worship chamber. Both Carlo and Simon removed their shoes and put on their black robes. Simon was so excited that his stomach began to loudly rumble.

"Control yourself!" Carlo said angrily.

Carlo pulled the brass bowl and the sharp utensils out from under the shelf. *Yes!* Simon thought. *Another sacrifice!*

Soon two of Carlo's servants showed up with another plastic bag, heavily laden. Only this time it was a young boy about 16 years of age. Simon could hardly contain himself. He had a taste for young boys as well as for blood.

Carlo did not waste any time on this particular sacrifice. He had learned the hard way on the last one. He would not lose another soul to Jesus. He quickly killed the child and offered the basin full of blood up to Satan.

Simon was thoroughly disappointed by the speed at which they killed the boy. No torture, no abuse. *What a shame,* he thought.

The room began to shake and Simon fell to his knees. "Father!" cried Carlo. "Are you pleased with my sacrifice?"

"What is it that you want, my Son?" the Devil asked.

Carlo began to cry and wail aloud. "Father, I don't want to die! I know it is coming soon, and I don't want to go through it."

"It is foretold that you must be mortally wounded, but after a short while you will rise again," said Satan.

"Father, why can't we allow Simon to be killed and then you can raise him from the dead?"

At this Simon looked up at Carlo—he was crying and pleading in a pathetic fashion. *Kill me? That's not part of the plan!* Simon thought.

"Enough!" said Satan as he shook the room. "It is your destiny to die and be raised as the ruler of the world. It must happen according to plan. Simon will be given power to rain down fire from the sky and to act on your behalf. You will rise up immortal for all time," said Satan.

The room grew quiet as Simon stood to his feet. Carlo began to remove his robe while Simon stared at the murdered young man. "What a pity," he said in a whisper.

Carlo knew he would have to go through this death. He didn't like the idea at all. Maybe even worse was not knowing when or how he would die. "We need to go back to Rome," said Carlo.

Simon just stood there staring at Carlo and the still warm body of the young boy. "Well!" Carlo shouted. "Don't just stand there. Make the arrangements now!"

Carlo's rage frightened Simon. *I'll be glad when this assassination thing is over with,* Simon thought as he ran from the room to arrange the escort back to Rome.

Chapter 16: Mortally Wounded

D ay 900, December: It was another horribly cold and snowy winter for Europe. There would be no crops this year either. Peter and Yvette had for many months now been slowly recruiting doctors and nurses into their group. This was not an easy task in the least. There was a continual paranoia on Peter's part that the word would get out that an underground medical organization was being developed.

The Lord, however, continued to bring medical experts across Peter and Yvette's path. It seemed that in each case the Lord had through visions and dreams inspired these people to come into the small clinic. In one case a very elderly male doctor came into Yvette's clinic early one morning and stood staring down the narrow hallway.

"Can I help you?" Yvette inquired.

The man began to walk slowly through the small rooms until he finally reached the main ER where Peter stood inspecting a mild second-degree burn on the arm of a little child. Yvette stood back and watched as the man observed Peter's work. Suddenly the man spoke up in Italian. "It's you!" he said.

Peter turned to look at the man with the unfamiliar voice. "Excuse me?" said Peter in his one and only language, English.

"It's you. You're the one!" said the man, this time in English as well.

"I don't understand. What do you mean?" said Peter. The man moved forward to inspect the small child's burn. "That doesn't look too bad, but I would apply a topical antibiotic all the same."

"Thanks!" said Peter. "I'll do that. Now do you mind telling me who you are?"

The old man stuck out his hand and said, "I am Bruno Shire, Dr. Bruno Shire."

Peter shook the man's hand. "I am Peter Bastoni, and this is Yvette Lewis." The man smiled kindly at Yvette.

"I saw you both in my dreams last night. I saw this building, and I knew I had to come down here. The Lord has told me about your work, and I am to help you if I can."

******

That had been many months ago, and now there were some 30 medical doctors, nurses, virologists, and lab technicians all meeting weekly at the small clinic. Peter had been elected unanimously as their leader, although it was a responsibility that he was not very comfortable with. So far there really had not been a need for any of these talented people, but each man and woman was under a conviction from God to be prepared. They knew something was coming and that they would be desperately needed. They just didn't know what or when.

Peter was not the only one who found himself busy as well as paranoid. Joseph had made a decision to begin the process of sending out warnings to the Catholic community. This procedure was complicated and dangerous. Joseph knew if he were ever found out, he would be killed.

It took Joseph months to develop a sophisticated code. It was important that *Deacon's Horn* read just as it always had. It was imperative that it remain in a Latin text, but it was also important that it be laced with a hidden series of messages warning the world about Carlo, Simon, and what was to come.

Joseph combined two methods to accomplish his task. First he designed a series of alternate words for every word written in his paper. He also designed a sequence to these written words. Only the third, fifth, and seventh words in each sentence were a part of the actual code. It would be far too difficult to write a complete and informative newspaper with each word in the sentence having a hidden meaning.

Joseph found that his method of word substitution and sequencing allowed him to easily write his paper as usual. This paper was a monthly issue, and because it was not a long paper, Joseph decided that he would have to be patient and embed only a portion of a message each month. His goal was to eventually include the entire truth and then issue the final newspaper with the code clearly displayed. Of course, by that time Joseph would have left the country and gone into hiding.

Now it was the eve of Joseph's last issue of *Deacon's Horn*. He had all but finished the newspaper, yet for some reason he hesitated to take it down to the publisher for the final print and distribution. He wasn't worried about any of them reading it and figuring out what he had been doing. He knew well enough that none of the men in the print shop would be able to read Old Latin. But for some reason Joseph felt apprehensive.

There was a knock at Joseph's door, startling him greatly. He slid the paper into his desk drawer and walked to his office door. Joseph was surprised to see Simon Koch as he opened the door. Simon greeted Joseph with an eerie smile. "Hello, Father!" said Simon. "May I come in?" Joseph swallowed hard and stepped aside to allow Simon access to his office.

Simon strolled through the office and plopped down into one of Joseph's comfortable leather chairs. "What can I do for you?" Joseph asked nervously as he walked back to his desk. Simon stared into Joseph's dark eyes until Joseph finally had to look away. Simon smiled dimly. He loved his new power—his ability to intimidate people.

"Mr. Ventini would like you to attend a celebration in his honor this evening. This is an invitation-only party and will be held at the Hilton International Hotel."

"Why does Mr. Ventini want me to attend?" Joseph asked passively.

"Because he likes you!" smiled Simon in a very fake manner. "You've been so helpful to our cause."

Joseph swallowed hard again. *Have I been helpful to their cause?* he wondered. *Have I been working for the Antichrist?*

"Can I bring a guest?" Joseph asked.

"Father, you don't mean a woman, now do you?" Simon asked with lust in his eyes.

"Well, yes. She is a woman and a friend of mine."

"Bring her along. This will be fun."

After Simon left Joseph collapsed in his chair. He pulled his newspaper back out of his drawer and reviewed it one last time. *Tomorrow it begins,* he told himself.

******

Joseph waited patiently at home for Yvette to show up. He didn't want to go to Carlo's party, but he also didn't want to be late and draw unnecessary attention to himself either. "How have I helped Carlo Ventini?" Joseph asked aloud to himself.

Suddenly it hit him like a lightning bolt. At the same time there was a soft knock at his front door.

Joseph let Yvette into his house without really even looking at her. He was so engrossed in the thought that plagued his mind. Yvette was disappointed. She had gone to great lengths to dress up for the occasion. Yes, she was going to a celebration for the son of Satan, but for some silly reason she still wanted to look her best. "What's the matter, Joseph?" Yvette asked.

"We need to run by my office before we go to the hotel." Joseph grabbed Yvette's hand, and they quickly left his apartment.

Yvette held onto the car's door handle for dear life as Joseph raced through the streets toward the Vatican. Joseph never spoke a word other than to say, "How stupid of me! How stupid."

Joseph parked the car and climbed out. "Come on," he said. "I need your help."

Joseph nearly ran up the steps into his office building. He unlocked his door and headed straight to the far closet. Pulling the door back, he revealed a four-foot pile of bound printer paper.

"What is all this?" Yvette asked.

Joseph looked at her intently. "These are the remnant, or at least many of them must be."

"What do you mean?" Yvette inquired.

Joseph put his hands on Yvette's shoulder. "Don't you see? These people didn't go to Heaven during the Rapture. They still have to choose and follow God, and many of them will, but they are a threat to Carlo and Simon. They will take these names and hunt these people down. We have to destroy these lists."

It took two trips for Joseph and Yvette to get all the names out of Joseph's office and into his Fiat. "What will we do with all of this? Won't they come asking for it soon?"

Joseph looked at Yvette in a very serious manner. "It is time to plan our escape."

******

Simon was already quite drunk when the majority of the guests arrived at the hotel banquet room. It felt so good to be alive. He owned the world and soon Satan would give him even more power—miraculous power—as promised. Throughout the room were photographers and reporters invited to the celebration by Simon to capture the moment. In addition there was a moderate contingent of security agents strewn throughout the room and at every entrance.

Joseph and Yvette entered through the side door and were waved past by a security guard. Quickly they found a table at the back of the room and just as quickly Simon found them. He stumbled up, intoxicated. "Father Bastoni, what have we got here?" he said as he pointed to Yvette.

"Mr. Koch, this is Yvette Lewis, my friend."

Simon grabbed Yvette's hand and attempted to kiss it. Yvette was instantly repulsed and pulled away. Just the touch of Simon's hand made her feel ill. Simon grinned, "Father, you have nice taste in women."

Joseph stared blankly at Simon.

"Nice party, isn't it?" said Simon. "By the way, Father, I'd like to send someone by tomorrow to pick up your list of good Catholic patrons."

Joseph nodded compliantly as the hair on his neck stood up.

"Have a good night, Father," said Simon with a wink for Yvette as he stumbled by Joseph and off to the bar again.

"Isn't he horrible?" said a disgusted Joseph.

"What are we going to do?"

"I'm not sure yet," said Joseph. Suddenly a tap on the shoulder surprised Joseph. He turned around quickly to see Scott Turner standing there.

"Father Bastoni," said Scott. "It's been a long time."

Joseph introduced Yvette. "This is the man I told you about. Remember the story about Zach Miles?"

Yvette nodded and smiled at Scott.

"What are you doing here?" Joseph asked.

Scott stared him down carefully before answering the question. "I am here with Ruth Jefferson to report on the European President's successes." Scott pointed across the room to where Ruth stood.

"Why are you here?" Scott asked. Joseph could tell that Scott was fishing for something.

"We were invited," said Joseph with little enthusiasm. He was hoping that Scott would pick up on his mannerism and pursue it. He wasn't sure if Scott was a follower of Carlo. He had to be careful, very careful.

About that time there was an announcement that the Pope was in the room. Soon after came another announcement that the European President himself was also in the room. The crowd stood as Carlo Ventini and Pope Peter John walked down the main corridor. Yvette's eyes met those of the Pope, and he graciously smiled back at her. Joseph observed this gesture with a mind full of confusion. He knew that the new Pope was working for the Antichrist, but he also knew that he was Yvette's uncle and that she loved him.

Scott watched Carlo closely as he walked by. He wasn't sure if he was the Antichrist, but Ruth had him convinced that it was possible. Joseph noticed Scott's fascination with Carlo. *He knows,* Joseph thought to himself.

All of the cameras in the room turned and focused on Carlo and Pope Peter John as they walked amiably down the marble pathway to the stage. The Pope smiled cheerfully and waved his hand in a saintly way. Carlo was a bit more apprehensive, looking from side to side. He knew that someone would eventually try and kill him, but he didn't know when or where. This knowledge was really starting to affect him personally, as he now spent most of his time paranoid and frightened.

Unexpectedly, as Carlo approached the place where a swaying Simon stood ready to greet him, there was a shout in the crowd. "You are the Devil!" screamed the voice. Carlo and Simon both looked up to see a man perched in the center of a very large air duct. The duct protruded from the wall and the screen had been removed.

Suddenly there was a flash of light followed by a loud boom. Instantly Carlo was lifted off his feet and violently crashed to the ground.

The security guards all simultaneously fired their weapons at the assailant. The man dropped his rifle and tumbled out of the duct, falling some 30 feet onto the nicely decorated platform.

Ruth was no more than five feet away from where Carlo lay motionless. The left side of his head was a mass of red and white-flecked tissue, and there was a large pool of blood forming around his body.

People from the audience began to scream and to cry out in surprise and sorrow. Simon ran from the podium and knelt over Carlo's lifeless body. Tears filled his eyes, and he was enraged. "Get a doctor now!" Simon screamed.

Ruth motioned her cameraman to zoom in on Carlo. "Do not take your camera off him no matter what," said Ruth sternly. The cameraman was nauseated and had to close his eyes as he filmed the ghastly scene. This was a live broadcast and around the world people watched in horror as the scene unfolded. In an instant the world was in mourning for the man they had grown to love—the man they had admired as a savior to the world.

Joseph stood next to Scott and Yvette watching as much of the scene unveil as possible. It was hard to really see anything with all the security and reporters around Carlo.

"Watch what happens next!" Scott whispered.

Joseph turned and looked deeply into his eyes. "You know?" he asked. Scott nodded. "You too?"

Joseph nodded.

Simon was in total rage. He stood and raised his hands towards Heaven and screamed out a curse towards God. At that moment Satan filled Simon's body with immense and evil power. He could feel his hands shake and clench as this power rushed into his body. Simon turned and looked at Carlo's dead assailant. He stretched out his hand towards the man and instantly the man's body ignited in flames. People began to scream and move away from the burning corpse.

Again Simon lifted his eyes towards Heaven. With his hands raised, he ignited the beautifully painted ceiling, melting away the picture of angels with outstretched hands. The room began to fill with smoke, and the guests began to leave in a panic. In homes around the world people sat by in total awe and fascination as this scene unfolded. Ruth's cameraman began to back away from Carlo. Ruth put her hand on the man's shoulder and said, "Don't move an inch! Keep the camera on Carlo."

Simon stood over Carlo with tears in his eyes. "Lord, my lord, rise again and show the world your glory!" Simon bent over Carlo and placed both hands firmly on his wound. His fingers sank into Carlo's mutilated flesh as he did. It was a grotesque sight that made many of the people sick, including Ruth's cameraman. He began vomiting and, as he did so, he lowered his camera.

Ruth quickly took the camera from him and turned it towards Carlo again. Soon Carlo's body began to quiver and then to shake and his once fatal wound began to heal itself right before her eyes.

Then slowly Carlo rose to his feet and stood before the people with little support from Simon. The crowd—what was left of them—stood fascinated, looking on in disbelief at the sight they had just witnessed.

By this time the podium was completely engulfed in flames and the room was full of smoke. The images on the televisions around the world were becoming blurry, but even so it was an amazing sight. Undeniably Carlo Ventini had risen off the floor where he had fallen after having been mortally wounded by a large caliber bullet to his brain.

Simon wanted Carlo to say something—something remarkable—to the audience and camera—maybe declare himself as god, but Carlo was disoriented and wanted to leave. "Take me out of here," was all he said.

Simon, Carlo, and the Pope exited the burning room amid a mass of security personnel and a crowd of stunned people. Soon after every person in the room cleared out except for the man who had shot and killed Carlo. Under a deception from Satan himself, the poor man had been convinced that he was saving the world by killing the Antichrist. Satan had whispered into the man's thoughts the truth of who Carlo was but also the lie that this man could somehow put an end to his plans. If the man could only have imagined the eternity in Hell that now awaited him.

Scott met with Ruth in the lobby as the firefighters ran by. "Ruth, this is Joseph Bastoni, and this is—" Scott had forgotten Yvette's name.

"My name is Yvette Lewis," she said with a warm smile for Ruth.

Joseph looked around the hotel lobby at the chaos ensuing, then back to Scott. "Do you two want to come back to my apartment for a while?"

Scott and Ruth both nodded affirmatively.

******

Back at Joseph's house Peter was completely unaware of what had just transpired. He had put in a long day at the clinic, and all he wanted to do was to lie on the couch and relax. He was pleased with the size and depth of his group of medical personnel. *We will be ready,* he thought as he began to drift away into sleep.

The door handle jiggled and squeaked as Joseph, Yvette, Ruth, and Scott stepped into the small apartment. Peter was startled from his light slumber. "Wake up, Peter. We've got some things we need to discuss." Peter sat up attentively as Joseph made the introductions.

After informing Peter of the night's incredible events, the topic turned to what the next thing for them to do was. "How do we tell the world?" Yvette asked. "What's going to happen next?" Joseph held Yvette's shaky hand in an attempt to sooth her nerves.

Joseph looked at Scott and Ruth. "I don't believe it is a coincidence that you two are here. I think God planned it that way, but for what purpose?" he said.

Ruth spoke up first. "God has given Scott and me an insight into all of this. He has put us in a position to report this to the world, although most will reject it."

Ruth's statement sparked a thought in Joseph's mind. He rose from the couch and went directly to his briefcase. When he turned to face the small group, he held a single copy of *Deacon's Horn* in his hands. "I've been holding onto this paper all day. In my heart I knew I needed to send it out, but something made me resist that impulse."

"What is it?" Scott inquired.

Joseph explained the messages that he had already sent out and the code that was embedded in each. "This is the final paper. The code is spelled out in this. When I send it out, the entire Catholic community will know that Carlo is the Antichrist. They will know what is to come, and they will know that I foretold the truth about Carlo being killed and raised again weeks before it actually happened."

Scott took the paper from Joseph's hand. He stared at it carefully and then grinned. "Not just the Catholic community, but the whole world!" he said. "You do have copies of the other coded papers that you sent out, right?"

Joseph nodded.

Ruth spoke up. "This is why God brought us here. We will take this paper back with us and report it to the world. *Deacon's Horn* will find its way into every hand around the world. We'll have it written in every language, describing how and when it came about, and then we'll send it out to news broadcasters and news distributors everywhere on the globe. *Deacon's Horn* will be a loud trumpet warning for sure."

"But they will trace it back to you," said Yvette as she looked at Joseph in a very frightened way. The look on his face told her that he had already thought about that.

"You will have to hide, Joseph," said Ruth.

"But where?" said Peter.

Scott stood and began to pace. For the first time since Zach Miles had died, Scott felt alive and energetic. "You will come with us. We can sneak you out of the country on our private jet, and we can hide you in Chicago." Ruth obviously liked the idea.

"I can't go without Yvette," said Joseph.

"She can go, too, but it will be very dangerous for you both." Ruth looked at Joseph and Yvette, concerned for their safety.

"Ruth, we are living in the last days. What do we have to fear? We need to warn the world, and we need your help to do it," said Joseph.

Ruth spoke softly. "Yes, you are right. It won't matter soon anyway."

"Pack your stuff!" said Scott enthusiastically. This caused everyone in the room to laugh.

"I need to get this paper to print tomorrow." Joseph looked at his watch. It was 4:00 a.m. "No! Make that today. What time is your plane supposed to leave?" Joseph asked.

"By 9:00 a.m.," said Scott.

"Yvette, let's get you home and packed. I can be ready to go in just a few minutes, but the print shop does not open until 8:00 a.m.," said Joseph.

Peter sat back and watched Joseph as he planned their escape. He was never more proud of his little brother than at this moment.

"Peter, do you need to go to the clinic at all this morning?" Joseph asked.

The small group of people stared at Peter, waiting for his answer.

There was a long pause before Peter finally spoke. "I can't go with you, Joseph."

Joseph stared at his big brother. He understood what Peter was thinking. He knew that his brother had a job of his own to do. Their time together was over. It had been such a joy for Joseph to have his brother by his side over the last two years. He had missed Peter's company and friendship through the many years of separation.

Joseph nodded to Peter in a way that touched Yvette's heart.

"You can't stay here!" said Yvette. "They'll come after you too!"

"It's okay, Yvette," said Peter. "I will stay with one of the other doctors on our team. I will quit working at the clinic and wait for God to tell me what to do."

******

It was just past 8:00 a.m. and Joseph was at the print shop with Peter and Scott by his side. Ruth and Yvette were at Yvette's house packing for their getaway. Joseph's hand trembled as he handed the master copy to the print tender.

"Send the copies to the usual locations?" the man asked.

"Just like usual," said Joseph softly as he turned to leave the tiny print shop.

Back in the car Joseph spoke, "I want to run by my office and grab a couple of things real quick."

Scott looked at his watch. "Make it really quick!"

******

Peter and Scott sat in Joseph's car waiting and watching as he climbed the last stair leading into his building. Joseph stood in his office doorway reflecting on his past life.

So much time lost, he thought. *So much time spent looking for truth in all the wrong places.*

Joseph entered the small office and grabbed a picture of his mother and father from his wall. Suddenly he felt a presence in the room. He turned to see two creepy-looking men standing in his doorway. "Father Bastoni?" one of the men asked.

"Yes," said Joseph.

"We have come to pick up the list of names."

"What names?" Joseph asked as if he didn't know.

The two men moved closer to Joseph. Evil looks covered their faces. "The Catholic memberships," said the other man with an extremely deep voice.

"Oh, those names!" said Joseph. "Sure, why don't you two take a seat and I'll get them for you." Both men sat in a very rigid fashion staring at Joseph as he walked out of the office.

Swiftly Joseph sailed down the stair and out into the courtyard at a dead run with a picture of his mother and father in his hand as he headed for his car. The two men heard Joseph running down the stairs. They looked at each other with surprise and anger. Quickly they got up to look out of the window just in time to watch Joseph as he ran across the courtyard. They had been tricked, and they both knew it.

Peter caught sight of Joseph as he ran towards the car. "Something is wrong," he said in a whisper.

Joseph slid behind the driver's seat and cranked on the ignition key. The Fiat rumbled to a start. "We have to go!" said Joseph all out of breath.

As the car backed out of the parking lot, Scott spotted the two men running towards Joseph's car. "Uh oh! We've got company!"

Joseph sped away. "We need to get to my apartment and pick up Yvette right away!"

"But first," said Peter, "you'd better drop me off down at the clinic."

Joseph looked at his brother. His heart sank at the thought that their time together was over. They both knew it. Joseph nodded to Peter and said, "I'll be there in two minutes."

Peter reached over and patted Joseph's hand. "Thank you for everything, Joseph." Tears ran down Joseph's face. The scene was so touching that even Scott began to cry.

The car pulled over to the curb. "Take care of yourself, Peter." Both men knew what was in store for each of them, but it helped to pretend. Peter opened his door. Joseph reached over and gave him a strong hug. "I love you, brother."

"I love you too," said Peter with a handsome smile.

Peter stood and waved as Joseph drove away. As he looked in his rearview mirror, Joseph was sure that he was seeing his brother for the last time—at least until they both got to Heaven. "God give us strength," he whispered as he wiped the tears from his cheeks.

******

Yvette and Ruth were waiting when Joseph and Scott pulled up. Quickly they loaded Yvette's luggage and Joseph's small bag and drove off. About that time the two strange men pulled onto the block where Joseph's apartment was. Joseph drove through the melted snow that filled the street, right past the two men heading in the other direction. The men saw him at once, but the street was so narrow they could not turn around. Joseph took numerous side streets to confuse the men. Eventually all four of them made it to the airport without getting caught by their pursuers.

Getting Joseph and Yvette onto the plane was a bit tricky, but it seemed that this was an area in which Scott excelled. He created enough diversion and confusion with the airport security that they no longer knew who was coming or going onto the private plane. Once aboard Scott knew there would be one last security review. He understood they would be looking at passports. Joseph had a U.S. passport, so his would not be a problem, but Yvette was a native of Italy. Hers would be a problem.

As soon as they were on the plane, Scott took Yvette by the arm and led her into the restroom. "There is an equipment panel back here that you can hide behind."

"But they know I came on board," she said.

"Yes, but I'm hoping that they were confused by all of the reporters and cameramen we had going back and forth."

"And if they're not?" Yvette asked. Scott just smiled in a dumb sort of way. What he really hoped was that the security guard didn't bring his dog on board, but he didn't want to share that concern with Yvette.

The guard's visit was brief, and if he had seen Yvette earlier, he certainly had forgotten. He looked at Joseph's passport and handed it back. "Have a nice trip, Father," said the guard.

Once in the air Yvette sat next to Joseph with her hand clasped in his. "What happens now?" she asked.

"Well," Joseph smiled. "In a few hours *Deacon's Horn* will begin to reach millions of people. We will be hated and sought after, but many will know the truth and be saved because of it." The two then closed their eyes in silent prayer.

In the airport parking lot Joseph's Fiat was full of smoke as the Catholic memberships burned in the back seat, having been set ablaze by Joseph and Scott.

Chapter 17: Churches and Temple Rise

Day 1000, April: Izuho sat on the cold concrete floor shivering from a high fever. He had been imprisoned in his cell for months now. Izuho drifted mercifully into a deep sleep. He began to dream about a better time in life, a time when he was working hard for God.

Thinking back, he had become a very busy man over the last couple of years. He had many new Christian contacts, and he was attending home fellowship meetings in five different homes on a regular basis. This wasn't the busiest part of his life by any means, however.

Izuho had become connected with a small group of smugglers. Their primary cargo was Bibles. Izuho had been sailing cases of books across the Yellow Sea to China's borders for quite some time now. This was particularly risky since China had just recently declared war on all organized religions throughout the country. Izuho knew the consequences of getting caught, but his need to share the gospel was compelling, and his heroic efforts had piped in thousands of Bibles, helping to forge new churches throughout most of Mainland China.

He made one or two trips per week, always at night. His instructions came from within his home fellowship group. There was rarely a drop in the same place.

Izuho was seeing the harvest of his labor. He yearned to attend one of these churches, but he knew that he could not afford to take the risk. He had a purpose—a very important purpose—and until it was fulfilled, he somehow had to avoid getting caught.

The Chinese government was aware that Bibles were coming into the country, and they despised it. Try as they might, however, they could not find the source. They had discovered and destroyed some of the underground churches, killing all in attendance, yet they still had no idea where all of this organization and literature was coming from.

Finally the Chinese government got a break when they got wind of a new church forming in a small coastal province. One of the government agents responsible for finding and destroying these churches was a middle-aged man named Chang Liao. It was he who first noticed that every church discovered had its origins in a coastal province. A plan began to emerge. Chang Liao decided he would move himself into one of the smaller communities on the coast. He would take a job as a fisherman and watch and wait. If his hunch proved true, he would soon discover any Christian activity, and if he was patient enough, he might even discover the source of the Bibles.

Over the next few months Izuho continued to make his usual voyage across the sea. Good weather or bad didn't matter to Izuho. He knew that God would take care of him until His mission was completed.

During this time Chang Liao continued to network his way into the small coastal community. He worked hard as a fisherman, and in his spare time he played in the streets with the children. He even gave them a portion of his catch of fish. Soon the town's people accepted Chang as a kind and loving man.

One day as Chang sat in the middle of a small field playing a make-believe game with a few of the children, he heard an unusual sound. In fact, it was a song. One of the children around 14 years of age was humming the Christian song, *Amazing Grace*. Chang had been to the United States before, and he knew America's passion for worship and especially this song.

Over the next week or so Chang befriended this child and his family. Finally one evening when he had been invited over for dinner Chang confessed that he had a belief in a foreign god. He said he was afraid of the Chinese government because he knew that they hated religion. "But," he said, "I can't help but follow after Jesus."

This word got the attention of everyone in the room. There was complete silence for a moment or two. Looks of confusion and apprehension filled the eyes of the parents and the children. The father spoke up first saying, "'In the beginning was the Word, and the Word was with God, and the Word was God.'"

Chang smiled brightly. "Amen!" He said.

From that day on Chang Liao attended a very small church hidden in the woods behind the village. He sang songs and listened to the preaching. He was especially encouraged by the fact that there was only one Bible among all of the people and the senior member of the church held it carefully. He was an extremely old man with a sparkle in his eye and gentleness in his voice.

If there is only one Bible now, then perhaps more will be coming, Chang thought. He had to find a way to get connected to the actual drop-off of Bibles. He needed to be there when they came in. Chang needed to network a little harder.

Weeks went by for Chang Liao, but there was still no sign that he was connected well enough with the small group to be trusted with such a responsibility as smuggling Bibles. Chang finally decided to create an image for himself that was sure to convince the people that he was trustworthy.

Chang wrote out a plan and sent it off to one of his partners in the agency. He mailed the letter from the next town to ensure nobody would get suspicious. One week later two men came into the small town and started asking questions about Chang. They described him carefully and insisted that he was a known enemy of the Chinese government.

While all of this was happening, Chang was out to sea fishing as usual. In the late evening as his boat was returning another boat approached. The captain pulled up alongside, allowing one of his passengers to board Chang's vessel. Chang knew the man. He was the one who had invited him into the church in the first place.

"You must come with us," said the man in a very serious way.

"Why?" Chang asked.

"There are two men in town looking for you. They say you are an enemy of the government. They say you are a Christian. You must come with us. They are waiting for you to return."

Chang protested, saying that he did not want to endanger any of his new friends and that he was prepared to die for Jesus. Eventually he surrendered to the man's request. His plan was working perfectly.

Chang traveled by sea for a couple of hours before the boat finally began to turn towards the shore. It was nearly dark when they made port. A young woman about 20 years old greeted Chang Liao at the dock. She was a gentle and attractive girl. *What a pity that she is a Christian,* thought Chang.

The young girl, who introduced herself as Lyn Lee, drove Chang through the mountains for nearly an hour before she finally pulled off to the side of the road and parked deep in the woods. "From here we walk," said the young lady.

Chang followed as best he could. The girl was fast and agile, and it was dark and hard to see. She obviously had been there before. Chang finally reached a small compound hidden in the trees. The young girl introduced Chang to a small welcoming committee who greeted him politely and with something that Chang had not expected. They greeted him with love. Their kindness and gentleness was more than Chang had ever seen. This caused him to feel a little shame, but only for a moment. *I can't let them get to me,* he told himself.

After two weeks in the camp Chang had become a contributing member. He hunted and gathered food supplies. He sang and prayed with the rest of the Christians. He was blended in perfectly. One night late a senior member of the camp approached Chang and told him about a shipment of Bibles coming in for distribution. Chang could hardly believe his ears. After so many months he was finally getting the information he wanted—the information his government so badly wanted.

"We need your help," said the old man. "Tuesday around midnight in the fishing port of Fuzhou."

"How will I recognize the boat?" Chang asked.

"You will not, but Lyn Lee will. You will go with her, and she will lead you to the man who has the Bibles. These books must come back here to be distributed to all of our churches." Chang could not believe his luck. He was sure to become famous after this. He had not only discovered the source of the Bibles, but also the governing church body and most likely many of its smaller churches. "This is a dangerous journey. If you do not wish to go, we will understand," said the man.

Chang tried not to sound too excited. "No, I think it is important for me to help out however I can."

"Good then!" said the man. "You will leave Fijjian tomorrow night."

Chang sat in his cabin alone. "How will I get this information to the agency?" he whispered quietly. There were no phones and there was no way to send a message from the camp. Somehow Chang had to sneak out of the camp and make a phone call.

He knew that the nearest town was nearly an hour's drive. He could never walk there and back before dawn. There was only one car in the camp, and it was dedicated to errands. He just could not find a solution. There was a knock on his cabin door. "Come in," said Chang in a depressed tone.

Lyn Lee stood in the doorway. The moonlight behind her made her look like an angel, but of course, Chang didn't believe in angels. Somehow he had to get her to take him to town, but how? Everything they needed was available in the camp. "Try asking her," said a small voice in Chang's head.

What am I thinking? he wondered. Then suddenly it occurred to him. "I need to make a phone call," he said softly. Lyn was a little suspicious. She knew that Chang had been informed about the shipment of books coming in. "Today is my mother's birthday, and I am afraid that tomorrow I may die and..." Chang's voice trailed off pathetically.

Lyn thought about it for a second and then finally said, "We have a phone." Chang was surprised to hear this. "It is for emergencies only, but maybe I could sneak it to you for a quick call."

Chang beamed. "You are so kind," he said convincingly.

Five minutes later Chang was dialing the number to another one of his agents. Lyn stood by momentarily until Chang began to speak as if he was talking to his mother. Lyn began to feel like an eavesdropper, so she stepped outside of the cabin. "Make it quick," she grinned. Chang winked at her. One minute later he had fully downloaded all his new information. The plan was set, and the trap would soon be laid. He hung up the phone and, with a smile, deleted the number he had just called.

******

It was a choppy sea, not unlike many of the other nights when Izuho approached the coast of China, but it did seem much darker—or maybe it was just Izuho's mood. Lately he had begun to feel his time was running out. Each trip brought him one day closer to getting caught.

So far this delivery seemed as routine as the others had been. Oh, sure, they all felt dangerous, but Izuho always managed to return home safely. Fuzhou was a small port and not one that Izuho enjoyed coming into. There were just too many opportunities to run into something solid. It was also a difficult port to depart in a hurry if the need arose.

How many of these trips have I made? Izuho wondered as he clung to the ship's wheel. Another large wave hit the side of his boat, causing it to list momentarily. "Well, at least it is not raining anymore," said Izuho aloud. When he got the word that he was going to make another delivery to Fuzhou, he was excited, because it meant he would get to see Lyn Lee once again. Their visits were always brief—no more than 30 minutes or so—and he probably only frequented Fuzhou every 60 days at best. Just the same, it was enough time for these two to fall in love.

Normally Izuho would be excited to make this trip. He didn't really understand his own anxiety, but the feeling tended to overshadow his anticipation of seeing Lyn Lee. All week long Izuho had a sense that something was going to happen soon. The bow of his craft dipped heavily as another large set of swells dropped Izuho's boat a good 15 feet. Then quickly the boat rose above the waves once again. Even Izuho was starting to feel a little seasick.

Suddenly the cabin of the small cruiser was enveloped in a soft, white glow. Instantly he felt the presence of God. "You have done well!" said the powerful but gentle voice of the Lord. "My child, you have one more trial awaiting you. Be strong and know that I am always with you." The light faded as Izuho clung to the wheel. A sense of peace replaced his fear. *What trial?* Izuho wondered. *Whatever it is, may God's will work through me. Nothing can be too bad if God is with me, right?* Izuho was not entirely confident in the last part of his thought.

******

Lyn Lee and Chang Liao traveled slowly down the mountain on their way to Fuzhou. Neither of them spoke a word. They just drove along silently listening to a worship tape that Lyn had inserted in the car's player. As Lyn began to hum the chorus, Chang looked into the face of the young woman. She smiled back brightly. Again Chang felt the pains of his betrayal. His mind began the process of rationalizing his own actions once more. *They are the real traitors, not me. They are betraying their own government,* Chang thought to himself.

"I love the next song," said Lyn softly. "Do you know it?" she asked Chang as the song began to play.

The only worship music Chang had ever really listened to was the music he heard over the last few months as a pretend-Christian. "No, I don't know it," said Chang. "So tell me, what is going to happen tonight?"

Lyn turned the stereo down a bit and looked over to Chang. "Tonight we will meet a man named Izuho. He is originally from Okinawa, but now he lives in Japan. He will be bringing the Bibles into the port of Fuzhou in a small cabin cruiser. We'll load the Bibles into this car and head back to camp." Lyn smiled at Chang and said, "Simple as that!" Chang could see by Lyn's eyes that she was masking her own fear. He knew she understood the danger she was putting herself in.

"Just like that!" laughed Chang.

Lyn nodded affirming.

"Who is this Izuho?" Chang inquired.

Lyn's eyes sparkled and her face lit up at the thought of Izuho. This did not go unnoticed by Chang. Lyn proceeded to tell Chang Izuho's story as he had told it to her. She told him about the tidal wave in Okinawa and how Izuho was spared at the last minute. She told Chang how God had actually spoken to Izuho and directed his path.

"Has God ever spoken to you?" Chang interrupted.

Lyn collected herself momentarily, taking her mind off Izuho. "The Lord talks to my heart," she said.

"But have you ever really heard his voice?" Chang asked. He was searching for something and Lyn understood this, but she did not know what.

Lyn said a silent prayer for guidance for just the right words to help Chang.

"Chang," said Lyn as she reached for his hand and held it lightly, "God is not a man we can talk to face-to-face. We do not have to hear Him audibly for Him to talk to us. He talks to our hearts, our minds, and our spirits."

"How do you know when He is talking to you?" Chang asked with a real curiosity.

Lyn smiled at the thought. "I feel His love, His peace, His presence all around me, and I am happy—even if life is hard or I am suffering and hurt. God still gives me peace and joy. This is how I know He is here with me."

Chang sat quietly and pondered all that Lyn had said as she drove carefully through the night, singing joyfully as she went. *What is it exactly that is so bad about these Christians?* Chang wondered. *Why is my government so afraid of such kind and gentle people? What is their real threat?*

******

Izuho navigated the pitch-black harbor slowly. The only visible light came from a small lantern at the end of a pier. Lyn Lee held the lantern up at the sound of the boat. Izuho nervously gripped the wheel as he inched his boat into the dark, narrow port.

Chang Liao's stomach began to tense as the boat approached. He was going to be a hero, but for some reason he felt remorse and guilt. *These people were nice to me, and I really don't see the harm in their beliefs,* he thought.

The reality of what would happen to Lyn and Izuho if they were caught started to sink into Chang's heart. "They will be killed," he said in a whisper. Chang tried to push these thoughts out of his head. The fact was he had a job to do. His government was counting on him. *These people are counting on you also,* his mind whispered. He looked at the young girl as she strained to hold the lantern high. He felt pity for her. She was so kind to him.

Chang found himself suddenly speaking, "I can't do this. Send him away. Hurry!"

"What?" Lyn asked.

"It's a trap! Send him away and run! They'll be here in a few minutes."

Lyn turned and looked at Chang. "You?" she asked.

"Yes!" said Chang bitterly, shamefully. "I am an agent of the Chinese government."

Lyn signaled Izuho to abort with three long up-and-down motions of the lantern. "Oh no!" said Izuho with a moan. He reversed his engines and tried to cut the wheel sharply, but there just wasn't enough room. His boat crashed into a piling, ripping his bow wide open. The boat began to sink instantly. "Dear Lord, what do I do now?" Izuho asked. He had no choice but to jump into the water.

Lyn ran toward the sinking boat. "I have to help him!" she shouted.

"You have to leave now!" said Chang. "They will catch you and kill you!"

"Then I will die with him. And I will go to Heaven with him."

These words changed Chang's life forever. He had never seen such faith or love in his life. Unexpectedly, Jesus was now real to him, and the awareness that he had betrayed Him was real also. Lyn dove into the water and swam over to Izuho. Together they approached Chang. About that time lights came on from every direction and hundreds of armed soldiers approached the pier. Lyn and Izuho were dragged from the water and beaten before Chang's eyes.

"Stop!" said Chang. "Leave them alone."

"Are you getting soft?" one of the men asked harshly. "Did they get to you?"

"You don't need to beat them," said Chang.

Lyn and Izuho were arrested and taken to the government headquarters in Changzhou for interrogation, accompanied by Chang. He, too, was questioned as to the location of the main camp and all known churches. Chang Liao refused to open his mouth. He was severely beaten for his disobedience, but still he never said a word. Finally he was thrown into the same cell as Izuho and Lyn. Lyn stared at Chang through her swollen eyes, and then suddenly she smiled at him. This broke Chang's heart, and he began to weep bitterly. Izuho walked over to Chang and put his hand on Chang's shoulder. "Soon," he said, "we will be in a better place."

******

It was another hot and windy day in Newcastle. Stan continued to struggle with each sheet of plywood. The wind drove him out of position time and time again. This was the third church he had helped to build this month. It was an incredible experience to see these small buildings rise up over the course of just a few days. It was even more rewarding to see them filled with people hungry to praise God.

Stan, Ruby, and their six children had moved from Quilpie to Sydney over two years ago. At first they had no idea what to do. They had little money and no place to live. Stan had built a makeshift shelter to house his family, and for more than a month they lived in this lean-to, washing in the stream below them and eating off the land. Stan fished and also set snares to catch rabbits and did whatever else he could to feed his family. Stan's older two boys found work in town doing odd jobs and yard work. This helped to provide a small income. What Stan needed most was patience, but it was not part of his nature. The waiting became very painful. Both Stan and Ruby found themselves in despair over the way they had to live and especially their children's misery.

One day Christopher, Stan's oldest living son, came back to the lean-to after a long day of mowing lawns and picking up trash. As he neared his home, he encountered an old woman as she walked along the dirt road. The woman smiled at Christopher and asked him where he was going. "Home," said Christopher without any enthusiasm.

"Why the long face?" the old lady asked.

Christopher looked into her eyes. They held his gaze for many seconds. It was as if she were not really old. When he looked directly into her eyes, she seemed to change into a young and beautiful woman. "I don't know," he said. "Just sad, I guess."

"I could use some food. How about you?" the old woman asked.

Christopher wasn't sure if she was asking him to come with her to her home for a meal or if she was asking him to feed her. He didn't know what to say.

"Do you have food at your house?" she asked.

"Yes, but not much," said Christopher.

The woman stared deeply into the young man's face and smiled cheerfully at him. Finally Christopher spoke, "Would you like to come with me and get something to eat?"

The old woman's smile grew even brighter, revealing pearl white teeth and a very young-looking profile. "That would be lovely," she replied.

Ruby was the first to spot Christopher walking along with the old lady. "Chris is back," she said, "and he's brought a friend." Stan looked up from where he stood just in time to see Christopher and the old woman stop in front of the entrance to the lean-to. Stan stood beside Ruby and all six of their children as the old lady introduced herself as just an old lady. Christopher whispered into his mother's ear. "She is hungry, I think."

Ruby nodded and then smiled towards the woman. "Would you like to come in and have something to eat?"

The woman followed the Evans family into the small shelter. "I hope you don't mind sitting on the floor," said Stan. The old lady simply grinned and dropped down on the dirt floor with surprising agility. Ruby brought forth a little rodent stew and some day-old bread and handed it to the lady.

"Thank you, Dear!" said the woman. "What a beautiful family!" she said softly. "And so kind of you to feed a homeless person even though you have little more than I."

Stan's youngest daughter, Carrie, stared intently at the old woman.

"Come here, Dear," she said as she curled and uncurled one of her old fingers towards little Carrie. "What is it you want to ask me?"

Carrie was a little shy but spoke up boldly just the same. "I don't think you are real," she said. "I mean, you are real, but something is not real."

"Touch me, Child," said the old woman. Carrie reached out carefully and touched the old woman's cheek. A smile lit the child's face. She now understood what the rest of her family never truly would. The old woman was not from this world.

The woman looked at Ruby and with a gentle, soft voice she said, "I am sorry for the loss of your other four boys." Ruby looked at Christopher for clarification. Had he met a complete stranger and yet shared this much personal information? The look on Christopher's face told Ruby he was just as surprised as she was.

"How did you know that?" Ruby asked.

"I have seen two of your boys, and they are wonderful, but," she paused briefly, "the other two—" she simply shook her head sadly.

At this Ruby began to cry. This brought about Stan's anger. "What gives you the right? How do you know this?" he said angrily.

Knowing that two of her children had died as infants, Ruby understood that these two children were fortunate enough to be under the age of accountability in the eyes of God and were with Him in Heaven, but the other two—*Dear Lord*, she thought. *What have we done?* The pain in Ruby's heart was tremendous.

The woman looked at Stan. "You have the responsibility as the head of your family to see to it that you do not lose any more of these precious children. Make sure that you purge your mind of all deception and doubt," said the old woman.

"Who are you?" Ruby asked as tears streamed down her face.

The old woman handed Carrie her small bowl of stew and stood quickly. "Go into town today as a family. You will meet a man who will direct you. God's purpose will be done!"

Stan stood next to his wife as the woman stepped forward and placed her hands on both of them. She looked at the children and then towards both parents. "Satan may be able to kill their bodies, but their souls will be safe with the Lord. Have courage and faith until the end." The woman turned and pulled back the blanket to the shelter's entrance. A few seconds later the Evans family stepped outside to watch her walk away, but she was nowhere in sight.

******

That had been more than two years ago. Stan had taken his family to town as instructed, and he did meet a man who provided a home for the Evans family and a job for Stan. From that day forward he had been building churches, town to town. Each month the family would pack up and move to the next location.

Today Stan fought the wind as he tried to close the walls of the small church. He had a sense of peace that he was performing God's will for his life. The recent event in Europe with Carlo Ventini appearing to rise up from the dead was just another indication that time was short. *We need to fill these churches and tell people what is to come before it is too late,* Stan thought, except Stan did not fully understand what was to come.

Ruby had been reading to him nightly from the King James Version of the Bible. He was taking it in and he was learning, but it was slow for Stan. There was just too much false doctrine already in his mind, making it hard for him to hear and understand the truth. "This is going to be a matter of faith," Stan had told his wife one evening after she finished reading Chapter 12 of the Book of Revelation. "I just don't understand what I am hearing," he said. Ruby consoled Stan as best she could, but it was never enough.

The concerned parents worked hard to reeducate their children to the reality of Jesus Christ and to the truths of the Bible. All of the children seemed to understand that the time was short and that they soon would have to suffer and endure persecution in the name of Jesus. Ruby new that in order for each of them to be able to stand up under such persecution, they would need to have God's promises planted deeply in their hearts. They would have to stand on faith alone. So as a family they read the Word, as a family they prayed continually, and as a family they prepared each other mentally for what was to come.

There was one more thing that the Evans family did on a constant basis, regardless of where Stan's work took them. They all preached continually the promises of God. From the youngest to the oldest, each child and adult gave his or her personal testimony to whoever would listen.

Witnessing and building churches seemed like a reasonable penitence to Stan. He was content to continue on this path until the Lord called his family home. He assumed this was the call that God had placed on him and his family.

What he didn't realize at the time was that there was an event ahead involving his family that would say and do more to further God's kingdom than anything Stan could have imagined.

******

Australia was not the only country building new churches. In Jerusalem new and improved synagogues were being added on a regular basis. It seemed the whole world was interested in the spiritual things. People were aching for some mystical power to guide and direct them. Also in Jerusalem there was a huge effort to rebuild the *Mosque of Omar,* commonly referred to as the *Dome of the Rock.* This temple had been completely destroyed during the massive earthquake at the time of the Rapture.

The effort to rebuild was a remarkable one since it included both Jews and Muslims. Due to the treaty that had been forged—thanks to the efforts of Carlo Ventini and Simon Koch years earlier when they first began to distribute food to all parts of the world—the PLO and Israelis would cooperate on a regular basis or risk losing their monthly food rations. To avoid fracturing this new, very strong treaty, both governments agreed to unify the new temple into a worship place for both religions. There would be separate rooms of equal design, and all would have access to the temple. It was a remarkable show of fair play between these two natural enemies.

It was approaching the three-year mark since the *Dome of the Rock* had fallen into a pile of rubble. It would be another six months before all of the new construction was complete, yet Muslims and Jews alike were already working to rebuild all of their instruments of worship. In particular the Jewish leaders had begun an effort to rebuild the *Ark of the Covenant* and all of their sacrificial tools. Their half of the new building would look very much like *Solomon's Temple,* minus the presence of God, of course.

Chapter 18: Declarations of Jubilee and Infamy

Day 1020, April: Scott and Ruth sat in his office examining the morning news before their broadcast. They did this daily as they looked for clues of what Carlo would do next. They knew that a time would soon come for them to run and hide, leaving the news business behind for Simon Koch's propaganda puppets to recite.

Ruth began to read from a fax from the United World Leader, Carlo Ventini, and his assistant, Simon Koch, that had been forwarded to all news broadcast radio and television stations. Ruth pored over the fax and read to Scott who was intently listening. "'Greetings to the World,'" she read. "'We wish to celebrate Mr. Carlo Ventini's coronation with an act of divine kindness.'"

Ruth stared at the fax as her mind drifted back to the day after Carlo's assassination. The world was bubbling over with excitement. By now virtually the entire civilized world had seen the numerous news replays of that fateful event. There were many questions as to whether or not this was a hoax or if it had somehow been staged. To date Carlo had not come forward to speak to anyone.

Simon drew the most attention, although it was Carlo the people had grown to love. It was Simon that everyone had seen raise Carlo from the dead and ignite the body of Carlo's assassin. The people wanted to know more about this man who could call down fire from the sky.

While the world was waiting to hear from Simon and Carlo, Simon was sitting outside Carlo's bedroom, standing guard over his leader until further notice. Carlo had been asleep for over 12 hours, and Simon was starting to worry. He had so desperately wanted to address the world and declare Carlo as god and himself as second only to Carlo, but for some reason Carlo was not in the mood to talk to or see anyone at the moment.

This new mood of Carlo's worried Simon greatly. An idea then came to Simon. He would go to Carlo's private chamber and talk with Satan himself to see what was next. He slipped away from Carlo's room and wandered down the long hallway until he finally got to the large, ominous-looking door. Simon had seen Carlo punch in the code before, and he remembered the sequence. After two tries the heavy latch slid forward making a screeching metallic sound that scared him. Simon inched his way into the room. *What a good day for a sacrifice,* he thought to himself. *What a pity there are none available.*

Simon stood in the center of the dark room when suddenly the heavy door slammed shut with a clang. Simon held his breath. He could feel the presence of evil in the room—oh, how he loved that feeling!

"What do you want?" boomed a voice that shook the ground where Simon stood. Simon fell to his knees. He wanted to speak, but he was so afraid. He also had a dilemma on his hands. He had never been in Satan's presence without Carlo. He had never addressed Satan personally, so he wasn't sure what to call him. *Should I call him Satan, Lucifer or the Devil, or can I call him Father like Carlo does?* he wondered.

"It is time to let the world know," said Satan. "It is time to declare Carlo as lord over the earth. You did well, Simon!"

Simon beamed with pride—a son's pride. "I tried to get Carlo to talk to the people, but he just sleeps," Simon whined.

"Do not presume that you know anything!" Satan boomed. "My Son will step forward in his own time. Your recognition will have to wait."

Simon suddenly felt like a scolded child. "I am sorry for being presumptuous," said Simon cautiously.

"Tomorrow you and Carlo will stand in the center of Vatican City and declare my Son the chosen one to rule the earth," said Satan. "Now leave me!"

Simon bowed his way out of the room. *Tomorrow I will be declared assistant to the ruler of the world,* he thought and smiled broadly.

******

It was a freezing cold, snowy morning, and yet the crowd was already gathering. Literally tens of thousands of people lined the streets awaiting the approach of Carlo and Simon. Simon had been given direction from Carlo to alert the media and to prepare for a public broadcast. Carlo's heart was pounding as he sat back in the limo. He was finally getting excited about what was to come. The trauma of being shot and killed was nearly behind him, and he was finally ready to assume his divine position over the world. Simon peered out of the tinted window into the rising sun. He was as excited as a child on the first day of school.

"Contain yourself," said Carlo with a smile.

Simon grinned back at Carlo. This was going to be his finest hour. He was finally going to prove to all those people who hated him, including his own family, that he was greater than they could ever imagine. The limousine pulled under the awning and was quickly surrounded by an armed security escort.

Pope Peter John stood by the entrance to the building waiting for Carlo to step out of the car. The crowd was really pressing in now, nearly overpowering the security forces that were trying to contain them.

Suddenly there was an enormous roar as Carlo stood and turned towards the crowd. Next Simon popped his head out, and again the crowd cheered loudly. The sound was deafening, and Simon loved it all.

"I have a room prepared for your conference," said Peter John.

Simon started towards the building when he heard Carlo say, "No! We will do it over there," as he pointed to a statue of the Virgin Mary in the center of a large courtyard.

Carlo headed towards the statue with a peculiar grin on his face. The thousands of people clapped loudly as he walked along with a parade of security guards on both sides. Carlo turned and held up his hands towards his armed escort. "Stay here," he said.

Simon ran to catch up with Carlo. "What are we doing?" Simon asked.

"We are addressing the people!" said Carlo in an annoyed fashion.

Carlo stood in front of the Virgin Mary and stared at the marble statue. His heart was full of hate for everything this woman represented. Slowly he turned to face the crowd. Cameramen moved in towards Carlo and Simon, and as they did they zoomed in on the small scar on Carlo's left temple. It was the size of a quarter and light pink in color. This view would be seen around the world, as literally billions of people would be watching. Simon could hardly control himself. He was anxious to hear Carlo say the words, *I am god,* but Simon was soon disappointed.

"People!" Carlo said as he hushed them with a wave of his hands. "I stand before you grateful for your show of love and appreciation. It is hard to explain, really, but the miracle that has brought me back to life has also changed me greatly. These changes are not fully understood by me yet, but I am sure they have a greater purpose for all humanity. I believe my rebirth is divinely inspired and intended for the good of the world. You might say, in fact, that I have died for the entire world and now I am made new and better, and, through me the world will be made better."

Carlo turned towards Simon. Not a sound could be heard from the audience. "This man has been given to me as my personal aide, to support me as I care for all of you. He has been given special powers over death and over the earth as many of you have already seen. Together Simon and I are at your disposal. You, the people, choose for yourselves what, if any, help and support you would like from us."

Simon turned towards Carlo and looked into his face. *What is this man saying? Where is the declaration? Why is he not declaring himself god and making me second only to himself?* fumed Simon. *Carlo had taken the moment and given it back to the people. Why should they have a choice in anything? We are the rulers of the world,* Simon thought.

Carlo could see that Simon was upset and surprised, but he couldn't care less about what Simon wanted. He knew what was best. Let the people feel they have a choice. And soon they would play right into his hands.

Three days later under the influence of Satan the world leaders organized a new government and established Carlo as its head. Still there was resistance from a few countries, but collectively they didn't have enough power to refuse the decisions of the other countries. They had to passively submit to this new government and its new rules. President of the New United World Organization was an impressive title, but not the one Simon had hoped for. He wanted Carlo to take the title of god.

******

Ruth put the first page of the fax down and picked up page number two. "'We wish to inform each country of Mr. Ventini's first decree as the divine and benevolent world leader. Over a period of the next seven months prisoners throughout the world will have their sentences remitted entirely, and officially by December 25 they all will have been released, leaving jails and prisons empty and thus fulfilling the promise of the *Day of Jubilee*. Furthermore, to all of the people of the world, any and all personal debt for loans, mortgages, and credit cards acquired before this decree will be wiped out completely.'"

As Ruth paused, Scott leaned forward saying "How can any economy survive this?"

Ruth looked down at the fax and continued to read. "'From this day forward December 25 will be known as the *Day of Jubilee*. Mr. Ventini believes in fresh starts and new beginnings for everyone. The United World Organization will work to restructure all lending institutions to ensure that they are adequately compensated during this year of Jubilee.'"

"He'll be a god to the world for sure after this," said Ruth as she picked up the last page of the fax.

"He already is!" said Scott sarcastically.

Ruth read the final page silently as Scott reviewed the previous pages. "This is amazing!" mumbled Scott as he read.

"Oh, my God!" said Ruth.

Scott looked to Ruth in surprise. "What is it?" he asked.

She read: "'Effective immediately all persons are to schedule themselves for the painless insertion of a personal ID tag that will allow them to buy and sell at their leisure without the need for cash. The savings from moving to a cashless society alone will nearly fund the entire *Day of Jubilee.*

Each person may fill out the necessary forms from any online computer station either from work, home, school, or the public library. Assistance will be provided for the elderly and indigent. Personal ID tag insertion stations will be set up at multiple sites in each town or city.'"

Scott found it all so remarkable. In less than 90 days after Carlo had been shot, killed, and raised to life again, he had been installed unanimously by billions of people and their respective governments as the leader of the world and given the title of President of the United World Organization. It was obvious that his new position was not just a mere title, but one that came with actual power and authority. Scott was anxious to share this news with Joseph and Yvette.

******

Joseph and Yvette had been cooped up for months, Joseph in Scott's apartment and Yvette in Ruth's home. Daily on Ruth's way to work she would drop off Yvette to keep Joseph company. Both Yvette and Joseph would have gone crazy if they had not had each other for support during this period of their lives. The word was out about Joseph, and he was a wanted man. *Deacon's Horn* had created quite a mess for Simon and Carlo.

Simon saw the article in the new edition of *Deacon's Horn* before Carlo knew anything. The article was encoded with information that would prove to the world that Carlo, Simon, and their plans were not what they seemed. Simon was irate, as well as frightened. How would he tell Carlo? Twenty minutes after reading the article Simon got a personal call from the Pope.

"Who did this?" Simon asked.

"Father Bastoni!" said the Pope angrily.

"Bastoni!" said Simon. "Yes, that would make sense." He knew his men had gone by for the list of Catholic members. He also knew that

Joseph had slipped away from his men. *I never liked that guy!* said Simon to himself.

"We will print a retraction of this inflammatory article this afternoon," said the Pope.

"Carlo is not going to like this one bit," said Simon. Pope Peter John shivered at the thought.

"We'll find Father Bastoni and correct this situation right away," said Peter John.

"Where is he?" Simon inquired.

"We don't know for sure, but we believe he left the country with a news broadcasting crew from Chicago."

"Find him! I want his head!" Simon screamed as he slammed the phone down on the Pope.

Peter John looked at his personal aide, Paul Laruso, who was standing next to him during his conversation with Simon. "We need to find Bastoni now!"

"What do we know about these news teams from Chicago?" Paul asked.

"Nothing," said Peter John. "But I have been told that my niece is also a part of this. She apparently was seen leaving Joseph's apartment with him, and I saw her with Bastoni together the night Carlo Ventini was shot. See if she is home. And if you find her, bring her to me right away," said the Pope angrily. He was very dismayed over Yvette's choice of company. Regardless of the evil in Peter John's heart, he did truly love Yvette like his own daughter—which, in fact, she was.

******

Joseph picked up the phone after the second ring. He was always a little nervous when he had to answer Scott's phone. "Hello," he said lightly.

"Joseph," said Scott, "are you sitting down?"

In truth, Joseph was sitting, and right next to him was Yvette. Joseph blew a sigh of relief. "Hi, Scott. I am sitting down. What is it?"

Scott proceeded to read the three-page fax to Joseph. Yvette could tell by the look on Joseph's face that whatever Scott was telling him was big—very big! "It's almost time for us to leave, I think," said Scott.

Joseph was heavy into thought at the time. "What? Leave to go where?"

"Leave, run, get out!" said Scott.

Joseph looked at Yvette and smiled weakly. "Yes, I see what you mean."

"We, Ruth and I, will be home in about an hour. We'll figure it out then."

Joseph knew that sooner or later they would all have to hide. Sooner or later Simon would find out how Scott had filtered *Deacon's Horn* through various news agencies to distribute it around the world while preventing or at least reducing the chance that Simon could trace the origin of the paper back to Scott and then back to Joseph.

To date the small paper had not only had a disturbing, but also a very damaging, effect on Simon and Carlo's efforts to deceive the world. Daily this small paper would show up in various countries in numerous small communities. *Deacon's Horn* had been rewritten to include excerpts from all the original monthly editions. It also included the final code and an explanation of how it had come to pass.

Many read the articles and quickly understood their importance. Most understood the reality of these predictions coming to pass well before Carlo ever got shot. Others ignored the paper as an elaborate hoax perpetrated by some excommunicated evil priest, as Simon's media puppets portrayed Joseph.

The world was on the lookout for Joseph. There was a large reward coming to the person who could help Pope Peter John find this evil liar. There were even threats that anyone found harboring such a criminal would be held accountable. Simon made arrangements to make it appear like Joseph was also somehow a co-conspirator in Carlo's shooting. This was easy to do since the real assassin was dead and buried. Who could refute Simon's fabrication?

******

Three months had gone by slowly, and Paul Laruso was finally narrowing in on Joseph and Yvette. It had seemed like an easy task in the beginning. Paul knew the names of all the news reporters that had attended Carlo's fatal celebration. He even knew the flight information for each corporate jet that left Rome that morning. The problem was there were three separate Chicago-based news broadcasters in attendance at Carlo's celebration and coincidentally all three had left Rome within an hour of each other on the same icy December morning months ago. The guard on duty that morning had been questioned numerous times. He had been shown pictures of all the news reporters and staff members. He did recognize some of them, but for the most part he could not put faces together with names, and in particular, he could not put these faces together with Joseph and Yvette.

The guard had no idea what plane if any they might have gotten onto. Finally out of anger Paul went a little too far during his interrogation. In a fit of rage and frustration, Paul beat the poor airport security guard until he died from internal injuries.

During the last few months Paul had systematically tracked and monitored each Chicago reporter who had attended the celebration in Rome. This was a painfully slow process, and with so many people to track simultaneously, it was going to take time and luck before he could target in on Joseph.

"How's it going?" Pope Peter John asked over the phone.

"I have narrowed it down considerably," said Paul. Today I am following a news reporter named Ruth Jefferson. It is possible that she has something to do with this."

"That's what you said about the last five reporters!" Peter John yelled through the receiver.

The pressure was really on the Pope. He had been put to the test by Simon to deliver this betrayer, as Simon liked to refer to Joseph. Simon's mood was getting worse as each day another edition of *Deacon's Horn* would emerge in some foreign country. Carlo had soundly chastised Simon for this continual nuisance.

"Why is it that you cannot do such a simple task as finding the source of this paper and its author?" Carlo asked.

The heat was on, and Peter John knew it was only a matter of time before Simon took control of the situation himself. "Follow her then," said Peter John of Ruth, "and for your sake, I hope she is the one." Then he hung up the phone with a slam.

Paul Laruso stood in the phone booth. *I hope she is the one, too, or next it will be me they are looking for!*

******

"Let's get ready to move out of here," said Joseph as he looked into Yvette's beautiful green eyes. Her frightened countenance touched his heart. He put his hand against her rosy cheek. "It will be okay. God will help us."

"What has happened?" Yvette inquired.

"The mark of the beast," he said with a whisper. "Carlo has published a declaration that all people must register all their personal information into one of his databases, and then they will have to go to a convenient location for the insertion of an ID tag that will allow them to purchase items such as food."

"So why do we have to leave now?" a very confused Yvette asked.

"Yvette, the Bible states that all men will have to take the mark of the beast or be prepared to die a martyr's death."

"What's a martyr's death?" Yvette asked.

Joseph looked at her carefully. "If we are caught and refuse to take the ID tag, we will be killed for sure. This martyr's death, according to the book of Revelation, is to be beheaded for your faith."

Yvette put her hand up to her throat and gasped. "Then I guess we run," she said with a weak smile.

Joseph moved into Yvette and hugged her tightly. "It will be all right," he said reassuringly, although he knew it was just a matter of time. Even if he and Yvette managed to escape Carlo's ID tags for a season, they still had the other issue to contend with. They were wanted people. They had become traitors and, with the help of Simon and his news media coverage, hated by the world. As Joseph stood with his arms clasped around Yvette his mind drifted back to Peter.

It had been four months since he had last seen Peter. He really didn't ever expect to see him again on this earth, but Joseph was still very worried about his big brother. How will he know not to take the ID tag? Where is he? Have they caught him? Are they even looking for him? Joseph understood that Simon knew about Peter. He knew Peter lived with Joseph, and it only made sense that Simon would be looking for him as well.

******

In fact, Simon had been looking for Peter. He was working his own angles to try and isolate Joseph and capture him. If he found Peter, he would likely find Joseph not far behind. He had a burning desire to make Joseph a public example. He wanted to show the world how he and Carlo would deal with such a traitor and blasphemer. Simon had scoured the city of Rome for Peter, but he was just not anywhere to be found.

Peter had slipped back into his small clinic the same morning he and Joseph eluded Simon's henchmen. Peter gathered up all of the medical supplies and equipment he could. He had also removed all traces of phone numbers and the names of every person working with him to prepare for whatever medical crisis might arise. Peter was still worried. He had made and received calls from many of the new members of his staff, and undoubtedly these calls would be traced. He was also certain that over the last six months or so many people would have witnessed members of his staff coming and going from the medical facility. *They will be able to identify many of these people,* Peter thought.

Peter picked up the phone to call Dr. Bruno Shire, the elderly doctor who had first approached him at the clinic months earlier. Bruno was the first and without a doubt the strongest member of Peter's staff. Peter drew comfort from the senior man's maturity. Dr. Shire had wisdom and a sense of peace that Peter gleaned from him.

Abruptly there was the sound of footsteps approaching from behind

Peter. Quickly he slid behind the door and hid himself. The footsteps continued until he could actually hear the sound of someone breathing. He had no weapon, so he began to look around. Three feet away was a small tray of medical instruments laid out in a neat little row. Among them was a moderate-sized scalpel, if only he could get to it.

Peter held his breath as the steps moved past the door. He could now see the back of a large man with gray hair walking past the door. Suddenly Peter lunged towards the scalpel sending the tray and all instruments flying in every direction.

"Peter!" said the man with a heavy Italian accent.

Peter recognized the voice instantly and turned around to see the face of a very concerned Bruno Shire. "What is going on here?" Bruno asked.

"They are after us!" said Peter. When he calmed down, he explained everything to Bruno who listened carefully and quietly.

"We have much to do!" said Bruno.

Peter was so relieved to have this man on his side. The two of them worked out the details, and eventually all the members of Peter's team were notified. They all gathered their personal effects and medical supplies along with their families and moved away from Rome into a small warehouse in the city of Latina where Bruno had grown up as a child.

In his youth Bruno had played in this old building. During World War II the building had been turned into an armament factory and was one of the few that actually survived the war without being bombed by the Allies. After the war the building was abandoned and once again Bruno and his brothers would make forts and play all day in the old factory. Bruno used to enjoy climbing the fire escape onto the roof where he could look out at the Tyrrhenian Sea and watch all of the fishing boats moving in and out of the harbor.

As Peter and his teammates hid, safely tucked away, Simon was enraged. He had exhausted every lead in an attempt to find Peter. Soon he began to understand that every person who had been seen frequenting the small clinic had disappeared. Even those whose phone numbers Simon had traced had gone. Every person and family were gone without a trace.

Why were so many medical professionals missing? Why had they all disappeared into hiding at the same time? What are they up to? Simon wondered.

******

Ruth went directly to her apartment and gathered her clothing and Yvette's. On the way out the door she stopped for one last look. *I will never be here again,* she told herself. Ruth walked over to her coffee table, picked up a small picture frame, and stared at it for a moment. Her beloved mother and father were in Heaven already. She knew that she would soon be there as well. Ruth tucked the picture into her luggage and headed out the front door.

Across the street sitting in a small, light blue car was Paul Laruso. He had followed Ruth from the studio and was now sitting patiently to see if she was the one—the one who was hiding Joseph and Yvette.

Paul ducked his head as he observed Ruth heading to her car with an armload of luggage. *Where is she going?* Paul wondered. Ruth was a full block ahead before Paul pulled away from the sidewalk. Caution was necessary. He didn't want to tip her off. He was getting desperate, as he was nearly out of leads.

******

Joseph sat reading the fax as Scott packed in a hurry. "Ruth will be here any minute. Are you sure you are all packed?" Scott asked with both excitement and panic in his tone.

"Yes," said Joseph. He had already answered this question three times.

Frankly, the last few months of living with Scott had been a test of perseverance for Joseph, not only because he could not leave the house, but also because Scott was a bit of a twerp as far as Joseph was concerned. He liked Scott and greatly appreciated all he had done for Yvette and him, but the young man could get really annoying after a while.

Yvette held onto Joseph's hand tightly as she sat quietly next to him. Suddenly just as Scott stepped into the living room loaded down with luggage a cool breeze blew across the room. Joseph knew instantly that a heavenly presence was in the house. A glow began to fill the room. Scott was frightened greatly, as was Yvette. Scott dropped his luggage with a thud. "What is it?" he asked in fear.

"Joseph, you have done well, and now it is time for you to leave this country," said the voice. "You are in great danger here now!"

Joseph did not recognize the voice. It was not the Lord. "Who are you?" Joseph asked.

"I am an angel of the Lord. You all must leave now through the back door. Take only what you can carry. You do not have much time. Hurry!"

At that very moment Ruth stepped into the house through the front door. She saw the glow and was frozen where she stood.

"Joseph, you and Yvette have a destiny awaiting you in Jerusalem. You must leave and go there now."

The light faded and the presence was gone.

"What was that?" a fearful Ruth asked.

Joseph did not wait to answer her. He quickly went to the front window and peered out from behind the curtain. He observed Paul Laruso closing his car door and crossing the street towards Scott's home. "Let's go!" said Joseph as he hurried across the floor and lifted Yvette out of her chair and onto her feet. "Out the back door now!" yelled Joseph. Scott reached for his luggage and quickly reconsidered, taking instead the smallest of the bags.

Paul Laruso knocked on the front door and waited. Looking at his watch he knocked a second time. Behind the house Joseph hoisted Yvette over the brick wall dividing Scott's house from the apartment building next door. Ruth scaled the wall quickly without any help. Finally Joseph cleared the wall.

"Where to?" a nervous Scott asked. Joseph had not considered this part of the equation yet.

"We have to get to Jerusalem," said Joseph.

Scott smiled intently. "Follow me!" he said.

Sometimes you just have to love the guy after all, Joseph thought to himself.

Paul Laruso checked his watch again. His patience was gone. With his right hand Paul tested the front door. It pushed open easily. Paul stepped into the hallway and stopped. Opening his coat, he pulled out his large revolver and began to inch his way into the living room. Five minutes later after searching the house twice Paul dropped onto the couch out of frustration. *How will I tell this to Peter John?* he wondered.

Chapter 19: Freedom for Some

Day 1065, June: Calvin could not believe his ears. After nearly three years in prison, he was to be released in a mere 48 hours. Each prisoner was to be given a new suit and $500 to start life over again. Also they were each to be given a certificate from Carlo Ventini himself.

The certificate read: *"This is the first day of the rest of your life. I forgive you, and the world forgives you."* Calvin did not know who this Carlo guy really was. He had seen the news like everyone else, but once again a limited Biblical understanding prevented him from comprehending the whole truth.

Staring out of the cafeteria window, Calvin watched as delivery trucks pulled up to the compound. The first truck was a custom shoe truck. The second was a custom suit truck. They were bringing in the promised clothing. Before the day was over each prisoner would be fitted and ready to go. A third truck pulled up, but this one did not have a name on the side. Two men stepped out of the cab and proceeded to the back of the trailer.

"I wonder who they are," said Cory Parker to Calvin.

"I don't know," said Calvin as he shook his head.

A heavy, redheaded security guard stepped up to the window beside Calvin and watched as the two men unloaded a crate of equipment. "They must be the security tag guys."

"What security tag?" Calvin asked.

"Haven't you heard?" said the guard. "The world is going cashless. We and everyone else are supposed to have an ID tag inserted into our right hand or forehead."

"What for?" asked Calvin.

"Like I said, so we can buy and sell without using money. Mr. Ventini is creating a new world for all of us. He believes in new beginnings. That's why he is letting all of you bums out of here."

"What if we don't want to have a tag inserted into our bodies?" Calvin asked.

"You don't have a choice!" said the guard with a stern little grin.

Calvin moved back to where Cory was now sitting. "We need to talk," he said.

"What is it?" Cory inquired.

"Trouble—big trouble!"

Cory and Calvin strolled casually out of the cafeteria and out into the exercise yard. The guards were all very relaxed. There really was no point in watching these guys anymore. They would all be free men in another day or so. There were at least 30 or so men standing around the courtyard talking or lifting weights as Calvin and Cory stepped out. "What's the matter?" Cory asked.

"It's the mark of the beast!" said Calvin.

"What is?" Cory asked.

"They are going to insert an ID tag into each of us—into our hands or even our forehead if we choose."

"Do we have to do it?" Cory asked.

"That's what the guard said." Calvin frowned.

"What happens if we take the ID tag?" Cory inquired like a child.

"It's the mark of the beast, and if we take it, then we can never go to Heaven. We will be doomed to Hell forever!"

"Forever!" whispered Cory. "How do you know this?"

The question surprised Calvin. *How do I know this?* he wondered to himself. "I guess as a kid I heard my mother and father talking about a day when the Antichrist would come into the world and would make everyone take his mark to buy and sell."

"So who is the Antichrist?" Cory asked intently.

Calvin thought for a moment and then said, "I guess it must be Carlo

Ventini!"

"Well, what are we going to do?" Cory inquired.

"We have to get to that ID tag equipment," said Calvin.

"And then what?"

"I don't know, but I will figure that out when I get to it." Calvin was an engineer as well as a fighter pilot. If he could get his hands on this equipment, he could probably disable it in some way.

The crate of equipment including air compressors, insertion guns, and tags had been taken to the main lobby where it would be used on each prisoner as they processed out of the prison. The two truck drivers had uncrated the equipment and driven away after giving the security guards brief instructions on how to use the small hand-held gun.

"Can I get any volunteers for a demonstration?" one of the truck drivers asked.

The lean, black security guard stepped forward boldly. "I'll do it!" he said with a smile. The driver held the gun in his left hand and pointed it directly at the guard's forehead. The nervous guard giggled a little. With a light flick of the trigger, the tiny microchip slid underneath the man's skin without any pain or even a noticeable bump.

"Done!" the driver smiled.

"That was easy!" said the young guard proudly.

******

It was after midnight when Cory and Calvin convinced the nighttime guard to let them play one last game of basketball. "Why not?" said the guard. "You're out of here tomorrow anyway."

Calvin was the first to be let out of his cell. Next came Cory. "How about you play the game with us?" Calvin asked.

"No, it's not my game," said the guard politely.

"How are we going to get past this guy?" Cory whispered.

"Be patient," said Calvin quietly.

All the guards except this one were in the cafeteria drinking coffee. *Let the rookie watch these bums, because tomorrow we are all unemployed,* was their collective thought.

There were two teams of ball players—about eight men per side—rotating in and out. The guard stood along the chain link fence watching the game. Calvin whispered to Cory, "We need to knock him out without getting caught."

Cory nodded. The next time he got the ball he charged down the court at full speed. Suddenly a single bump from another one of the players sent Cory directly towards the guard. Cory hit him under the chin with one of his forearms which was as big as the guard's leg. The man crumpled to the ground and was out like a light.

The rest of the prisoners had no idea what was going on. They came over to the guard to try to move him, but Cory held them back. "Leave him alone, and if he starts to wake up, knock him out again."

Calvin and Cory took off towards the lobby. The prisoners just stood there completely confused. "But we get out tomorrow!" said one man loudly.

Looking through the corner of the glass window, Cory could see a security guard hunched over his desk. To his left was the small platform containing the equipment that would be used tomorrow to seal their fate. He opened the door slowly, and just then the guard turned his head to the other side and let out a loud snore. Together the men tiptoed into the lobby and walked directly in front of the guard. Cory could see the man's gun clearly in its holster. He had killed before to protect the innocent, and he knew that he could again if need be.

Calvin tugged on Cory's arm as if he had read his thoughts. Cory followed Calvin over to the equipment. Calvin picked up the ID tag insertion gun and studied it closely. *If I disable it, they will just find someone to fix it,* he thought to himself. *I need to make it look like it is still working.* Calvin studied the load chamber. It was full of thousands of ID tags. These little green tags frightened him very much.

First he unscrewed the end cap and looked directly into the barrel of the gun. Then he began to look around the room for a tool to help him. Finally he spotted a ballpoint pen lying next to the security guard. Calvin crept slowly towards the pen. "Please, God!" he whispered, "Keep this guy asleep until I can break this thing." He stood over the guard and gently picked up the pen, then slowly made his way back to the gun. Quietly Calvin unscrewed the pen and removed the spring and washer. Together he reformed the two small pieces into a mechanism that would prevent the ID tags from sliding down the barrel under the pressure of air. The washer would restrict them from moving into position and the spring would deflect them, giving the appearance that a new tag was entering the chamber with each pull of the trigger.

Calvin reassembled the gun but was dissatisfied. He really needed to see the thing operate to be sure that it would work and especially to ensure that no tags blew through the barrel. Calvin looked at Cory. "I need to test it," he whispered. Cory nodded and walked slowly towards the guard. Calvin was afraid Cory would kill the guard, but he didn't know what else to do. He had to fire the gun, and that would be noisy. Calvin flipped the switch on the air compressor. Instantly the guard lifted his head and Cory clobbered him, probably before his brain could even register who was in the room.

Calvin held the gun out and pointed it toward the wall. Gently he pulled the trigger and to his surprise a small, green microchip shot out. Calvin swallowed hard. Again he pulled the trigger, but this time nothing came out. The gun sounded the same and it looked through the chamber as if it was working but, in fact, it was broken. "Must have been one left in the chamber," said Calvin with a little grin. Powering down the equipment, he and Cory retreated to the courtyard where the young guard was still fast asleep or maybe in a coma. Who could tell?

******

The next morning Calvin stood in line behind Cory waiting his turn to process out. Both men—like every other prisoner—were dressed in nice new suits. As each person stepped forward the security guard asked him where he wanted the ID tag inserted. "In the forehead or in the hand?" he would say. After a blast of air passed through the gun, each man would receive $500 and his pardon papers and then be directed to one of the large buses.

Cory was next, and he was nervous. What if this thing was working again? He didn't have a lot of confidence after seeing that first green chip fly out when Calvin pulled the trigger last night.

"Hand or head?" the guard asked. Cory stuck out his right hand and said a silent prayer. He closed his eyes just as the guard pulled the trigger. "You're kind of a big baby, aren't you?" said the guard. Cory couldn't help but smile. He knew that nothing had entered his hand. Besides, the bump on the guard's forehead was consolation for his rudeness. He apparently had no idea who it was that had inflicted the massive blow, and for that Cory was also glad.

Cory stood outside waiting for Calvin to process out. *What do I do now?* he wondered. He didn't want to go back to Mississippi where he had grown up. There was nothing left there for him—no family or friends. In fact, the only friend that Cory had was Calvin.

Calvin stepped up beside his big buddy. "It worked!" he said with a smile. Cory nodded. Calvin could tell that his friend was preoccupied with a thought.

"Where will you go?" Calvin asked.

"I don't know," said Cory without looking up.

"I'm going to California," said Calvin. Cory looked up, and it was obvious to Calvin that he wanted to go too. Calvin had to laugh. Sometimes it amazed him how much Cory tended to act like a little child. He was a huge, intimidating man, but inside he was kind and scared and confused. "Would you like to come with me?" Calvin asked. "I don't know where I'm going exactly, and I don't even know who will be left—"

"I'll go!" said Cory even before Calvin could finish his explanation.

******

Tina Glover stood in the corner of the small lab, stewing. She couldn't stand the idea of Tommy having a girlfriend. Although his relationship with Dr. Sara Allen was not a typical boy-girl relationship, it was still romantic, and it made Tina jealous.

Dr. Dedrick Bishopf stared through the microscope at the intricate little microchip. "This is amazing," said Dedrick. "Where did you get it?" He had been trying to get one of the little ID tags for many months now. Even though he had been a member of Carlo and Simon's Unified Science Organization after his being unanimously elected at the L.A. science convention, he still had had no success obtaining a single tag. They were all well guarded after that little prison incident at Leavenworth.

Dedrick had even been flown to Rome to meet with Simon and Carlo. Of course, there were hundreds of scientists there for that brief meeting. Yet Simon did single out Dedrick in a direct, one-on-one conversation. "So you believe that Mother Earth is just experiencing growing pains, is that correct?" Simon asked.

Dedrick had little choice as to what he could say, so he simply nodded and said," Yes, that is correct, Mr. Koch."

Simon giggled like a child. "Well, let's hope she's all grown up now!" he said as he walked away snickering. This was the confirmation Dedrick was looking for. Simon gave him the creeps. With his wild eyes and condescending attitude, he conveyed to Dedrick that he knew the truth about what had happened that fateful day when the world shook.

Dedrick understood that Simon and Carlo had predicted all the natural disasters. They were ready to come to the aid of the world just in time to make them look like heroes. *Now they have all the power,* Dedrick thought. *The world is doomed.*

That had been nearly two years ago, and during those last two years Dedrick, Tommy, and Sara had been working underground with scientists from nearly every country. They had been sharing scientific facts about the real condition of the world. They had also developed an underground church full of scientists. It was slow and dangerous at first.

"How will we ever know who to trust?" Tommy asked.

"We will have to test everyone carefully and slowly until we know who is open to the truth," said Dedrick.

This was a tedious process. Scientists are not known for their willingness to take any fact based on faith, but slowly Dedrick, Sara, and Tommy had networked a good portion of the world's scientific community into an underground church. The real breakthrough came from the live footage of Carlo being assassinated, followed up by numerous and insightful articles from a small paper called *Deacon's Horn.*

It was more reasonable to believe the article proclaiming Carlo as the Antichrist, especially since it described what would happen to him before it even happened. This prophecy began to take these scientists back to the Bible where they found remarkable insight as to the disasters that had already come and those yet to follow. They began to see the light and understood who and what Carlo was, but what could they really do about it? How could they help the world to understand the truth?

Maybe the answer was in one of those little green tags that were being inserted into the hand or forehead of every person on the plant. Maybe there was a way to help the world understand what this tag was really for.

"A friend of mine from the Creation Institute gave the tags to me," said Sara.

"Can you tell how they work?" Tommy asked.

"I'm not an electrical engineer," said Dedrick, "but I can tell you that this is nothing like I have ever seen before. We need some expert help on this."

Since the science convention Tommy, Sara, and Dedrick had been spending a lot of time together. Dedrick had heard Tommy's testimony and was convinced that time was running out. The three of them had been watching television together when Carlo Ventini rose from the dead. They understood that he was the foretold Antichrist, and they knew that they would have to try to warn the world against his deception—but how?

Bored with the whole thing, Tina drifted out of the lab and wandered down the hallway until she found a small patio café. The smell of fresh coffee attracted her attention. Tina stepped out into the clean cool air and up to the counter.

"What can I get you?" the young handsome employee asked.

"What is that smell?" she asked brightly.

"Oh, that's our new hazelnut blend," said the young man with a grin. "Would you like to try it?"

"Is it any good?" she asked.

"No!" said the man with a laugh. "But it smells good, don't you think?"

At this they both laughed.

"I'll just have some good, old fashioned, regular coffee please," said Tina with a charming smile of her own. *This guy's kind of cute,* she thought to herself. Besides, Tommy was so busy with Sara, his new girlfriend, that she felt she needed to meet someone for herself.

"How do you take it?"

"Black, one sugar, please," said Tina.

The young man handed Tina her coffee. "Here you go. Enjoy! And by the way, my name is Mark Singer."

Tina extended her hand in a friendly gesture. "Hi! I'm Tina Glover."

Mark shook her hand lightly and smiled. "Nice to meet you, Tina. What brings you out here so early? I haven't seen you before, have I?"

Tina's intuition told her to keep her mouth shut about what she was doing and why she was at the technical wing of UCLA at 6:30 a.m. However, the sense of anger that she felt over Tommy's activities and his new girlfriend was stronger than her own good sense. "I am working with a few other scientists to try to understand how these new implantation devices work."

"What implantation devices?" Mark asked.

"The ones that everyone is having inserted into their hands or foreheads."

Mark scratched his forehead and said softly, "I hope there isn't something wrong with them."

"My brother seems to think they are a tool of the Devil, but I don't think there is anything wrong with them at all."

Mark looked into Tina's dark brown eyes. He could see her bitterness, and he could sense her jealousy. "Are you a scientist too?" he asked.

"Yes, but not the kind you're probably thinking of."

"What kind are you then?"

"I am a volcanologist," said Tina.

"Really!" said Mark as he poured Tina another cup of coffee. "Tell me what a volcanologist does."

Tina was really starting to like Mark, but she was afraid that her education and position in life might scare him away—after all, he poured coffee for a living. How compatible could they be?

"Enough of me. Let's talk about you," she said.

"Like why I work in this coffee shop?" said Mark.

He's perceptive, she thought, *and really good looking. I hope he likes me.*

"I am paying my way through medical school, so every day I get up at 5:00 a.m. and come down here to make and serve coffee to the students and the staff. It helps pay the bills," he said with a grin, "but it doesn't help much!" He laughed.

******

The stage was set. Daily Tommy, Sara, and Dedrick would come into the lab to work on the microchip, and each day Tina would follow along and then slip away to the coffee shack to meet Mark Singer. Their relationship had not extended to any actual dates, but Tina was optimistic that soon Mark would ask her out. So far she had hidden her relationship from Tommy. She really didn't know why, but for some reason she wanted Mark to be her own little secret.

Work in the lab was slow. Dedrick had found a brilliant, young electrical engineer to help the team understand how the microprocessor worked, but even so progress was slow.

"This is the most unusual chip I have ever seen," said Brian, the young engineer. "I wish we knew who made it."

"That information is being guarded carefully. We have no clues," said Dedrick. "It is like our own Treasury Department and the security measures used to safeguard printing plates to prevent counterfeiting."

"Well," said Tommy, "the one thing we do know is that this chip is half organic. It actually begins to grow into the nerve and muscle tissue and other connecting tissues around it. We have no idea what happens when we try to remove one, but based on the study we are doing now, it looks like the chip actually becomes a living part of the body."

Brian nodded slowly as he listened to Tommy's explanation. "I have noticed," said Brian, "that this chip appears to have a small signal embedded in it. I can't be sure without other chips to compare it to, but it looks like this chip actually has a small tracking system built in."

"What does that mean?" Sara inquired.

"I don't know," said Brian, "but if I were to guess, I'd say that each frequency is tuned specifically for each chip, making each unique."

"And then?" Sara asked.

"Then," said Brian, "all you would have to do is note the person who wears the chip and you could track them with a global satellite positioning system."

"How far could they be tracked?" Sara inquired.

"Anywhere in the world, I suppose," said Brian, "but I can't be sure of this without another chip to look at."

"Tommy," said Sara, "I gave you two chips. Where is the other one?"

Tommy looked over toward Brian and then to Dedrick. "We do have one more chip, but we have been running a different type of test on it."

"Where is it?" Brian asked. Both Sara and Brian looked inquisitively at Tommy.

Tommy looked towards a door at the far end of the room. "In there."

Sara and Brian followed Dedrick and Tommy into a small room attached to the lab. Tommy flipped the light switch on and stood looking at the table in front of him. Brian stopped and stared as well. "What is this?" said Brian.

Sara turned away. She could not stand to see the horrid sight. "It is an important test," said Dedrick. "We wouldn't have done it if we didn't have to, but it was necessary."

On the table strapped down with leather restraints was a large chimpanzee. Across its mouth was a piece of gray strapping tape. It had wires and tubes coming out of every part of its body, and an EKG monitored its heart rate and rhythms. The top of the chimp's skill had been removed and its brain was exposed to the room air. Two large wires were attached to the base of its brain, and another extended from its neck. All the wires fed back into a little black box with a small, green LED on the top.

Sara turned back around to the chimp. Its large eyes looked at her pleadingly. It was obviously terrified and in great pain. Sara turned to Tommy. "Why have you done this? Why didn't I know? How could you?" she cried.

"Sara, you have to understand. We only had two chips, and we needed to get as much information out of them as possible."

"I know how many chips we have! I gave them to you, remember?"

"We need to know how they work if we are going to stop Carlo," said Tommy softly.

Sara interrupted. "You cannot stop him! No amount of knowledge will prevent these chips from being implanted into nearly every person on this planet. Even we will have to take them by the January first deadline or we will be arrested and then they will forcibly insert a tag into us."

"We have to do something, Sara. We cannot just sit back and let this happen without warning the world against these chips."

"But this is horrible," said Sara as she pointed to the poor chimpanzee.

"You are right, Sara," said Dedrick. "We will take the ID tag out of the chimp, and then we will put it to sleep."

Dedrick stepped forward and grabbed a small scalpel. As he approached the chimp, its eyes grew even more fearful and it twisted and pulled against the restraints. Brian watched Dedrick carefully as he began to slice away the remaining skin on the forehead of the little ape. Brian began to feel nauseated and had to turn to leave. Sara cried audibly, and Tommy tried to put his arms around her to comfort her, but she pushed him away gently.

"I'm sorry, Sara. We had to do it," said Tommy.

Sara nodded. She understood the times they were living in and their desperate need for answers, but still she hated to see the torture of this small animal. As Dedrick began to pull against the chip, he noticed that it would not move. Looking at it from another angle he was amazed at what he saw.

"Come and look at this," he said softly.

"What is it?" Tommy asked as he approached the table. Sara and a nauseated Brian followed him. All three stood next to Dedrick as he pointed to the chip.

"You see," he said, "the microprocessor has grown into the connecting tissue and is completely attached to the brain."

"How can that be?" Brian inquired.

"We knew it was partly organic," said Tommy, "but we didn't know to what extent."

"It becomes a part of you, literally," Sara noted.

Dedrick made a small incision at the base of the chip. Like filleting a fish he began to remove the connective tissue from around the chip, and when he did, the monkey began to react violently, quaking and writhing as if it were in tremendous pain.

"What is going on?" Tommy yelled.

"I don't know!" said Dedrick. He leaned over and took another large slice out of the tissue. As he did this, the monkey went rigid and the LED on top of the small, black box began to flicker off and on. At the same time the EKG equipment started to beep. The wavy pattern on the screen turned to a flat line.

Brian flicked a single switch, turning off the blaring alarm. All four scientists stood over the poor, dead chimpanzee in total awe at what had just happened. Sara had a stream of hot tears rolling down her cheeks. Tommy moved over to console her. This time she allowed him to put his arms around her. Dedrick removed the bloody chip from the monkey's skull and handed it to Brian.

"Find out what you need to know, Brian. We already know all we need to on the organic side of this chip," Dedrick said as he lowered his head with a sigh.

******

Tina walked out of the small coffee shop with a bright smile on her face. Mark had finally asked her out to dinner for that very night. She really liked him very much. Now she just had to make up another excuse for Tommy and then she could sneak away and meet Mark as planned. This wouldn't be too hard. Tommy was so busy with Sara and his new friends that he hardly noticed Tina anymore. He never even asked her where she went whenever she left the lab.

Chapter 20: A Pale Horse Called Plague

Day 1200, October: Jasmine sat on the steps to the Bethlehem Public Library for yet another day. *Is this really what God wants us to do?* she wondered. For the last month she and Elisha had stood daily at the entrance to the library speaking boldly: "Do not accept the ID tag. It is the mark of the beast! Listen to what the book of Revelation says in Chapter 13:16. 'He also forced everyone, small and great, rich and poor, free and slave, to receive a mark on his right hand or on his forehead.' This is from the Devil himself!" Elisha shouted.

Jasmine was proud of Elisha. Over the last few years he had really grown into a big, strong man, and he was truly dedicated to doing God's work. *I'm dedicated too,* Jasmine thought, *but these people just continue to ignore us. They continue to go into the library and receive their ID tags regardless of what we say.*

Jasmine walked up the steps to Elisha and placed her hand gently into his. "Let's go home. I've had enough for the day." Elisha could plainly see Jasmine's frustration, and he felt the same way. However, the reality that people were walking into the library as free people and walking out bound to Satan for eternity was torturing his young mind.

"Why won't they listen?" Elisha asked out of total frustration.

"I don't know," said the tired, young girl. Jasmine led a dejected Elisha down the steps and back towards Benjamin Cohen's deli.

******

"How much longer?" Jasmine asked as they entered the front door to Benjamin's house.

"How much longer until what?" a young David asked as he entered the room.

"Until we don't have to do this anymore," said Jasmine. Elisha ignored both of them, walked into the living room, and plopped down on the couch next to Benjamin.

Benjamin put his arm around Elisha. "Another rough day?" he asked.

Elisha just nodded and sighed loudly.

"Come here, all of you," said Benjamin. The children gathered around waiting for him to speak.

Maybe he has some good news, Jasmine thought. *We sure could use some.*

"Sit!" said Benjamin. "I have been reading and studying the book of Revelation, and if I am not mistaken, our time here is just about over."

"What do you mean?" Elisha asked.

Benjamin patted Elisha's hand lightly. "I found it in Chapter 11."

"Found what?" Jasmine demanded in her usual impatient tone.

"Forty-two months," said Benjamin.

How cryptic, David thought. *Is Benjamin losing it or what?*

"Forty-two months from the first day of the Rapture is the time God allows the Antichrist to mock Him and deceive the world."

"And then?" Jasmine asked.

"And then," said Benjamin slowly as he tried to calm Jasmine down, "and then the Antichrist will reveal himself as the god of this world."

"How will he do this?" David inquired. He, too, had grown over the last two years. He was now 15 years old and at least an inch taller than Benjamin.

"You are all aware that the Jews and Muslims have rebuilt the temple, the *Dome of the Rock*, and they have rebuilt it right over the site of the *Holy of Holies, Solomon's Temple*," he said. All three children nodded agreeing. "This is where the Antichrist will reveal himself during the dedication of the temple."

All four of them had come to realize that Carlo Ventini was the son of Satan, but for some reason they never focused specifically on this fact.

Now it was all coming together. Soon the Antichrist would be in their country, and soon he would declare himself as lord of all.

"What will happen after he declares himself god?" Jasmine asked.

Benjamin sat forward, and with a very serious look on his face he said slowly, "Child, God will pour out His wrath on this planet. Disasters, death, and suffering beyond what we have already seen are coming to all who are left here."

"That means us!" said David.

Benjamin nodded and pulled the three children into him and hugged them tightly.

"How much time do we have?" Elisha asked.

"I have counted since the first day of the Rapture. Today is the 1,200th day, so according to the Bible we have another 60 days. On the 1260th day the Antichrist will be presented to the world as god!"

Elisha started counting in his mind. "Christmas Day!" he said.

Benjamin nodded. "Yes, that is the day that the new temple will be dedicated, and Carlo will be there for the presentations."

"Well," said Jasmine with a tough little smile, "then I guess we have 59 more days to warn the world about the ID tags. Maybe we can save a few."

******

"We are not getting maximum participation in our ID tag program," said Simon as he read the latest percentages to Carlo.

"Which countries are the worst offenders?" Carlo asked with a growl. Even with all of his own success, Simon still cowered whenever Carlo spoke to him in this tone of voice.

"The United States has less than a 65 percent compliance rating," said a frightened Simon.

At this Carlo sneered. "Soon they won't even matter. Who's next?"

Simon swallowed hard. He knew that Carlo was going to come un-glued at this next bit of information. "Western Europe," he whispered.

Carlo grabbed the report from Simon's hand. He stared at it in disbelief and then ripped the paper to shreds. "All right, if that's how they want it!" Carlo stepped across the room and pulled out a small black book. He tossed the book to Simon who juggled it before he finally caught it. "Call Alexis Kurpov and set up a meeting for tomorrow."

******

Peter stood in the center of the small warehouse. There were literally hundreds, maybe even thousands, of bodies lying everywhere. Moans of pain, screams of death, and cries of sorrow could be heard so clearly that it began to burn into Peter's mind.

He bent down to examine one small child—a beautiful little blonde girl of maybe three years old. The young girl was just lying there whimpering as he examined her chest with his stethoscope. Abruptly the girl began to choke to death on her own blood. Peter held the child and cried aloud as he looked around the room at all the dying people.

Suddenly there was warmth all around Peter. He quickly sat forward and realized he was in his own bed. It was just a dream—just a horrible dream.

"Peter," a calm voice whispered.

"Yes," said Peter as his voice trembled. His forehead was covered with perspiration. "Is that You, Lord?" Peter asked.

"Peter, the time is coming. Death and misery are coming to you. Be strong. Be prepared. I will give you the ability to slow this plague, but it must come to pass as it is written."

The light in the room faded, and Peter knew that he was alone again. *It is coming,* Peter thought to himself, *soon—very soon!*

Unable to sleep, Peter wandered around the makeshift lab that he and the others had put together. They had good equipment—state of the art—and many talented people to operate it, but somehow Peter knew it would not be enough. It would never be enough.

******

Alexis Kurpov stood at the entrance to the airport ramp for the second time. He didn't want to do this. He didn't want to see Carlo and Simon ever again, but what choice did he have? The leader of the world had requested that Kurpov meet him personally at the airport outside the city of Tver. Alexis couldn't possibly say no.

Simon was the first one down the ramp as usual, but this time he came up with a small escort of military police. Both Carlo and Simon traveled with this group of Special Forces everywhere they went. It came with the job, although Carlo was certain he personally could never be hurt again. Just the same, it looked good. Besides, Simon could still be hurt or killed.

Simon smiled brightly to Alexis. "Hello, Mr. Kurpov. Good to see you." Simon stuck out his clammy hand to Alexis who looked at it for a couple of seconds before he felt compelled to shake it.

Next Carlo strolled down the ramp towards Simon and Alexis. Carlo's gaze captured Alexis', and he stared the frightened man down for a few seconds before speaking. "Let's go!" said Carlo. "We'll ride with you, Mr. Kurpov. Our security can follow along behind. You did get the escort vehicles I requested, correct?"

Alexis nodded and increased his step to keep up with Carlo.

There was very little conversation as they rode in the back of Alexis' limo. Finally Carlo spoke up. "How are the Russians doing these days?"

"Like the rest of the world, I imagine," said Alexis.

"Oh, how so?" inquired Carlo.

"We are slowly starving to death, and with this horrid weather we are also either freezing to death in winter or dying in the intolerable heat of summer."

"Yes," said Carlo. "The weather has been very uncooperative these last few years."

Simon almost giggled at this. *What a pity,* he thought as he sneered at Alexis. "By the way, you wouldn't happen to be taping this conversation, would you?" Simon asked with a smile.

Alexis looked pale. He could still remember the last time he had tried this. He had learned his lesson. "No, we are not taping this conversation."

Simon looked at Alexis' driver and winked.

Things hadn't changed at the Kurpov home. It was still decorated in a very patriotic fashion, and even the housemaid was the same. Simon smiled brightly at the young lady as she led them into the study. One thing that went with Simon's new job was the ability to have just about any woman he wanted, whenever he wanted. All he had to do was request their presence and someone on his staff would bring them to him. What could they do, say no? Hardly! Whenever Simon wanted a woman— or a little boy—or whatever his disgusting mind would desire, he would just make the request.

This had gotten a little out of control recently until Carlo interceded. He caught Simon one time beating a young woman as he prepared to rape her. Carlo chastised Simon greatly saying, "Control your pathetic urges, or would you prefer that I take this before my Father?" Simon was afraid of the threat, yet in his heart he suspected that Satan would gladly approve of his behavior. Still, out of obedience to and fear of Carlo, Simon slowed his activities down some, although the urge burned inside him constantly.

"Leave us," said Alexis to his housemaid. He closed the door himself. "Have a seat, gentlemen." He really hated this. He had no idea what they wanted this time, but he was certain it meant more suffering for some poor country.

Carlo sneered at Alexis. "How have you been, Alexis?" he asked.

The look from Carlo bore right through his chest, causing him pain. The pain was really out of fear of Carlo and what was behind his smile. "I am fine."

"So tell me about plagues," said Carlo.

"Plagues!" whispered Alexis. "What plagues?"

"Are we going to have to do this again?" Simon asked.

Carlo raised his right hand slightly to quiet Simon. Simon hated it when Carlo did this. Always during the big moments it seemed that Carlo took away Simon's fun.

"What do we have to choose from?" Carlo asked.

What is the point? Alexis wondered. *I cannot defeat these guys. I cannot resist, but I can't let them have one of these plagues. They will kill millions.* Alexis made up his mind he would remain courageous to the end. *They will get nothing from me,* he decided. *I've done enough already.*

It was as if Carlo could read his mind. "Resisting me will not stop us from getting what we want, but it will cost you your life."

Alexis was afraid. He had rarely ever been afraid of anything, but at this very moment he was terrified. He knew he would not come out of this alive. "I will give you nothing!" he said as his voice wavered.

"Oh, yes, you will!" Simon growled.

Carlo raised his hand towards Simon one more time. "Bring them in," said Carlo in a loud voice. Suddenly the door to the study opened, and in walked a small security force with Alexis' housemaid and chauffeur. Behind them came another security officer leading a small child.

Alexis stood. "Let her go!" he demanded.

"How come you didn't introduce us to your daughter the last time we were here?" Carlo asked. "I understand that your wife died two years ago giving birth to this little one. She is your wife's legacy and such a beautiful little girl. Don't you think so, Simon?"

Simon grinned and licked his lips. "Very beautiful!" he said in a low monotone voice.

Alexis loved his daughter more than anything in life, but he had a dilemma on his hands. *If I give him what he wants, millions will die because of me,* he thought. The grief Alexis felt as he looked at his little girl was overwhelming.

"Let her go to her father," said Carlo.

The security guard let go of the child's small hand, and she ran to her father and hid behind his legs. Alexis was all the protection she had in the world.

"Now to show you that we mean business," said Carlo as he turned towards one of the security guards, "we will let you choose which one of these two people you want us to kill first." Carlo waited patiently. "What, no choice? Okay then, Simon, you choose!"

Simon loved this, and he was very grateful to Carlo for letting him be involved. Simon stood and walked around both the maid and the driver. The fear in their eyes was tremendous. The young lady began to cry as Simon caressed her cheek with the back of his hand. Finally Simon turned to Alexis and glared at his little daughter. "I hope you are not planning on taking a drive anytime soon." Simon giggled.

Carlo nodded to the security guard who pulled out his handgun and put it against the temple of the driver. The man's knees began to buckle with fear as the security guard prepared to pull the trigger. Out of the blue the room was full of smoke as the sound of the gun resounded through the study. Blood splattered on the maid who quickly fainted from fear, falling to the floor with a thud. The young child began to scream aloud.

"Shut her up!" said Carlo angrily. "And now who should we kill—or are you ready to give us what we want?" said Carlo.

Alexis stood silently as he stared at his driver dead on the floor with blood pouring from his mutilated skull. He had served Alexis for over 20 years faithfully.

"Stand her back on her feet," said Simon as he pointed to the young maid.

The maid swayed back and forth supported by two of the guards. "Well, what is it going to be?" Carlo asked.

Alexis remained speechless as his little girl clung tightly to his leg. He knew his daughter loved the maid like a mother, and in fact, she had raised his daughter since her birth.

Carlo nodded to the security guard. The young woman spoke a simple word in English, "Jesus!"

"No!" Alexis yelled, but it was too late. The shot rang through the room as the woman fell backwards against the wall and slid slowly down to the hardwood floor with a bullet hole squarely in the middle of her forehead. Her eyes were still open, and on her face was an odd sort of smile as the blood trickled down her cheek. Alexis' daughter screamed uncontrollably at this point, and nothing was going to quiet her.

"Bring her to me!" Carlo said.

Alexis picked his daughter up and gripped her tightly in his strong arms. It took three security guards to separate his daughter from him. The little girl screamed uncontrollably.

"Tape her mouth shut," Carlo demanded. "Okay, what's it going to be?" Carlo asked as he looked into Alexis' dazed eyes.

Alexis knew that he and his daughter were probably going to die no matter what. He didn't want to be responsible for the deaths of millions by giving Carlo what he asked for, but he could not just stand by and watch them torture his daughter.

He walked to a bookshelf in the corner of the study. Two of the Security guards pulled their guns and pointed them at Alexis. He lifted two large books and set them on the desk. Next he reached in and began to twist his wrist back and forth. Suddenly with a light push the bookshelf swung inward, revealing another small room just within.

"It's in here," said Alexis flatly.

Carlo held the little girl as he walked into the small room. It was dark, but still Carlo could see racks on the walls loaded with guns of all sorts, from the very small to the extremely large. Alexis walked over to a large wall safe and turned the tumbler back and forth. Finally he clasped the large chrome handle and pulled the door open.

Carlo's eyes were nearly acclimated to the light in the room, enough to see two small boxes sitting in the center of the safe. "What do we have here?" he said brightly.

Alexis reached in and pulled out both boxes. "This is a biological agent called T20, and this is an antidote for it, but it only works if it is given within 24 hours of exposure."

"What does this agent do?" Simon asked with a little giggle.

Alexis swallowed hard. He could still remember the reports coming across his desk when they first began to test this agent. It had a mortality rate of 100%. Exposure was death. In fact, many of his lab technicians and a couple of the scientists had had a terrible accident with just a trace amount of this agent, and within two days they were all dead. "It attacks the lungs like tuberculosis, but much faster. It results in a bloody, terribly painful cough and eventually the victim drowns in his own blood."

"How is it transmitted?" Carlo inquired.

"It is a Level IV agent. It will travel by contact or by air. If you come in contact with it, you will be dead in 48 hours for sure."

"How long will it stay virulent?" Simon asked.

"We don't know. We couldn't stop it or kill it. So we isolated everything we could and ended the program."

Carlo nodded to his security guards. Two stepped forward and took the boxes from Alexis. "Thank you once again for your support," Carlo said as he smiled and handed Alexis back his daughter.

"Such a pretty girl," said Carlo as he patted the child's head.

Carlo walked over to one of his remaining guards and pulled the man's revolver from its holster. He then turned towards Alexis. "Okay, I guess we'll be seeing you then," he said with a smile. With that Carlo shot the little girl in the face, leaving Alexis just enough time to see his daughter die and to feel the pain of her death before Carlo shot him in the stomach and then in the chest. Alexis died holding his beautiful daughter in his arms.

******

Brian studied the chip carefully. He was now certain that these chips had specific frequencies assigned to each one. They were, in fact, tracking devices. "From anywhere in the world," said Brian, "they can find you if you have one of these in you."

None of this was interesting to Tina. She couldn't care less whether or not these chips could take their owner to the moon. For months they had been working in this small stuffy lab, and for what? *Who cares! It is just a chip so we can buy food and the things we need to live. It's a good idea,* she thought.

"We need to get this information out so the people will know the truth," said Tommy.

Sara nodded in agreement. "We can use our underground connections, write a technical report, and feed it to the people. They need to know this before it is too late."

"Too late! Too late for what?" said Tina. She really didn't like Sara, even though Sara had never done anything to her. "It is already too late. Everyone has one of these so they can buy stuff. In fact, we are supposed to have one by now, and if we don't, then we will starve."

"Tina," said Sara, "don't you realize what this chip is?"

Tina glared at Sara. "Yeah, it is a piece of glass, and it lets the world buy food."

"No! This is the mark of the beast, and if we allow it in our bodies, we will be condemning ourselves to Hell. That is why we have to warn those who have not taken this ID tag yet."

"How do you know this is the mark of the beast—if there is such a thing?"

"All right, Tina. That's enough!" said Tommy. "We are trying to prevent people from going to Hell. Where are your priorities, anyway?"

Tina turned and stomped out of the room. *None of this is from God,* she told herself. In the hallway Tina could smell the coffee, and it somehow brightened her up. *I'll go see Mark and see what he thinks,* she told herself.

Back in the lab Dedrick finished typing the last page of the memo. He had been corresponding with scientists from other countries. Daily he fed them more information about the microchip. So few chips had found their way into labs that virtually nothing was known about them until now. With a click of the send button, the message was off at the speed of light. *Hopefully, it will help,* Dedrick thought.

"What's next?" Tommy asked.

"Let's see if we can do something to modify or destroy the chip while it is inside of someone without killing them," said Dedrick. None of the team except Sara seemed to fully comprehend what he was saying. *There are limits to everything. Yes, understand what we can, and warn those we can warn. But to alter the path of age old prophesies foretold in the Bible? That is another matter altogether,* she thought.

Tina walked onto the patio and stood watching Mark serve a customer who was sitting at a distant table. Mark's profile struck her as Greek. He was so handsome. They had been seeing each other for weeks without Tommy ever suspecting a thing. Mark turned toward Tina and smiled. "Good morning!" he said. Mark could tell that Tina was in another somber mood. She was a pessimistic person—not one he would ever consider spending his life with—but for now he felt like there were some advantages to placating her and leading her on.

"How are you this morning?" he asked.

"Fine, I guess," said Tina, "but my brother is driving me crazy!"

"How so?" Mark asked as he stepped back behind the counter.

"They are still working on those chips. They are looking at them and—"

Mark interrupted, "What chips?"

"You know!" said Tina, "One of those ID tags that everyone is having implanted. I told you about this already."

Mark wiped his forehead. He could remember how easy it was to have his chip implanted. "Oh, those chips! What are they doing with them?" he asked.

"That's what I'm trying to tell you," said Tina. Mark poured her a cup of coffee and leaned back to listen. "They think that the chips are the *Mark of the Beast* as foretold by the Bible. They are studying them to see how they work so they can warn the world not to take them."

"What do you think?" Mark asked.

"I think they are chips, and if you don't take one, then you don't eat."

Mark smiled. "So then you have yours already?"

"No!" blurted Tina. "Tommy won't let me get one. They are sending messages around the world warning people against the implantation of these tags."

Mark looked down at the half folded newspaper below the counter. The headlines—which he had already read earlier in the day—were titled *"Good Citizen Policy."* Mark could still remember the article. It was an international press release from Simon Koch. In summary, the article stated that not everyone has seen the importance of taking the ID tags as requested and some have even gone to the extreme of damaging or destroying equipment located in various places. Simon requested that, as a good citizen, each person should report all people known to be avoiding the ID tag insertion and any person engaging in criminal activities to hamper the insertion effort. Simon offered a reward for being a good citizen. Mark could use that money to pay off his student loans and help subsidize his income until he finished school. *I knew that Tina would work to my advantage sooner or later,* he told himself with a grin.

Of course, the international government of Carlo Ventini could and would track every person who did not comply with his or her ID tag requirement, but that was not the point Simon was trying to make. He wanted to pit those who had taken the tags against those who had not— a kind of international peer pressure.

******

The first signs of the plague hit England on a Sunday morning. By noon every hospital in London and the surrounding area was full of people young and old, coughing and choking on their own blood. By Tuesday over a million people were dead.

Simon and Carlo decided not to use very much of the virus. It was completely fatal without the antidote, which only they possessed. They decided instead to plant small amounts of the dreaded chemicals in various strategic locations where they had received the least amount of compliance for their ID tag implantation.

The plague was inserted into Western Europe, the east and west coasts of America, East Germany, Russia, China, and Australia, and in many other densely populated smaller countries and islands. It was Carlo's plan to step forward with an inoculation in the nick of time to save the world once again. But what neither he nor Simon fully understood was how quickly this deadly virus would spread.

******

Dr. Bruno Shire was the first among Peter's team to see a small outbreak of the virus firsthand. He was in Rome for the day picking up supplies when he watched a young man collapse before his own eyes.

The man coughed and choked until his mouth ran red with blood. Bruno had heard of the outbreak in England and America. He desperately wanted to get his hands on a sample of the disease so it could be studied in his lab. Bruno bent over the young man, and with the edge of his handkerchief he dabbed the boy's mouth and then placed the handkerchief into a plastic bag.

Bruno raced back to the hideout as quickly as he could. As soon as he arrived he called Peter and the rest of the medical staff into the lab. "What is it?" Peter asked. He could tell that Bruno was worked up about something.

"I think I have a sample of the virus," he said as he held up the plastic bag. Many of the lab workers stepped back. They had already heard how deadly this plague was.

"Well, let's get to it then," said Peter. "If you don't have a reason to be in the lab right now, clear out. The fewer we expose the better."

"The way I see it," said Bruno, "the virus kills its victims in 48 hours tops, which means that I am probably exposed and will probably die tomorrow evening."

Peter stared the old man down.

"Don't worry, Peter. If we find an antidote within 24 hours, I will be okay."

"How do you know 24 hours will be enough time? What if you don't respond after given an antidote? What if it is too late?"

"Then it will be too late, but at least we will have a cure to use on others." Bruno smiled at Peter. "Now let's get dressed in our decontamination suits and get to work!"

In fact, even as they were speaking Bruno could already feel a change in his own chest. Something had taken up residence there, and it was only a matter of time before it would kill its host unless they could find a cure.

Suited up and in the lab ready to go, Bruno pulled the bloodied handkerchief from the plastic bag. Just the sight of it frightened Peter and the other two lab technicians that were in the room.

"First thing we need to do is get this under the microscope," said

Peter.

"No!" said Bruno. "The first thing we need to do is to pray for guidance."

Peter nodded gently, and all four workers held hands and prayed to the Lord for guidance and protection.

Now six hours had gone by with every worker in the lab intensely focused on his or her task and by now the virus had been run through every piece of lab equipment. They understood what it was completely, but they were not sure how it worked—not yet.

Bruno coughed lightly. This had been going on for the last hour or so. Peter knew the old doctor was infected. Peter also knew Bruno would die if they could not understand how this virus worked and soon. In fact, Peter suspected that Bruno had probably infected all of them. *The virus must be airborne,* he thought. He was beginning to feel a change in his own chest.

"Okay," Bruno said, "let's talk this through. We know it has RNA, and we know the glycoprotein of the outer shell. Its morphology appears crystalline in structure, yet it attaches itself like a fungus or bacteria."

One of the lab technicians spoke up. "It seems to replicate by pulling out the salts from its victims. It utilizes this salt as a method of self delivery."

"In other words?" asked Peter.

"In other words," said the technician, "it acts very much like chemotherapy. Let me explain. When a doctor wants to treat a site where there is known cancer, he has to find a carrier to deliver the poisons to that specific location. If he doesn't, then he will administer toxic chemicals to the healthy good cells of the body and the chemo will kill them instead of the cancer cells that he is trying to eliminate."

Peter nodded. He understood this well enough from medical school, although he had never studied oncology beyond that.

"This virus is riding the salts in our body until it gets to a location that is highly capillary such as the lungs. The humidity and heat available in the lungs, combined with the significant amount of oxygenated blood, provides a perfect environment for these chemicals to divide and replicate."

"How does this virus kill the host?" Peter asked.

"Good question!" said the technician. "I think these chemicals act as super desiccators, so to speak. In other words," the technician mused as he read Peter's expression of confusion, "these chemicals are so absent of any H_2O that they quickly supersaturate in the presence of moisture, and like we all learned in basic chemistry, liquids such as water will migrate from an area of high concentration to an area of low concentration until they achieve equilibrium. These chemicals are so dense and so dry that they pull out all the moisture from the lungs, actually bursting the individual cells, collapsing their membranes, and causing them to bleed out, filling the lungs with blood and body fluids—in effect, drowning the victim."

Peter was impressed. It was one thing to be a doctor and to know how to diagnose and fix mechanical problems with the human body, but it was something altogether different to understand the chemistry and physics behind God's creation. "Can they be stopped?" Peter asked.

"Yes!" said a young, female technician from the other side of the lab. She stood holding a report fresh off the printer that was attached to a piece of equipment. All three men walked towards her. Bruno coughed heavily as he crossed the floor. "I have subjected these chemicals to the presence of the following list of elements and compounds, and in each case this virus was completely unaffected."

A look of disappointment covered each man's face.

"Except for one!" the young lady smiled. "I remembered something as I was running these tests—something I learned in graduate school. It seems that about 20 years ago the Russian government was experimenting with a super-dehydration technique, supposedly to develop a process of preserving food that would last eons.

My professor told us that he was part of a group of scientists sent over to Russia by the United States as part of a special fact-finding team investigating the development of biological agents. They found nothing, of course, because the Russians had plenty of warning. However, my professor said what struck him as unusual was the proximity of their super-dehydration equipment to their animal laboratory."

Bruno, now becoming weaker by the minute, listened attentively, hoping they were coming close to an answer that would save him and the millions of others infected by the aggressive virus.

"My professor also said that he had run into a Russian scientist who he had worked with once on a joint venture—something top secret having to do with space and extended sleep or something like that. Anyway, this Russian scientist seemed to be under both moral and religious conviction due to what he was working on. He said that a couple of his friends had recently died experimenting with a small set of crystalline chemicals and super dehydration. To make a long story short, I was told that if you take the right chemicals and virtually any ordinary virus and dehydrate them together—I mean really dehydrate them until there are absolutely no water molecules in them at all—they will form a new compound. This compound has no enemies and only a single objective—that is, to replicate—and for that they need a specific environment."

"Like our lungs," said Bruno as he coughed severely. Peter knew he could not go on much longer.

"Sit down, Bruno, and rest," said Peter.

"If we don't find an answer soon, I will have plenty of time to rest."

"What do you have there?" the other technician asked as he pointed to the paper in her hands.

"It is not the nature of any single chemical to just simply replicate. This requires something with a will to survive," said the young woman.

"Such as?" asked Peter.

"A virus like the flu or a simple cold virus," said the young lady. "I suspected that they collapsed one or two specific crystalline chemicals around a simple yet strong virus, encapsulating the virus in a crystal chamber or crypt, so to speak. I thought if I could somehow permeate the crystal lattice, then I could kill the virus inside, preventing the chemicals from replicating."

"What did you find out?" Bruno inquired.

"It looks like a simple acetone works, but it would be deadly for humans because of the quantity of acetone necessary to kill these fast-replicating chemicals," said the female technician.

"Well, what do we do then?" Peter asked out of frustration.

"We don't need to actually dissolve the crystals. We need only to place gaps in them, and then we can deliver another biological agent like a vaccine that will kill the virus, and then we can stop the replication before it fully dehydrates the lung," the technician said hopefully.

******

Twelve more hours went by as they desperately tried various combinations of solvents and various vaccines. It was looking hopeless. Every time they found a solvent to break up the chemicals, it would also destroy the antigen. Peter turned just in time to see Bruno hanging from the corner of a table. He was about to collapse entirely. Peter ran to him, catching him before he hit the floor. "We need to get you out of here," said Peter as he, too, began to cough.

"No!" said Bruno. "I will infect everyone. Leave me here, and if I die, bury me in this suit."

Peter moved Bruno up against the wall and went back to work at a feverish pace. "We need an answer now. God help us!" Peter whispered.

Naphthalene, a whisper resounded in Peter's mind. "Naphthalene," Peter said aloud.

"What?" the young lady asked. She, too, was feeling ill and would not be able to continue much longer.

"I don't know," said Peter. "Naphthalene, I guess!"

Both technicians looked at each other and smiled.

"What is naphthalene?" Peter asked.

"Mothballs!" the young girl grinned.

The male technician explained to Peter that naphthalene, also known as mothballs, is often used to increase octane. "They are used in the distillation process of making gasoline, and they do an excellent job of cracking one compound into more refined compounds," he explained.

"Can it be that simple?" the woman asked.

It took 45 minutes to create a mixture of mothballs and antigen. Each time they tried they would destroy the antigen until they finally dropped it in favor of a simple sulfur drug. By this time Bruno was completely unconscious yet coughing uncontrollably.

Blood began to spew onto Bruno's facemask as he continued to cough terribly. "We can't wait for the results!" said Peter urgently. "We need to try this on Bruno or he will die!"

"How much would you say he weighs?" the female technician asked.

"About 180, I'd say," said Peter. The other technician nodded in agreement.

The young lady filled a syringe with 25 milliliters of the hopeful antidote and handed it to Peter. "It may kill him," she said softly. Peter nodded. He understood that the responsibility was his alone. He cut Bruno's suit at the elbow. "This better work or we are all dead," said the male technician with a cough. Peter injected the medicine directly into Bruno's vein.

An hour later Bruno was sitting up with his mask off taking a slow drink of water. He was horribly dehydrated, and it would be weeks before he was strong again, but the antidote worked. Now the task would be to mass-produce it and get it to the world without getting caught.

"Thank you, Lord!" Peter whispered as he sat back and closed his tired eyes.

******

Hector Roundtree gazed out of his observatory window. He had been alone forever it seemed, especially since his mother and sister disappeared. He had no life other than the Goldstone facility. He rarely went home except for a change of clothing. He slept and ate right in his office, and over the last couple of years it was unlikely Hector had more than a dozen conversations with any person. He ignored all news and newspapers, and he decided a year ago not to take the ID tag as required. He ate for free at this facility, and he had a huge supply of gasoline at home for his automobile, so what was the point as far as he was concerned?

Tonight Hector stared up to the stars and spoke softly, "Mom, I miss you very much. You too, Sis." About this time a loud blare could be heard from within his office. Over the last year it seemed that the heavens were in a constant uproar. Hector assumed this would be another one of those alerts—a near comet or small asteroid passing earth's orbit.

Hector sat down and turned his guidance system on high gain, and at once he was made speechless by what he saw. He typed in a couple of commands and then went to another screen for a closer look. Hector took control of the Hubble scope and redirected its lenses to a precise set of coordinates. "How can this be?"

Hector ran to a large filing cabinet. "Where is it?" he yelled to himself. He pulled out a file dated July. On it was written a code: ED14 S-class. Hector plugged in the report data. *This asteroid is not supposed to be there,* he thought. *It is supposed to be in the Kuiper belt.* Maybe it was a different one. But after the computer analyzed the data on ED14, it confirmed this was without a doubt the same asteroid. "How did you get here?" he said aloud.

Hector spent the night studying over his calculations, and they continued to bear out the same results each time. Eventually Hector dropped his pencil and calculator. "God, help us!" he said.

He took one more set of measurements. *If this thing is fully metallic, then it will come in just over six miles wide,* he thought, *but perhaps it is not a full metallic asteroid, in which case...*

"In which case," said Hector aloud, "we still die!"

Hector asked the computer some basic questions: When will it hit? Where? The answer came back quickly: in 60 days at 2:18 a.m.—location 15 minutes north of Lebanon, Kansas. Hector flicked the computer switch off. He had a protocol for this type of disaster, but what was the point? He was sure that other sites like the Jet Propulsion Lab in California would have seen it by now anyway. Yet it turns out that none of the other working sites were on. It would be at least another month and a half before ED14's new course was discovered. It would be even longer than that before the general population understood that a star was falling from the sky right on top of them.

******

The sun was just beginning to set over the Pacific Ocean. It was one of the few remaining peaceful sights left on earth. Calvin Fraser for many months now had gone up and down the coastline preaching to whoever would listen. This evening he and Cory Parker stood inland at the center of the Stanford University campus right next to the statue of Saint Augustine. The trees were red and yellow with the colors of late fall. This school meant a lot to Calvin. It had been his dream as a young man to attend there. Eventually through a terrific amount of hard work he did fulfill his dream, although he never considered that it would end up this way.

From the first day that Calvin and Cory had arrived in Palo Alto they began to preach a message of salvation. More often than not they were mocked and made fun of by each passing crowd, yet they were not deterred. Perseverance sustained both men. That and a deep friendship kept them moving from town to town. Calvin took Cory to his home and, as suspected, it was abandoned. He had not heard a word or received a letter from his parents since the day of the Rapture, and although he missed them both, he rejoiced in the fact that they were in Heaven with Jesus.

The one thing that Calvin and Cory lacked was money. The $500 they each received when they left the prison had lasted them for a couple of months, but now they were destitute. Even now as Calvin spoke, his stomach ached from the hunger he felt.

This particular night the crowds were unusually ugly and the insults came from every direction. "Can't you read the signs of the times?" Calvin asked. "Don't you realize that the end is coming soon? The Antichrist is already here, and he is Carlo Ventini!"

Shouts rang out. "You are the Antichrist and you are the evil one! Mr. Ventini has saved the world."

"No!" said Calvin. "Ventini has deceived the whole world. Can't you see that his ID tags are the mark of the beast? Do not take one or you will be damned to Hell for eternity."

At this the crowd pressed forward with a roar. "You are not a good citizen!" they shouted.

"There is a reward for turning in creeps like you," said one young coed.

"Hey! That's right!" said another. "Let's get this guy and collect the reward."

A handful of jocks stepped forward to grab Calvin, but before they could get a good hold on him Cory Parker—all 6' 8" of him—interceded on Calvin's behalf. He stood between the college students and Calvin.

"Hey, Mister, we are not afraid of you," said one of the boys as he backed up a foot or so. About this time Calvin could hear sirens in the background, and he knew it was time to leave. *Do not cast your pearls before swine,* he thought. Cory glared at the young men as he helped Calvin down from the table where he stood. The students had lost their courage all of a sudden. There wasn't one of them willing to challenge Cory. Apparently they did have at least some wisdom.

Calvin and Cory ran through the campus and ended up on the edge of El Camino Real and Page Mill Road. "Well, where to now?" Cory asked.

Calvin didn't know. He didn't even want to think about it. All he really wanted right now was a warm bed and some hot food. "Lord, help us!" Calvin cried.

Cory overheard this. He understood his friend was worn out and needed rest, but where could they go? For months they had slept under bridges and in libraries when they could. There were no shelters or free food facilities anymore. It was hard enough for the well-to-do to stay fed, and it was impossible for the homeless.

The sun was gone now as Calvin and Cory wandered down the block. Just a few streets over they encountered a very old man who appeared to be a drunkard. "Got a dollar?" the man asked in a crackly voice. Cory reached into his pocket and came out with 50 cents.

"All we have is a little change," said Cory softly.

"Are you willing to give it to me?" the old man asked. Cory noticed brightness in the man's eyes and sharpness in his voice. *Peculiar for a drunkard,* he thought.

Cory looked at Calvin who nodded lightly. "May as well," said Cory. "It won't buy us anything."

As Cory stepped towards the man, the old man began to glow. He actually began to grow and alter his appearance until he was nearly seven feet tall with a massive set of outstretched wings as white as snow.

Cory covered his eyes to protect them from the bright light. Both Cory and Calvin were frightened by the angel and frozen where they stood. "Fear not! I am here to help you. The Lord is pleased by your faithful service, but now is the time for you to move on."

"Move to where?" Calvin asked, but before he could get an answer to the question, he found himself with Cory standing on a hill overlooking a brightly lit city. Cory turned and looked to the angel. "Where are we?" he asked.

"Las Vegas," said the angel.

"Las Vegas!" Calvin exclaimed. "What for?"

"There is work here for the both of you. Together you will find food and shelter for a season. By this time next week, all paper currency will be outlawed and you will never again be able to buy any food without the mark of the beast. You will be safe here for a while. Preach the message of God to these people. Some will listen. Time is very short! Now go down there and place your two quarters in any slot machine. Pull the handle. God will provide!"

Suddenly the hillside was pitch black; the only light came from down in the valley below. "Okay then!" said Cory. "I guess we go down there and find a little work and maybe some food." The food part sounded good to Calvin. His stomach rumbled for lack of nourishment.

Both men walked down the hill and into the first casino they came to. The suits both men were wearing did not look so new anymore, and this drew attention to Cory and Calvin quickly. But before any of the hotel security could approach, Cory dumped his 50 cents into a tall slot machine just in front of him. With one pull of the lever, he stood back and watched the wheels turning. Wild cherry, wild cherry, wild cherry! Suddenly a loud alarm went off and lights began to flash. Soon the sound of coins falling on the floor could be heard throughout the casino. Management and casino security approached Calvin and Cory as they stood watching the silver coins pile up on the ground.

By the time the slot machine emptied out Cory had won over $1,500. But better than that the casino manager asked both men if they would be interested in working for the casino. Room and board would be provided at a great discount. Naturally both men accepted the offer.

******

Scott stared at the Wailing Wall. It was an impressive sight to him. *Just imagine,* he thought to himself. *This is part of the original wall that protected Israel, rebuilt by Nehemiah thousands of years ago.*

"Come on, Scott. We'll be late if we don't hurry!" said Ruth. Curfew came at 10:00 p.m. in Jerusalem and all surrounding areas, and anyone not authorized who was caught outside after this time would be arrested.

Back at the apartment Joseph sat silently staring out of the large plate-glass window. Life had changed and become so bizarre over the last few years that it was all just a blur to him now. He thought back to the day he met Zach, and again to the day of the big earthquake. It all would have been so much easier if he had only believed and followed after Jesus.

He also wondered about his big brother, Peter. Was he alive? Where is he? Would he ever see him again? All these thoughts ran through his mind. Yvette slid in next to Joseph and picked up his hand. "Are you okay?" she asked softly. Joseph wiped the tears away with the back of his hand and turned to her and smiled weakly.

"Is anyone really okay?" said Joseph out of frustration. "Millions have died from this plague and from starvation. The world is a total wreck, and very soon it will get much worse."

"Well, maybe we can make it a little better," said Yvette.

"How can we make this any better?" Joseph asked.

Yvette smiled brightly and kissed Joseph tenderly. "Maybe we could get married and then—" At that moment there was a knock at the door. Joseph jumped up and instantly there was a look of fear in Yvette's eyes.

They had narrowly escaped Paul Laruso back in Chicago. They had even managed to sneak off in Scott's company jet and fly halfway around the world to Israel, but they knew it was only a matter of time before Simon's men found them again. Joseph was a thorn in Simon's side, and he would not quit until Joseph paid for the information he had printed in *Deacon's Horn.*

The knob turned slowly. There was nowhere to run, nowhere to hide. The apartment was one room, and they were in it. Suddenly Scott walked in with Ruth not two feet behind him. Joseph blew a sigh of relief and Yvette began to cry from fear. It was all just too much for her. For many months now she had been running from Carlo's grip with the others. First in Chicago and now since May she had been locked up here in Jerusalem. Every day she feared the inevitable—getting caught. As it was she and the rest of her small party were in this country pretending to be a news crew from the United States, here to report on any outbreaks of the plague. They had sent their jet back to the United States and were hoping that its flight plan would not be tracked back to Israel which, of course, it had been.

Paul Laruso has been given one last chance to find Joseph or to pay the ultimate cost for his failure. The pressure was also on Pope Peter John. Simon had warned him that if he failed to find Joseph, Carlo would have to take some kind of action against the Church.

"You have disappointed me for the last time!" said Peter John as Paul walked into his office two days after Joseph had escaped his grasp. Paul knew he would die if he was not successful next time.

******

Back in Chicago Paul retraced Joseph's steps. He had entered the country originally with Scott Turner and Ruth Jefferson. He had traveled with Yvette Lewis and all four of them had left Italy on Scott's company jet. It seemed reasonable to Paul that wherever they had gone, they had use of the company jet. After a few calls and a bit of retracing the jet's path, Paul figured out that for some reason Joseph must have gone to Israel. *If he is there, I'll find him,* Paul thought.

******

Paul had been in Israel in the city of Jerusalem for months. The city was very small but densely populated. He had to systematically eliminate each hotel and apartment complex. He started with the more rural hotels on a hunch that Joseph would be too bright to stay in downtown Jerusalem. After months without a single lead, Paul decided it was time to change some of his tactics. He had issued a statement along with a small picture of Joseph that he gave to the local media. The statement read: "Joseph Bastoni, the author of *Deacon's Horn*, a slanderous religious newspaper, is believed to be in Israel, possibly in Jerusalem itself. A reward is offered to the person who can provide sufficient information leading to the whereabouts and arrest of Bastoni. He is a criminal and a liar. He has attempted to destroy Carlo Ventini's credibility as our world leader." Additionally Paul inserted his cell phone number. He would let the local community help him find Joseph.

Finally he decided it was time to move to Jerusalem. Apparently Joseph was stupid enough after all to go straight into the big city instead of hiding out in one of the smaller suburbs. *He fooled you, didn't he?* Paul thought to himself in anger.

Ruth handed Joseph a copy of a local newspaper. "I saw this on the way back. I can't read Hebrew, but I recognize the picture."

Joseph studied the newspaper. His picture was plastered right in the center along with the article. "What does it mean?" Yvette asked. Joseph gazed at her beautiful face. He loved her so much. *If only times were different,* he thought to himself.

"It means we have to leave!" said Scott.

"No, it means I have to leave," said Joseph.

The room was quiet for a few seconds. "It is for the best. I can move easier if it is just me. I can blend in, but all of us together look too obvious." What Joseph said made good sense, but nobody wanted to listen to it.

"We'll stay together," said Ruth, "and just trust in the Lord to provide."

Scott nodded in agreement, although in his heart he, too, felt Joseph should try to sneak away quietly before they all got caught. Joseph continued to peruse the paper. He was the only one among them that could read and speak Hebrew. It was his job to keep everyone informed of current events.

Joseph held his finger to a notice just beneath his own article. "We have more troubles," he said.

"What now?" Yvette asked.

"It says here that all currency and credit cards will be disallowed worldwide as of November 30 and all people will be expected to buy and sell using their personal ID tags."

"Which none of us have!" said Ruth.

So far they had survived on cash alone while they were in Jerusalem. Thanks to Scott's wisdom they had stopped at a local bank in Chicago and pulled out thousands of dollars to tide them over for a while, but now the money was all but gone.

"All we have left is credit cards," said Scott. "I have avoided using any because I didn't want anyone to trace us here, but soon we'll be out of food. And by the end of next week I will have to pay for another month here in this apartment. What will we do?"

"Okay," said Ruth, "we need a strategy and pronto!"

The four weary people studied their dilemma well into the night. It was obvious that they would have to move because Joseph had been seen too many times by the locals in the neighborhood shops. "We have no car and no money, and in a week we won't even be able to buy anything to eat. What are we going to do?" Yvette asked.

"Scott, your credit cards still work today," said Joseph.

"Yes, but they will trace them back here," said Scott.

"They already know we are here, so it doesn't matter. Let's buy a bunch of food and rent a car and drive away."

"Drive to where, Joseph?" Ruth inquired.

Joseph shook his head. He had no idea where to go. In fact, he had no idea why God had requested that he come to Israel in the first place. "You're right," he said. "Where would we go, and how long could we hide before they catch us?"

"Well, at least it is a good idea for us to use the cards to buy food. That much we can do," said Scott. "I think I can also find another apartment, and we can sneak you in at night."

"How will you pay the rent?" Yvette asked. She, too, was starting to see the big picture, and it was hopeless.

"I'll pull cash off my cards and then pay for the rent," said Scott.

"That will buy us one month anyway," said Joseph.

"Better than nothing!" said Scott.

Joseph nodded compliantly. "Why don't you and Ruth go see what you can find and buy something to eat too."

As soon as Scott and Ruth left, Joseph walked over to the large window and stared out at the early morning sky. The sun's rays were just beginning to connect the east to the west. "I have to leave," said Joseph somberly.

"I know," said Yvette as she walked over to Joseph.

"Scott and Ruth have risked their lives for me too long. They can hide out for another month without getting caught if they move from here. Soon it will all be over anyway," said Joseph as he dropped his head on Yvette's shoulder.

"Joseph," said Yvette, "I want us to get married today. I want to be your wife. I want to be one with you like any good wife would. Please say you will marry me."

"How can we get married? We have no license, and we can't show identification to even get one," he said. "Who would marry us anyway? Who would be seen worthy in God's sight to say the marriage vows?"

"You would, Joseph. I would. God knows we are husband and wife already. The formality and ceremony of marriage is man made. We just need to ask God to marry us and to honor our vows."

Joseph wasn't sure about this at all. Apparently he still had some religious tradition left in him, event though he knew Yvette was right. "What if God sees this as sin and adultery?"

Yvette walked away from Joseph long enough to pick up his Bible from the table. "Marry us, Joseph," said Yvette.

Joseph knew that there were no formal marriage vows in the Bible, no formal sayings that should be read at all weddings. The Bible described the commitment of a man and woman and the purity of the marriage and its bed. It says that a man and a woman will join and become one flesh and that no man should try to separate their covenant.

Yvette pulled the clip from her hair and let it fall onto her shoulders. "Okay, I'm ready!" she said.

Joseph had to laugh. Her enthusiasm and determination to marry him was unswerving. "Lord, if this is wrong, please let us know," said Joseph.

"It is not wrong," said Yvette. Then with a little smile she added, "Trust me!"

Joseph did trust her, and he did love her, but he wasn't entirely sure why they didn't just get married years ago when they first met. *So why now?* he wondered.

Yvette knew the reason. It was obvious to her that their time together was coming to an end. Life as they knew it was nearly over. She was determined to be his wife before it all fell apart.

Joseph held Yvette's hand while he placed the Bible in the palm of his other hand. "Okay then, are you ready?" he asked.

"Yes!" Yvette answered excitedly.

Joseph felt stupid and a little corny, but he went through with it all the same. "Lord, we commit ourselves to You and to each other. Lord, if You are willing, please allow us to be husband and wife for as long as we both shall live," which Joseph figured wasn't all that long.

Joseph and Yvette felt a rushing wind enter the room, and fear filled Yvette. *Maybe I was wrong,* she thought suddenly.

"I will pour out My blessing onto this covenant for as long as you both shall live and into eternity. Now you must leave tonight and go to Bethlehem. There you will meet whom I shall bring you."

Yvette clutched Joseph's strong hand tightly. "Bethlehem? How will I get there?" he said.

"How will we get there?" said Yvette.

"A way shall be made known to you very soon. Be ready tonight," said the Lord.

The wind stilled in the room and the presence of God was gone. Joseph turned towards Yvette. The look in her beautiful green eyes told him that she was totally committed to her man. "That's right! How will we get there, Wife?"

Joseph closed his arms around Yvette and kissed her passionately. Finally after so many years Yvette and Joseph would be able to consummate their relationship the way God had designed and intended for marriages.

******

From two blocks over an elderly woman sat behind her coffee counter and read the paper from the night before. Business in her little shop had been lousy for the last year, and very soon she was going to have to close down her establishment. For 20 years she had served coffee to the locals in the community, but now this was a luxury that the citizens just could not afford. On the front page the woman spotted the picture of Joseph, and she studied it closely. *I know this man,* she thought, *he was in here just two days ago.* The woman continued to read the article. "A reward!" she said aloud.

******

Paul Laruso was up early driving through the city of Jerusalem. There were so many small apartments and hotels there—how was he ever going to find Bastoni? Suddenly Paul's cellular phone began to ring, startling him. Paul picked up the phone and held his breath. He was certain it would be Peter John. Time was running short for Paul Laruso.

"Hello?" said Paul. To his surprise, it was the voice of an old Jewish woman. Her English was not very good, but then neither was Paul's.

Fifteen minutes later Paul walked into the coffee shop and introduced himself. The woman explained that she had seen Joseph with a young woman many times and as recently as two days before. Paul showed the lady a picture of Yvette. "Is this the woman?" he asked. The old lady studied the picture closely. Apparently her eyesight was not very good.

This did not overwhelm Paul with confidence.

"Yes, that is her. I see her two days ago," said the woman as she poured Paul a cup of hot coffee. "I get reward now, yes?"

"No," said Paul, "not yet. Let me check this out first, and if it turns out to be true, then you will get your reward."

The woman was obviously dissatisfied with Paul's answer. As he turned to leave she demanded that he pay for his coffee which he had neither asked for or drank. Paul stuck his right hand in front of the woman's scanner and then turned and walked out.

Laruso drove around the neighborhood surveying the apartments. There were no hotels any closer than a mile away, so Paul felt certain that Joseph was nearby. *Which apartment?* he wondered. Logic dictated that Joseph's apartment was probably no more than a block or two from the coffee shop, so Paul decided he would continually circle this area until something clued him in.

******

It was early evening when Scott and Ruth knocked on the door. Yvette answered it carelessly without even asking who was there. She was in such a pleasant mood that she seemed to be unaware of the danger around them. Joseph was napping on the sofa when Scott walked in with an armload of groceries. Finding food was not impossible yet, but being able to afford it was another matter. The two shoppers had managed at great cost to buy canned goods and even a little dried meat, but there would be no fresh vegetables or fruits for any of them and certainly no dairy products. The noise from the grocery bags startled Joseph, causing him to sit upright. "Hungry?" Scott asked.

In fact, Joseph was starving. Next Ruth walked in with another armful of food. "This ought to hold us for a little while," said Ruth. "By the way, there are a few more bags in the car."

"What car?" Joseph asked.

"We rented a car," said Scott. "We couldn't be expected to hunt for an apartment far away from this place and shop for a month's groceries all on foot now, could we?"

"Good point!" said Joseph. "I'll get the rest of the food for you."

"Let me help," said Yvette.

About this time Paul Laruso was just turning the corner leaving this particular block when through his rearview mirror he caught sight of Joseph and Yvette as Joseph handed her a small bag of supplies. Paul hit the accelerator hard. He would circle the block and finally capture these two renegades. The Pope would be especially pleased if he caught both of them. Ruth stood and looked out of the large window. She watched Yvette and Joseph working together as they gathered all the groceries. "They sure love each other," she said aloud.

Scott walked over to Ruth and peered out of the window. "Yes, they do!" he said mildly. Scott watched Joseph close the car door and follow Yvette up the stairs. He was about to walk back to the food on the kitchen counter when he observed a small white car pulling in behind his rental car. "I wonder who that is?" said Scott.

Yvette came in laughing with Joseph close behind. "I think we have company," said Scott. Joseph ran to the window in time to catch a glimpse of Paul as he walked under the stairwell.

"I think it's him!"

"Who?" asked a worried Ruth.

"The man that followed you to Scott's house back in Chicago."

"How can he be here?" said Yvette.

"He's tracked us down," said Joseph as he walked towards the kitchen.

Joseph set the groceries down, and turning to his right, he spotted a large, cast iron skillet. It was the only potential weapon in the room. Joseph moved quickly toward the door, and as he did the knob began to turn.

Joseph waved the two women away, and they backed up into the kitchen to hide. The door flung open suddenly and Paul Laruso stepped in with his gun fully extended. Joseph aimed the skillet and clobbered Paul's gun hand, obviously shattering the small bones. The gun dropped to the floor, and both Joseph and a surprised, greatly angered Paul stared at the revolver. Paul started to dive for the gun, but before he could reach it Joseph walloped him hard on top of his head, knocking him out.

Scott stepped in and pushed against Paul's body with his foot. "He's out cold," said Scott. Joseph's hands shook nervously as he dropped the skillet with a heavy thud. Scott bent down and picked up the gun. He turned towards Ruth and Yvette who stood there amazed at what had just happened. "What do we do now?" Scott asked.

"We go to Bethlehem," said Joseph.

"Bethlehem! Why Bethlehem?" Scott asked.

"The Lord paid us a visit right after we got married!" said Yvette.

Scott and Ruth both looked at Yvette. "You got married?" said Ruth.

"God visited you?" said Scott.

"Well, you guys had a busy day!" Ruth beamed.

Paul Laruso began to stir. "I think he is waking up," said Scott. "We'd better tie him up."

Joseph ripped one of the sheets from the mattress into strips and bound Paul tightly around the wrists and feet. "Let's gag him too," said Scott. Joseph nodded and tied a strip of cloth around Paul's mouth. Paul opened his eyes slightly—just enough to see Joseph and Scott standing over him.

"What do we do with him now?" Ruth inquired.

"Nothing!" said Joseph. "We leave him here, take our food, and go to Bethlehem."

This was an error in judgment on Joseph's part. Paul heard every word they said. He knew where they were going next, and as soon as he freed himself from this particular mess, he would track Joseph down and kill him.

Chapter 21: Inquisition and Persecution

Day 1215, November: Carlo stared at the morning headlines as rage filled his evil face. Simon sat quietly by. He had already seen the news. He knew that Carlo was going to hit the roof over this one. The headlines read that the plague—although terrible and deadly—had been contained and many lives were being saved on a daily basis by a mysterious antidote that was being shipped to locations around the world. "It is confirmed that these shipments are originating from Italy, but it is not believe that this antidote is coming from Mr. Carlo Ventini or Simon Koch. It is thought that some underground scientific community is responsible for this life-saving medicine. Whoever you are, we, the world, are eternally grateful."

Carlo slammed the paper down. "Who is doing this?" he shouted.

Simon had a large file in his hand. He was prepared to give Carlo a report that he was sure would send Carlo into a massive fit of rage. "We have various groups that could be responsible for this," Simon replied as he opened his file. "There are many underground Christian activities going on. The scientists listed in the paper are the most likely source of the antidote. We have a lead as to how this underground network operates. We think its origins come from somewhere in Los Angeles. We'll know more in a few days. There are also many small organizations around the world distributing Bibles and building churches. We even have numerous evangelists preaching against—" Simon paused.

Carlo glared at Simon. "Preaching against what?"

Simon rephrased his comment: "They are preaching salvation messages from the Bible."

Carlo stood. "Call Peter John and get him out here today! It is time to
turn up the heat on these Christian radicals," Carlo said as he walked
away angrily.

******

Three hours later Peter John and Simon stood before Carlo as he sat
back staring out of his window at the small, white-capped waves coming
off the Adriatic Sea. "I have made a decision. It is time to condemn
Christianity and outlaw it altogether."

The Pope stood speechless. What would he do for a living? It was his
job to be the government for his people—the right hand of God.

"We will do this in phases. First we will destroy many of our Agripods."

"What?" Simon asked. "We can't do that!"

Carlo raised his bony hand. "We will destroy them and blame it on
radical Christians. Furthermore, we will blame this plague on the scientists. We will say they started it and then developed an antidote to make
themselves look good."

Simon was beginning to see the big picture. He liked it very much.
Yet the Pope was still very worried about his personal future. "After the
celebration and dedication of the temple in Jerusalem, I will declare myself as the lord of this planet, and then you will serve as my religious
leader." Upon hearing this Peter John smiled brightly. This was an even
better job than the one he already had.

Within 48 hours the television and newspapers were full of fabri-
cated monstrosities portraying Christians as the evil destroyers of the
world. Simon's statements were bold lies. "These so-called Christians are
nothing more than a bunch of terrorists," said Simon in a public address
broadcast around the globe.

Simon stood outside a burned out Agripod facility in Spain. "This is
one of seven facilities that have been destroyed in the last two days," he
said. "If we, the people of the world, do not stop these Christians from

destroying all of our good work, then we will starve to death."

Additionally Simon went on to explain that he and Carlo had solid evidence that an underground group of scientists was responsible for the most recent plague that had already killed millions. "It is believed," said Simon, "that these scientists developed this deadly disease and then the antidote so they could pretend to help the world, but we are not falling for these lies. We know they are responsible for the deaths of millions of innocent people."

"Furthermore, it is believed that this scientist network originated in the United States, but there may be underground groups in nearly every country. Presently we are trying to find the source of the virus and its creators. It is our opinion that it has originated somewhere in Italy."

Within a few days after Simon's news broadcast the word was out and people from all around the globe were uniting for a single purpose— to find and eliminate Christians and scientists alike. Churches were burned to the ground, sometimes with a congregation still inside. It seemed that even the local governments were supporting nearly every tactic necessary to destroy any semblance of Christianity.

Carlo had three more Agripods destroyed, and once again he blamed this destruction on the radical Jesus followers. Simon issued a statement that food supplies would be reduced by nearly 25 percent as a result of this terrorism—more fuel for the fire.

With a smile Simon read the latest report to Carlo as Peter John stood by. "Nearly every mission in Africa has been destroyed. There is a campaign to burn churches in Australia and in Europe. The Chinese government has stepped up its effort to find and eliminate all Christian activities."

"What about the United States?" Carlo asked.

"They are much slower to react," said Simon, "but we are beginning to see some activity. Our good citizen policy is starting to pay off. Many Christians, scientists, and those who have refused our ID tags are being turned in to their local governments routinely by our good citizens." Simon laughed out loud at his own comments. "They are being treated as criminals and prisons are starting to fill up again."

Carlo almost smiled. "What about the scientists who are sending out this antidote? Have you found them yet?"

"Not yet," said Simon, "but we have narrowed in on their location, and we'll have them in a day or two." Simon knew this was a sore subject for Carlo. He wanted to be the one to give the world an antidote, and he wanted to be the one the world viewed as its savior yet once again.

******

Izuho, Chang, and Lyn Lee had been in prison for over a year and all were in terrible shape. None of them had enough strength to walk more than 10 feet. They were subsisting on rice and water with an occasional piece of meat that was probably snake or some other reptile. They had not received any fruits or vegetables at all during their time of incarceration, and as a result they all had scurvy and other terribly painful, bloody bowel problems. Also, they had not seen the light of day in over a year.

Yet regardless of these present conditions, they continued to sing praise songs, much to the dismay of the security guards. Each one of them continued to pray for strength, and they continued to witness to whoever would come around.

The personal relationships between Chang, Izuho, and Lyn Lee had grown strong. They loved each other greatly. Today as the food was brought in, Chang tried to give a portion of his much needed rice to Lyn Lee. She was becoming very ill, and soon she would die without more food. An elderly security guard saw this act of kindness and was completely amazed.

The next day the same security guard came in while all three prisoners were singing to the Lord. Instantly they all quieted down. They had learned the painful lessons about singing in front of the guards. The old guard handed each of them a bowl of rice and then stood back. Again Chang tried to give some of this rice to Lyn Lee, as did Izuho. The old man's eyes began to fill with tears. These acts of kindness were more than he had ever seen in his 30 years of prison security.

The guard opened his coat and took out three large slices of bread and handed them to the prisoners who just stared at him in disbelief.

Next he dug into his pockets and pulled out three small pears, giving one to each person.

Finally he handed Chang a small, brown plastic bottle. Chang turned the bottle over and read the label: *Vitamin C 500 mg.* The bottle was full. At this Chang began to cry out in gratitude to the Lord and stood to hug the guard.

The guard, however, put up his hand for Chang to stay seated. Then he smiled, turned, and walked out of the cell, locking the door behind him as he went.

******

Dr. Bruno Shire was still not a well man, but he grew stronger every day. His primary function now was to distribute as much of the antidote as possible to the four corners of the globe. This was not an easy task. It was difficult to know whom he could or could not trust. He and the other doctors couldn't just simply step forward and announce a cure for the plague. They were all wanted men and women. Also, if they gave out the formula to the antidote, it was likely to end up in the wrong hands— hands that would deliberately prevent people from receiving it. The problem was one of trust, and every day this issue grew.

Presently Bruno was relying on his associates from the underground scientific community, the network that Tommy Glover and Dedrick Bishopf had developed. So far it had not been breached by any of Simon and Carlo's followers; at least it didn't appear as if it had. Bruno would use these contacts to distribute the antidote, but he made up his mind not to share the recipe with any of them in case of a break in security. *Oh sure, they will reverse engineer it eventually,* Bruno thought, *but until then we will make the world's supply of antidote right here.*

The job of mass-producing enough of the antidote for the billions of people was a horrific challenge. First of all it had to be made known that this antidote was not an inoculation. It only worked after an infection, and it would not prevent reoccurrence.

This meant that an ample supply would always be needed, or else the virus would return. There was no way of knowing how or if the virus could ever be eliminated. This was the lesson the Russians had learned 20 years earlier.

Peter ran shifts around the clock as they synthesized and packaged vial after vial of the medicine. He used a small workforce to drive far distances to post offices and Federal Express offices to ship out the medicine, but it would not be long before this pattern was fully understood and transportation stopped. So far, however, nobody seemed to care. Post office boxes were established in every country as a security measure. In this way, if a medical shipment was traced, it would not disclose the true location of each receiver. The problem with these shipments was that they had to go where there were known scientists from the underground who could distribute and administer the antidote, but unfortunately there were not contacts in every country.

This created a real dilemma for Peter. He knew people were dying, and he knew he could help, but if he stepped forward with an antidote in hand, he would be captured. They all would be captured, and maybe that was the thing to do, Peter considered. But once again, what would happen to the antidote if its secrets were revealed? The risk was too high. He would have to find other ways of getting the medicine into those countries.

It so happened that the very next day one of Peter's drivers didn't return on time. No one could be sure, but it was a safe bet that the young man had been captured. This worried everyone greatly. If the driver had been captured, then it would only be a matter of time before the bad guys found the warehouse and the lab full of born-again scientists.

In fact, the young man had been taken prisoner. Simon had sent the word to every post office in Italy: "Anyone shipping large packages should be detained until the package contents can be analyzed to ensure it is not antidote."

As soon as the postal worker saw the man step into his office with the three large boxes, he became suspicious. The deliveryman knew that something was wrong when the postal worker turned and picked up a phone. Perspiration began to emerge on the man's forehead. *Should I run?*

he wondered.

The postal worked turned and asked the man what was in the boxes. "Oh, just some chemicals, I guess. I don't really know. I just deliver the stuff," he answered. Now he really began to sweat. The postal worker took out a sharp knife and began to cut the tape on the box, and as he was doing this, the driver turned to run. He didn't get far, however, because right behind him stood two large men, both carrying side arms. The young driver was beaten and tortured for over an hour before he revealed the location of Peter's medical facility.

When a second driver was also reported missing a mere 10 minutes later, Peter threw up his hands. "It's over!" he said loudly. "We need to leave now!"

All the members of Peter's staff quickly shut down their facility. Peter went inside the lab to see Bruno. He was on the computer sending more delivery information through the underground scientist network. "We've been found out!" said Peter. Bruno stopped typing and looked up at Peter. He was proud of the young doctor. Peter had done so much to help the world, but now it was over.

"You did well, Peter," said Bruno.

Peter smiled weakly.

"Let's give them the recipe before we leave this place," said Bruno.

Peter nodded in agreement, and Bruno began to type on the keypad once again.

Suddenly there was the sound of gunfire.

"Oh, no!" said Peter. "They're here!"

"Go, Peter!" Bruno yelled. "Go now!"

"I can't leave you!" said Peter.

"Peter, I have to get this formula sent out or millions more will die. Besides, I am far too weak to run. Now go—leave me!"

As Peter turned and looked at the door, he could hear screams and more gunshots.

"Peter, you have to go! You've done all you can. God will need you again. Now run!" Bruno shouted as he desperately urged Peter to flee to safety.

Peter stepped up to Bruno with tears in his eyes and grabbed the old man's hand. "I'll never forget you."

Bruno nodded. "Peter, God will protect you. I feel you have more to do. Go through here and follow the trail down to the sea." Bruno pointed to a small recirculation vent about three feet off the floor. "When I was a child, my brothers and I used to slide down this, and out the back of the warehouse we would go."

Peter ripped the face of the vent off and turned to look at Bruno one last time. Without saying a word he slid down the shaft and disappeared.

Bruno replaced the vent cover, turned back to the terminal, and began to type rapidly as the sounds of gunfire echoed through the lab. Finally there was a loud crashing sound as two men kicked in the door to the laboratory. Bruno looked into the eyes of both men and then back to the terminal. They raised their guns to fire, but not before Bruno clicked the send key. The last thing Bruno heard was the sound of rapid gunfire.

Outside Peter crawled down a steep bank behind the warehouse. He, too, heard the gunfire coming from the lab, and he knew what it meant. Forty-five minutes later he was wandering around by the pier. *What do I do now?* he wondered. "Lord, help me!" Peter cried.

Go home, Peter! a voice in his mind whispered.

******

Simon was elated to share the good news with Carlo. The raid on the laboratory was a near success. The only disappointment for Simon was that there was still no sign of Joseph Bastoni's brother, Peter. Simon was sure capturing Peter would lead him to Joseph, and he really wanted to get his hands on the priest. He had made Simon look bad, and that just wasn't something Simon would tolerate now that he was the second most powerful man in the world.

Simon read the report to Carlo. "We have captured or killed all of the doctors and scientists that were a part of this antidote project. Additionally we have seen a great increase in the burning of churches and the persecution of Christians everywhere in the world," Simon sneered.

"It is not enough," said Carlo in a low and angry voice. Simon was confused. He thought that Carlo would be very pleased with all the efforts and results. "I want them all dead! I want all churches destroyed, and every Christian must take my mark or die." Simon listened carefully. It wasn't often that Carlo showed this much passion as he spoke. "And I want all Bibles outlawed and destroyed," he growled.

From over in the corner of the room, Peter John cringed when he heard Carlo say this. How was he to do his job if Carlo took away his Bible?

"How?" Simon asked. "How will we get people to burn their Bibles?"

"If they have to suffer long enough, they will burn them," said Carlo with an eerie smile.

Carlo instructed Simon to reduce shipments of food even further. He also instructed Simon to dispense more of the plague. Yes, there was an antidote out there, but it was not likely that very much of it would be available since the raid on Peter's laboratory stopped all production. All of this combined with more anti-Christian propaganda from Simon made being a Christian very unpopular.

*****

Stan and Ruby stood next to an old eucalyptus tree staring out in disbelief. This was the ninth church they had seen burned to the ground. Many of the workers that had helped Stan build these churches had gone into hiding or had been arrested. Some had even converted to Carlo's way of thinking. They had seen all of Simon's lies on the news and had begun to believe them.

"What will we do now?" Ruby asked.

"We will rebuild it!" said Stan angrily. He wasn't giving up regardless of Simon's tactics.

Ruby looked into Stan's weary face. She knew that he was tired both physically and mentally, time was running out, and there just wasn't a solution. Trouble was coming to the Evan's family soon, and they both knew it.

Ruby walked with Stan back towards their small home. "Stan," said Ruby, "I am so scared!" Stan stopped, turned to his wife, put his strong arms around her, and hugged her tightly as she wept bitterly.

"God will sustain us," said Stan.

"What's to become of us and the children?" she said.

Stan wasn't sure of anything anymore, but he had a good idea as to what was to become of his poor family. *Why have I failed them so miserably?* he wondered. *Why was I so deceived by false doctrine? Look what this has done to my family,* he thought to himself in total dismay.

When Stan and Ruby arrived home, they found the front door broken and wide open. "Oh, no!" moaned Ruby. Stan entered the house slowly and carefully went from room to room.

"They took our babies!" Ruby cried hysterically.

Stan, startled by the sound of wood cracking behind him, turned to see a frightened Christopher standing in the doorway.

"What happened, Dad? Where is everyone?"

Ruby went to her son, put her arms around him, and began to cry loudly. Stan stood in the center of the empty house. It was deathly silent except for the weeping of Ruby crying for her children who were no more.

******

Peter's legs ached, but he had no way to stretch them out. He had been squeezed into the small crate for nearly 24 hours. The rocking of the boat had calmed him enough to allow him some much needed sleep, but now with the cry of his bladder and the aching in his nearly numb legs, his rest had come to an end. He had wormed his way onto the boat just as the sun was beginning to set with no way of knowing where the freighter was going. All he knew for sure was that it was moving away from Latina and, hopefully, away from Rome as well.

Another two hours and Peter could stand it no more. He had to get up and move if his legs would allow it. The sounding of the ship's horn told Peter that they were approaching a port. *But where?* he wondered. The big ship began to shudder as its propellers spun in reverse to slow the tons of steel. It was terribly painful for Peter to stand, and with a grimace on his face he climbed out of the crate. Slowly he worked his way out of the cargo bay and onto the deck. The sun was bright orange and just starting to descend in the sky. From where Peter stood he could see the entrance to the port. There were other large freighters docked all around. *Where am I?* he wondered.

Peter hid in the shadows of the ship until it was fully moored. As soon as the dockworkers came aboard to unload the vessel, he saw his opportunity to disembark and mingle in with the other workers as if he was one of them.

At first nobody seemed to notice, but finally a large, hairy man stepped up to Peter just as he was about to walk down the ramp. The man was obviously addressing himself to Peter but in a language Peter could not understand. Peter knew he had heard it before, and he knew it was French, but what the man was saying was a complete mystery to him.

Again the man spoke, but this time he also pointed to a large toolbox sitting alone on the deck of the ship. Peter nodded, walked over to the tools and picked up the few remaining wrenches, put them into the box, and locked the lid down. Next he picked up the heavy box and walked down the ramp past the large man. As soon as Peter cleared the dock, he dropped the tools and ran off.

Peter made it to the nearest train station where he stood looking up at the signs. He could not understand anything he read. He wasn't even sure where he wanted to go until he saw a small sign with a picture of an airplane and the words: *Charles De Gaulle. Yes, the airport. That is where I need to go,* Peter thought. Very soon Peter found himself sitting back and looking out of the train window as it sped through the surrounding countryside.

The train arrived at the airport a mere 30 minutes before the last United Airlines flight left for Chicago. Fortunately for Peter he carried his passport at all times and had enough money to buy a coach seat. Moreover, it was lucky for Peter that they still took cash, because in just one more day that was going to come to an end forever.

Peter arrived in Chicago some eight hours later. It was late in the evening when he rented a car for the drive to Appleton, Wisconsin. It felt good to be back in the United States. Everything appeared to be normal to Peter as if none of the last few years had even happened. As usual the people at the airport and on the freeways seemed to be in a hurry, yet they all seemed to cooperate with each other. *Just like the good old days,* Peter thought. But quickly the reality that this was nothing like the good old days sank into his mind. In fact, very soon all of this would come to an end.

******

It was 2:00 a.m. when Peter pulled into the driveway to his mother's home. The place was a total wreck. The lawn was tall and covered with leaves and the windows seemed to have a thick cover of dirt over them. Even the paint looked to be peeling off the sides of the house as far as he could see in the headlights. There was a large red sign on the front door that read: *Foreclosed.*

The house was fully paid for, but during the last three years Peter had neglected to pay any property taxes, so the house had reverted back to the state. Peter got out and walked up to the front porch. His own shadow cast from the rental car headlights startled him momentarily. Peter turned the knob to the front door, but the door was locked. He stared at the handle for a few seconds. Life in this house had been good for Peter. In retrospect, it had been very good. He and Joseph had strong, loving, godly parents. *What a shame we didn't listen better to what they told us,* he thought to himself.

As Peter turned to leave, he remembered a spare key that he had stashed a lifetime ago. Reaching his hand up above the ledge of the door, Peter's fingers grasped a cold piece of metal. He smiled as he looked at the key. He could still remember placing it there years before. Peter had a bad habit of locking himself out, and it was not a very easy house to break into—not to mention that it had gotten a little embarrassing to call the locksmith out on a regular basis. Peter inserted the key and turned the knob. The door slid open with a very loud, squeaky sound. Peter hesitated before entering, uncertain of what he would find.

The house was dark and even the headlights didn't help much because the windows were caked with years of accumulated filth. Peter stood in the living room. It was completely empty. There wasn't even a log in the fireplace anymore. He felt anger at the thought of someone coming in and taking all of his parents' things. "You've been gone a long time, Peter," said a soft voice from behind.

Peter turned quickly to see an old and very short man standing in the doorway. "Do I know you?" Peter asked.

The man smiled and spoke up, "No, Peter, you don't know me, but I know you."

"Who are you then?" Peter asked.

The man stepped into the living room, and as he walked he began to glow and to change. Soon he was much taller than Peter, dressed in white, beautiful, with two huge wings perched above his head. Peter shaded his eyes from the brightness. "You have been courageous. The Lord is pleased!"

"What do I do now? Where do I go?" Peter asked in fear.

"You need to go to Israel," said the angel boldly, "to Jerusalem. There you will see Joseph."

"Joseph!" said Peter enthusiastically. "That will be wonderful! He's okay, then?"

"Joseph is a hated and wanted man. *Deacon's Horn* has cost Carlo Ventini many souls, and Simon will not stop until he catches him."

"But he hasn't caught him yet, right?" Peter asked optimistically.

"Not yet but, Peter, you must hurry!"

Abruptly the glow in the room was gone and so was the angel. All that remained were the dim headlights from the rental car and a cold, empty house full of faded memories. "Israel," said Peter aloud. "How will I ever get there?"

Peter drove away from his old house uncertain as to what to do next. *Where do I go now?* he wondered. The thought of Melissa, his ex-wife, came to his mind. *Would she even help if she could? Did she still live nearby, or did she go in the Rapture?* He knew the answer to the question almost before he thought it. Melissa didn't go in for God or religion and all that stuff. She believed in living for today—for the right here and now. A few minutes later Peter pulled into Melissa's driveway. There was a Mercedes parked beside him, and it was one he didn't recognize. He had no way of knowing if Melissa still lived there or if she had remarried. He was apprehensive as he approached the front door. *What choice do I have?* he thought.

Peter knocked lightly on the front door. It was 3:00 a.m., and he didn't want to wake the neighbors. He could hear the barking of a dog from within the house. Soon he would know who lived in this house. The porch light flicked on. "Who's there?" said a pleasant, female voice. Peter recognized the quality tone of Melissa's voice right away.

"Melissa, it's me—Peter!"

He could hear latch after latch turning. Then suddenly the door opened, but only slightly. "Stand by the light," the soft voice commanded.

Peter stepped towards the door and smiled. "Melissa, it's me!"

Melissa opened the door and folded her arms around her bathrobe. "What in the name of God are you doing here?"

"That's exactly why I'm here," said Peter. Melissa looked confused, yet she invited Peter into her house. Melissa had gotten older, but she was still attractive. Her hair had gone gray and her face had some new wrinkles. Peter suspected that he looked older too. "Hello, Melissa. How are you?"

"Peter, what are you doing and where have you been all these years? I thought maybe you had disappeared with all the other people."

"No, Melissa, I didn't, but I wish I had!"

Peter and Melissa spent the rest of the morning getting reacquainted with each other. Peter shared the events of the last three years with her, but it was obvious to him that she was not buying his story.

"I read about Joseph. He is a wanted man?"

Peter nodded.

"Are you wanted too?" she asked suspiciously.

Peter stared at Melissa and did not answer the question. She understood the meaning by his lack of response. "What do you want, Peter?"

"I need to go to Israel, and I need your help to do it. I have to get a plane ticket."

"Why can't you buy your own?" she asked.

"Melissa, all I have is cash and not very much of it."

"You can't use cash anymore as of today," she said.

"I know, Melissa. That is why I need your help."

"Don't you have an ID tag?"

Peter looked into Melissa's pale eyes. "No, do you?"

"Of course, doesn't everyone?" she said.

Peter's heart sank. There was nothing he could do for Melissa. She was doomed. There was no point in continuing his conversation with her. Peter got up to leave. "Well, I had better go."

"Wait, Peter!" said Melissa. "Maybe I can help you. But why do you need to go to Israel?"

Peter wasn't sure what to say. He knew she would never believe that God wanted him to go to Israel. "I am meeting someone," he said.

Melissa stared into Peter's dark eyes. "Really! Anyone special?" Melissa asked with some jealousy in her voice.

Peter was a bit surprised by her tone. She wasn't the jealous type, and in fact, she had never really shown Peter a great deal of interest even when they were married. "Yes, someone very special!" he said.

Melissa walked over to her computer and turned it on. "Where exactly do you want to go?"

"Jerusalem."

Melissa scanned through the net until she found what she wanted. "There is a flight leaving tonight. It's $3,000 dollars for a business seat!"

"Coach will be fine."

Melissa wrinkled her eyebrows. "Business class, Peter." Melissa ran her right hand across her ID reader and hit the enter key. "Done! You can pick up the ticket at the counter at O'Hare."

"Thank you, Melissa," said Peter.

"What is going on, Peter? Has the world gone mad? Do you really believe all this God stuff?"

Peter felt a pain in his heart for Melissa. She was lost and nothing could change that, but she had been his wife. He had loved her and still did if the truth were known. "Melissa!" said Peter, "I—" Peter paused and sighed heavily. "Thank you for your help," he said.

Peter drove back towards O'Hare in a somber mood. Life was crazy and getting worse all the time. Melissa had been deceived and would pay the ultimate price for it, and there was nothing anyone could do. At least he would get to see Joseph soon.

Chapter 22: On the Lamb

Day 1240, December: Scott paced the floor impatiently. "We've been here for weeks and for what?" Joseph, Yvette, Scott, and Ruth had driven away from Paul Laruso in Jerusalem and on to Bethlehem as requested by God, but for what? They had ditched the rental car weeks ago. Scott and Ruth had rented the apartment without Joseph or Yvette around, so nobody saw them sneak in. They were hidden away safely, but now they were about to run out of food again, and in another week their rent would be due. This time there would be no way to pay it. It would be impossible for them to hide out without this apartment.

Living arrangements were tight. Yvette and Joseph had the only bedroom. Scott and Ruth shared the hide-a-bed. Ruth laughed once saying, "If my mother saw me sleeping in this bed with a young white man, she'd never let me hear the end of it."

Scott smiled and said, "Just make sure you stay on your own side." They both laughed themselves to sleep over this. Frankly, they had become very accustomed to each other. Scott looked up to Ruth, and she in turn tolerated his many little quirks.

Yvette snuggled under Joseph's arm. She didn't care if they were cooped up in the apartment. She was content to be there with him. "It's safe here," she said.

Joseph knew he would have to leave the room sooner or later, but until God prompted him, he wasn't going anywhere. At least that was his thought weeks ago, but now even Joseph was starting to feel like a caged bird.

******

Ruth came through the front door; she had been wandering around the city all morning. Earlier in the morning Ruth and Scott had flipped a coin to see who would be able to escape the captivity of their small apartment for the day. "Another day in here and I will go crazy," Ruth had said.

Fortunately she won the toss. Scott wanted to go, too, but Ruth thought it best that they not leave together to avoid drawing too much attention. A tall, striking black woman with a young white male would draw attention, especially in Bethlehem.

"Well, how was it?" Scott asked impatiently.

Ruth understood Scott's tone of voice. She had felt the same way hours earlier. News reporters are used to action and a fast-paced life. Sitting back for weeks on end was killing Scott, and she knew he needed out. Ruth elaborated on the sights and sounds of Bethlehem until Scott thought he would die from envy. "I have to get out of here!" said Scott.

"Yes!" Joseph said. "You are right. We all need to get out for a while." Yvette turned towards Joseph with a disapproving look.

"Yvette, God brought us here for some purpose, and we are not going to find it here in this apartment. Tomorrow we will all go sight seeing."

******

Scott was the first one dressed. He continued to nag the others impatiently as they got ready. "Can we go now?"

"Soon, Scott. Just give us a few minutes—please!" said Yvette.

By noon all four of them had seen many of the sights in Bethlehem. It was nice to be out of the small apartment even though Yvette was still very apprehensive about the whole thing.

It was Joseph who spotted David and Benjamin standing at an entrance to a public building. They were obviously getting a lot of attention from the gathering crowd.

Joseph stepped closer so he could hear what the old man was saying. "The end is coming soon!" said Benjamin. "The Antichrist is already here, and soon he will desecrate the temple of the Lord."

"You are the reason we have no food, old man!" shouted someone in the crowd.

"Yeah, and the plague came from the Christians too!" said another.

David grabbed Benjamin's arm and tried to drag him away from the crowd, but it was too late. Others had already moved in to attack him. Someone from the crowd hit Benjamin squarely on the side of his head, knocking him to the ground. "What about you, kid? Are you with him?" another person from the mob asked.

Joseph worked his way into the center of the crowd and bent down to lift the old man up. "Who are you?" a woman standing in the midst of the angry rabble asked. Joseph turned and spoke in Hebrew to them, and suddenly they all backed up.

Benjamin looked up to Joseph in fear. Whatever Joseph had said to frighten the crowd had also frightened Benjamin and David. Ruth pushed her way through the crowd and stood next to Joseph. She bent to help him lift the old man. Joseph walked Benjamin from the center of the startled mob as they stood by watching. Joseph said something else to the crowd in Hebrew, and they all quickly left the scene.

Benjamin's legs were wobbly and the side of his head was bleeding badly. Yvette stepped in and pressed her handkerchief to the wound. *Once a nurse, always a nurse,* Joseph thought. "My name is Joseph Bastoni," he said in English this time. "Do you understand?"

"And you work for Carlo Ventini?" David asked carefully.

The small group looked to Joseph. He smiled brightly. "No, I lied. I had to say something or they would have killed you both."

"Well, we had better get out of here before they figure it out and come back," said Ruth. "Someone might have recognized you, Joseph."

David led the group back to Benjamin's deli, and along the way he asked Joseph a number of questions to ensure that he was telling the truth about who he really was. "So you were a priest and now you're not, right?"

Joseph smiled. He liked the young boy's doubting, suspicious mind. "Keep asking questions. It will keep you from being deceived," said Joseph with a smile for the boy.

Once inside the house Yvette proceeded to repair Benjamin's wound. "It really needs stitches," she said, "but I guess this tape will have to do."

They all spoke until late in the evening, sharing their experiences since the Rapture. Benjamin and David were fascinated with Joseph. He was the only person they had ever met that actually knew Simon and Carlo, and furthermore, Joseph, Yvette, Scott, and Ruth had all been there when Carlo was shot and then had risen from the dead. All of this helped to build their faith.

"But tell me, how did you come to be Christians?" Rush asked in her standard news reporter fashion.

Benjamin told in great detail all that he knew about Elisha and Jasmine. He talked about how he came to know all the children and how Elisha had witnessed to him about Jesus. He told them Elisha and Jasmine's story of survival in the desert. All this fascinated Joseph, and he really wanted to meet them.

"Where are they?" he asked.

Benjamin looked to David for the answer. "They left this morning early. Elisha said he wanted to try one more place before it was too late."

"One more place for what?" Scott asked.

"For souls!" said Benjamin.

Hours went by as Scott elaborated on their financial dilemma. Benjamin understood. He, too, was running out of supplies and could not buy anything with cash. "But at least you have a house to live in," said Scott.

"And now so do you. So do all of you!" Benjamin smiled at Yvette.

"Thank you!" she said gratefully as she hugged him.

It was past curfew, and Elisha and Jasmine were still not back. Benjamin was very worried. "What could have happened to them?" he said out of desperation.

"Would you like us to help you look for them?" Joseph asked.

"I wouldn't know where to look, and besides, we would all get arrested. It is after curfew."

Soon the front door swung open and Elisha stepped in carrying Jasmine. His mouth was bleeding and one of his eyes was swollen shut. Jasmine looked to be unconscious. "Bring her over here," said Yvette. Elisha did not recognize Yvette or the others, so he stood rigid, unwilling to move.

"It is okay, Elisha. They are with us," said Benjamin.

Elisha was hesitant but carried Jasmine to the couch all the same. Yvette examined her carefully.

"Is she going to be okay?" Elisha asked. Yvette didn't answer. She was still inspecting Jasmine's body. The young girl began to stir as Yvette placed her hands on her abdomen.

"Get me some ice!" said Yvette.

David returned with a towel loaded down with ice cubes. Yvette placed the towel on a huge bump in the middle of Jasmine's forehead. "They threw rocks at us. We barely got away," said Elisha.

Joseph stared at the young man. Although his eye was swollen and his mouth was cut and bleeding, Joseph could tell by his countenance that this was a handsome, strong young man of God. "My name is Joseph Bastoni. I think God sent me to meet you."

"To meet me—why?" asked Elisha suspiciously.

Although he wasn't entirely sure why, Joseph felt impressed by the Lord that there was something special about Elisha. "There is something I need to share with you—something that will help you in the future, but frankly, I am not sure what it is."

Soon the young, injured girl began to stir as Yvette held the ice on her forehead. She whispered softly to Jasmine, "It's okay. You are going to be fine." With that Jasmine opened her eyes and stared into Yvette's smiling face.

Jasmine began to panic and turned her head to look for Elisha. She was remembering what had happened earlier in the night, and she was afraid Elisha would not be there. He had faced off with a large crowd proclaiming Jesus as the Truth and the only way to Heaven. The group had become very angry with the two bold evangelists. It seemed that recently everyone they met had become very unreceptive to God's Word—to the point they often threatened violence. This time they did more than threaten.

Jasmine could remember everything up to the point that someone hit her across the head with a bottle. She remembered the group as they tried to separate Elisha from her. They were going to beat him, but Jasmine would have none of that, so she stepped in and fought for her young man until suddenly the lights went out.

Now as she lay in Yvette's lap she felt a great panic that Elisha would not be there. "Elisha!" Jasmine whispered.

Elisha moved in towards Jasmine and looked into her worried face. His expression was one of love and great concern for his brave young girlfriend. "I'm right here!" he said softly as he reached out and took Jasmine's hand into his own. She smiled in relief and then began to cry.

Tears filled Elisha's eyes and ran down his cheeks. He loved her so much. "It will be okay, Jasmine. Everything will be all right."

Yvette looked over to Joseph. The look on her face matched his own. These two young children had touched their hearts. Sorrow filled Joseph's mind, and he suddenly understood what God wanted him to share with Elisha. He understood that he was passing the gauntlet, so to speak.

Elisha and Jasmine had much more to do for God. They had much more suffering and trial to endure, and Joseph began to wonder what specifically he needed to share with Elisha.

What is it that I can impart to these two young people that will help them in the future? *he asked himself.*

******

Laruso drove through the tiny city of Bethlehem one street at a time while anger consumed him. He had a literal hate for Joseph. He would find him if it was the last thing he ever did, and in fact, it would be the last thing he ever did if he didn't find him soon. Peter John had issued his last ultimatum. He, too, was under great pressure from Simon to find Joseph. This whole thing had become a personal quest for all three men for their own varying reasons.

Paul had lain tied up in Jerusalem for nearly two days before the owner of the apartment came by when he got suspicious after having seen Joseph's picture in the newspaper. To the owner's surprise Paul lay there on the floor covered in his own body waste, seething with anger and in pain from his broken wrist, complements of Joseph. After a shower and some medical treatment, Paul was on his way to Bethlehem. He found Scott's rental car within a couple of days parked just a few miles south of Bethlehem, but Paul would not fall for any more of that. He knew Joseph was hidden in the city somewhere. It was a small place, and he was determined to find him at any cost.

Paul's cellular phone rang. The sound rubbed his nerves raw. *Who could this be?* he wondered. He had not taken out a new advertisement on Joseph although he was considering another article in the paper. Since Jerusalem was only five miles away from Bethlehem, he felt certain that the paper had circulated that far at least. "Hello?" said Paul as he held his cellular phone up to his ear with an arm that had been immobilized in a small splint.

On the other end of the phone was the Pope. "Any luck?" Peter John asked in a derogatory fashion. He was really beginning to doubt Paul's ability to find anyone.

Paul wanted to lie. He wanted to say anything positive, but there just wasn't any good news to share. "Not yet, but soon!" said Paul.

"Of this, I am sure," said the Pope. It was a double meaning which Paul understood well enough. Either he found Joseph soon or he, too, would have to run from Peter John and Simon Koch.

"I have another assignment for you temporarily," said the Pope.

******

Earlier that day the Pope had received a call from an angry Simon Koch who was very dissatisfied with Peter John's inability to capture one simple ex-priest. "I have some information which may help you in your feeble attempt to find Bastoni," said Simon. "I have tracked down his brother, Peter Bastoni."

"Have you captured him?" the Pope asked optimistically.

"No, not yet, but we know exactly where he is."

"Where?" asked Peter John.

Earlier in the week after Peter had eluded Simon during the raid on his medical facility, Simon had posted an airline alert giving the name and description of Peter Bastoni, M.D. Simon had missed Peter as he flew to Chicago from Paris, but just barely! However, he now had Peter, and there would be no escape.

"He is in a plane on his way to Jerusalem," said Simon.

"Jerusalem!" said Peter John. "He must be going there to meet Joseph."

"You really think so?" said Simon in a condescending fashion. "I want you to pick him up and see if he doesn't lead you to Father Bastoni," he growled. "Oh, one more thing, Your Holiness," said Simon. "If you screw this up, they will be looking for a new Pope by this time tomorrow." Simon hung up the phone as Peter John shook with fear.

"We have found Joseph's brother, Peter," the Pope said now to Paul.

Paul was surprised. For some reason he had forgotten the fact that Joseph even had a brother. "You do know that Joseph has a brother, right?" said Peter John.

"Um, yes, of course!" Paul mumbled.

"Good! Well, he is flying into Jerusalem as we speak."

"How do you know this?" Paul asked.

"I have my ways!" said Peter John in his own arrogant way.

"Where is he?" Paul inquired anxiously.

"He will be landing in Jerusalem in about two hours."

"I'll be there to greet him," said Paul.

"Make sure that you are," said Peter John. "Maybe he can help you find Joseph since you can't seem to do it alone." This comment cut Paul like a knife. He prided himself on his ability to find people, but he had to admit that taking nearly a year to find one simple man was a bit much.

Paul turned his car around and pointed it north. He would be there to greet Peter as he stepped off the plane. Then suddenly the thought occurred to him that he had no idea what Peter Bastoni even looked like. His heart sank at the thought that this man could slip through his grasp as well. Paul had a lead on an apartment complex he really wanted to check out, but he figured he'd better get to the airport first. Later he could come back to Bethlehem. Besides, it was past midnight and he would have to wait until morning to find someone to talk to. Paul was authorized to be out past the mandatory curfew, with the help of the Italian government. The only other people allowed out after 10:00 p.m. were those with a specific travel destination permit—that and city government officials and police officers.

******

Peter slept for most of the flight. He was exhausted, and thanks to Melissa the business seat that he sat in was large and comfortable. Peter's mind drifted in and out of dreams. Like a broken film projector his thoughts went from Bruno to Melissa to Joseph, and eventually he found himself running through a desert with thousands of men chasing him. No matter how fast he ran, he could not escape the evil-looking troops as they closed in. Finally as Peter struggled against the deep sand, the ground suddenly opened up and swallowed him completely. The next thing he knew he was in a dark cave surrounded by thousands of frightened people, all looking to Peter for help. His heart was full of compassion for them, but he didn't know how he could help any of these poor, scared people.

The flight attendant's voice came over the loud speaker, startling Peter back to reality. "We will be landing in about 30 minutes," said the attendant. Peter took this as his cue to get up and use the restroom one more time before they landed. He grabbed the toiletry kit that the airline had given him and wandered down the aisle to the bathroom. Peter stared at his face in the mirror. *Boy, have the last few years aged me!* he thought.

As he shaved and brushed his teeth, he wondered what was to come next. How was he ever going to find Joseph? *God, You will have to do this because I am lost.*

******

Paul stood next to one of the customs agents waiting for the passengers to deplane. He knew that Peter would have to come through one of these 12 lines before he would be allowed to leave the airport and enter Jerusalem. But Paul had no way of knowing what line Peter would use. He had tried to get the security guards to cooperate with him by detaining Bastoni as he tried to clear customs. Paul dropped big names like Pope Peter John and Simon Koch, but the guards didn't seem overly impressed.

They did, however, give Paul permission to stand behind one of the counters during the customs inspection. Maybe he would get lucky and Peter would pick his line. He had a 1-in-12 chance anyway. Paul patted his hip. He felt the cool steel press against his body, and he was grateful for this gun even though it was not his favorite. Scott had taken Paul's primary weapon, but luckily for Paul he always brought two of them whenever he traveled.

A massive group of weary-looking travelers rounded the corner towards the customs counters. Paul began to scan the group carefully. It was difficult because they were all swarming as they battled for position in the empty lines. Everyone looked alike to Paul. He began to fear he would never find Peter in this mob.

The first couple of men through his line were obviously Palestinian, as were most of the travelers—that and Jewish. Finally one man stepped up to Paul's line and dropped his United States passport down on the counter. Paul followed the passport up to its owner. He was startled by the family resemblance as he looked into Peter's dark, tired eyes. The custom's agent looked at Peter's passport and then to Laruso. Paul nodded and the guard stamped Peter's passport. "Have a nice stay," said Paul as he motioned Bastoni by.

Peter headed straight toward the bus terminal. *Strange,* he thought to himself, *that man almost sounded Italian instead of Hebrew.* About that time Paul pulled up behind Peter and placed the revolver in the small of his back. "Mr. Bastoni, you are under arrest!" Peter turned to see the very man he was wondering about.

"You are Italian!" said Peter lightly.

Paul nodded. "That's right, and you are Joseph Bastoni's brother."

Paul escorted Peter out of the airport and into his automobile. Peter was wondering what God would do to help him find Joseph, but this seemed a little extreme. Paul climbed into the car and closed the door while still pointing his gun at Peter. "Okay then, where is he?" said Paul.

"Where is who?" Peter asked.

Paul jabbed the barrel of his gun into Peter's chest. "Don't play games with me. Where is Joseph?"

"I thought I was under arrest. You're not a police officer!" said Peter.

"That's right," said Paul. "I work for Pope Peter John and Simon Koch. Maybe you've heard of them?"

"Yeah," said Peter, "and they work for the Devil himself!"

Paul raised his gun and crashed it down on the side of Peter's face, cutting his cheek wide open. Blood ran down his face and rage filled his eyes. He wanted to attack Paul, but Peter knew he would be killed if he moved an inch toward him.

"Where is he?" Paul yelled.

"I don't know!" said Peter.

Paul was about to hit him again, but for some reason he restrained the urge. "Why are you here?" he asked.

"I don't really know," said Peter. "God told me to come."

This answer angered Paul, so he hit Peter in the mouth with the side of his gun, splitting Peter's lip open, and once again blood began to gush from the wound. "Where is he?"

Peter slumped back in his seat. "I don't know!" he yelled back to Paul. "God told me to come to Jerusalem, so I came. I have no idea where Joseph is."

Paul did not believe Peter's comments about God, but he was beginning to believe that he had no idea where Joseph was. "Would you tell me if you did know?" Paul asked.

"Never!" said Peter bluntly.

Paul smiled. *He doesn't know anything,* he thought to himself. "Well then, I will tell you where he is," said Paul. "He's in Bethlehem, so let's go find him!"

******

Once again Tommy and Sara sat alone in the front part of the laboratory while Dedrick and Brian ran another series of tests on the ID tags. So far they had learned a great deal about how the tag worked, both as an organic implant and as an electronic device. This information they shared daily with their underground connections.

Their hope was that there would be some way to disable the device, but so far all they had come up with was enough information to inform the technical community about how the tag worked. Yet at least this data had some value. It gave the underground scientist network information that could be published and viewed by the world.

If nothing else it planted doubt and confusion in the minds of many who had not yet taken the ID tag. The information that was distributed in leaflet form and through the Internet was very specific. It stated that if an implant was put into the body of a person, it could never be removed without killing the human in the attempt. Their statement also included the fact that each ID tag had a tracking system built in, making it impossible to hide from Carlo's evil government.

Sara was becoming disgruntled with their effort as she had said once before, "Because some things can never be changed because God has decided to allow them to happen." In the case of the ID tags Sara was convinced that there would never be any technical solutions to counter the eternal damnation associated with receiving one of these tags into the human body. Once there the host was doomed to Hell forever according to the Bible, and that was all there was to it. "This is God's will," she said to Tommy as they sat quietly by waiting for Dedrick and Brian to reach the same conclusion.

"Where is Tina?" Sara asked. Not that she really cared much. Tina had become increasingly hostile towards her. It was evident that Tina was completely consumed with jealousy. She did not like for one second the idea that Sara and Tommy had fallen in love and were now spending all of their time together.

It had been Tommy and Tina for nearly 30 years, and now Sara had come between them. Tina's only comfort was in the form of Mark Singer. She had continued to see him daily as Tommy and the rest worked in the lab. She also snuck around in the evenings with Mark on a regular basis. She was very attracted to him, and yet she was still dedicated to Tommy. However, since he no longer seemed to care about her, she had decided to put more effort into her growing relationship with Mark.

Today Tina was disappointed when she entered the coffee shop because Mark was nowhere to be found. She had been out with him just the evening before. He had said nothing about not working today, although he had been acting a little peculiar lately—almost preoccupied with something.

Tina thought it had something to do with the fact that she and Mark had not attempted a physical relationship to date. She was afraid she would lose Mark if she did not give in to his sexual desires, yet Mark had not even approached her about this. She was completely inexperienced in this area. Tina had never been with a man, but she was a woman, and she was attracted to Mark—maybe even falling in love with him. She wasn't sure about this either, since she had never been in love before or even had a legitimate attraction for a man. Tommy had protected and sheltered her. She hadn't needed anyone other than him until now.

******

Mark Singer made his phone call to the Good Citizen hotline four days ago, but he hadn't heard anything until early yesterday evening. A call came to him while he was working in the coffee shop. The call came from Simon Koch himself. Mark felt honored that the second most powerful man in the world would want to talk to him personally.

"Mr. Singer," said Simon. "I have received some information from you that is very interesting and of concern to me." Mark stood with the phone frozen to his ear. "It seems that you have a small group of scientists there on your campus who are performing illegal operations with our ID tags. Is this correct?" Simon asked in a very formal yet gentle way.

Mark spoke up cautiously. He hadn't really thought this thing through completely. He just wanted the money for the reward, but now he was talking to Simon Koch. He knew that he was betraying Tina and that she would be in serious trouble over this.

But then again why hadn't she complied and taken the ID tag like everyone else? Why was she a part of a group of rebel scientists that were doing criminal acts against Carlo Ventini—and after he had done so much to help the world?

"Yes, Mr. Koch. I have heard from one of the scientists that they have two of your ID tags and that they have been studying them and sending this information through an underground scientist network that they developed."

Simon began to get excited. This was possibly the nexus of the underground Christian activity he had been looking for. "What are their names, Mr. Singer?"

Mark paused for just a brief second.

"Mr. Singer, you have a tremendous reward coming to you for your allegiance to Mr. Ventini and myself," said Simon encouragingly.

"They are Tommy and Tina Glover, Sara Allen, Dedrick Bishopf, and some other guy named Brian, but I don't know his last name."

"Where can we find them?" Simon asked.

"They are here daily in the laboratory just down the hall from the coffee shop."

Simon pondered his new information. He knew Dedrick Bishopf personally, or at least he had met the man in L.A. and then once in his own office in Rome. He had never liked the old man in the first place, and the thought of getting his hands on that presumptuous Sara Allen was nearly too much for Simon. "Okay, Mr. Singer, do not say a thing to anyone. We will take care of this situation tomorrow morning. Do everything as normal so that nobody suspects that you know anything. Oh, one more thing!" said Simon. "You can expect your reward within the next few weeks." Simon smiled as he said this to Mark. He knew that in just a few weeks everything Mark Singer held dear would be destroyed forever.

Mark grinned as he hung up the phone. He wiped the perspiration from his face and then sat back and began to dream about what he was going to do with his reward.

******

Tina considered waiting for Mark. *Maybe he's just late,* she thought. After all, they had been out last night until the early morning hours. Tina moved over to the coffee bar and took a seat on the stool. The room was dimly lit and deathly quiet.

The usual smell of fresh coffee was absent from the air. Tina noticed a small white note pad placed carelessly on top of a newspaper. With one hand she slid the paper and the pad towards her. Orienting the pad, she stared at the names written on it: *Tommy and Tina Glover, Sara Allen, Dedrick Bishopf, and Brian. What is this all about?* she wondered. She picked up the paper which was folded in half, and as she opened it she read the caption: *"Good Citizen Reward."* Tina's eyes filled with tears as she read the article.

She began to realize that Mark had used her. He had betrayed her. Suddenly a thought struck Tina's heart. "No, I betrayed them!" she said aloud.

Tina dropped the paper and ran out of the coffee shop. She had to tell Tommy. She had to warn them all before it was too late. Tina rounded the corner to the edge of the lab and stopped. From behind she could see Mark Singer walking with six armed men. *He's leading them to the lab,* she thought in total despair. About this time Mark began to turn in Tina's direction. Instinctively she ducked into the women's restroom. She hid in the closest stall and began to cry. *What have I done?*

******

Sara was the first to see the men enter the lab. Instantly she knew they had been found out. Before she could speak a word to Tommy, the men came crashing through the glass door and into the front part of the lab itself. "Freeze!" said one of the men as he pointed a large shotgun at Tommy. Fear and hopelessness filled his heart.

Sara moved over and grabbed Tommy's hand tightly. "I love you!"

she whispered.

Tommy smiled weakly,."I love you too!"

Brian heard the commotion from the other room and opened the heavy door to look out. He was stunned to see Tommy and Sara surrounded by many armed men. Brian slammed the door and locked it as quickly as he could.

"What is it?" Dedrick asked.

"Trouble—big trouble! We've been found out. Who are they?" Brian asked.

Dedrick didn't have to see the men to know who they were and what it would mean to be taken captive. "They work for Simon Koch, I am sure," said Dedrick.

One of Simon's men started to pound against the heavy door. "Unlock the door or we will blow it open!" said the man.

Dedrick smiled at Brian. "Our work is done. Let's move this hydrogen bottle over by the door."

Brian understood the meaning of Dedrick's gesture. The hydrogen was in a huge bottle, under pressure, and tied directly to another large bottle of oxygen. "This is going to make a very big boom," said Brian.

The two men placed the heavy bottles directly in front of the door and stood back. The pounding on the door continued for another few minutes before the man finally had enough.

"Okay, then, we'll just blast our way in!"

Dedrick turned and opened the main file directly on his computer and highlighted all files. With one stroke of a key he deleted all files that could link other scientists back to Dedrick and Tommy.

The entire building shook all around Tina as she heard the terrible explosion. Unknown to Tina, a bottle of hydrogen and oxygen had blown the outer wall right out of the lab killing Dedrick, Brian, and one of Simon's men instantly. The others, including Sara and Tommy, had been thrown into the far wall and were all unconscious. Fire began to consume the lab. Any usable evidence that could link Dedrick and Tommy to other scientists was sure to be destroyed. That was the good news.

The bad news was that as soon as Tommy and Sara regained consciousness, they were lifted to their feet and marched out of the building. From the bathroom window Tina could see and hear Mark Singer speaking to two of Simon's men. He described Tina as tall and moderately attractive, lean and bony. Her mind was full of hate for Mark and for herself. *I caused all of this!* she thought.

"Two of them are dead," said one of the men.

Tina's heart nearly stopped. "Oh, God, please help me!" she whispered under her breath. She was sure that Tommy had been killed; then suddenly she caught sight of a bloody and dazed Tommy and Sara being escorted to one of the two vans in the parking lot.

"What will happen to those two?" Mark asked.

"The same as all traitors!" said one of Simon's men. "They will be taken to Simon Koch, and then he will personally kill them."

Mark seemed to be completely unmoved by the sentence that was soon to follow for Tommy and Sara. "So when will I get my reward?" Mark asked.

The men looked at him and laughed as they walked off. Mark Singer didn't understand their humor. He wanted money. He figured he had done his part as a good citizen, and now he wanted what was coming to him.

Tina backed her way out of the restroom and ran down the far hall until she found another exit out of the school building. By this time fire trucks and police cars were racing into the parking lot creating a massive distraction, allowing her to wander off completely unnoticed. Tina walked aimlessly through Los Angeles. She felt so alone and lost. For the first time in her life Tommy was not going to be able to help her. *And why?* she thought. *Because I've betrayed him! I've killed them all!* Tina's desperate mind cried out.

Finally Tina found her way out to the highway where she managed to hitch a ride back to her motel. Once inside Tina fell face first onto the bed and cried out to God. There was no hope as far as she could see, and the sense of guilt over her foolish mistake in judgment was too much.

Suddenly there was a startling knock at the door. Tina went to the balcony, and looking down she spotted one of the vans that Simon's men had taken Tommy away in. Again there was a loud bang at the door.

"Open up!" a man shouted. "We know you are in there!"

At that moment all options left Tina. She was alone and death was coming to her just like it had for Dedrick and Brian and just like it soon would for Tommy and Sara. The grief and horror was too much for her. Tina walked out on the ledge and climbed up on the rail. "God, forgive me, please!" Tina cried hysterically.

From within the van Tommy could see the driver staring up at the balcony above his room. Tommy looked up just in time to see his sister launch herself off the balcony, falling some 30 feet onto the concrete.

"Oh, my God! No!" Tommy screamed in anguish. There was no way for him to escape from the van to get to his sister, and even if he could, Tommy knew what his eyes would behold. All Sara could do was to reach over to Tommy and hold him tight as he cried.

******

Elisha spent the afternoon with Joseph. It seemed they had so much to share—so many things to talk about. Joseph was impressed with the young man's strength and courage. Elisha actually made Joseph feel a bit guilty that he had been in hiding all this time. He hadn't made a single attempt to personally witness to a nonbeliever. Although he knew that he had caused considerable damage to Carlo Ventini by writing and publishing *Deacon's Horn*, it was not enough.

Elisha led Joseph up the side of a small hill that overlooked the city. It was the same location that Jasmine and Elisha had found themselves in the day they were met by Philip, an angel of the Lord. They stared down at Bethlehem quietly. The sun was just beginning to stretch against the sky, giving it an eerie red hue. A cool breeze blew across Joseph, causing him to shiver momentarily. He turned towards Elisha and looked into the intense brown eyes of the brave child. "God has more for you to endure, I am afraid."

"What do you mean?" Elisha whispered.

Joseph put his strong hand on Elisha's shoulder and pushed him gently to the ground. Both men sat and looked down at the city. There was a sense of calm mixed with a greater sense of sorrow and a certainty of a destination yet to come for both men. "We are nearing the mid-tribulation point," said Joseph.

Elisha looked into Joseph's tired face. He did not know this man, but he felt a genuine love for him. He could sense Joseph's greatness—his will to do whatever God commanded. He had learned from Joseph that he was the author of *Deacon's Horn*, and Elisha had seen the articles like most of the world had. Suddenly he was proud to be there with such a brave man—a man who had done so much to warn the world against the Antichrist.

"You mean the desecration of the temple?" Elisha asked.

"Yes," said Joseph, "but much more than that Elisha—much more!"

"What do you mean?" the young man asked.

Joseph sighed and began to elaborate for Elisha from the prophecy of Apostle John in the book of Revelation. "You have already seen the beginning of Christian persecution," Joseph said. Elisha nodded as he followed along. "You will see much more than this. Soon after the temple is desecrated, God Himself will begin to pour His own wrath out on this world. There will be so few Christians left—so few that have not yet taken the mark of the beast—and in every case these people will have to hide or they will be found and killed."

"What is God's wrath?" Elisha asked.

Joseph's face intensified as he spoke. "Soon after the Antichrist reveals himself proclaiming to be god, a third of the world will be destroyed in a massive global disaster. A third of the people will die, a third of the earth will be burned up, and a third of the sky will be blocked out by smoke and dust."

"How?" asked Elisha with great concern in his voice.

"The Bible says a star will fall from the sky—an asteroid—and it will cause incredible damage. After that even worse disasters will come on earth." Elisha looked to Joseph for more clarification.

"Satan will be set free to torment mankind, and evil creatures from the abyss of Hell will be let loose to torture the people. Again Christians everywhere will be sought out and killed." Both men were quiet for a few moments before Joseph spoke up again.

"You will have to remain strong. You will have to hide from Carlo Ventini and eventually from Satan himself. It will be even more horrible than today by far."

"When should we leave? Where should we go?" Elisha inquired.

Joseph's heart was full of compassion for the brave young man. "You should leave soon, but we will not be going with you."

"Why not?" asked Elisha. He needed Joseph's wisdom and strength. Benjamin had become a great support for Elisha, but Benjamin was not knowledgeable or strong like Joseph.

"We have a different destiny than you. I believe God brought us here to share with you all we have done and all that is yet to come, and also to encourage and warn you to be prepared. It is only by the witness of another Christian, one to another, that you can draw strength—hopefully enough to survive what is to come."

"What about you?" Elisha asked. "What will happen to you?"

"I don't know, but it doesn't really matter. God will be with us." Joseph put his hand on Elisha's shoulder. "Something great is waiting for us all, and I feel it is coming very soon."

Elisha felt like a scared little boy that needed courage to face what was coming. Over the last few years he had grown so much, but he was also worn out. Joseph sensed the young man's fear. "You have a young, beautiful girl down there," said Joseph as he pointed to Bethlehem. "She is counting on you, Elisha, so be strong and know that it is all in God's hands regardless. Stay faithful and focused on Him and you and Jasmine will be fine. Heaven is waiting for you both."

Elisha felt better, strengthened by these words and by the realization that he had Jasmine to go through life with. He loved her so much!

Joseph and Elisha stood to leave. "There is one more thing," said Joseph. "There will come a time when two men will enter into Jerusalem and proclaim Jesus as God. These men are prophets sent from Heaven. They are two witnesses from the Lord. Look for them because they will be a marker for you to gauge the time you have before Jesus returns. They have power from God, and it will not rain a single day until they are killed and then raised from the dead after three days. When you see this you will know that Christ is coming very soon. Then there will be a great battle in the Kidron Valley in Meggido marking the end of mankind."

Joseph was desperate to give Elisha knowledge—information that Joseph had always seen as useless until the day that Zach Miles disappeared. Now he wanted the young man to be prepared as best he could.

******

Jasmine walked Yvette to the end of the block. She wanted Yvette to see what had become of the site where Jesus had been born. Yvette walked along silently. She was amused by Jasmine—such a hard little girl—but still something about her was kind and gentle. "Look what they've done to this," said Jasmine.

Yvette stared at the building. Outside the walls were covered with painted graffiti, all of the small windows had been broken, and the building stood completely abandoned. "Inside," said Jasmine, "is a small cave marked by a star on the floor. This is where it is believed Mary gave birth to Jesus, and even if it is not, look at how the people have treated this place!" Jasmine showed her anger.

Yvette liked her passion. "Keep your anger focused on the evil that has done this, but don't let it consume you, or you will be like them," said Yvette.

Jasmine liked the Italian lady—accent and all. She had cared for Jasmine when she was wounded and had shown great love to her over the last couple of days. "What is going to happen to us?" Jasmine asked.

Yvette's heart broke as she looked into the frightened eyes of the beautiful girl. "I wish there was good news, but there isn't. Things will get worse, but in the end we will be in Heaven with Jesus, and then nothing can ever hurt us again." Yvette smiled. This helped Jasmine, but not much.

******

Peter walked in front of Paul as they climbed the stairs to the small apartment building. Paul was following up on a lead he had received the night before. Someone from the apartment complex had called his cellular number with information. They had seen Joseph leave the building earlier that week with three other people. Paul was hopeful that he would catch them all sleeping. He had no intention of knocking but instead moved Peter to the side and began to pick the lock. Peter considered this his chance to run, but before he took a single step forward Paul cocked his revolver and pointed it at him.

"Move and you're dead!" said Paul.

Peter froze where he stood.

Paul turned the doorknob slowly, and with a light push he cracked the door open about three inches. Peter screamed as loud as he could, "Joseph, run!" Paul turned and whacked Peter hard on the side of his head with the butt of his gun, causing Peter to collapse against the door, swinging it wide open. Paul stepped over Peter and moved into the room. Nobody was present, but there were clothing and food in the apartment, indications that someone was still living there. Sitting on the edge of a coffee table was a King James Bible. At the base of the book stenciled in gold was the name: *"Joseph Bastoni."* The Bible was a high school graduation gift given to him by his mother many years ago. Paul smiled. He was optimistic that they would return at some point, so he dragged Peter into the house and locked the door behind him.

Many hours later Peter still had a massive headache and another nasty cut on his face. He was beginning to look like a prizefighter with battle scars everywhere. Paul was near exhaustion. He had tied Peter up, much the same way he had been tied up by Joseph. Paul hoped that he could get some sleep without worrying about Peter trying to escape. The best he could do, however, was to catnap 15 minutes at a time. Peter was grateful that Joseph had not returned. *Maybe he saw Paul enter the building and was staying away on purpose.* Peter hoped this was the case.

Looking out of the apartment's only window, Paul stretched as he stared out at the sky. It was going to be a beautiful day, but for Paul there would never be another nice day until he captured Joseph and delivered him personally to Simon Koch. Paul turned to look at Peter, then quickly back to the window. He stared out in surprise. "Can I be so lucky?" he said aloud. Walking down the street towards the apartment was a young, dark-skinned teenage girl with a tall, middle-aged woman with dark red hair. Paul knew at once from the picture he had studied for nearly a year that this was Yvette Lewis, the Pope's niece.

Paul said nothing to Peter. He didn't want him to make a sound, but Peter could sense that Paul had spotted something. "I need to go to the bathroom," said Peter.

"Tough!" said Paul. There was no way he would let Peter get up and make a single sound that would clue Yvette in to their presence.

"Who do you see out there?" Peter asked. "Is it Joseph?"

"No," said Paul. "Now shut up!"

Peter began to rant loudly. "Why do you want him? What has he done? Don't you know Carlo and Simon work for the Devil?"

"Shut up!" said Paul as he pointed his gun at Peter's head.

"It won't matter if you kill me. I am going to Heaven soon anyway. Where are you going?" asked Peter.

Paul raised his gun to hit Peter once again when suddenly the front door to the apartment opened wide and Yvette and Jasmine stepped in. Paul pointed his gun at Yvette. "Move and I will shoot you dead!"

The two women were completely caught off guard. Yvette thought that she and Jasmine could slip in, grab some clothing and food, and be back at Benjamin's deli before Joseph and Elisha returned. This error in judgment was going to cost her greatly.

******

Paul parked the car behind the deli. "Everyone out now!" he said as he opened the car door for his hostages. All three of them had their hands tied behind their backs, but none of them were gagged. "Say a word and I'll shoot all three of you."

Inside the house Joseph, Benjamin, and Elisha sat on the couch studying the Bible. Joseph was pointing out as much of the meaning of the book of Revelation as he could explain. Benjamin told Joseph and Elisha that the girls had gone for a walk but that he had sent David out to look for them to ensure that they were okay. "Scott and Ruth went into the city to see what is going on. They will not be back until lunch," said Benjamin.

Yvette led the way into the house crying large tears with every step. Jasmine had very little understanding as to what was happening other than the fact that whatever it was, it would not be good for any of them. Paul pushed Peter with the barrel of his gun. "Say anything and I will kill all of you!" Peter knew that Paul was not bluffing.

David rounded the corner in time to see Paul and Peter walk though the back door and into the kitchen of Benjamin's deli. David saw the sun reflect against Paul's gun. "We are in big trouble," David whispered to himself.

Elisha was the first to see Yvette as she walked in with her hands behind her back and a grimacing face. Next came Jasmine in much the same fashion, and finally Peter and Paul entered the room. Joseph looked up in time to see Paul push Peter up against the wall. Seconds went by before anyone said a word. Joseph finally spoke up, "You came for me, so let these people go, and I will come with you."

"I don't think you are in a position to negotiate anything with me! I'll take whoever I want and kill anyone I want!" said Paul as he swung his revolver around the room.

Joseph and Elisha both stood simultaneously. "Sit down!" Paul yelled. "You think you are so smart to hide from me? Now what are you going to do?" Paul grabbed Yvette, and she let out a shriek. Joseph stood again. This time he approached Paul to within a foot or so.

"How would you like me to blow her brains out right here and now?" Joseph froze.

"I don't know who all of you are, and I don't care, but you three are coming with me," said Paul as he pointed to Peter, then to Yvette, and then Joseph.

Joseph nodded, "Yes, we will come with you. Just let these people alone. They know nothing about us."

"Don't tell me what to do!" said Paul angrily. Suddenly he really wanted to shoot one of the others just to make his point. He stepped over to Elisha and placed his gun against Elisha's left temple. "I'll kill whoever I want!"

Jasmine screamed out, "No! Please, no!" Paul stopped and looked into the face of the tough little girl. She reminded him of his own daughter back home. Paul lowered his gun and grabbed Yvette's arm and pushed her into Peter and Joseph. "Let's go!" he growled.

Joseph whispered to Peter, "How did you get here?"

"It's a long story, but let's just say God sent me to you," said Peter.

"Shut up!" said Paul as he pushed the two men out of the back door and into the parking lot.

Just then David crept out from behind the dumpster and jumped on Paul's back. "Run!" he yelled to the others.

Paul threw David off his back, crashing the boy's small body into the dumpster with enough force to knock the wind out of him.

Peter turned to kick the gun out of Paul's injured hand, but instead Paul clobbered him with his gun with enough force to make a loud thud. Peter dropped to the ground, knocked out cold. Then Joseph turned to attack Paul, but he wasn't quick enough. Paul put his gun against Yvette's neck. "One step and she's dead!" Anger filled Joseph's mind. He could do nothing to Paul without killing Yvette and probably himself too.

"Get in the car—her in the back and you in the front with me."

Paul looked down to where Peter lay and made the decision to leave him there. "He's not important to us anyway."

Peter lay unconscious on the ground as David sat gasping for air. Paul's tires squealed as he drove off with Joseph and Yvette.

******

It was another two hours before Scott and Ruth returned to hear the news, and by this time Peter was nearly recovered, sitting on the couch next to David. Peter explained the ordeal to them, including the part about the plague and how he came to be in Israel. "But now I have no idea what God wants from me or why I am here," said Peter with his heart full of anguish. He hadn't had the chance to say more than a word to his little brother and, who knows, maybe he never would again.

******

"What do you want me to do with them?" Paul asked as he spoke to Peter John on his phone. He had pulled his car off to the side of the road not even a block from where Scott and Ruth had just been taking in the sights.

"I'll call you back," said the Pope. "Try not to lose them this time!"

These words burned into Paul's heart, and he turned his hatred onto Joseph. "Take your shoe laces off now!"

Paul tied Joseph's hands behind his back and shoved him in the back seat with Yvette. "I can't wait to hear what they are going to do to you," Paul grinned.

Yvette was terrified, but having Joseph in the back seat with her began to calm and comfort her. "What is going to happen to us?" she whispered.

"I don't really know, but God will take care of us," said Joseph softly.

"Shut up back there!" said Paul as his phone rang once again.

"Take all three of them to Jerusalem to the new temple," said the voice on the phone. It was Simon himself. Paul swallowed hard. He did not have the nerve to tell Simon that he had left Peter in Bethlehem. *Well, then I will just go back later and get him,* said Paul to himself.

Simon was elated that Joseph had been caught, yet he was unwilling to listen to Peter John's plea to bring them back to Rome or to at least bring Yvette back to Rome.

"She is my niece," said the Pope.

Simon laughed loudly. "No, she is your daughter, and she stays in Jerusalem. She made her choice and now she will pay. Would you like me to send you there too?" Simon asked.

Peter John shut up quickly after Simon's threat.

"Well? Answer me!" Simon commanded. His authority grew daily, and as the great day approached, he really began to feel powerful and godly himself.

"No!" said Peter John.

"Smile and be happy. Soon you will be the chief priest for the true god of this world," Simon said. This did comfort Peter John. He was going to be a powerful man himself very soon.

******

Paul took Joseph and Yvette to the new temple. There two men— one a Muslim and the other a Jewish rabbi—met him. Paul followed them into the temple through a side entrance, shoving and prodding Joseph and Yvette along.

Yvette was terrified, and Joseph knew it. He wanted to hold her hand, but there was nothing he could do. "It will be okay, Wife!"

Yvette smiled at the word *wife*. "Okay, Husband, I trust you." This did not comfort Joseph since in his heart he knew it would not be okay at all.

The inside of the temple was elaborately decorated with fine paintings of religious icons such as Abraham, Ishmael, and Isaac. The walls were a pearl white—nearly glowing—and the floor was a dark jade. The tables were marble, and tons of gold adorned nearly everything. Joseph had to admit the temple was a beautiful sight even if it was not a temple of the true God at all.

Paul followed along as the two men led the group down a narrow flight of stairs. At least three flights below the staircase ended at a large metal door. One of the men pulled out a key and unlocked the door and pushed it aside. The room was dimly lit. It was decorated nothing like the previous floors. Everywhere Joseph looked was covered with brick and mortar. At the far wall there was another small door. The men led Paul directly to this door and again used a key to unlock it. "In here," said one of the men.

Paul pushed Yvette and Joseph into the room. Yvette was petrified, and even Joseph began to perspire. There was absolutely nothing in the room other than a small overhead light 10 feet up—not even a bed or a mat for the floor. The only appliance in the room was a small toilet in the corner. Joseph understood this room to be a prison. But what was it originally constructed for? A thought occurred to him that maybe this was intended for holding human sacrifices—future human sacrifices. "We will be the first!" Joseph whispered. Yvette did not understand this cryptic comment from Joseph, but the two men who led them to the room certainly did.

Joseph and Yvette were untied and pushed into the room, and with a loud thud the door was locked behind them. Yvette ran to Joseph and fell into his arms. He held her tightly as she cried.

"The Lord is our Shepherd," he whispered softly as he caressed his terrified bride.

Chapter 23: Martyrs

Day 1245: Calvin and Cory had been working in the MGM casino for two weeks. Calvin worked by night as a janitor while Cory worked keeping the peace as a bouncer. Both men were given a room to live in and three free meals each day. The arrangement was perfect. By night they worked and by day they traveled around the city witnessing to anyone who would listen. For some reason the mood of the people in Las Vegas was much more tolerant of Calvin and Cory. There were very few angry crowds, yet there were also very few converts, but with hard work the two men began to see their harvest.

There were probably as many as 70 or so new followers of Jesus as a result of their efforts. Many of them were employees from other hotels who had not taken the ID tags like they were supposed to. Since they all had free room and board, it just didn't seem necessary.

Calvin and Cory found it challenging to find people who had not taken Carlo's mark, and soon it would be nearly impossible. Yet they both held out hope. They knew that throughout the world there must be men and women just like them—witnesses for God. Certainly there had to be more people who knew that Carlo was Satan's son.

On this particular morning Calvin and Cory stood at the edge of an elaborate park speaking to a few passers-by. Calvin explained, as usual, the deceptions that the world had fallen victim to. It was all the evil trickery of Carlo and Simon, he explained. Additionally he told them that soon Carlo would declare himself god and the people would suffer greater things than they already had with the plague and starvation.

One young black woman named Leasa Moore stood by silently listening to Calvin. She had seen and heard him speak before. What he had said continued to run through her mind. Just the day before she had stood in line to get an ID tag inserted when the warning from Calvin began to scream out loudly in her thoughts. *If I allow this, I can buy some food, but if I do take it, what does it really mean?* The thought hounded her. As Leasa stepped up to a man holding a small insertion gun, fear began to fill her soul. She looked at the man and mumbled that she had forgotten something and then turned and left.

Today Leasa stood at the edge of the park listening as Calvin spoke. Something in his voice seemed to comfort and draw her in. It was like he possessed a confidence and a passion that she had never seen before.

Unfortunately for Leasa, she had seen far too much passion. She left her home in Seattle at the age of 16 and somehow found herself in Las Vegas working in nightclubs as a dancer. Yet even this income did not provide enough money to support her drug habit. After a few years of working in clubs, Leasa eventually turned to prostitution to meet her financial needs. However, since the Rapture and subsequent plague and famine, business had slowed greatly. Today there was no longer a point to her particular profession. Shortly after Carlo Ventini introduced his ID tags the drug trading worldwide had been virtually stopped, and for a young prostitute of only 29 years of age, it was now impossible to get any drugs.

Leasa suffered greatly for a time, but eventually she overcame her addiction. However, the only life she knew was prostitution, and now even that was impossible since there was no way to pay for her services. Leasa felt hopeless and lost.

"Christ loves you so much, and He does not want any of you to suffer an eternity in Hell. Won't you accept Him into your life as your Lord and Savior?" said Calvin gently. Leasa began to break down. She wanted hope, she needed love, and she needed Jesus to save her pathetic life.

Calvin offered a sinner's prayer to the crowd, but all of them laughed at him and walked away—all except Leasa Moore who stood there crying out in despair. "Help me, please. I have nothing," she sobbed.

Cory walked over to her and put his huge arm around her shoulder to comfort her. "It will be okay now. Jesus will take care of you." Cory led Leasa to Calvin who stepped up to the young woman and greeted her with a smile. Calvin lifted Leasa's chin towards his own face. They were virtually the same height—which was average for her but short for Calvin.

"What is your name?" Calvin asked with a smile.

"Leasa Moore," she whispered.

"Leasa, do you understand who Jesus is and what He wants for your life?" asked Calvin softly.

"No, not really," said the young woman.

Calvin looked around and located an empty bench. "Let's have a seat," he said. Just as Calvin spoke a police car drove slowly through the park. Calvin paid it no attention, but it made Cory nervous. He knew that what they were doing was considered by many to be illegal, and in some countries it truly was. The United States was a bit slower to stop free speech and to outlaw Christianity. However, they did support the legal requirement for tag insertion. This law would be enforced as of January 1, and since money was already obsolete, there were very few who had not taken the ID tag as required.

Calvin and Leasa sat for quite some time talking as Cory stood guard. It was his ambition to protect Calvin at all costs. Slowly hope began to fill Leasa's heart. Calvin had painted a picture of Heaven for her. He explained what was to come of the world and what Jesus had planned for all believers. Finally Calvin asked Leasa if she was ready to accept Christ as Lord of her life. Leasa nodded slowly, affirming that she wanted God to save her from the pit of Hell.

"Then let's say a sinner's prayer together," said Calvin.

At this Cory moved in next to Calvin and knelt beside Leasa. He picked up her delicate hand, placing it into his own. His closed fist completely swallowed her hand. "Lord," said Calvin, "we come before You and humbly ask You to forgive our sins. We ask You to wash us in Your cleansing blood. Jesus, we acknowledge You as the Son of God and the only way to Heaven. Holy Spirit, we ask You to come into our lives and to guide us all the rest of our days. We commit all to You and follow after You. We praise Your holy name and thank You for Your grace and mercy.

Amen."

Leasa turned and smiled at Cory and then at Calvin. She felt a release of burden and sorrow, and for the first time in year, she had a sense of hope. *But what will I do now?* she wondered.

"Leasa," said Calvin, "The Holy Spirit of God will fill your body today because God loves you. He will sustain you through faith and through His Word. The truth of Jesus is enough for you."

"What do I do now?" she asked.

"Do you have a job and a place to live?" Cory asked.

Leasa shook her head and said that she did not have any place left to go—that she had used up all of her options. And now she didn't have a roof over her head or even any way to buy food.

Cory looked to Calvin much the same way a young child who had just brought home a stray dog would, hoping his mother would let him keep the animal as a pet. "She could stay with us," said Cory optimistically.

Leasa felt a little uneasy as Cory spoke. She had been around men all her life, and in every case they all eventually took advantage of her. It always tended to end the same way. They would befriend her and allow her to stay with them, and then at some point in time they would begin to make advances towards her, pressuring her to have sex with them as payment for helping her out. Calvin seemed to sense this fear in Leasa, although Cory missed it altogether. "Leasa, you will be safe with us. We understand your past, but it does not apply to your future. Come home with us."

Lease followed Cory and Calvin back to the MGM casino. "How do we get her in?" Cory asked. Calvin had no idea. The entrance was monitored, and nobody entered without scanning either their ID tags or their employee badges. These casinos were now very exclusive. Only the richest of people could afford to gamble and entertain themselves while the rest of the world struggled just to find food and survive the horrors of this present life.

Inside the casino next to the employee entrance a young man sat on a stool while leaning back against the wall. It was his job to scan the forehead or hand of each person entering the building or to validate the picture ID of any employee who had not yet taken Carlo's mark. A sense of calm came over the young man as he closed his eyes.

Simultaneously the latch to the back door slid forward unlocking the door. Calvin and Cory had prepared to knock when the door slowly opened. Both men stood to the side expecting someone to walk out, yet there was no one there. Cory peered in and saw the man leaning against the wall snoring loudly. "He's asleep," said Cory. Slowly Leasa, Calvin, and Cory tiptoed their way into the entrance and up the back stairs to their room.

"You will be safe here," said Cory, opening his arms as if to give Leasa access to any part of the room. "If you are hungry, we have a little food in the refrigerator." Cory smiled as he pointed to the small icebox in the corner.

"We have to get ready for work now, but you can make yourself comfortable. We get off at 6:00 a.m. I think it would be safest if you do not leave the room." Calvin beamed brightly at Leasa saying, "God has blessed us with a harvest today. Praise the Lord!"

******

Simon sat in the back of the large limousine directly across from Carlo. Excitement filled his heart as he and Carlo prepared for the final scene of their elaborate deception.

Simon had published many news articles in the last week. He had also held two separate news conferences, and in all cases he was deliberately trying to antagonize people from around the world. He was trying to unite them, to bring out their hate, and to focus it back on the Christians. He had footage of massive piles of dead bodies all consumed by the plague. From this view, he panned the camera to the scene in the warehouse in Latina where he took credit for seeking out and destroying the center of the plague's development. "We have caught the so-called *born again* scientists in the midst of making more of their evil plague. As you can see here, we have burned and destroyed all of their monstrous equipment. Additionally we have captured two of their leaders from the United

States. They have been arrested and are being sent back to me personally for interrogation. Simon smiled at the thought of confronting Dr. Sara Allen. Oh, how he would enjoy torturing this young, eye-catching scientist.

Additionally Simon had illustrated how the good people of Sydney, Australia, had rallied around Carlo Ventini and had burned all churches in that large city and surrounding areas. Simon had agreed with the Australian government to visit their country prior to going to Israel for the dedication of the temple.

"Give me the status of the world," said Carlo passively. He was distant from Simon and very preoccupied.

"Let's start with Asia," said Simon with a smile. "The Chinese government has weeded out nearly every Christian organization, arresting literally thousands. They have also agreed to a public demonstration designed to show the people their intolerance for this kind of behavior."

This got Carlo's attention. "What does that mean?" he asked.

Simon grinned. "They are going to execute some of the Christians on public television as a deterrent to their people."

Carlo liked the idea greatly. "Maybe it is time to do this very thing around the world," he said.

Simon nodded in agreement and proudly spoke up. "I have already made arrangements for executions in Australia tomorrow."

"You will be there for that yourself then?" Carlo asked.

Simon's smile broadened at the thought. "Yes, I will assist in this myself," he said.

"Not too actively!" said Carlo sternly. "What else is going on?"

"We have distributed the plague to many new locations and have limited the antidote to areas where we have already killed many. We also have reduced the food shipments to Africa and Russia, and we have eliminated them to America completely."

Carlo smiled saying, "They will not need it soon anyway."

Simon laughed at this and continued to speak. "Europe has been given a little more food, as has South America and Australia, but we also gave them a double dose of the plague. We have made Christianity illegal in virtually every country and island other than America, Europe, and South America, but they will follow suit very soon."

Carlo was sure of this, but he was still a little concerned about the predicted outcome of his divine rulership. He too understood the Bible and its predictions that Jesus would come back and defeat him in time. Today this thought plagued Carlo's mind. He so wanted to rule for an eternity.

"Finally we are rewarding people with food for turning in Bibles, and in most countries the local governments have made possessing Bibles illegal and subversive. They are putting people in jail for the crime."

"How are we doing on our ID tag compliance?" Carlo asked.

Simon had hoped to avoid this question. "Things are getting better!" he said.

"How much better?" growled Carlo.

"Worldwide we have nearly 90 percent compliance," said Simon.

"Who's giving us trouble?" Carlo asked weary of Simon as he continued to dodge the real question.

Simon sighed. "Europe is still very slow to comply. They are at 78 percent, and America is at 73 percent. But remember that next month it will be a law, so I am sure that after you declare yourself as god and this law goes into effect, everyone will comply."

"Comply or die!" Carlo roared. He was getting tired of this resistance to his power. *This will change,* he thought angrily.

Carlo's limo stopped in front of an extremely large, old building at the edge of Vatican City. Simon had given orders to have Tommy and Sara delivered directly to Peter John's office. He had planned on using the Pope's influence as they condemned Sara and Tommy for murder and conspiracy.

Simon was on a tight schedule. His personal jet would leave Rome in two hours and head directly to Sydney, but not before he got his chance to abuse and murder Sara and her young friend, Tommy.

Carlo let Simon out of the limo as Peter John stood outside waiting to greet him. "I will meet you in Jerusalem one week from today," said Carlo as he closed the limousine's door and drove away.

Peter John was exceptionally nervous today at Simon's visit. It was only last night that he had gotten the word from Paul Laruso that Peter Bastoni had escaped. This, of course, was not entirely true, but Paul had no intention of telling the Pope that he had left Peter unconscious in Bethlehem because he considered Joseph to be the real prize and Peter to be an unnecessary nuisance. Peter John knew that Simon intended to display all three of these criminals to the world. He would have to tell Simon somehow but decided it would be best to wait until Simon satisfied some of his bloodthirsty energy on Tommy and Sara.

******

Sara and Tommy sat chained wrist to wrist on a flat, metal, cargo bench inside the hollow belly of a C130 aircraft. They were both terribly sore from the explosion, and neither of them could hear much of anything as of yet. Raw nerve and fatigue consumed them. They knew their friends, Dedrick and Brian, had been killed during the lab explosion— and worse yet for Tommy was the death of his twin sister, Tina. He could not bring himself to consider what would become of Tina's soul now that she had taken her own life. All he could do was to pray and hope God would have mercy.

"What is coming next?" Tommy asked.

Sara looked into his tired and worried eyes. *Such a gentle man,* she thought. Sara understood Tommy's pain and sense of guilt over Tina. She wanted to help, but she knew that worse things were yet to come for them both. "I don't know," said Sara softly. But the look in her eyes confirmed for Tommy what he already knew.

"I am glad I have had this time with you," he said as he leaned in and kissed Sara's cheek.

Sara laid her head on Tommy's chest and began to cry. "Maybe God will help us somehow," she whispered. Tommy had not heard from God since that one morning in his motel room nearly three and one half years ago.

Now in Rome the two were shoved into the back seat of a Mercedes as the driver and his partner closed their doors and drove away from the airport. "Simon Koch is looking forward to meeting you two!" said one young man as he smiled at Sara. The other man—much older—laughed until he began to cough from his 40 years of smoking. The lung cancer had not advanced to the point that he could notice it yet, but soon he would not be laughing anymore.

The car drove into the city and was speeding down a cobblestone street when suddenly from the side, a large truck crashed into the Mercedes, instantly igniting the automobile. The driver's neck was broken. His partner was still breathing but unconscious. The front of the car was nearly torn in half. Sara and Tommy were completely unharmed but confused as to what to do. *The keys—get the handcuff keys!* said a loud voice in Tommy's mind. He leaned over to the driver and reached into the man's pocket. He had seen the young man place the keys inside his coat after cuffing Sara and Tommy together. Smoke filled the car to the point that Tommy could hardly see Sara.

Finally he found the hole and slid the key inside and turned it, freeing them both. Tommy kicked the car door open and pulled Sara away only seconds before the car exploded into a ball of fire.

Tommy surveyed the car wreck and noted that the truck had pushed the car into a narrow alley. The fire and smoke provided an excellent cover, hiding Sara and Tommy from the crowd that was gathering around the truck. Tommy squeezed Sara's hand and began to run away from the fire and towards the other end of the alley. The two of them wandered into the late hours of the night heading north. Eventually they entered a large freight yard where there was a fully loaded train just getting ready to depart. "Let's get on this and see where it takes us," Tommy said.

The glow of the December moon was all the light Tommy had to navigate. He surveyed the boxcars until he found one that would suit his needs. He hoisted Sara up and then climbed aboard. They both slid between two large canvas covers that had been put down to protect the plywood beneath from bad weather.

"Where are we going?" Sara asked.

Tommy smiled weary and said, "I have no idea!"

******

Simon waited impatiently for Sara and Tommy. He was running out of time. His plane would leave in an hour, and he didn't want to rush what he had planned for Dr. Allen and Tommy Glover. Fifteen minutes later Peter John received the call that his car had been destroyed in the fire. "Is everyone dead?" he asked.

"We believe so, but the fire was consuming and so hot that we are only now able to get close enough to view the scene," said the police officer.

Peter John hung up the phone and swallowed hard as he turned towards Simon. "What is it?" Simon asked impatiently.

Simon interrupted before the Pope could speak. "Don't you tell me they were killed!" Simon's eyes glared red at Peter John.

Peter John was terrified. It was going to be bad enough to tell him that Peter Bastoni had escaped, but now this. "Yes, they were burned to death in a car fire," said Peter John in a trembling voice.

******

Paul Laruso felt a sense of accomplishment combined with a sense of irritation. He had finally captured and delivered Joseph and Yvette after nearly a year of chasing them. But now anger welled up inside as he considered his own blunder. Why had he left Peter lying there in the alley behind Benjamin's deli? Paul decided to get a bite to eat and then he would return to Bethlehem and recapture Peter Bastoni and deliver him to the temple.

Thirty minutes later Paul was back in Bethlehem. He pulled into the alleyway behind Benjamin's deli, but not all the way into the parking lot. Paul figured Peter and the others would still be there. *Where else would they go?* he thought. Just the same, he wanted to sneak in without them running away. He was in no mood for a chase.

Paul tested the back door, and it was unlocked. He pulled out his gun and slowly opened the door. A few minutes later Paul stood in the center of the empty house as a sense of doom overcame him. He would have to call and explain this to Peter John and Simon. This was going to be bad for him. He had lost Peter Bastoni, and he hadn't a clue where to begin looking.

******

Elisha was the first to speak. "We have to get out of here! He will be back soon."

"What for?" asked David. "Why should he come back?"

Jasmine spoke up before Elisha could say another word. "He's been here once. He'll be back again."

Benjamin helped Peter off the couch. "Let's pack up as much food as we can carry and leave this place."

"Where will we go?" Peter asked. "And how will we get there?"

Benjamin handed David a set of keys. "Go open my shop," he said as he pointed in the direction of his small wooden shop outside. David ran off to do what he was told.

"I have some friends in Jerusalem. We can go stay with them for a while," said Benjamin.

"How come we have never heard of these friends?" Jasmine asked.

Elisha put his hand on Jasmine's arm as if to warn her away from pressing this issue too hard.

"Jasmine, these people are not friends. They are family, but I have not seen or heard from them in 10 years," Benjamin sighed. Elisha knew this story already. Benjamin had shared it with him many months ago.

"Who are they?" Jasmine asked with a little more caution and less persistence in her voice this time. Elisha nodded as her tone became acceptable to him.

"It is my son and his wife," said Benjamin.

It seemed that over 20 years ago Benjamin and his only child, a son, had an argument that ended their relationship. After Benjamin's wife died, he found himself alone with no family for comfort. Benjamin's son was so full of anger that he didn't even attend his own mother's internment. Benjamin had not talked to his son since the day his wife had died.

David came back into the house smiling. "It's a car!" he said proudly. Benjamin looked to Peter. "How are you feeling?"

"I'm okay," said Peter, but he didn't look or feel okay. He looked and felt more like a man who had just played a game of tackle football without a helmet or padding.

"Good! You drive," said Benjamin.

Peter's heart was so heavy with grief over Joseph and Yvette. He wished that Paul had taken him too. At least that way he would have been with Joseph.

"How are you going to get all of us into one car?" Ruth asked.

Benjamin hadn't thought about it, but Scott already had. "I am not going," said Scott.

"What do you mean?" Ruth asked.

Scott had been very quiet ever since their return from sightseeing. He was consumed with an idea that came to him shortly after hearing about Joseph and Yvette. He wanted to rescue Joseph. In his life he had never done anything heroic. Everything was always about taking care of himself. Now his friends had been taken away. Scott just knew that Paul would return for the others. He had to do something. There had to be a way to get to Joseph.

"You guys go on ahead. I am staying here for a while," said Scott.

Ruth was dismayed. She felt an urgent need to leave like all the rest, but she could not leave without Scott. Somehow over the last couple of years she had grown to love him even with all of his quirks. He was a little brother to her, and she could not leave him here to fend for himself. "Then I am staying too!" said Ruth.

Scott smiled at Ruth. She was a brave woman, and he was grateful that she wanted to be by his side—no matter what.

Peter was still a little fuzzy in the head, but he understood that Joseph's friends were not going to run. He wanted to stay too, but who would drive the car?

******

Peter pulled into a narrow driveway and stopped the car. The house, like all houses in Jerusalem, was sandy brown and very small. Benjamin turned and looked at the three children stuffed into the small rear compartment. "Well, let's see how this goes," said Benjamin. The 75-year-old man climbed out of the car and walked slowly up to the front door of his son's home—or what had once been his son's home. He could not be sure that Daniel Cohen even lived there anymore.

The door opened even before Benjamin knocked. It was Jill, Daniel's wife and Benjamin's daughter-in-law. She smiled at Benjamin in total surprise. "Papa!" she said as she wrapped her arms around the old man's neck and hugged him tightly. Peter and Elisha stood outside the car watching this event unfold. Next a middle-aged man of maybe 45 years stepped into the doorway. He looked like Benjamin only younger and taller. Benjamin stared at his son.

Benjamin noted that the years had changed his boy, and sorrow filled the old man's heart. What had he done? Why had he allowed this separation between him and Daniel? All those wasted years—and for what? Life was never going to be the same.

"Hello, Daniel," said Benjamin with a cautious smile.

It took a few seconds before Daniel spoke. He was obviously not sure what to think about the whole scene. He had never expected to see his father again even though his heart yearned for this day. "Hello, Papa," he finally said.

Jill looked past Benjamin and directly at Peter and Elisha. "Who are your friends?" she asked.

"It is a long story," said Benjamin. "May we all come in and talk about it?"

Jill looked to Daniel for the answer. She smiled at Daniel, urging him to take this flag of truce from his estranged father. "Yes, Papa, come in and bring your friends."

Benjamin breathed a sigh of relief as he waved to Peter and Elisha to come forward. Jasmine and David climbed out of the back seat and followed the men up to the house and into the foyer. All seven people stood in the living room of the small, brightly lit home.

Elisha saw all of this as amusing. He knew that Benjamin and Daniel had very hard feelings toward each other. He didn't really understand why, but he had felt the same way about his own father many times—though not to the extent that he would move away and never return, although it had actually turned out that way. The thought made Elisha sad.

"What is this all about?" Daniel asked. "What is going on, Papa?"

Benjamin motioned towards the couch. "Can we sit and talk, Son?"

Everyone found a place on the furniture or floor and sat down to listen to Benjamin. The conversation was cautious at first. Benjamin knew that his son was not a believer in Christ and would, therefore, not be easily convinced.

"The world is coming to an end. The Antichrist is already here, and he is Carlo Ventini. Soon Jesus will come back and defeat him, but until then misery awaits all of us." Benjamin continued to discuss the subject until he felt that he had said all he could.

Jill and Daniel sat back silently but with occasional looks of disbelief. Finally Daniel spoke up, "You believe Carlo Ventini, our world leader, is the Antichrist? You believe in this Jesus as the Son of God? Papa, what has happened to you?"

Benjamin sat quietly. He knew he would not be able to convince Daniel. His son was a hard man who required logic and proof of everything.

"Mr. Cohen," said Peter. "I know this is hard to believe. I was the same way once, but God has actually spoken to me." Daniel and Jill looked at Peter questioningly. Peter went on to elaborate about the last three and a half years. He explained the move to Rome and his efforts on the antidote for the plague. He further explained how and why he came to Jerusalem.

None of this seemed to help. In fact, just the mention of his involvement with the plague seemed to freeze Daniel and Jill where they sat.

"So you are one of those *born again* scientists," said Daniel, "here to confuse my father, no doubt?" Daniel's accent was not as heavy as Benjamin's, and Peter could easily detect his dislike of him.

"It is all true! What's the matter with you?" a frustrated Jasmine roared. Elisha put his hand on her arm to calm her, but she knocked it off and stood to speak. "We were in the desert when an angel came to us and brought us to Bethlehem. He told us about Jesus, and it is our job to tell everyone we can before the end comes!"

Jill did not like the young girl's tone of voice at all. How dare this Palestinian come into their house and speak to them like this. "What end? The end of the radical Christians maybe," Jill countered.

It was no use. Benjamin knew this. He had regrets about ever coming here now, but what choice did he have? There was no other place to go. In just 10 more days Carlo would dedicate the temple, incurring the total wrath of God, and then the world would know the truth. At least those who had doubts about Carlo would know the truth.

"We need a week," said Benjamin. Everyone in the room quieted and listened as the old man spoke. "Regardless of what you believe, Daniel, in just 10 days Carlo Ventini will desecrate the new temple and God will respond severely. We need a place to stay until then."

Jill looked at Daniel and shook her head. She had no intention of allowing any of these Christian rebels into her house to stay, especially for 10 days. They barely had enough food just to keep the two of them alive.

Daniel received Jill's message loud and clear and then turned and looked into his father's tired old eyes. He stared at the man who used to carry him to bed and read to him from the Torah nightly—the same man that for the last 20 years he had been mad at, mad enough to avoid him completely. But now his father had come back and was in need of his help. Even if Daniel thought Benjamin's cause was ridiculous, he would not abandon his father again. "Yes, you and your friends may stay here, but I do not want my neighbors to see any of you, so you must not leave the house. And I would like you to respect our rules. We do not have much food, but I guess we can find a way to buy some more."

"Do you have ID tags?" Elisha asked after hearing Daniel talk about buying more food.

"Yes, of course! Don't you?" said Jill.

Benjamin lowered his head as all the other Christians in the room looked towards him for his reaction. Pain filled the old man's heart. He knew his son and daughter-in-law were lost for all eternity.

"What is it? What is the matter?" Daniel asked.

"We brought food," said Benjamin without raising his tearstained eyes towards his son.

******

Paul turned to leave Benjamin's deli. He could not believe the mess he had gotten himself into by leaving Peter behind. After a year of chasing Joseph and Yvette around, it just didn't seem fair that he was going to suffer for this mistake because of Peter Bastoni! Paul pulled out his cell phone and called Peter John's direct line.

"What is it?" the Pope asked.

Paul swallowed hard and said, "I lost Peter Bastoni."

"Lost him! Where? What do you mean, you lost him?" Peter John shouted.

Paul explained everything as best he could, but the Pope was livid. "You find him today!" said Peter John as he hung up the phone.

Scott and Ruth had been in the closet listening to this entire conversation. That morning they had devised a plan. They would watch for Paul to show up and then hide in the closet until the right moment. Now Scott's hand shook as he held onto Paul's revolver, the one he had taken off him when Joseph knocked him out with a frying pan.

The top half of the closet was louvered to circulate air. This allowed Ruth the advantage of watching every move Paul made. However, since Scott was shorter he could not get the right angle to look down through the louvers. He had no idea how close Paul would be when he stepped out. Ruth grabbed the handle and pushed hard against the door, opening it quickly. The noise caused Paul to turn rapidly just in time to see Scott standing in the kitchen pointing his own gun at his chest. Paul raised his revolver and pointed it back to Scott.

It was a standoff—neither man blinked or moved an inch. Ruth stood by, amazed at the sight. This was not exactly what she and Scott had planned.

"Drop the gun!" said Paul.

"Drop yours!" said Scott, but not as convincingly as Paul.

Ruth backed up a step, knocking a large spice rack off the wall and distracting Paul for a fraction of a second, but it was long enough. Scott fired his gun towards Paul hitting him in the shoulder and causing him to drop his gun.

Ruth looked at Paul and then back to Scott. She was impressed with the little man. He had done well. "Okay then!" said Scott excitedly. "Now we want you to take us to where Joseph and Yvette are."

Paul looked at Scott with eyes full of rage and surprise. He wasn't terribly wounded. He knew he would not die from the small hole in the flesh of his shoulder, but he had lost his advantage. Scott had his gun pointed more accurately this time and Paul knew he would use it if necessary.

"Ruth, get his gun," said Scott with a bit of pride and forcefulness in his tone.

Ruth walked up to Paul and leered at him as she bent to pick up his revolver. "Where is Joseph?" Scott asked.

"In Jerusalem at the new temple," said Paul.

Ruth stood and turned toward Scott, but before she could say a word, Paul grabbed her and the gun, forcing it up to her head. A look of terror filled her face. She had gotten careless, and now she would pay for it with her life. "Drop the gun!' said Paul.

Scott looked into Ruth's scared eyes, hoping for an answer. "Don't, Scott. He will kill us anyway!"

Scott understood this, but he had no choice.

"Put the gun down now!" Paul yelled.

Ruth gave Scott a stern, motherly look. "Shoot him, Scott!"

"I can't!" Scott said. "I'll hit you!"

"Shut up!" said Paul. "Drop your gun now or she is dead!"

The situation was hopeless. Scott started to lower the gun. Just then Ruth dug her finger into Paul's bullet wound. He yelled out in pain and released his grip on her. "Shoot him!" Ruth screamed. Simultaneously, Paul and Scott fired. Ruth could nearly feel the bullets speeding by her in both directions. Paul fell first, pulling Ruth down with him.

Ruth looked into Paul Laruso's dying face. "I wish I had never heard of Joseph Bastoni," he whispered. Suddenly Paul's chest made a loud gurgling sound and out of his mouth a large bloody bubble emerged. Paul died with his eyes open as if he were looking at something terrible.

Ruth sat forward. "You killed him, Scott!" Getting no response from Scott, she looked up just in time to see him falling against the far wall and down to the ground, leaving a trail of blood as he went.

"Oh no, Scott! You're shot!"

"There's news!" Scott whispered with a weak smile.

Ruth ran to Scott's side and held his hand tightly as tears flooded her dark brown eyes. "You saved my life, Scott," Rush whispered.

Scott looked into Ruth's grief-stricken face. He had grown to love Ruth very much. She had so much strength and wisdom. "Thank you for taking care of me all this time," Scott coughed. "I would not have made it without you. I'm going to see Zach Miles very soon," he smiled. Scott closed his eyes as Ruth pulled his limp body into her own.

The room around Ruth began to glow brightly as a rush of cool air blew through her hair. "Do not grieve for him," said the voice softly.

Ruth began to sob uncontrollably. "What do I do now?" she moaned. "What will happen next?"

"Child, there are many trials ahead for this world. Very soon evil will consume the earth, but only for a season. You must stay here until Christmas Day, and then you will go to Jerusalem for the dedication of the temple."

Ruth held Scott tightly, crying all the while. "Then what will I do?" she asked.

"Just as you did for Scott, you will lead people to Me and away from the *Lake of Fire*."

The glow in the room faded, leaving Ruth alone with two dead men. Ruth surveyed the kitchen looking for anything that would help her deal with her present situation. On the far wall next to the closet where she and Scott had just hidden was a very large metal door. *It's a freezer,* Ruth thought. She laid Scott down gently and walked to the door. Inside the freezer was nearly empty except for a few large beef briskets. Benjamin used the meat locker to hold his monthly order of beef and lamb, but since the beginning of the famine his locker grew less and less necessary. Ruth dragged Paul into the room and placed him against a far wall. Next she carefully pulled Scott into the meat locker and placed him carefully in the other corner. Ruth bent down and kissed Scott tenderly on the forehead. "Now you are truly happy. I'll see you soon!"

******

Chang led the way with Izuho and Lyn Lee stumbling behind him. The crowd threw rocks and pieces of wood at them as they were paraded onto the stage. Tailing the procession was the elderly guard who had been giving them extra food. He knew what was about to happen to these three young people. It saddened his heart greatly. Over the last month or so he had really grown fond of all three of them. He even became receptive to their preaching of the gospel and began to believe what they spoke.

Lyn Lee grabbed Izuho's hand out of fear as she stood before the crowd of literally tens of thousands of angry onlookers. "I love you!" Izuho whispered with a brave smile for Lyn Lee. She smiled back weakly.

Chang was checking out the cameras. They were placed everywhere. It was obvious that this was going to be broadcast around the world. Chang's eyes also caught sight of a small table with a large whip and a long sword-like knife laying on it. The display was ominous. Chang knew the tools were to be used on the three of them, and fear filled his body. He stared at the small, sharp pieces of metal tied to the end of the whip. "Lord, give me courage," said Chang softly, but not so softly that the old guard did not hear him.

Lyn Lee, Chang, and Izuho were stripped of all their clothing as the crowd cheered loudly. Two guards led each person to one of the three large poles in the center of the stage. They were all tied tightly with sharp wire as the executioner, dressed in red, stepped up to the stage and over to the small table.

The crowd roared as the man picked up the long whip and snapped it into the air. Izuho understood the sound. He knew what was coming next, but for some reason he did not have any fear. He knew it would hurt and he would die a horrible death, but his only concern was for Lyn Lee. She was so frail already. "Lord, please take Lyn Lee now so she doesn't have to suffer this with us," he prayed.

Lyn Lee looked into Izuho's eyes. She loved this man greatly. "Thank you!" she whispered and smiled back to Izuho.

About that time the old guard stepped up to the three poles as if to inspect the work of his men. The man whispered his appreciation for the Word that Chang had planted in his heart. Next he went to Izuho and stood between him and Lyn Lee. "God hears your prayers," he whispered. As he did this, the others on stage stood back and watched, not fully sure of what the man was doing. The old man pulled a long knife from his pocket and held it close to his body. He had already thought this through even before he heard Izuho's prayer. *They must die, but why must they suffer?* he thought. He also hoped God would forgive him for taking matters into his own hands, or perhaps he was an instrument for the Lord in the first place.

Izuho saw the reflection of the sun coming off the knife, and so did one of the other guards. The old guard turned towards Lyn Lee revealing his lethal blade. She looked into the man's face. She saw his grief and torment and understood that he wanted to spare her the torture that was to come.

Lyn Lee looked to Izuho and Chang and smiled brightly. "I love you both and I will see you in Heaven in just a few minutes from now." Lyn Lee then nodded to the guard who altered his position so he could thrust his long blade underneath her ribcage and directly into her heart. A shout came from one of the other guards warning the older man to stop, but he ignored the warning and pulled his blade back for leverage. A gunshot rang out as a younger guard fired his weapon directly at the old man, but not before he inserted his blade fully into Lyn Lee's chest cavity. The young girl looked into Izuho's eyes and then toward the eyes of the old guard. Both Lyn Lee and the guard died quickly.

The crowd became unruly at the sight of what had just happened. They could not believe that the old man would do such a thing, preventing the girl from dying the tortuous death she deserved. They had no concept of the love and compassion that the guard had shown to Lyn Lee. The crowd now had a lust for blood, and they began to chant to the men on the stage, "Beat them...Beat them!"

Izuho was first to be tortured. With each snap of the whip, the flesh was torn from his body, spraying blood onto Chang. Izuho refused to satisfy the crowd by screaming out in pain. Instead he gritted his teeth and held onto the pole as tightly as he could as the metal wire sliced through his wrists. It was another five minutes of horrible whipping and tearing at Izuho's body before he lost enough blood to become unconscious. Before this happened, however, he looked towards Chang compassionately and blinked his eyes goodbye. Chang cried uncontrollably. He had made such a mess of things. He felt this was entirely his fault. He felt he deserved what was coming to him. Lyn Lee and Izuho had been such pure-hearted people, and now they were dead because of him.

After Izuho's death the guards pulled down his body and Lyn Lee's and threw them into the crowd along with the old guard's lifeless body. Yells and screams of delight could be heard from every direction as thousands of people raced to get to the bloodied corpses of these martyrs. Fights ensued as many wrestled for an opportunity to be a part of the excitement.

Next the guards turned towards Chang as the executioner walked around the pole slowly snapping his bloody whip. Unexpectedly the man called out to the guards to have Chang untied. He was enjoying the response from the crowds, and he was sure that the home audience watching from their televisions around the world also approved of his work thus far.

Now he thought that he would really show them something. Chang was stretched between two of the poles facing the crowd. The man in red walked up to Chang, looked into his eyes, and smiled a hideous grin.

Instead of getting the response of fear he expected from Chang, he got a smile and the words, "God loves you!" This shook the man's confidence momentarily, causing him to strike Chang in the face out of anger. The crowd roared at this, but then they did not hear or see how Change had reacted to the man. "He still loves you!" Chang smiled through tears of pain.

The audience at home was rendered speechless by this man's bravery and confidence in a God they knew nothing about. This was not having the effect that Simon and Carlo would have hoped for. This was turning into a testimony of faith and love, both of which they and the world hated.

The executioner walked over to the table and picked up the large sword-like blade and turned back to Chang. "Let's just see how much your God loves you!" With a swipe of the blade, the man spilled Chang's intestines out of his stomach cavity. The crowd stopped their grotesque activities on Izuho's and Lyn Lee's bodies long enough to appreciate what had just happened to Chang. They clapped and cheered wildly, but what they didn't see was the fact that Chang was dead even before the blade touched his body. God had chosen to remove Change before his torture. The only one who knew about this was the executioner who realized that as his blade slit open Chang's body, there was no life in him at all.

The crowd cheered for more. They wanted Chang to scream out in pain as his intestines covered the ground where he was tied, yet they heard nothing. They became quiet. What had just happened? Why was this man not screaming? The executioner knew he needed to do something and quickly. He turned sideways, and with a rapid swing he decapitated Chang and then bent down and picked up his head by the hair, waving it to the crowd who once again were thrilled with the executions.

******

Sara slept on Tommy's lap while the train continued its perpetual *thud, thud, thud* as it sped through the countryside. It had been a long night for Tommy. His mind had drifted in and out of thoughts. Often he found himself thinking of the good times he and Tina had shared as they went through college together and then into the field to work as volcanologists.

Tommy thought about how over the last couple of years he and Tina had continued to grow apart. It seemed to start right after his visitation from God. Tommy could still remember God's warning that Tina's heart was not the same as his own. Why hadn't he paid more attention to Tina? Why hadn't he spent more time trying to convince her about the reality of Jesus?

A thought occurred to Tommy. What was missing from the beginning for Tina was the Word of God itself. He and Tina had never gone to church or read the Bible. Even after his encounter with God, Tommy still never spent a moment reading the Bible. He understood now that there was no way Tina would ever have come to know the Lord without the Scriptures having been placed carefully in her heart. It was not enough for her to take Tommy's word about God. She would always require more proof.

The train began to slow. Tommy pulled the canvas back to see what was going on. The sun was beginning to rise over his left shoulder. He had no idea where he was, but he was certain that he was going north. The further north the better as far as he was concerned.

Twenty minutes later the train came to a complete stop. Tommy woke Sara gently. "We need to get off here," he said softly. Sara looked into Tommy's weary face. She knew he had stayed up all night watching over her. She loved him very much.

Tommy lifted Sara off the train and led her around the boxcar and into a heavily wooded forest. "What do we do now?" Sara asked.

Tommy looked around slowly. "First I think I will use one of those trees if you don't mind." Sara smiled as she had the same idea in mind.

A few minutes later Tommy and Sara found themselves walking down a moderate slope, clear of the woods. Below them was a small, yellow house at the base of a long, narrow meadow. There were no other houses anywhere around. In fact, it was an odd sight just to see this home there. It seemed completely out of place, as if its owners were flown into the middle of a large forest and just simply built a dwelling right in the heart of it. There was a dirt road leading away from the house, stretching over a small hill, and disappearing into the woods below. Tommy and Sara were both starving, but could they risk the chance of being caught by whoever lived here?

"Perhaps God has led us here," said Sara as if she was reading Tommy's mind.

"Yes, and perhaps not," said Tommy cautiously.

"Well, there is only one way to find out," said Sara as she marched on towards the house. Tommy followed along nervously. The last thing he wanted to do was to get caught and sent back to meet Simon Koch.

Before they reached the house an elderly woman with cotton white hair stepped out onto the front porch. Even though Tommy was a good 50 yards away, he could still tell that something was odd about this lady. She was very old, but not just old. She was different somehow.

Sara stopped about 25 feet away from the woman and smiled at her. Tommy watched this exchange carefully. If the woman were an enemy, he would figure it out soon enough. The old woman's smile was surprisingly white and somehow youthful. *Something is very unusual about her, for sure,* Tommy thought. Next an elderly man stepped out on the porch beside the woman. "We've been waiting for you two. Come on in," he waved.

Sara looked to Tommy for an answer. She was just as confused as he was. Something was very wrong with these two people. They looked old and maybe even harmless, but somehow Sara and Tommy knew that things were not exactly as they appeared. Tommy held Sara's hand and walked up to the front of the yellow house. Both Sara and Tommy stopped at the base of the steps.

"How are you, Tommy?" the old woman asked. Tommy felt a jolt of electricity run through his body. He began to feel trapped. How could they know his name? Sara could feel Tommy's grip tighten. She knew they were about to run. She also wondered what she had gotten them into.

"It is okay!" said the woman with an Italian accent and a very squeaky voice. "You are safe here. We've been waiting for you."

The old man and woman walked down the steps together. It was obvious that Sara and Tommy were not going to come in. As they approached, Tommy noted that the woman's face was covered with deep cracks and her hair was nearly transparent. The old man looked much the same. These two were certainly as old as any person he had ever seen, yet as they walked, they seemed to give off a youthful appearance.

"How do you know me?" Tommy asked suspiciously.

"Won't you come in and have something to eat so we can talk about it?" said the old man. Sara's stomach rumbled at the thought.

"No!" said Tommy. "We will discuss it here— in the open."

The old woman walked up to Tommy and put her bony ancient hand on his arm. "Don't grieve over Tina. God has His own ways of judging the heart and giving each of us what we justly deserve."

Tommy's eyes filled with tears. "What is going on here? Who are you two?"

"We are your friends," said the old man.

"Won't you come in?" said the woman.

Tommy held tightly to Sara as they climbed the stairs and went into the house. The smell of delicious food found its way into their nostrils even before they entered the foyer. The house itself was very comfortable, but decorated with appliances and furniture from at least two centuries earlier. Even the painting on the wall of *The Last Supper* looked to be hundreds of years old. The chairs and couch were made from the leather of some animal that Tommy could not even guess by its appearance. Maybe it was age that did this, as well, but the couch did look comfortable—as did every piece of furniture in the room. The lamps were all oil, but the glass looked cloudy as if the sand had not fully melted.

"Over here," said the woman as she pointed to a dining room table made out of the trunk of a large pine tree. The table sat no more than a foot off the ground and all around the table were large pillows. "Won't you recline with us and eat?" the woman asked.

From behind the old man put his surprisingly strong hand on Tommy's shoulder and squeezed. "It is okay. You are safe now!"

Tommy and Sara sat on the floor between the pillows as the woman began to bring dishes of sweet smelling food into the room—plate after plate of meat, eggs, bread, and potatoes. The man began to serve Sara first and then Tommy.

"Eat up! We know you are very hungry." Tommy hoped that they were not being fattened up for the kill, but he could no longer resist the food and began to devour everything on his plate.

"Aren't you two going to eat?" Sara asked.

"No, Darling. We've had our fill," said the old woman.

"How do you know about me?" Tommy asked with a mouthful of potatoes. "And how do you know about Tina?"

"Yes, and why did you say you were waiting for us?" said Sara.

The woman looked to the old man to answer these questions. With a smile as young as her own, the man began to speak. "God told us. We have been following your activities for quite some time now."

Tommy was getting suspicious again that maybe they were fattening them up for the kill after all.

"Are you angels?" Sara asked.

Both old people began to laugh childishly. "No, we are not angels," said the woman.

"But you are something," said Sara. "Something not from this world!"

"No," said the man. "We are from this world, or at least we used to be."

"What do you mean?" Tommy asked.

"Eat up," said the woman, "and we will tell you our story."

"We were like you once, a long time ago," said the woman.

"A really long time ago," added the old man with a grin. At this both old people snickered like children.

"We were married for nearly 70 years," said the woman proudly as she looked to her husband. "But that was then and this is now."

"When were you married?" Tommy asked. He was detecting a theme that was worth exploring.

The old woman smiled as if she were still a newlywed. "What was it, Husband? 1826?"

"More like 1827, I think," said the man. The woman smiled at this, causing Sara to laugh out loud.

Tommy looked at the two old people and spoke. "You mean to tell me—"

"Yes!" said the man. "We have been dead for about 100 years."

Sara chimed in. "I don't understand. What are you doing here? How do you know us?"

"Let us try to explain, Dear," said the woman.

"The Lord has a use for all of us in His kingdom. Sometimes He uses angels, sometimes He uses live people to do His work, sometimes He does it Himself, and then sometimes He uses those of us that are already living in Heaven."

"It just depends on God's particular need at that time," said the old man.

"Why is God using you two now?" Tommy asked.

Both of the old people laughed loudly. Tommy and Sara did not see the humor, but their laughter was contagious. "Eat up!" said the woman.

"One hundred years ago Martha and I," said the old man as he pointed toward his wife who winked at Tommy, "were Catholic missionaries in Africa."

"It was hot and hard work, but very rewarding!" Martha chimed.

"Yes, Dear," nodded the old man. "Very hot. But we didn't mind. Daily we would walk from town to town and sit in the shade with the members of every tribe and witness to them from the New Testament. Sometimes we would get chased out of their villages."

"Mostly by Muslims," said Martha.

"Yes, Dear, mostly by the Muslims," said the old man as he tried to continue. "But over time we built a church and had children and adults coming every Sunday for service. It was wonderful," said the man looking up as if trying to remember what happened next.

"But then Harry, my husband, and I found ourselves in the middle of a tribal war," said Martha as she patted her husband's ancient hand.

"Yes, that's right. We found ourselves in the middle of a tribal war, and when it was over the Muslims were victorious."

Harry grew quiet for a moment. "One night they came into our town with torches and lit our church on fire." Martha stared at her husband as he spoke slowly as if remembering each little detail of that night over 100 years ago.

"Well, to make a long story short, they tied us up and threw us into the church while it was burning," said Harry as he closed his eyes.

Martha spoke quietly, "Harry and I had a few minutes before the fire and smoke consumed us. We both prayed to the Lord for help and asked God to keep us together for eternity. We asked God to let us see the day of His glorious return and to allow us to be involved wherever possible."

"So here we are!" said Harry proudly.

"What about us? How do we fit into all of this?" Tommy asked.

"God has more work for you two to do, but it will not happen until after the temple is desecrated by that monster."

"Until then?" asked Sara.

"Until then you'll stay here with us regaining your strength, because you have much to do," said Harry.

Tommy was a little frightened by the whole thing, but if it was what God truly wanted him to do, then he would be obedient.

******

Simon stood in the center of a grand stadium that had been built for the Australian-hosted Olympic Games. Today, however, there were no games to be played. This was serious business, and Simon was in a dreadful mood. Only yesterday after Simon landed in Sydney did Peter John call to inform him that it appeared as if Tommy Glover and Sara Allen had not died in the fire after all, but instead had escaped. Simon was livid, and the Pope was literally terrified that Simon would have him killed for this error. "Find Paul Laruso and have him track them down," Simon demanded. "And I don't want to wait a year this time!"

Peter John understood the warning, but he had already tried to call Paul three times with no response. Something was wrong, but what he didn't know. "Is that all you have for me?" Simon asked, irritated. The Pope paused on the other end of the phone. He knew the next thing he said might cost him his life for sure, but what choice did he have? He had postponed this long enough.

"Peter Bastoni has escaped," said the Pope softly.

"What?" Simon screamed, his face turning bright red. If Peter John had been with him, Simon would have killed him for sure.

"What are you doing about this?" Simon asked.

"I cannot seem to find Paul Laruso either. Something has happened to him and—"

Simon interrupted the Pope saying, "You are becoming extremely useless and disappointing to me. I will take care of this myself as soon as we are done dedicating the new temple in Jerusalem." Simon hung up the phone seething with the desire to kill this weak and stupid man. He only needed him as an icon to his people, and that soon would come to an end when Carlo declared himself as god. But for today none of this mattered. Simon had a new task before him, and it was one he was definitely in the mood for.

Simon walked by a news crew as they were hooking up all of their cables to their sound and camera equipment. This was going to be a worldwide spectacle for sure. He had not seen the Chinese video on Izuho, Chang, and Lyn Lee yet, but he was sure his would be better. Simon's security escort cleared a path through all the construction activities and led the way to the stage. Simon stood in the center of the stage looking out at the massive stadium. He could easily squeeze a 100,000 people into this place. "What fun we will have tonight," said Simon aloud as he walked off the empty platform.

******

Stan and Ruby were devastated when their children were taken away. All through the night they cried and worried about what had happened to the five of them. Ruby was the first to speak what both she and Stan were thinking. "We need to turn ourselves in. At least that way we can be with the children."

Stan was in agreement, but it was not that easy. They had no idea where their children had been taken, and they also had Christopher to worry about. Stan did not want to consider turning in his eldest living son along with them. Stan looked to his son. "We can't leave the children by themselves," he said.

Christopher nodded. He understood that his parents had to attempt to find his brothers and sister. "I'll go with you," said Christopher.

Ruby spoke up abruptly. "No, Chris, you cannot come with us."

"Why not? Where else can I go? What will become of me in the end anyway?"

Ruby and Stan had been reading the Bible to their children every night since the Rapture. All six children understood the times they were living in. They also understood that it was only a matter of time before they would not be able to resist Carlo Ventini without paying with their lives. That day had finally come, and now Christopher saw no reason to avoid it further. His argument was a good one. Stan had no idea where his son could go or how he would survive, not to mention that he, too, would eventually be captured and killed. What was the point in putting this off any longer?

Stan was about to give in to his son's request. He was proud of the boy. To follow his parents into a situation that would surely cost him his life was a brave thing to do. Ruby spoke up again. "The job is not complete. There are still others that need to know about God. Just possibly God does not want Chris to come with us and that is why he was not taken with the other children, not to mention that there is always the Millennium. Chris may survive after all."

"Do you really think so?" Stan asked hopefully.

"Why not? The Bible says people will be here for the Millennium. Chris could be one of them, couldn't he? " said Ruby desperately. She knew if Chris came with them, he would also die, and this thought broke her heart.

Chris was opposed to the idea. "Where will I go? How will I survive?"

"You could go back to our home," said Ruby.

"Our home was burned to the ground," said Christopher.

"The survival pod," said Stan with a smile. "You can stay in our survival pod!"

Ruby nodded.

"It has food and water enough for a year for a family of eight. You can make it, Son. You can make it!" said Stan with a new determination in his voice.

Suddenly the room took on a soft white glow as if the sun were coming up, but since it was not even dawn yet, that was not possible. "Say goodbye to your parents, Christopher," said a gentle voice as Philip, the large black angel, appeared.

Ruby was terrified, but as all mothers can be, she was brave. "They took my babies!"

"Be comforted. You will be with them soon. Stay strong. God will not leave you even through the trials ahead. Your family will serve His purpose."

"What is to become of Christopher? Should he go with us?" asked Stan as his voice trembled.

"God has a different path for Christopher. Say goodbye to your parents. I am taking you back to your ranch."

Ruby reached over and took hold of her son, crying as she hugged the boy tightly.

Stan also hugged his son. "I love you, Boy! Stay strong and faithful. God will not leave you."

Christopher cried desperately and held tightly to his mother. "I don't want to leave you, Mom, or you, Dad. I love you!"

Christopher disappeared even before the sound of his voice faded from the room. "He is safe in your survival pod. Now take courage and be strong. Your love for each other and your children will carry you until the end," said a calming voice. The light faded from the room. Stan hugged Ruby as they both wept for their children. Suddenly there was a loud knock at the door, startling them.

"Who could that be?" Ruby asked. Stan knew who it was, and he was glad. He wanted to be with his children.

******

Stan and Ruby sat on the floor of their cell with all five children around them. They had been there for a week. Carrie, Stan's only daughter, sat on his lap as he wrapped his strong arms around his little girl. "What will happen to us, Daddy?" she asked.

"Well," said Stan. "You remember all the things we've read to you about Heaven and Jesus?"

The child nodded.

"Soon we will be there, and we will not have to be locked up in this stinky little jail."

"Are we going to die?" one of Stan's sons asked. He was the second-oldest living son, and he was all of 14.

Stan thought about the question for a few seconds. "If it is God's will for us. We will die to serve a purpose for Him, but then we will all be in Heaven where we can never be hurt again."

"Will it hurt?" Carrie asked. At this Stan began to cry. He could not stand the idea of this sweet little girl and all the rest of his children in pain and fear due to the evil people that awaited them.

******

Simon stood back on the stage once again. The stadium lights were bright, and the massive crowd cheered as he walked across the stage to the microphone. "Good evening, my good and loyal friends," he said with a large, fake smile. "Tonight we will together rid the world of evil. As you fully understand, the Christians around the world have been attacking all of us with their subversive tactics. They have taken the food right out of the mouths of our own children. They have poisoned us with this horrific plague, and they continue to destroy our every effort to make this world a great place of peace and prosperity. They refuse the ID tags that we have provided to improve the economy and to eliminate drugs and criminal activities that come with paper money. They have even tried to kill our own leader, Carlo Ventini, but as you have seen, they will never succeed. Tonight we will make a world demonstration, sending a clear message to all Christians that we declare war on them, their Bible, and their God." At this the crowd clapped and stomped their feet for nearly five minutes.

Simon turned to see Stan and Ruby being escorted on stage along with their five children. Stan wanted to hold Carrie, but his hands were tied behind his back. Ruby kept her children close together as she walked beside her husband. "I love you, Stan. We will be home soon." Stan nodded. It was all he could do because of the grief that filled his heart. If only he had not been deceived by the false doctrine of his church, he would not have had to put his family through all this. It was all entirely his fault and he knew it.

Simon walked up to Stan and glared at him, but Stan did not back down. Simon could kill him and his family, but he was no longer going to be afraid of any man. God had given him courage and strength to endure this. His lack of fear made Simon angry, and he hit Stan in the mouth with the microphone. At this the crowd went wild. Their enthusiasm only fueled Simon's thirst for blood. "This man and his family are Christians. They are responsible for building at least 20 churches. These churches were the center of many terrorist activities until we found out and burned them to the ground. This man and his family led much of this evil activity. They are the reason so many of us have suffered. What would you like me to do with them?" Simon shouted.

"Kill them!" the crowd chanted. The sound of so many voices in unison created a wave of energy focused directly towards the Evans family. It was literally a physical sensation as the voices channeled into a single roar: "Kill them all!"

Stan's children were terrified and began to cry, all except the oldest boy who stood proudly by his father's side. Simon grabbed the young man by the arm. "You will be first, tough guy." He led the boy over to a table where two men stood by with chains. The men stripped him of his clothing and lifted him onto the table, chaining his arms and legs down. Next they threw a bucket of water on the boy's naked body. The crowd watched carefully on the many big screens throughout the stadium while huge satellite dishes fed the airwaves with each and every event as they unfolded.

Next wires were taped to the boy's thighs, armpits, and neck. As soon as the men stepped back, completing their tasks, Simon reached over and turned a large, black knob clockwise. Instantly the boy began to convulse and scream out in pain. Ruby screamed with him, as did the other children. This went on for a few minutes before Simon turned the knob to full power. The boy's body nearly levitated off the table. Smoke began to pour from his skin as he screamed horribly.

Stan could not take another second of this. His heart was exploding in his chest. "God, let him die!" Stan cried. Just then the boy's body ignited into a ball of flames and his screaming finally came to an end.

Simon walked away from the smell and back over to where Stan stood. He looked at Stan again, this time expecting to see fear, but once again it was not there. Simon saw hate and sorrow, but no intimidation at all. In fact, it seemed that Stan had a new determination. This angered Simon greatly, so he reached out and grabbed Carrie by her dark brown hair and dragged her over to where the men now stood. Ruby let out a loud moan and passed out. She could not handle any more of this. God was merciful to allow her to shut down, but Stan stood and endured the death of each and every child, horrified by their pain and agony, but unable to do a thing about it. The torture was different for each one: electricity, whips, decapitation, intestines cut out, whatever it took. In all cases it was horrible and painful beyond belief, yet now each of his babies were in Heaven, and it was now his and Ruby's turn.

Simon had been so engrossed in what he was doing that he had not noticed that the crowd had become deathly quiet. The people's opinion was changing with each child's death. This same reaction was felt in homes around the world. People were sick at what they saw. How could this man be a friend and yet do all of this to children?

Finally Simon had Ruby lifted onto a table and stripped of all her clothing. She was in and out of consciousness. It was just too much trauma for her mind to understand. Simon had chosen to use the electricity on her. He had decided it was the most painful and the least messy.

Just as Ruby began to scream Stan broke free of his guard and came running as quickly as he could with his hands tied tightly behind his back. Simon was so focused on Ruby as he turned the black control knob that he didn't even see Stan until it was too late.

Stan rammed into Simon throwing him into the electrical equipment, causing him to turn the knob to full power. Ruby's body leapt up on the table as the electricity surged through her at over 20,000 volts. Stan looked at his wife's lifeless body as it began to smoke. He jumped up with as much force as his legs could muster and landed directly on top of Ruby. Instantly the current transferred into his body killing him almost upon contact.

Simon stared at the table and reached over to turn off the black knob before Stan died, but the knob would not move. No matter how hard he tried, he could not turn the power down. Finally both Ruby's and Stan's bodies ignited into flames pushing Simon back from the table. Before his very eyes he saw the black knob back down from full power to zero all by itself. This sight frightened him. Simon's face was plastered on television screens around the world. All who watched the final execution saw his evil look of frustration and fear.

******

The Russian media was the first to leak the information. The American government had gotten an assurance worldwide that no country would say anything. The United States needed more time to assess what damage would come as a result of the asteroid. They had only discovered its path 10 days earlier, even though Hector Roundtree had spotted it well over a month prior. There was so much disarray on earth that nobody was really looking to the heavens.

Finally the President of the United States made a public address. Alongside him stood Dr. Raymond Hyder, the world's foremost expert in catastrophic events. The President urged people to remain calm. He assured them that the United States military had a viable solution that would prevent the asteroid from approaching any closer to the earth.

"We are going to fire three rockets at the asteroid. They will bore into its surface and deploy three solar sails which will redirect the asteroid away from earth."

"What happens if this doesn't work?" one of the news reporters asked.

"It will work, I assure you!" the President said sternly.

"But if it doesn't?" said the persistent reporter.

The President turned the conversation over to his expert who had already been briefed not to cause a panic by giving too much negative detail. "ED14 is a semi-metallic asteroid. Presently it is approximately six miles across, but we believe that if it enters our atmosphere, it will burn up and reduce in size considerably," said Dr. Hyder.

"Which means what?" another reporter asked.

Hyder looked to the President and then to the reporter. He wanted to tell them all to run away as fast as they could. He knew that the asteroid would be at least one or two miles across as it came crashing into the earth. He was sure that it would destroy a large portion of the United States, Canada, and Mexico. Furthermore, it would have a global effect on the earth for many years to come. This impact would surpass a full-scale nuclear war.

"It means," he said, "that within a specific parameter there will be great damage, but outside of this area life will continue as normal." Dr. Hyder felt like he was betraying all 265 million Americans as he spoke.

Of course, there were numerous reports from other scientists disagreeing with the President's expert and with the chosen path forward, so what ensued was total chaos for all Americans, especially after the deployment of the three sails failed miserably.

There were no options left. There was just not enough time to implement any of the ridiculous contingencies that the United States had developed over the years. The final blow came for the Americans when a report came out that the President and his family, as well as many other rich and politically powerful people, had left the United States in the middle of the night bound for some unknown location.

******

Carlo Ventini watched the live broadcast from the television in his private jet. He knew the man was lying, and he understood why. A smile crossed his face at the thought of what was to come. He would no longer have to feed any Americans or tolerate their lack of obedience to his ID tags. More importantly he would not have to suffer their faithfulness to Christianity any longer.

******

The word was out. Kansas was the target, and people were leaving in a big hurry. That was three days ago and now from Colorado to Iowa people continued to stream out on every highway trying to get as far away from ground zero as possible. Only the wealthy could afford to fly since all the airlines had raised their rates to an unrealistic price for the average person.

Hector Roundtree received never-ending odd looks as he drove east continually. Many of the state highways had been converted to single direction traffic, making it difficult for Hector to stay on the main roads. Often he had to use alternate routes, but eventually he found his way to his goal—Lebanon, Kansas. The entire state was a ghost town. Only the homeless and the mentally ill were left behind to roam the streets.

Hector parked his car in an open field and sat back looking at the night sky. "Twenty-two more hours," he whispered to himself as he looked at his watch. Gazing up at the stars, Hector knew he would be able to see the object as it entered the earth's atmosphere. It would be quite a spectacle.

Chapter 24: Great Declarations

Day 1260, Christmas Day: Pope Peter John followed the rabbi down the flight of stairs until he came to the small metal door. As the door opened, Peter John's eyes slowly adjusted to the dimly lit room. Yvette sat in the corner next to Joseph. She was surprised to see her uncle there in her cell. "Yvette!" said the Pope. "What have you done? And you, Joseph, a priest! How could you?"

Yvette and Joseph stood as Peter John walked into the room. Joseph watched him as he walked over to Yvette and kissed her on the cheek. The rabbi stood at the entrance of the cell as if posting guard. Peter John looked back to the man. "Close the door!" he commanded. The rabbi closed the door with a solid, clanking sound.

"What is it that you two think you are doing?" the Pope asked.

Joseph had a real hate for the man. He knew that he was working for Carlo, and even if by chance Peter John wasn't sure who and what Carlo was, by this time he had to know how evil the man was. "You know why we are here!" said Joseph as his temper flared.

"Yes, I do!" said Peter John. "You are here because you two are enemies of Mr. Ventini—and the world, for that matter."

Yvette could not believe that the man she had adored as a child could now be saying these things to her. What had happened to her uncle? "You know that is not true!" said Yvette. "We are not enemies of anyone. We are trying to warn the world that Carlo Ventini is the Antichrist, and you know it!"

Peter John smiled brightly. "I know nothing of the sort. Carlo Ventini is a savior to the world."

"Only Christ is a savior to the world, or maybe you have forgotten who you are supposed to be working for," said Joseph angrily.

Peter John slapped Joseph across the face. "How dare you talk to me like that? I am the Pope! I am God's personal disciple to the world."

Joseph's eyes burned as he glared at Peter John. "You may be the personal disciple of Satan himself, but you are no man of God."

Peter John grinned at Joseph. "That's where you are wrong. I am a man of God. Carlo Ventini is god, and he has chosen me as his head priest."

"You will spend an eternity in Hell for this decision," said Joseph.

"If I were you, I wouldn't say too much. After all, if your God loves you, then why didn't He take you during the so-called Rapture?"

"I was not a true believer. I had doubts, but God has shown me mercy, and now I serve Him with all my heart," said Joseph.

"Well, let's see if He shows you mercy now," said Peter John as he looked to Joseph to see if the man had any fear, which he did not.

The Pope looked back to Yvette. "You should have chosen better company to spend your time with."

"You too!" said Yvette with a little smile.

This angered Peter John greatly. "I could have had you spared, you know."

"No, thanks!" said Yvette. "I will die with my husband, and we will both walk into Heaven side-by-side."

"Husband! When did this happen? From priest to husband—such a man of God!" said Peter John as he walked towards the metal door and knocked once. The rabbi opened the door and let the Pope out. Both men turned and stared at Joseph and Yvette briefly before slamming the heavy metal door shut.

Yvette looked to Joseph with eyes full of tears. "What happened to him? He used to be such a good man." Yvette would never know how wrong she was.

******

Simon met Carlo at the hotel in Jerusalem. Simon had not seen him in over a week, but he was sure that Carlo would be pleased with all he had accomplished in such short time. The temple was ready for the dedication. Joseph and Yvette were captured and waiting for Carlo. With the exception of the escape of Peter Bastoni and the two nasty scientists, Tommy and Sara, everything was perfect. When the dedication was over and he was declared second only to god, he would find a way to recapture all three of these people. *Oh, how I will enjoy that day,* he thought.

Simon walked into Carlo's suite and greeted him with a broad smile. In return Simon got a hideous glare from Carlo filled with more anger than he had ever seen before. Something was wrong! Somebody had done something that Carlo did not like, but who?

"What's wrong?" said Simon cautiously.

Carlo threw the evening paper down on the table before Simon. On the front cover was a picture of Simon standing next to a child who had just been decapitated—one of the Evans' children. Simon swallowed hard. "I told you not to get too close to this!" Carlo roared.

"They were traitors, and I was teaching the world a lesson," said Simon as he tried to convince Carlo that what he did was proper and necessary.

"They were children! You did not teach the world a lesson about the evils of Christianity. You taught them a lesson about how psychotic and out of control you are!"

This statement wounded Simon. Sure, he loved the killing and torture, but he did it all for Carlo's sake—or at least that is what he told himself. "I am sorry, Carlo, I thought—"

"Enough!" said Carlo. "I don't care that you killed them, but I will not have you damaging my image as the benevolent leader of the world."

Simon nodded with a face full of rejection.

"We will deal with the media after the dedication," said Carlo. "Now tell me about our plans."

"There will be leaders and media from all around the world except for the United States which will have its own issues to deal with about that

time." Simon grinned hoping to distract Carlo's anger. "The Muslim and
Jewish religious leaders will be there, and they will perform their own
ceremonies. Then the stage will be set for you to speak to the world and
tell them that you are their god."

At this Carlo smiled. He had his own plans and speech prepared for
the night. He did not like the idea that other ceremonies designed to
worship God would take place before he made his speech, but it would
be the last time anyone ever worshiped Jehovah. From here on it would
be Carlo Ventini as lord of all.

"What kind of resistance will we get?" Carlo asked.

Just as Carlo asked the question, his suite began to shake violently.
The room began to fill up with evil creatures as they materialized in the
presence of Carlo and Simon.

"There will be resistance, but it will be futile!" the voice of Satan
boomed.

"Father!" said Carlo with a smile.

"The Jews and Muslims will dispute your claim. They will attempt to
attack your credibility, but Simon will stand in for you. He will be given
additional powers in time to convince the world that you are their god."

"Will we defeat Jesus, Father?" Carlo asked with concern and doubt
in his voice.

Satan roared at the mention of the Son of God. "Yes! His people
have abandoned Him already. The world belongs to me, and I give it to
you to rule for me."

Carlo was encouraged by this and was now firmly convinced of his
rightful place as god over the earth.

******

In Las Vegas Cory and Calvin were amazed at the careless and thoughtless behavior of the many patrons in the MGM casino. It was as if they
had no concept of the coming disaster that was only hours away. There
were even bets being placed as to how far the damage from the asteroid
would extend, how many people would die, and how big the asteroid

would be. It seemed as if the world had finally grown accustomed to death and destruction.

Cory and Calvin finished their shift and headed upstairs to their room. As they entered the apartment they could hear Leasa Moore singing a happy little tune. They were both amused by this. Leasa turned away from the small stove and looked at the tired men. "I've made some breakfast out of what I could find. I hope you're hungry." On the table sat a few pieces of chicken, some day-old fruit, and a large piece of cheese, all of which the two men had snuck back to their room from the buffet downstairs.

Cory and Calvin sat down to breakfast as Leasa served them both. She so wanted to thank them for their kindness, for the hope she now possessed. Cory was the first to take a bite of the day-old food. The look on his face told Calvin that he was not in for a treat, but out of gratitude the men ate all she had prepared for them.

Leasa stood back and smiled, but it was obvious her smile was full of confusion and fear. "What will happen next?" she asked. "I was watching the news, and I guess this ED14 asteroid—or whatever it is called—is really going to hit here in the United States. How will we survive?"

"God has taken care of us so far!" said Cory with a smile. He was much braver and more confident than Leasa was.

"Leasa, these things are foretold in the Bible. We cannot stop them, and if it is God's will that we die as a result, then so be it," said Calvin.

These were not exactly the words a new believer wanted to hear. Suddenly a rush of wind blew through the apartment and a silhouette of a large, white angel appeared. "It is time for you to move," said the angel. "You are not safe here anymore."

Leasa was terrified at the sight of Barthemaus, an angel of God. She began to wobble as if she would fall to the ground, but Cory caught her arm and steadied her. "It's okay," he whispered.

"Where will we go?" Calvin asked.

"Go to the park and gather the Lord's followers. Then I will guide you to safety," said the angel.

The rushing wind stopped just as quickly as it had started, and

Barthemaus was gone. A quiet hush fell on the room as Cory and Calvin stood in awe of what had just happened. But Leasa was left holding onto Cory's massive arm as she shook with fear.

"Well, I guess that answers your question, Leasa," said Calvin. "Let's pack up what we can. I have no way of knowing where we are going to next."

A few hours later Calvin stood atop a park bench as both familiar and unfamiliar faces began to gather around him. He and Cory had spread the word about God throughout the city, and now this message had been carried on to many more.

The people had organized themselves and were in the park to pray for guidance from the Lord. They had planned on praying all night until the asteroid hit. For some reason Calvin and Cory had heard nothing about this gathering. *Probably,* Calvin thought, *because we have been busy with Leasa for the last few days.*

"Listen to me, people," said Calvin loudly. "We need to leave here."

"And go where?" one panicked believer shouted.

"I don't know where we are to go, but I know that God is going to lead us. Now go home and gather those essential things you can carry. Be back here in one hour," said Calvin boldly. The power of the Lord surged through him.

******

Over 200 people left the park as directed by Calvin, but only 150 or so came back. "I guess they don't all believe in you," said Cory.

Calvin knew this to be the sad truth.

March them to the north, a small voice in Calvin's head whispered. He still had no idea where he was going, but out of obedience he led the people through the streets of Las Vegas and out into the desert. It was quite a sight to see—so many people walking along side by side. The line of believers stretched an entire city block. People came out to see the spectacle and began to ask those in the procession where it was they were going. "Wherever God leads us," answered one of those marching along.

At this the crowds began to mock Calvin and his people. They hurled insult after insult at them, condemning Christianity. "You are all fools and traitors! We hope you rot out there in the desert," said one man. Calvin felt pity for the mocking crowds, but Cory was inclined to want to hurt someone. He restrained himself, however, and followed along beside Calvin and Leasa.

******

It was starting to get dark, and Calvin's people were all tired and thirsty. "We need to stop," said Leasa. "Everyone is exhausted."

Calvin looked at his watch, and it was nearly 4:30 p.m. They had been walking through the rocky terrain for more than eight hours. All the while Calvin still had no idea where he was leading them. "It looks like there is a stream down there about 300 yards," said Cory as he looked down the ravine. To his left the sun was nearly below the horizon, so they had maybe 30 minutes of light left, and they had not found any shelter yet.

The crowd gathered around Calvin quietly. "We will go down there," said Calvin as he pointed into the small valley below.

"What's down there?" someone in the crowd asked.

"There's water for sure, and we can rest for a while until we figure out what to do next," said Calvin.

Cory knew that Calvin had broken a major rule of leadership. *You never let your followers know that you do not know where you are going,* he thought.

"You mean you do not know where we are?" said three people at once.

The crowd began to whisper and shuffle around where they stood. "An angel came to us today," said Leasa, "and he told Calvin to lead us away from the city, so have faith. God will take care of us somehow."

Calvin was impressed with the growing faith of this young lady. He began to walk down the ravine, and without a word the mass of people followed along. At the base of the valley was a shallow but clear stream of water. The people spread out to fill their bottles and jugs with water, then sat down on the ground as the sun began to fade out. It occurred to Cory that this might be the last sunset he would ever see.

Calvin and Cory watched the orange shadow of sunlight reflect against the cliff before them. Simultaneously both men saw a glassy reflection from about a third of the way up the cliff. "What was that?" Calvin asked.

"I don't know. The sun was shining on it and reflecting it back, but dirt doesn't reflect light," said Cory.

Cory stood. "Let me go take a look while there is still a trace of light."

Calvin nodded and watched as Cory waded across the stream. He began the reasonably easy climb up the side of the opposing cliff. Cory stopped after climbing up maybe 100 yards. Before him was a sign that read: *Colton Silver Mine, No Trespassing.* "What luck!" whispered Cory. "This might be the answer to our prayers."

Cory nearly ran as he headed back down the face of the angled cliff. Calvin and Leasa watched him splash his way across the stream and back up the bank towards them.

"It's a mine!" said Cory with a huge grin.

The crowd of people began to stand and move closer to hear what the big man was excited about. "A silver mine," said Cory.

By this time the sun was down and it was nearly too dark to see anything. "Who has a flashlight?" Calvin asked. Numerous people stepped forward with lights.

"Okay, great!" said Calvin. "Now let's get a fire built so we can stay warm and see each other."

Five young men volunteered to take on the task. *Now we're cooking,* Calvin thought.

"Cory, you take a few of these men and go look in the cave. See if it is big enough and safe for all of us."

Cory nodded in agreement.

Leasa spoke up, "I want to go too!"

Cory smiled at her and looked to Calvin for the okay sign. He nodded in agreement. "But be careful!"

Leasa grinned and followed Cory and three other men across the stream. The water felt soothing to her tired feet. She was amazed at how this week was turning out. Just a few days ago she was only seconds from taking the ID tag, and now she was surrounded by people who had marched out into the desert at the direction of God.

The entrance to the mine was boarded up. It was obvious that nobody had been there for years—maybe decades. Cory tore the wall of wood down and flashed his light into the cave. Instantly hundreds of bats flew out towards the night sky. "Wow!" said Cory, "just like in the movies."

"I hope there are no monsters or bears in there like in the movies," said Leasa.

Cory laughed as he stepped into the cave. "Me too!" he said as he flashed the light deep into the mine.

After 15 minutes of wandering through the old mine Cory, Leasa, and the other men turned to leave. "This place is big enough for hundreds of people," said Leasa.

This was certainly true. The mineshaft wound all through the mountain creating small pockets or rooms along the way. In the center was a large, hollowed out area big enough to park three Greyhound buses. Below that the ground began to slope down leading to another shaft with similar compartments. The air in the cave was surprisingly fresh, as if there were an airshaft or two feeding the whole cave. Cory suspected that there was such a shaft somewhere which would account for the bats in plenty.

"Well, I guess this is home," said Leasa. At this all the men laughed.

"Let's get back and tell Calvin what we've found," said Cory.

******

Benjamin and David sat at the dining room table beside Jill and Daniel. There was no conversation and, in fact, over the last 10 days Jill had said no more than a few words, and none were positive. Daniel had tried to make conversation with Benjamin from time to time, but it was all too painful for his father. Benjamin knew that his son and daughter-in-law were doomed to Hell, and he just could not bear to talk to his son with the pain he felt.

Finally Jill spoke up. "Today is the day, right? The day of the temple dedication?"

Benjamin nodded compliantly.

"Then I guess you will all be leaving today after the dedication?"

"Jill!" said Daniel.

"What? You know I am right. They need to leave, and they need to do it today before we all get into trouble. We don't even know most of them. They could be criminals. One of them is a scientist and may be responsible for the plague that continues to kill so many," said Jill.

"Yes," Benjamin whispered. "We will leave today." Benjamin had no idea where he and the others would go, but it was certain that they could not impose on Jill and Daniel any further. He was grateful that they had all managed to stay civil for as long as they had.

David looked at Benjamin and spoke. "Then we had better go out and warn the people here in Jerusalem one more time before today's dedication."

Benjamin was proud of the young man. He wished he could feel the same way about his own son, but he could not. "Yes, we will go out and preach the Word one more time," said the old man.

At this Jill looked away in disgust. She had truly hardened her heart towards Christianity. Daniel stood to leave the kitchen. "Be careful, Papa! People are not very happy with Christians right now, and you might get hurt."

"I've been hurt before," Benjamin whispered so quietly that Daniel did not hear him as he and Jill walked out of the room.

Benjamin informed Elisha and Jasmine that he and David were going out to witness before Carlo made his announcement to the world. Jasmine was anxious to get out of the house, and she wanted to go with David and Benjamin. For some reason Elisha felt that he and Jasmine should wait for Peter to get up before they did anything. "We will be back in a little while," said Benjamin as he kissed Elisha's and Jasmine's cheeks.

"What time is the temple dedication?" Elisha inquired.

"1:00 p.m.," said David.

"We need to leave by noon then," said Jasmine.

Benjamin nodded. "If we are not back by then, go without us and we will meet back here after it is over." Benjamin had no real desire to go to the temple. He understood well enough what was to come, and he really didn't want David or the others to see it, but he knew that Peter and Elisha felt compelled to be there.

Elisha agreed. He, too, understood Benjamin's lack of desire to go to the dedication, but for some reason he and Jasmine just had to be there. He was sure of that.

Peter entered the room just as David and Benjamin started for the front door. "Where are you going?" Peter asked still groggy from his restless sleep. Since Joseph and Yvette had been taken away, Peter had gone into his own shell. He rarely spoke, and nightly he had terrible dreams about Joseph and Yvette being tortured to death. This had really affected his sleep. He wanted so greatly to see his brother one more time, but that, too, was in God's hands.

"We will be back by noon." David smiled as he closed the front door behind him.

Peter turned to Elisha. His eyes told the young man that he was grief stricken. Elisha felt compassion for Peter, but he didn't know what to say. "Today is the day," Elisha whispered.

Peter nodded in agreement. He felt in his own spirit that something big was about to happen—something that would change everything in his world.

******

Ruth drove Paul Laruso's car slowly towards Jerusalem. She had said her goodbyes to Scott. She knew that she would never be back to Benjamin's deli. The feeling that she felt in leaving Scott's body behind made her cry as she drove. Ruth tried to remind herself that Scott was in Heaven, but somehow leaving his poor cold body locked up in that meat locker next to Paul Laruso just didn't allow Ruth the resolution that her heart needed.

What am I doing? Why am I even going to this temple ceremony? Ruth wondered. Yet she continued to steer the course. Somewhere out there was her destiny. She had felt it strongly all morning. Ruth wondered what Peter was doing and if she would see him or Joseph and Yvette again. *Were they even alive?* Ruth had no answers.

******

Joseph and Yvette sat nestled together. Joseph felt in his heart that their time together was just about gone. Until Peter John showed up, Joseph had no real concept of time. He and Yvette were fed on a regular basis which gave him a sense of night and day, but because they were closed into the dimly lit cell without even a watch, they had lost track of the days. They would both be surprised to find out that they had been in the jail for over 10 days.

"It's going to happen soon, isn't it?" Yvette asked.

Joseph looked into her emerald green eyes, and his heart broke for her. He loved her so much, and he was afraid of the pain she would have to endure this very day. Joseph lifted Yvette's face to his own and kissed her softly. "Soon," he said.

"I wish we had more life together, and I wish I could have children for you and live in the country to raise them. I would love to watch you grow old and maybe even become a grandfather." Yvette smiled through her tears.

"You would have made a great mother. I am sure of that," said Joseph through tears of his own.

"Tell me about Heaven," Yvette whispered.

Joseph smiled at his lovely wife and kissed her on the forehead. "Heaven is where all our dreams will come true. It is a place where we will never feel pain or sorrow again. We will never age, and we will always be together. We will be with God, surrounded by His love forever."

Yvette beamed at Joseph. "Do you think God will give us our own house so we can live together?"

Joseph laughed with Yvette. "I don't think we will need it, but I'll ask, okay?"

All of a sudden the dim, cold cell was engulfed in a warm presence. This time Yvette did not feel fear but a total sense of peace and joy. "You have done well. Stay strong to the end and know I am with you both."

The light faded from the room and just then the large metal door opened and Simon Koch stood before them with a broad, evil smile on his face. "Father Bastoni, so good to see you again!" laughed Simon.

"Likewise," Joseph glared.

Simon's anger flared up and he wanted to hurt Joseph, but then he remembered the severe tongue-lashing he had received from Carlo. "I understand you two are married now. May I ask who performed the ceremony?"

Joseph refused to answer the question, but Yvette could not resist. "We did it ourselves, and God Himself was there and blessed our marriage for all eternity."

"Well, wasn't that nice of Him. Your eternity will be here before you know it," said Simon with a grin. "It's time to go. You have a lot of fans out there who want to thank you for your articles in *Deacon's Horn*. They will be glad to know that their favorite priest is now married too!"

Three security guards stepped in behind Simon carrying handcuffs. "You don't need those. We will come with you without any struggle," said Joseph.

"Yes, I am sure you will but, frankly, it looks better this way," said Simon sarcastically.

Yvette and Joseph were cuffed and led up the stairs. Joseph wanted to hold Yvette's hand to comfort her, but that was not possible, so he spoke to her softly in the presence of the guards and Simon. "Heaven will be wonderful. Soon we will be free of these earthly bodies, and we will not have to tolerate the evil of this world."

"Shut up!" said Simon angrily.

Joseph ignored Simon. In fact, he continued just to spite him. "We will not have to suffer an eternity of torture in Hell with Satan, Carlo, and Simon."

At this Simon turned around and backhanded Joseph across the face. Joseph's lip was split and bleeding, but he smiled at Simon just the same.

"You lose! Nothing you can do will hurt us after today, but you will suffer greatly for all time. Christ will defeat you in just three and one half years from now," said Joseph boldly.

"Maybe there are other ways to hurt you," said Simon as he turned to Yvette. "How about it, men—wouldn't you like to have some of this right now?" said Simon as he pulled Yvette's blouse down, exposing her breasts. The guards looked at Yvette lustfully. "Yes," said Simon, "maybe there is enough time for Mrs. Bastoni and us to—"

"They're calling for you!" said a voice at the top of the stairs.

Simon looked up to the rabbi. *What lousy timing,* he thought. "Okay, well, I guess it will have to wait until you are dead," said Simon as he fondled Yvette while rebuttoning her blouse. Tears filled Joseph's eyes. He was angry beyond his ability to express, and he was also scared for Yvette. They had narrowly escaped a horrible situation with Simon, and Joseph knew he would have been the cause of it all since he chose to antagonize Simon.

The two of them walked quietly until they reached the main floor of the temple. There stood a huge gold altar that had been built to the exact specifications used in *Solomon's Temple.* At the center of the altar was a replica of the *Ark of the Covenant.* It was covered in thin sheets of solid gold and at the top were two winged cherubim facing each other. At the entrance to the altar was a small golden table with several loaves of bread and a vial of oil. Gold-plated dishes and pitchers adorned the top of the table. At the edge of the table was a large candelabra with flames burning. The lamp stand looked like a flowering branch of an almond tree. All seven of the oil lamps on the lamp stand were made out of pure gold, as were their wick trimmers and trays.

Simon stopped at the entrance to the room and watched a rabbi who was wearing an ancient ephod of purple and gold with a breastplate covered in multicolored stones signifying each of the original 12 tribes of Jacob. The priest read from the Torah while waving a bowl of incense.

Today will be the last time anyone reads from that book as well, Simon thought.

Joseph was impressed at the detail that was given in the recreation of the holy temple of God. Everything was done as closely as possible to the descriptions given in the book of Exodus. He thought, however, it was odd that they did not include the bronze washing-basin at the entrance of the temple—a simple oversight, but an important one. These rabbis felt no need to consecrate their sinful life to God before coming into His presence, but then God was not in this temple, so it really didn't matter. Had this been the original temple and a rabbi or priest come into it without washing and purging his sins, God would have destroyed him instantly.

Simon waited impatiently for the rabbi to finish his ceremony while the world watched via a television feed. Earlier the Muslims had dedicated their portion of the temple while reading from their Koran, another book that would soon be removed from society. Soon it would be Carlo's turn. Simon's stomach rumbled with excitement.

******

Peter paced the floor in Daniel's living room. It was already noon and there was no sign of David and Benjamin. "We have to leave!" said Peter impatiently.

Elisha nodded in agreement. He was worried about David and Benjamin. Jerusalem was not exactly the same as Bethlehem where the citizens were used to discussions about Jesus. The people here could be more dangerous. He prayed that they were okay wherever they were.

Daniel and Jill stood at the front door, and without saying a word they let Elisha, Jasmine, and Peter out of the house, and without a goodbye, they closed the door. Jasmine understood that their obligation was over. They would never be allowed in the house again. She tried not to think too far ahead, but she could not help but wonder where she would lay her head tonight.

Elisha followed along with Peter as he headed towards the temple whose towering peak could be seen above the other buildings in Daniel's neighborhood. Peter wound his way through every side street keeping the temple in view whenever possible. It was no more than a one-mile walk.

By the time Peter stopped it was 12:45 p.m. Crowds extended out in every direction. Peter's heart sank. There would be no way he could get close enough to see what was going on. Then suddenly there was a blaring siren behind Peter that startled him greatly. Peter, Elisha, and Jasmine stepped aside as a small police truck inched its way through the crowd. Elisha noticed the bed of the truck was open, so he pulled on Peter's sleeve and pointed to the truck. Peter understood right away and smiled to Elisha. All three sat on the tailgate of the truck as it moved in towards the center of the temple. Eventually one of the officers leaned out of the cab and told the three to get off, but by this time they had managed to draw within 20 yards of the temple's entrance.

Peter surveyed his new location, and although it was much closer, it was still just a parking lot. All of the action was going on inside, which was where Peter felt compelled to be. He looked up to one of the big screens that had been placed around the parking lot, and to his disbelief he saw Joseph and Yvette standing next to Simon Koch. Peter's heart was grieved at the sight of his little brother in handcuffs beside his fearful bride. Elisha caught sight of what Peter was looking at and let out a moan of disappointment. "I am sorry, Peter," said Elisha.

"We have to get in there somehow!" said Peter.

Jasmine and Elisha followed Peter as he pushed and shoved his way towards the entrance of the temple. Peter stopped five feet before the front of the building. He could go no further. There stood a massive crowd lingering, and as if that were not bad enough, there was a security checkpoint with numerous armed guards. "I don't think we can get any closer," said Jasmine lightly. She understood Peter's need to get inside the building and her heart went out to him, but there was nothing they could do.

Peter turned around to a tap on the shoulder. It was Ruth Jefferson. "Ruth!" said Peter in astonishment. "How did you get here?"

"I drove," said Ruth.

Peter pointed to the huge screen. "I need to get inside, Ruth!"

Ruth looked at the 30-foot image of Yvette and Joseph and nodded. "I think I have a way, but it will only work for one of you."

Elisha and Jasmine turned to listen to Ruth's plan. "I have these," she said as she handed Peter two news reporter passes. Both passes had pictures—one was a picture of Ruth and the other a picture of Scott.

As soon as Peter saw Scott's picture he began looking at the crowd. "Where is Scott?" he asked.

Ruth looked at all three people and then down at her feet. "He is dead," she said softly.

"What happened?" Jasmine asked.

"He saved my life. The man that took Joseph and Yvette came back and Scott shot him before he could kill me, but Scott was shot too," she said as tears began to fill her eyes.

Peter looked at the passes carefully. "How can we make this work for us?"

"Let me see them," said Jasmine.

Peter handed the passes to Jasmine. She studied them carefully before speaking. "Do you have a picture of yourself?" Jasmine asked.

Peter patted his pockets until he found his passport. "I've got this." Jasmine looked at the picture on Peter's passport.

"Elisha, give me your knife. Ruth, do you have any tweezers in that purse of yours?"

Ruth pulled the large purse off her shoulder and dug around inside until she came out with a shiny pair of metal tweezers. "And how about some clear nail polish?" Jasmine asked. The little terrorist had obviously done this before. Elisha was impressed at this young lady's ingenuity. Slowly Jasmine cut away the plastic from Scott's photo until she could get a solid hold on it with the tweezers. After extricating the picture she handed it to Ruth gently. Next she removed Peter's picture from his passport. He hoped he would not need to show this as well as the news reporter pass to get into the temple.

A little clear polish and a few minutes to dry and Peter Bastoni had a new ID as Scott Turner, a Chicago-based news reporter. "I hope this works for you," said Jasmine as she handed the ID back to Peter.

"It would work a lot better if you had a camera," said Elisha as he pointed to a white news van parked beside the security entrance. "I'll be back in a minute," said Elisha. Jasmine ran off behind him. She was not going to let him get into any trouble without her by his side. Peter and Ruth watched the amusing show as Jasmine climbed into the front of the van with the driver and asked him for a cigarette.

The man was obviously attracted to the young girl, and she played this to her advantage while Elisha slowly opened the back door to the van. On the shelf to his left, just out of his reach, was a large shoulder camera. Elisha crawled in, causing the van to rock slightly. The driver turned to look behind him. Before he could do this Jasmine grabbed his face with both of her small hands and kissed him firmly. She held the kiss for some time, allowing Elisha to grab the camera and escape out of the back. Jasmine watched Elisha's every move from the corner of her eye, and as soon as he closed the door, she released her kiss and dropped the cigarette into the lap of the driver. The man thrashed around looking for the source of the smoke while Jasmine climbed out of the van.

Elisha handed the camera to Peter with a smile. "Good luck!" he said.

"Thanks!" said Peter. "Will you be here when we come back out?"

"Unless God calls us away, we will wait right here," said Elisha.

Peter turned to leave, but before he could take a step, Jasmine pulled a sticker off the side of the camera. It was written in Aramaic. "I don't think you want this sticker," said Jasmine as she leaned in and kissed Peter on the cheek. "Good luck!"

******

Benjamin and David had encountered tremendous hostility everywhere they went. Benjamin pleaded with the people for understanding, but it all fell on deaf ears. "We'd better head back," said David.

Benjamin nodded in disappointment. If they had converted even one, it all would have been worth it. "Yes, let's get back before they leave for the temple."

Along the way David and Benjamin encountered a group of teenagers who were heading towards the dedication. Benjamin stopped the group and began to explain the truth of Jesus Christ to them. Instantly hate and anger greeted him. "You'd better shut up, old man, before you get hurt," said one of the teenagers.

"Come on, Benjamin," David urged. "We need to leave now!"

Benjamin Cohen wanted to reason with the young adults. He wanted them to know the truth. He refused to leave without giving them one more warning. "God's wrath will be poured out on the world this very day. You must listen to me!"

One of the boys grabbed Benjamin's beard and pulled him down to the ground while another boy kicked him in the face. David tried to shield Benjamin with his own body as the teenagers continued to pelt them. "Get rocks," said one of the kids.

Moments later Daniel and Jill turned the corner leaving their own block. Jill was the first one to see the teenagers throwing rocks at Benjamin and David. "What's going on?" she asked as she pointed in their direction. Daniel stopped the car in the center of the road. He was uncertain as to what to do. "You can't help them now!" said Jill. "Besides, it's their own fault!"

Just then one of the older boys lifted a large rock over his head and sent it crashing down on Benjamin's skull. By now David was already nearly unconscious from all of the physical abuse he took while trying to shield Benjamin. When Daniel witnessed the older boy drop the rock on his father's head, he instinctively gunned the accelerator and pointed his car in the direction of the teenagers. With his horn blaring he drove right up on the curb. This sent the unruly crowd running. Daniel got out of the car and ran towards his father while Jill sat quietly by. David was moaning as blood trickled down his face. Daniel lifted David off his father and laid him gently on the sidewalk. Next he knelt down beside Benjamin. His father's face was a mass of battered flesh, and all around his head was a pool of dark, red blood. "Papa?" said Daniel.

Benjamin could not raise his body towards his son. He simply touched him with one of his smashed hands and whispered, "I love you, Son."

Daniel began to cry aloud. "We have to get you to a hospital!"

"Son, promise me you will take care of David. He is a brave, young boy."

Daniel nodded in agreement as Benjamin closed his eyes for the last time. Daniel scooped him into his lap and held him there as he cried.

Finally Jill got out of the car and walked over to Daniel. She put her hand on her husband's shoulder as he rocked his father's lifeless body. "All of this for a ridiculous belief in Christ," said Jill.

Daniel looked into Jill's face. "Is it ridiculous, or are we the ones who have been deceived?" he asked.

Daniel and Jill put Benjamin and David into the backseat of their car and drove off to the hospital. David would be all right in a couple of weeks, and Daniel was true to his promise. He brought David back into his home and provided for his needs even though Jill was completely opposed to the whole thing.

Daniel had his father buried next to his mother in Bethlehem. Standing over their graves he spoke softly, "Now you two are together again." Daniel wept bitterly—so much time wasted and so many regrets.

******

Calvin had moved the large flock of Christians into the silver mine. He was grateful that the Lord had provided the shelter and the water they would need to survive. Cory broke the group down and assigned each of them necessary tasks. Some gathered wood for the fires, while others filled every available container with water from the stream below. Additionally Calvin had each member of his group hand over all of his or her food supplies. "We must share and ration this food," he said. So far everyone was cooperating with each command given by Calvin or Cory. They had legitimate authority from God in the eyes of the people.

Finally, when all the necessary chores were complete, Calvin had the group assemble before him. "We are here because God has honored our faithfulness. Before this night is over millions will die as God's wrath begins to pour out, and by tomorrow we will be living in an entirely different world. Nothing is ever going to be the same. From this day forward the Antichrist will be declared as god, and we, followers of Jesus Christ, will be declared an abomination to the world. They will hunt us down and kill as many of us as they can."

The group stood by quietly as Calvin spoke. None of them would have ever guessed that Calvin was by nature a reserved, timid person. But now the Lord had anointed him as their leader and had given him the wisdom to guide His people.

Calvin called Cory to his side. "This is Cory Parker. He has been with me since God first made Himself known to me. Cory is a veteran and an expert in survival. Please follow all instructions that he gives you and we will stay safe from harm while we are in this mine."

Leasa looked at Cory and smiled. She was proud of her new friend.

"Now," said Calvin, "I want to read to you from the book of Revelation. This is what it says will happen next. 'Then I saw another angel flying in midair, and he had the eternal gospel to proclaim to those who live on the earth and to every nation, tribe, and language and people. He said in a loud voice, Fear God and give Him glory, because the hour of His judgment has come. Worship Him who made the heavens, the earth, the sea and the springs of water.'"

"Today God will pour out His wrath on the world. Let us pray that we may be of some use during these last three and a half years. Let us ensure that we remain faithful until the end." Calvin dropped to his knees. Cory and Leasa and all the people knelt with him and prayed also.

******

Peter was sweating it out as he stood before the security guard. The man studied his ID carefully as Ruth spoke up. "We are late, and if we don't get some of this on video, we are going to be in big trouble back in the United States."

The man smiled at Ruth, then looked at his watch. "In another few minutes there won't be any United States." Ruth grimaced at the thought.

She, like all the rest of the world, had heard the news. But even now it was just too much to comprehend so she simply ignored the reality.

Once inside Peter pushed and forced his way towards the entrance to the altar. He just had to see Joseph one more time. There were bright red stanchions with cameras every few feet separating the viewing audience from the walkway into the holy place. Peter could clearly see Simon standing at the entrance, obviously waiting for someone. He was wearing a deep purple robe with a gold sash.

Suddenly all the heads in the room turned to look as Peter John dressed in his priestly vestments led Carlo Ventini along the walkway. Peter knew that Simon and Carlo had never seen him personally, but he was still nervous that they would somehow find him out. Carlo waved to the crowd as he walked towards Simon. His robe was pure white and nearly glowing. Across his chest was a golden plate with a number of symbols, each of which represented Satan himself. This was going to be his greatest day, and his body was full of excitement.

Simon raised his hands towards Carlo as he climbed the stairs to the altar. Blue electricity shot out of Simon's palms and filled the room. The colorful fire seemed to engulf everything around, yet nothing was consumed. Simon was surprised by what was happening. He could feel the surge of power flowing through him, but he knew it was not his own. Satan was using his body as a conduit to show his power. The audience gasped as they watched the streams of blue and orange racing throughout the room and up to the beautifully painted ceiling.

"Nice touch!" Carlo whispered as he walked past Simon. Simon Koch had never been more proud than at this very moment. His life had turned out to be much more spectacular than he ever dreamed it would. He was nearly a god himself. Simon closed his fists as the blue electricity dissipated.

Peter John walked over to the podium, and in the corner of the room he spotted Yvette and Joseph standing side by side in handcuffs like common criminals. The Pope stared at Yvette briefly and then without acknowledging his daughter turned toward the audience, "Ladies and gentlemen, it gives me great pleasure to be here with you. Today we are honored to have Mr. Carlo Ventini among us for this holy dedication. As the world waits in foreboding for the terrible asteroid to strike the United States, we cannot help but feel for those who will perish in such a horrible disaster. Mr. Ventini wants to assure all of you that this asteroid has a great purpose and was designed to serve warning on the world that our benevolent leader will not be mocked."

The audience, including many rabbis and Muslim religious leaders, stood by silently as they listened to the Pope continue to describe the character of Carlo. "I stand on record that I have been misled for many years as I directed my church to read and believe in the Holy Bible. I now know that this was an evil deception and that none of what is written in that book is true. I have been worshipping a false god."

A single gasp could be heard from the crowd. *What is this man saying?* they wondered. *Can he be saying that the Bible is false and the God of this book is not real?*

Simon escorted Carlo to the podium as Peter John stepped aside. Carlo looked over his shoulder to where Yvette and Joseph stood. With an evil, terrifying grin he sneered at them both.

Ruth and Peter stood silently watching every move that was made. *Somehow Joseph and Yvette are soon to be a part of this, but how?* Peter wondered.

"My children," said Carlo softly. "I stand before you today to declare that I alone am responsible for the asteroid that will soon strike earth."

Mumbles and whispers could be heard from the audience. Carlo looked directly into the large camera in front of him. He wanted to make himself clear to the world as it watched. "I have come to this world to rid it of lies and deceptions and all other forms of gods. I have come to reclaim my children and to put an end to suffering. Today I stand before you and declare for all to hear that I am the one and only true god." At this Simon raised his hands and the room shook violently.

A panic filled the audience as the floor around them swayed. "Fear not!" said Carlo as Simon lowered his hands again. "I am here to care for you, and all I ask is obedience in return. Life will never be the same, and now that I am here among you there will be peace and happiness for all who serve me as their god."

Simon waved for the guards to bring Joseph and Yvette before the altar. Peter's heart leaped as he observed Joseph step forward. "Do you recognize this man?" Carlo asked. "He is Joseph Bastoni, a priest from Vatican City, and this is his accomplice. He is responsible for sending out lies and propaganda around the world. He is solely responsible for the resistance that we have encountered as we have tried to help the people of the world. He is also linked to the scientific community, and it is his own brother who is responsible for developing the plague that has killed so many of your loved ones."

Peter's heart was full of anger for Carlo, as was Joseph's.

Simon stepped up to the podium with Joseph and Yvette by his side. "Now that we have captured these evil creatures, we will sacrifice them to His Holiness Carlo and appease his anger. He is a kind and merciful god, and he will put an end to the plague and bring peace and prosperity to the world." How he would actually do this Simon had no idea, but it sounded good all the same.

Joseph looked out into the audience, slowly scanning the room. He spotted Peter standing next to Ruth, and even from this distance he could see his brother's grief. He hated to see Peter in such torment. Joseph knew Peter had grown in the ways of the Lord, but he also knew that he still needed someone for support and understanding. He wished it could be him, but this was not God's plan. "Lord, protect him!" said Joseph aloud.

Simon looked to Joseph to see what he was talking about. He saw Joseph staring out into the audience at a man who looked very much like he did. *That is Peter Bastoni,* Simon thought. *I'll deal with him after this gets over.*

Peter looked into Simon's face. He understood that the man had figured him out, but somehow he just didn't care if Simon came out into the crowd and swept him up onstage or not. Peter looked towards Joseph and by this time even Yvette had spotted Peter.

"I love you, Joseph," said Peter softly, "and you, too, Yvette!"

Joseph nodded and mouthed an "I love you too!" in return, as did his wife.

As Simon turned to lead Joseph and Yvette towards the *Ark of the Covenant,* Joseph looked back to Peter and mouthed the words, "Leave now. Hurry!"

Peter nodded. He understood that Joseph did not want Peter to see him die. Furthermore, he did not want him to get caught by Simon.

Peter tugged on Ruth's sleeve. "We need to leave now!"

Ruth turned to Peter and put her soft, dark hand on his tear-stained cheek. "They will be with God very soon, and they will be filled with joy!"

Simon seated both prisoners on two wooden chairs facing the audience. Below their feet were two wicker baskets. The security guards strapped them tightly to their chairs.

Joseph looked into Yvette's eyes and smiled as he reached over as far as his hand could reach, just barely touching the skin of Yvette's wrist. "I wish I could have gotten you a wedding ring, Wife."

Yvette smiled boldly. "For our kind of love, no ring would ever do. I am proud to have you as my husband for eternity."

Tears streamed down Joseph and Yvette's faces as they stared into one another's eyes completely unaware of the two men standing behind them with large swords pulled back over their shoulders, one on each side of the prisoners.

******

Outside Elisha and Jasmine found a shady corner of the building to stand beneath. "Where will we go from here?" Jasmine asked in her usual impatient tone. Elisha smiled lightly and kissed her on the forehead.

"Wherever God wants," Elisha said confidently.

"I know that, you big dummy, but where?" Jasmine grinned.

"We need to go back and get Benjamin and David, and then we can strike out on our own. Do you remember Benjamin reading from the Bible, describing that people hid themselves in caves?"

Jasmine nodded.

"Well, we know where there is a really big cave with water," said Elisha.

"Yes," said Jasmine, "but don't you remember that the opening to the cave collapsed during the earthquake?"

Elisha had forgotten this, but he was not discouraged in the least. "Then we will have to dig it out."

A cool breeze blew past the two of them and they became still. They were now familiar with the presence of God and His angels. Philip appeared to the children. "May the peace of God remain with you both!" said Philip as he stood before them.

Even though the children were familiar with the angelic presence, it still did not diminish their reverent fear of the Lord. They both shook as they stood before Philip.

"What should we do now?" Jasmine asked.

Philip stretched out his hand to Elisha and placed it on his shoulder. Elisha could feel a sensation of tingling, and a sense of comfort and power filled his body. "The Lord has anointed you as a leader for His people. Today they will follow you out into the desert to hide from Satan, for today God's wrath will begin to pour out on this world. Satan will be let loose to torture and kill all that he can."

Jasmine was terribly frightened as Philip spoke. All of this had just become too real for her young mind.

"Fear not!" said Philip as he looked toward both children. "God has spared you, and victory awaits you both if you remain faithful until the end."

"When will it end?" Jasmine asked in a much more timid voice than usual.

"There will be three and one-half years of torture, death, and persecution for the Christians. It will be 1,260 more days until Christ returns again, but this time He will bring all the believers from Heaven with Him. Satan will be cast into Hell, and there will be a thousand years of peace with no death or suffering."

"Do we have to stay out in the desert for the next three and one-half years?" Elisha inquired.

"Satan will find some of you. You will always be on the move until the battle is won," said Philip.

"What do we do now? We need to go back to get Benjamin and David, but then what?" Elisha asked.

"No, Child, you will not find Benjamin, and David is where the Lord wants him to be for now."

"Benjamin is dead?" Jasmine asked with deep sorrow for the old man whom she loved greatly.

"No, Jasmine. Benjamin is alive forever in Heaven where he belongs." Philip smiled at the teary-eyed children.

"How will I lead the people? I am only 21 years old, and I have no experience. How will they know to follow me?" Elisha asked.

"You are God's chosen leader over Israel, just as King David was when he was a child. The people will follow you because they need a leader. They will follow you into the desert. Now be strong and have courage. Watch out for deceit and betrayal. Guard over your flock carefully," Philip said and then simply disappeared.

******

Hector Roundtree lay atop the hood of his pickup truck sipping on a small plastic bottle of water as he stared directly into space. The cold morning sky was full of stars, and the moon was brightly lit. He had been tracking the huge asteroid all night as it sped towards the earth. It was Christmas morning, but none like he had ever experienced before—no Christmas tree, no presents, and no family to share it with.

"Mom," said Hector out loud. "I am sorry I did not listen to you. I have missed you and Sis so much. Mom, what do I have to do to be in Heaven with you both?"

Hector looked at his watch. It was 2:48 a.m. "Any second now!" he said aloud. Just then the sky was nearly as bright as day. Hector dropped his water bottle and jumped off the hood of the truck. Staring directly overhead, he saw the most spectacular sight of his life. The sky was a red ball of fire. He could no longer even see the stars or the moon. Hector fell to his knees. "Lord, forgive me! I confess Jesus as Lord. Please let me into Heaven to be with my family."

Abruptly the ground shook and the air around him heated up tremendously. This was followed by an incredibly violent rush of wind strong enough to pick all 200 pounds of Hector off the ground and push him into his truck. Hector screamed in pain as the intense heat began to consume his body. He looked up in time to see a mountain falling right on top of him. Hector's body exploded from the intense heat and the force of rushing air as ED14 came crashing down on the earth. Instantly Hector was ushered into the presence of God and the family he missed so dearly.

******

Simon and the Pope sprinkled the blood from Yvette and Joseph's decapitated bodies over the *Ark of the Covenant* while chanting praises to Carlo who stood by in his flowing white robe. Peter John was somewhat nauseated by the sight of his own daughter's head laying in the wicker basket and the sight of her blood on the floor of the temple. *But it's not like she was my real daughter,* he thought. *Besides, she made her own choice to follow after Jesus instead of Carlo Ventini, the one true god.*

Just outside of the temple Peter and Ruth were reunited with Elisha and Jasmine. "Well, what did you see?" Jasmine asked. She was completely unaware of the tears still on Peter's face.

"Joseph and Yvette are in there," said Peter softly.

Elisha understood the meaning but as usual Jasmine didn't. Neither she nor Elisha had been looking at the big screen when Joseph and Yvette were murdered. "Can we get them out of there?" she asked.

Ruth put her hand on Jasmine's bony shoulder and looked into the young girl's eyes. "By now they are in Heaven," she answered.

Jasmine looked to Peter and whispered, "I'm sorry, Peter."

Elisha put his hand on Peter's back. "Benjamin is dead also," he said with grief.

"And David?" a startled Peter asked. He loved the brave, young boy very much.

"No, he is safe for now," said Elisha.

"How do you know this?" Ruth inquired.

Jasmine smiled and said, "An angel came and told us—the same one that brought us to Bethlehem."

"An angel!" said Ruth. "When did this happen?"

"Oh, about five minutes ago," said Jasmine nonchalantly.

Back inside the temple pandemonium began to break out as Simon sprinkled Joseph's blood over the Mercy Seat of the altar. Jews and non-Jews alike were offended by the desecration of their new temple. They began to cry out against Carlo and Simon. "There is only one God, Jehovah! Allah!" they said.

At this Carlo lifted his hands in anger towards the crowd and tore the front of his robe. Out of the blue the earth began to shake violently, spilling over the lamp stand and covering the floor with burning oil. The temple began to fall apart before the eyes of all who watched. Even those who watched from distant points on the earth felt the tremendous force of the earthquake as the asteroid buried itself some three miles deep into the earth's crust. An explosion could be heard inside the temple as a large piece of molten metal came crashing through the roof, then another and another. It was like a hailstorm of fiery rock. One of the six inch missiles struck Pope Peter John in the back, ripping his head off and draping his body over the small, golden table of bread and oil. These were small meteorites referred to as *tektites* from ED14, and they fell from the sky onto all parts of the earth.

Simon grabbed Carlo and led him down the back stairs of the altar. The rest of the people inside scrambled for their lives. Many were pelted by chunks of asteroid before they could get out of the building. Others were trampled to death in the panic.

Outside the crowds screamed in fear as they watched hundreds of large, glowing pieces of rock fall from the sky. Peter turned in time to see the face of the temple crumble into a pile of rubble.

"We need to get out of here now!" shouted Ruth.

Elisha led Peter, Jasmine, and Ruth to the outer edge of the parking lot. "Do you see that hill over there?" Elisha asked as he pointed east. "Beyond that about 50 miles or so is a cave, and it has water. We need to go there."

Behind Elisha stood a mass of people listening as he spoke. "Will you take us with you?" one very old man asked.

"Whoever wants to follow us can do so, but bring everything you can with you. We may be gone for a long time. We will leave in 30 minutes, so go and prepare what you can!"

About that time another wave of hot rock came flying into the parking lot, killing more people and completely destroying the temple.

"I hope we can survive 30 more minutes!" said Jasmine.

Chapter 25: Wanderers

The magnitude of the asteroid would never be fully appreciated, but needless to say, it was nearly two miles wide on impact. The force at which it hit the earth was so great that it created tidal waves in each of the Great Lakes. The explosive power generated by the impact was equal to hundreds of gigatons of TNT, and it completely destroyed the state of Kansas. In fact, the heat and shock from the explosion traveled as far as Colorado to the West, Texas to the south, Toronto to the north, and Illinois to the east. Melissa Bastoni, Peter's ex-wife, never knew what hit her as the explosion completely destroyed her home and incinerated her body.

The shockwave reached far into the Gulf of Mexico sending massive tidal waves out into the sea, destroying all of the Antilles and the southern portions of Mexico. Within minutes a massive dust cloud began to form. Soon it would cover the entire earth's surface, initially heating and then greatly lowering the planet's temperature while killing all remaining plant and animal life.

Ten days had not been enough time to evacuate Mexico, Canada, and the United States, and with little to no preparation for such a massive catastrophe, these countries were in total ruins. In just a few minutes time over 80 million people were dead and millions more were homeless throughout the United States and the Antilles. The death toll for Mexico and Canada was less than half that. but over time the effects from this asteroid would certainly cost millions of additional lives.

******

Calvin and all his followers were on their knees praying when ED14 struck Kansas. It was not a wise decision to be in a mine during times of earthquakes, but Calvin put his faith in God, so when Cory recommended that they all go back outside until the effects of the initial impact had passed, Calvin declined stating, "God will be with us."

There were moments in that mine when Calvin wondered if he had made a huge mistake in not listening to Cory, for as soon as the asteroid struck the earth, the mine began to quake violently. Dirt and large rocks began to pelt the people. Many were injured, but none too seriously. It turned out, however, that if Calvin had listened to Cory, many would have died, because just outside the Colton Mine literally thousands of small meteorites fell to the ground as speeding balls of fire exploded everywhere. This would not be seen until the next day when they all left the cave. At that time they would all be amazed by the destruction.

Leasa moved to the center of the mine where Calvin stood. "How long will all of this last?" she asked softly.

"Forever!" said Calvin plainly. "People!" shouted Calvin as he waved them towards himself. The crowd moved to Calvin and stood quietly as he spoke. "Today our work begins. There are still many people out there who do not know what is happening to their lives. They do not know who Jesus is, yet somehow they have not taken the mark. We have to find them."

"There must be other groups like us around the world," said one woman.

"Yes, and we need to find them and unite with them—one common purpose for us all. We have three and one-half years until the battle is won. Satan will find and kill as many as he can, so we need to find them first. This is a race against evil and against time. Are you with me?" Calvin shouted.

Cory raised his mighty fist high in response to Calvin's speech as the rest of the group roared with cheers.

Hidden away in a dark mine just above a recently cratered Nevada desert floor 150 people stood worshiping God while preparing themselves to do battle against the Devil. Many lives would be lost in the attempt, but souls would be won for God, as well, and that was all that mattered to any of them.

******

Martha and Harry stood over Tommy and Sara as they slept side by side on the floor of the living room. They, too, had felt the effects of the asteroid although Tommy and Sara slept right through it all.

"Well, Mama," said Harry, "I guess we have done all we can for now. These two will have to take it from here."

Martha beamed at her ancient-looking husband. "I suppose you are right," she said in her heavy native accent. "Maybe God will let us look in on them from time to time."

"I am sure of it, Wife. These two have a lot of work ahead of them, and who knows—maybe they will need our help again."

Harry and Martha turned and walked out of the room hand in hand and just disappeared. It would be many hours before Sara and Tommy awoke to find their hosts gone.

******

Christopher Evans sat alone and frightened clinging to the side of the survival pod as the earth shook. He missed his family greatly. Chris knew they were all certainly dead by now. He felt so alone.

Suddenly before his eyes Philip, an angel of the Lord, materialized at Christopher's side. "Be at peace, Child. You will become strong and powerful for the Lord, and you will lead many of the lost sheep back to God before they are consumed by evil," said Philip boldly.

"How can I do such a thing? I am just an 18-year-old kid!" said Chris with a heart full of confusion.

"You will become strong, Christopher—much stronger than you could ever imagine. The Lord will give you wisdom and power. Now be at peace! Stay here another week. I will come back to you with instructions as to what you must do next."

Philip disappeared from the pod leaving Chris alone and frightened. *How will I ever become strong and brave?* he wondered.

******

Elisha marched out into the desert with Jasmine by his side as usual. Behind were Ruth and Peter walking along quietly and occasionally gazing up at the sky as the blue continued to recede, being replaced by an ugly gray.

Behind Peter and Ruth were maybe as many as 2,000 people marching along quietly as they all tried to understand what had just happened to their lives. It was doubtful that these people—Muslim and Jew alike—had any real understanding of who Jesus Christ was, but Elisha was sure to fix this as soon as he could.

The journey they were on would take them far into the desert, and it would take at least a week to move this many people so far south of Jerusalem. Elisha was already wondering how he was going to feed and shelter these people as night began to fall. Jasmine seemed to sense his thoughts. She slipped her little hand into his and began to talk softly. "If the Lord wants you to lead these people, then He will provide. All you have to do is believe and be obedient."

"I am sure glad I got locked in the back of that van with you," Elisha smiled.

"And I'm glad I came back for you," said Jasmine.

"What do you mean, came back for me? I didn't know you had ever left."

"Well, I did, but for some reason I changed my mind." Jasmine squeezed Elisha's hand. "Like the rest of these people, I see something in you that can only come from God. You will lead them, and you will fight to save them from Satan, and I will fight to protect you!"

"I love you, Jasmine," said Elisha.

Jasmine looked into his bright eyes and smiled. "I know you do. I love you too!"

The sun was completely gone by the time Elisha finally held up his hand for everyone to stop. "Pass the word," he said. "We will make camp here tonight."

******

Hours later Elisha and Jasmine walked through the camp until Elisha came to a large rock protruding from the sand. Elisha climbed on top of the rock. From this vantage point he could see everyone and they could see him. "People!" said Elisha. The crowd, old and young, turned towards him and listened carefully. "The Lord has been gracious to us today. So many have died, but we have been spared." He paused to reflect on Benjamin, Joseph, and Yvette. "There are others—many more hiding around the world. Jesus spread His Word through 12 disciples in the beginning, and we have thousands right here. We can make a difference, but first we need to organize. I want one leader for every 100 people. Each of these leaders will report to me, carry out my instructions, and keep the peace over their respective groups." Elisha paused to consider how he might select one man from every 100. Over 20 men would be necessary. "Lord, please give me guidance," Elisha prayed.

Jasmine whispered to Elisha, "Have them line up into two long lines and then count off 1 to 100. Every 100th person will be the leader over that group."

How did she know I needed help figuring this out? he wondered. Jasmine smiled and winked at Elisha. "Okay," said Elisha. "Line up into two lines and count off 1 to 100. Repeat this until everyone in line has a number. Every time you get to 100, separate that group from the rest of the line. You at the end of both lines may not end up evenly at 100, so just remember your number."

It's working, thought Elisha as he watched each person count off and then separate into groups. Near the end of the lines he ended up with two smaller groups of 42 and 37. "Okay, every person whose number is 100 step forward." In every case the person stepping forward was a man—some very young and some very old. All Elisha needed to do now was to figure out who should lead the last two smaller groups. Looking down from the rock, Elisha noticed Peter and Ruth. *Yes! Thank You, Lord.* "Those two will be my leaders as well," said Elisha softly.

Elisha introduced each group to its new leader. This went off well until he introduced Ruth as the leader of the smaller group of 37. This was Elisha's first test of authority. Ruth was a woman, she was an American, and she was black. This caused instant strife among the group, but before Elisha could intercede on Ruth's behalf, she took matters into her own hands. "How many of you have been on the top of Mt. Everest? How many of you have spent months in the jungles of South America living off snake meat and boiled insects? How many of you have met with the world's most powerful leaders? How many of you have stood in the middle of a battlefield as bombs burst all around you? I can lead you and meet all of your needs if you will allow me. Personally I don't care what you think of me. I can take care of myself, and maybe someone else can come into this group and lead you. The choice is yours."

The group unanimously elected Ruth as their leader. Elisha looked at Ruth with a whole new respect. "Thank you!" he said.

Ruth smiled brightly and nodded.

Elisha met with the group leaders over dinner which in itself was a collection of odds and ends. Each man and woman sat cross-legged in a circle as the fire glowed brightly. Of course, Jasmine sat next to her man, but this time she was quiet. She knew she would have to start behaving a little differently around Elisha, especially in front of the others. He was God's chosen leader. She would have to learn some discipline. *This is not going to be easy,* she thought.

"We will be at the cave this time next week," said Elisha.

"And then what?" one of the younger men asked.

"We will wait on the Lord for our next set of instructions, but until then we will continue to sing His praises and read His Word to build faith among ourselves. I am worried that many of you do not know Jesus as Lord and Savior, as the Son of God. This must change. We will start with Bible reading daily to build your faith. This must be passed on to all men and women in this camp. We cannot survive without the knowledge of Jesus as Lord of all."

The journey would be hard for all of them, but it was not the first time God had led a tribe of people out into the desert to serve His greater purpose.

******

Simon and Carlo were back in Rome at the new world headquarters. The whole flight was stressful not only because Carlo was in such a bad mood, but also because of Simon's fear that another one of those small meteors might find its way into their jet.

Simon followed Carlo into his private office. Simon was afraid. He did not know how Satan would react to today's events. Had they done something wrong or was this the way things were supposed to go? If so, then why did Carlo seem so upset?

Carlo dropped to his knees as soon as he entered the room. "Father!" he cried out. "Are you displeased with me?"

The room began to shake like it never had before. Simon felt faint from fear. Maybe they had done something very wrong after all. Suddenly the room stopped shaking and a bright light appeared in the center of the room. In the midst of the light stood a very large figure. It was difficult for Simon to look at him because of the brightness around his body, but he knew this was Satan in the flesh. *He's beautiful,* Simon thought. The image of an evil-looking, twisted creature with horns fled from Simon. Satan was a massive and beautiful creature, but only because God had created him that way, though Simon didn't understand this fact. It was Satan's heart that was ugly beyond description, yet to Simon this was beautiful as well.

"You have not failed me, my Son," said Satan. "What has come to pass was expected, but it is the future that we will change. From here on the world will serve only me. We will seek out and destroy all opposition. There will not be a Christian left on earth. This planet is mine, and all its inhabitants will worship me. Nothing can stop that!"

"Then you are pleased with me, Father?" Carlo asked.

"Yes, but you have much more work to do. You have a world to unite and to lead according to my wishes."

Simon did not speak. He just listened carefully. *Why does Carlo get all the credit?* he wondered. After all, it was Simon who found Joseph, Simon who killed the Evans' children, Simon who terrorized the world, and Simon who had the power to call down fire from the sky. *My day will come,* he told himself. *Someday I will be a god, too, but in the meantime I will help to rule the world and rid it of any trace of Christ.*

Simon and Carlo listened to Satan carefully as they received instruction for what to do next. There were a lot of exciting things coming to the world, and Simon was glad to be part of it all. Very soon the world would be starving like nothing they had ever seen before. Disease and plague would be rampant. Weather changes would call for massive power consumption just to keep the people alive. Oil would become the most important commodity ever, much more so than in the past. Wars would be fought for control of this fuel. Death and misery would help to create a new world order, and at the heart of it was a trophy that Satan wanted for himself—Israel and all of God's chosen people. This was Satan's heart's desire, but God had always prevented this from happening in the past, and now it was going to have to be won through other means—lethal, evil means.

John 3:16

Printed in the United States
28225LVS00003B/37